MIDNIGHT WHISKEY

WHISKEY WITCHES PARA WARS BOOK 3

F.J. BLOODING

This is a work of fiction. All the characters, organizations, and events within this book are products of the author's imagination and are used fictitiously. Any resemblance to business establishments, actual persons, or events is entirely coincidental. The publisher does not have any control over and does not assume any responsibility for author or third-party websites or their content.

Whistling Book Press

Alaska

Printed in the United States of America

Published by Whistling Book Press

Whistling Book Press
Alaska
Visit our web site at:
www.whistlingbooks.com

Shifting Heart Romances

by Hattie Hunt & F.J. Blooding

Bear Moon

Grizzly Attraction

Here's the reading order to make it even easier to catch up!

https://www.fjblooding.com/reading-order

Other Books by F.J. Blooding

Devices of War Trilogy

Fall of Sky City

Sky Games

Whispers of the Skyborne

Discover more, sign up for updates and gifts, and join the forum discussions at www.fjblooding.com.

WHISKEY MAGICK & MENTAL HEALTH

Sign up to learn more about our books and receive this free e-zine about Whiskey Magick and Mental Health. https://www.fjblooding.com/books-lp

Paige dodged a lightning blast aimed at her head and frowned at her youngest daughter.

Rai grinned impishly, her eyes dancing with blue lightning. "You said."

Paige didn't disagree. She'd told her daughter not to hold back in order to get a good feel of where she was, but she didn't want to *die* in the process.

Margo leapt in, her wolf teeth bared, her black coat rippling. Her paws landed lightly on the ground before she launched herself at Leah.

Paige kept herself from protecting her oldest daughter, but it took every bit of overprotective strength she could muster. Her job was to train these kids to survive. It wasn't to baby them or protect them. Her kids were going to survive.

Leah blinked her blue eyes once, then a door opened between her and Margo, closing behind the wolf's puffy tail.

Before Paige could ask where Leah had sent Margo, the wolf leapt out of thin air closer to the rope bridge of the obstacle course. "Well done, Lee."

Ember fought with Ripley, who shifted effortlessly through the trees in her ghostly dog form. As a death dog, her shifted form was less solid and was a lot more… creepy.

But Ember's fire was still able to singe her fur. Something about him being a *rajasi* and how his fire could light a soul on fire, which was part of the reason the rajasi had been eradicated even from legend a millennia before.

Lightning tagged Paige on the shoulder, sending her body into the rigidity of electric shock. Her muscles tightened, snot streaming effortlessly from her nose. She thought she might puke.

But this wasn't the first time her daughter had hit her with bolts of lightning, so she knew how to recover quickly. Paige shifted into an elephant—the body mass taking most of the effects of the electricity and dispersing it—and charged her daughter.

Rai squeaked and shifted into a hawk, flapping hard to get away.

No way! Paige wasn't going to let her retreat that easily. She leapt into the air with her giant elephant feet, shifting into a gorilla—which was quickly becoming her favorite form —and reached, grasping her daughter's brown tail feathers.

Lightning wrapped around her thick-skinned hand as tail feathers released.

Rai continued to fly away, but this time as a true thunderbird, which meant she was getting serious.

Paige shifted into a pterodactyl, wishing she could shift into a dragon. She overtook her daughter in four wingbeats, her claws outstretched.

The thunderbird screeched, her wings shooting lightning.

Dinosaur skin reflected most of that, but not easily. The pain of the electricity made Paige's wings quiver. She dropped in altitude before she could correct her flight. Then she gathered the air under her wings and shot through the sky, intent on taking her daughter down. She didn't want to die in the sky. She wasn't afraid of the electric bolts shooting at her. She was afraid of the landing. She hated flying.

Rai turned in midflight, her wings going still as she called lightning from the clear blue sky.

Paige had never seen her daughter do that before.

If Rai hit her with that much electricity—

It was time to get to the ground. Now.

Paige turned tail and dove for safety, hoping Rai would remember she was attacking her *mother* and that she should hold back. The ground came in fast—faster than she liked. She shifted into a gorilla as soon as she came close enough because she needed better control.

Lightning hit her mid-shift.

Time passed Paige in a fog for a while after that, vague sights and sounds filtering through. The next thing she clearly saw was her bright-eyed daughter leaned over, her long dark hair spilling over her shoulders unbound.

Ember knelt beside her, his amber eyes dancing with worry, his hair a fiery wreath of energy.

Leah joined them, pulling her long blonde hair back into a ponytail, knowing full well she'd need it out of the way. They had wounded people on this obstacle course quite often. "Mom, you okay?"

Paige tried to grunt, but moving was...hard. The world was trying to destroy her, and here were her kids, the perfect weapons of destruction.

Bobby came over and flopped down beside her head. A golden light lit his hands as he placed them on her shoulders.

The light enveloped her, surrounding her with love and healing.

Her muscles realigned and healed. Bones she hadn't realized she'd broken snapped back into place.

It wasn't entirely pleasant, but after several moments, Paige was pain-free.

The light disappeared, and sound invaded.

"…sorry, Mom. I don't know what happened."

"—totally wicked!" Tyler's voice rang with his bardic power. "I've never seen anything—"

"—crap," Mandy swore as she raced over and tripped, tumbling to join them. "Are you okay?"

Paige knew Mandy well enough by now to know that she could have been asking about anyone being okay except for the person dying. She was unsurprised to see Mandy staring at Ember.

He frowned at her like she'd lost her mind and nodded, his head pulled back, giving him a double chin.

A naked Margo calmly walked toward them, her dark eyes taking in Paige, the scar on her cheek ticking. Her belly bulged slightly with her pregnancy. "Are you healed?"

Paige moved her arms, which was a little hard because the kids were crowded around her. "Seem to be."

"Dang, woman!" Ripley shifted into human form as she ran up fully clothed, a wild grin on her face. "That was impressive."

A large grizzly bear charged them.

Leah turned and slapped black energy at him with a frown. "Joe!"

He skidded to a stop, shaking his big bear head, and shifted into a tall, naked man. "I wasn't going to run you over, Lee."

"Yeah, right," Leah grumbled.

He'd done it before.

Paige held up a hand, feeling a bit like Frederic from *The Pirate Movie* in the coffin scene. "I'm fine, guys. If a demon couldn't kill me, my own kids can't." Which obviously wasn't the case. Her kids *could* kill her and almost had.

How scary was that?

She pulled herself to her feet, meeting Margo's gaze. "I think the training went well." But she needed to be done for the day.

Margo grunted, resting her hand on her belly. "I agree."

The kids took that as their cue to get up.

Paige rolled her neck. "Perhaps a little too well."

She moved her legs, working the kinks out. "I don't know what broke in the fall, but I'm certainly glad we have a healer."

Ripley broke out of Joe's cuddle with a smile on her lips and a hint of worry in her eyes. "You fell hard and in mid-shape. I think we found a weakness."

That information would be handy if they were preparing to battle shifter witches. But this was one weakness she just had to find a way to shield herself against.

Joe shifted back into a grizzly and wandered off with a roar, challenging the kids.

Leah raised her head and turned toward him, then followed. The other kids trailed behind her with a mixture of excitement and trepidation.

Rai's movements were subdued as she held back.

Paige grabbed her daughter's attention and flagged her over.

The girl's shoulders slumped even further, but she made her way to her mother.

If Dexx were there, he'd know exactly what to tell her, what to say to lighten the mood. But the last she'd seen or heard from him had been a news clip on the BBC, showing him and the Red Star team taking on some big demon in Parliament.

What the hell was her man doing in England, taking down a government that wasn't even theirs? If only she could *talk* to him.

But he hadn't called, hadn't texted.

And hadn't come home. Was he even *coming* home? Had she pushed too hard? They'd argued before he'd… Had he left? No. She couldn't go down that path. Dexx was handling something. He'd managed to send a bunch of information on DoDO. He hadn't abandoned them—her.

Paige shook off her worry about Dexx and wrapped a conciliatory arm around Rai as they walked toward the house with Margo and Ripley in tow. As much as she wished she had some answers about Dexx, she was worried even more about their kids. *Her* kids.

Paige gave Rai's shoulders a gentle squeeze with her good arm. "You did good up there." She ignored her other arm, which still ached. It must have been one of the broken things.

"I almost killed you," Rai whispered, her voice constricted and low as if a ball of tears was wedged in her throat.

An answering ball threatened to fill Paige's throat. "I gave birth to you, remember? You're not gonna get rid of me *that* easy."

"I heard your bones break."

"Well, yes. But you didn't *kill* me."

Rai stopped and pulled away from her. "What if Bobby wasn't here? What if I *had* killed you?"

Paige wished Alma was there to share some of her wisdom. What would she have said?

In that moment, Paige understood the position Alma had been in, being a strong witch in her own right, raising granddaughters who were stronger and more powerful than her.

But instead of being afraid of that power like Alma had been, Paige was going to show her daughter—all of her kids whether they were hers or not—that they didn't need to fear who they were. They simply had to hone themselves to do the most good.

She took her daughter's shoulders in her hands and waited until Rai met her gaze.

It took a while. Lightning danced in that gaze, wild and unfettered.

Afraid.

Paige's heart twisted. She cupped her daughter's cheek. A handful of months ago, Rai'd been a tiny baby. And here she was in the body of a teen. She gathered Rai into a hug, wrapping one hand around the back of Rai's head and tucking her close. "Be the best you can be. Do the best you can do. Don't die, and if someone tries to kill you…" Why was she quoting Malcolm Reynolds from *Firefly*? "You try to kill them right back."

Rai held onto Paige for a long moment.

Margo took in a deep breath, meeting Paige's gaze, her eyes saying they needed to be very careful, but also that she understood. She put her hand on Rai's shoulder, offering her silent support.

Paige smiled at the wolf gratefully.

Ripley bounced on her toes, looking uncomfortable. She reached over and patted Rai awkwardly on the back. "We have work to do?"

Paige pulled away and screwed on a mom smile. "You did great out there. Be scared. That's okay. Fear will keep you smart. But don't hide behind it. Don't allow fear to be your excuse to hide from life. Your thunderbird fought too hard to be freed to have her human keep her hidden."

Rai frowned for a moment, but then raised her chin. She nodded once then turned to follow Joe and the kids who were now climbing over the obstacle course.

"I worry they're too strong," Margo murmured, walking to a small shed and pulling out a robe.

Ripley tucked in the corners of her lips and blinked. But it was obvious from her wide eyes that she was thinking something sarcastic. "Then, we need to teach them how to control it."

She wasn't wrong.

Paige and Ripley made sandwiches while Margo got dressed in the main house. Then, armed with a light lunch, they all three piled into Leslie's SUV and drove into town. Ripley and Margo had their own business to attend to, as did Paige.

She was the Secretary of Paranormal Affairs in name only, but that didn't mean she got to slack on her duties. The reality was that even if the position wasn't real—because only the President of the United States could assign it to her —there was a void there and a need *for* the position, whether it was a granted title or not.

When Paige stepped out of the vehicle, Willow Mathews, who had taken point in controlling what got through to Paige and what she handled on a daily basis, greeted her. Willow had vollun-taken the position of being her executive assistant and was the only reason Paige was able to survive this incredible shift of responsibilities.

She and Willow handled some boring details on their way to Leslie's shop, taking time to stop at the coffee shop and drink their coffees at one of the patio tables. Within an hour, they had found solutions for the handful of people who'd waited for her to come to town and dealt with all the things Willow had on her plate for the day. Well, not necessarily dealt with? More like touched on each of them. Willow didn't bring Paige small issues.

All in all, daily operations were starting to run a bit more smoothly.

Paige walked into her sister's shop earlier than expected and with time to spare. That was new, and she didn't know what to *do* with her free time. She'd become conditioned to having each microsecond crammed full with world-ending doom.

Leslie looked up from her work at the counter, surprise shining in her green eyes, her dirty blonde hair in a messy bun of messiness. Like seriously more than normal. Some women could pull off that look and make it look effortless and cool. Leslie made it look messy. "Is the world on fire?"

"Not currently." Were there twigs in her bun?

Leslie frowned and glanced out her shop windows.

Paige had no idea what she was supposed to do in that moment. "Do you need help?"

"With what?" Leslie's tone rose with indignation and derision. "I'm sorry, baby sister, but I just put my shop *back* together for the last time. If it explodes one more time, I'm callin' it quits."

Paige held up her hand in surrender. "I just offered because I could maybe learn some stuff?"

"I don't have time to teach you." Leslie gestured to her shop. "This was stocked this morning. Look at it."

A few bars of soap remained here and there. The shelves where the lotions had been were bare. The wine was gone. Even the candles were gone. "Oh." Paige gave her sister a smile. "Well, that's good. Right?"

"Right. Yes." Leslie nodded with a disgusted sigh. "You want to help? Take this case." She set down her spiral notebook behind the counter and disappeared behind it. She came back up, whacking her head. She grunted but stood without so much as wincing, handing Paige a thick case file instead.

"You okay?" Leslie had a thick skull, but *that* thick? She'd hit it *hard*.

"Fine." Leslie waved off Paige's concern. "Ghosts are appearing all over town. They're possessing people. They're putting people into comas. Someone's torturing them to draw their energy."

"The ghosts?"

Leslie gave her a look like she was dumb.

Well, she'd obviously missed something.

"They're torturing the people to *death* and *making* them ghosts." Leslie's green eyes flared open, and her lips set in a tight line before she continued. "*Then* the ghosts are possessing people—maybe tryin' to get a message out? Don't know. The possessed people are falling into comas before the ghost can do anything. That's what I have."

Paige was certain there was more. Leslie was a wicked smart woman, but she was also the kind of person who needed to focus on what needed to be done, and it would be best if everyone else just left her alone while she did it. "You got the case because?"

"Red Star's missing." Leslie turned and headed to the back of the shop. "And you're busy, but now that you're here and you want to help, stay out of my shop and solve the case."

Paige blinked as Leslie firmly but resolutely shut the cloth "door" in Paige's face.

2

Paige checked in with Willow to make sure there wasn't anything new that had popped up in the past few minutes. There wasn't.

So, she headed to Red Star.

Ripley had disappeared, taking Margo with her. She'd come to town *not* to be Paige's bodyguard but to open her bar, and Margo was Ripley's bouncer. The two got along well, so that was great.

Paige took the case file to Red Star and went to her old office. The bullpen was alive with the greenery that she magicked there, but the entire place was silent. Sinking into Dexx's new chair reminded her that this wasn't hers anymore.

And it made her miss Dexx. She could smell him, feel him.

Cawli padded into the room in his tiny cat body and hopped up in the chair on the other side of the desk.

This was a new development Paige wasn't certain she liked. Cawli had been able to separate from her in order to materialize in the *Vaada Bhoomi*—the spirit animal realm—in order to protect her children. She'd assumed that when they made it back, he'd be reclaiming his role as spirit animal companion, riding inside her mind.

But he was still manifesting outside of her. Granted, not everyone could see him. Rai, Ember, Ripley, and Leslie were able to see him. And she was still able to shift per normal thanks to their bond. But she wasn't able to shift into animals as big or as powerful. No more massive T-rexes for her.

She did miss his dry commentary, though he had never been there as constantly as Hattie was for Dexx or Robin was for Leslie. She had a sense, though, that he was vulnerable being outside of her. It could be the fact that he was so tiny. He was the size of a house cat.

What is this? he asked, hopping onto the desk, his ethereal paws making no sound.

"A case." Paige opened the file and took out some of the notes. They were color-coded with OCD precision-placed sticky notes, and well-organized. Also, there were a *lot* of notes. "I think Leslie was trying to handle this."

It makes sense. He laid down beside the file, his feline eyes trailing down as if reading. *You were busy.*

"As were you." She wanted to ask him what he did when he wasn't with her. They weren't bonded like normal shapeshifters. She'd never been bitten by an alpha. He'd come to her outside of a church when someone had been possessed by a demon, and he'd offered his assistance. He'd often be "missing" from inside her head for long periods of time. "How *are* things going with…" She shook her head. "Whatever it is you're doing?"

He flicked his tail in irritation. *Not as well as I'd planned.*

Paige blinked and pulled back in surprise. It wasn't often he admitted anything to her. "Does any of this have to do with what's going on in Europe?"

It's just Britain. They're countries, not states, Paige. He laid his head on his folded paw and closed his eyes, his whiskers twitching. *Yes and no. There are consequences to letting the ancients out, things I hadn't considered.*

"Like?" The ancients were the big, mythological shifter spirits that had a lot of power and were hard to bond with because of their volatility. They hadn't been released to the world for thousands of years because the last time they'd been in the world, they'd been hunted for their power.

But thanks to Paige and Cawli, the ancients were being released back into the world.

He sighed. *There are power players moving in to try and tap into the ancients even if they don't fully realize what they seek.*

Huh. "Like Cooper?" He'd been the powerful "lizard wizard" Dexx'd taken on last year. He'd somehow managed to control some ancient stag or something.

Like him. But also—you need to know Dexx will return to you.

That was out of left field.

He's dealing with something big.

"That demon thing he got caught on TV fighting."

Yes, Cawli said with a whoof of frustration. *I hadn't realized exactly who Dexx was until it was too late. I brought you too close to a danger that nearly destroyed us the last time.*

"Come again, what?"

Cawli raised his head and met her gaze. *Dexx's first brother is the biggest reason we ancients went into hiding the last time. It was the only way to protect ourselves.*

What? That didn't make sense. Dexx only had one brother, and he'd been in a mental ward because the demon possessing him had been making him pay for raping a woman and getting away with it. He'd killed himself years ago.

His brother from many lifetimes ago. It's very complicated, but leave it to say that Dexx is a very complicated man, and he's trying very hard to protect you *from the danger he brings.*

Okay. That was kinda news.

And if I'd known earlier, I would never have brought the ancients to you with that monster so close to your lives.

"Just how bad is he?" And was Dexx enough to bring this guy down?

He's a major player, and with what Dexx is discovering now, he might very well be extremely tied to your own war. I do not want you going up against the First Brother, Paige. Whatever you do, do not volunteer yourself for Dexx's battle.

"But if he needs me—"

You will let Dexx fight his own war.

Well, Cawli obviously didn't know her very well.

Do you have time for this mystery? Cawli asked, letting his head fall to the side slightly.

Nice subject change, but he was letting her know the topic was closed. For now. "Nothing's going on currently."

I can tell you to enjoy this lull because it will be fleeting. He released a sigh that was half-purr. *I would make no plans to take this case on yourself. You are the Secretary of Paranormal—*

She laughed at him. "I'm the Secretary of nothing right now." But he *was* right.

She picked up her phone but paused as a sudden thought hit her. "Why did you present yourself to me as a tiger before? In the spirit cave?" When she'd been pregnant, she'd been summoned to the Spirit Cave in Utah to be judged by the spirit realm.

He gave her a cat glare that might have been scarier if he was bigger than a house cat.

She chuckled and dialed the sheriff.

While the call went through, she tried to touch Cawli, but he was like a ghost with no real form.

"Tuck," he answered his phone gruffly.

"Whiskey," she answered crisply. "I have a case."

"Congratulations." Something slammed on his end.

"I have no team." This could go bad quickly.

"Then make one." Papers made crinkly sounds as they were shuffled with a fierce hand.

"*You* have one." She understood what he was doing, pushing back on her.

"Get your old one back."

She couldn't. "They're fugitives right now? And it looks like they have an apocalypse of their own to deal with."

"You're not getting involved, are you?" Worry up-ticked his tone.

"Noooo." Maybe.

He sighed and slammed a metal file cabinet. "Then make another one. A temporary one. I'll send you the budget. Same email?"

He already *had* a temporary budget for this? This was the reason he was the boss. "Yeah. But where am I going to get—"

"Paige." Something slammed down on his metal desk that could have been a thick file or a stack of smaller ones. "I need you to understand something real quick. I'm busier than a one-legged man in an ass-kicking contest. You built the last one, and I didn't think it'd work, but it did. Do it again."

She had no idea how that was going to happen. She opened her mouth to say that when the line went quiet. She checked the screen. He'd hung up on her.

Great.

Okay, well, if she *was* going to handle the paranormal situation for the entire country—somehow—then she needed to find someone to take this case.

She *had* interviewed more than a few people when they'd first started Red Star, and there were two or three people who hadn't made it, but it'd been really close. She just had to find those files again.

Dexx had had this office for nearly a year, and all her files were still in the same place she'd left them, so at least there was that. On the one hand, it meant he wasn't *using* the files. On the other hand, it meant she could find what she needed. She pulled out the applications and found the three she was interested in, making a few calls and leaving a few voicemails.

But she hadn't managed to get ahold of anyone. She sent emails as well just in case.

Okay. She needed to at least get a little familiarized with the case before she potentially handed it off.

Staring at Leslie's case notes in a pile wasn't helping her see the big picture. So, Paige got up to go to the conference room and put the puzzle pieces on the whiteboard.

After several hours had passed with no return calls or emails, she grabbed the folder of applications and called the people on the "absolutely not" list as well.

Before she left her desk, she sent out a general job posting for temporary assistance.

She was so screwed.

She did have, maybe, Barn. He had been a coroner in Denver, but he had many talents. He could be a lab tech. He knew computers and databases. When he'd followed her to Troutdale, he'd set up shop with Leslie helping her diagnose paras who had illnesses because she hadn't been able to hire him full-time.

So, she sent him a message. *Got a case. Got time?*

After a few moments, she'd managed to get a map of the area hung up on the white wall and was starting to put up tacks. Her phone vibrated.

Barn's reply had a single word. *Leslie's?*

Hopefully, that meant he knew what was going on. *Yup.*

Coffee?

Bringing? At Red Star.

He didn't answer, so she hoped that meant he was on his way.

The case *was* intriguing. Tuck had called Leslie in on it because people had been attacked by ghosts then falling into comas. Apparently, he'd attempted to create a new Red Star on his own using Leslie as his anchor. So that's why he already had a budget prepared.

Little did he know just how busy Leslie was. It might not have looked like she had a lot going on, but she had almost more than Paige did. It was just that Paige's issues were world-sized, and Leslie's were family-sized. Which probably wouldn't have been as ginormous if she hadn't been a Whiskey. The Whiskey family was a *large* extended family and with an even larger "found" family that seemed to be getting bigger by the day.

Also, there was the fact that Leslie dealt with *details*. Paige... really didn't. She'd moved into a point in her life where she could delegate some of those. This was the first time since she'd made so many changes in her life that she really *noticed*.

She had minions.

And now, she needed investigative minions.

"Hey," Barn called from the front door. "S.O.S. received. Got the coffee."

Paige stepped out of the conference room, not fully focused. She was still trying to connect all the pieces mentally so she could get a better understanding of what was going on. The two cups in his hands caught her eye, but they weren't paper. "They both for you?"

"Nah. Jill's going green, so less waste." He handed her the yellow travel mug. It had a copper octopus on it and the logo of the coffee shop. "Also, your favorite color. I'm claiming extra points for that."

Barn was a tall guy—well, taller than Paige who was average. But he was a *big* man. Big around the waist and with broad shoulders. His calves were well-defined and amazing, but the rest of him was pretty soft. He was a man who spent more time in his brain than on the track.

Which was exactly where Paige would be if she wasn't a shifter. She knew that, so she wasn't about to judge him.

She was super glad to have him. Seeing his round face and black-rimmed glasses sent a jolt of joy through her that the yellow coffee cup only added to.

She listened to him blabber on about his latest group of miniatures, which she took to mean had something to do with dolls? She didn't quite know. It was about some game, and he was really excited because there was in "instream" of "cool" people, and he was fixing to "DM" some "campaign." She couldn't tell if he was running for political office or starting a craft club. But he was excited about it, so she was happy for him.

"Which brings me to the case," he said, dumping his stuff. The man never packed light. He would go from one building to the next with a full backpack, his leather messenger bag, and a jacket. "If you look at this as a single case, it's confusing. Like seriously, super conf—" He held up both hands and reassessed his words. "Rolling straight natural ones on all perception checks. Mass confusion."

She had no idea what he'd just said, but she took that to mean that a one was bad. "Talk to me in a language I know."

He gave her a look that asked her what kind of sick person she was to *not* understand him.

She sighed and gave him a look that said he needed to get serious.

His eyes narrowed behind his thick lenses as if telling her that he was and that she needed to up her game.

She rolled her eyes. "What did you see?"

"When you take a look at the case from a distance, including the current events into the information cycle, you see things a little different."

Paige folded her arms over her chest and studied the board again, but this time, she pulled her mind out a little, focused a little less on the details she had, and included current world events.

The paranormals were being rounded up—or had been—and were incarcerated.

She checked the timeline as Barn continued to talk, setting up listening filters to trigger if he said a code word that needed her attention.

The first ghost attack had occurred three days after DoDO's paranormal round up.

The second ghost attack had occurred three days later.

Then a battering of three attacks in one day, which had occurred the night she'd defended the elven city that had been invaded by DoDO.

Barn stepped in front of the board and opened his hands in a wide gesture with a beaming grin on his face. "See? What do you think?"

She *had* been listening to him. Kinda. He'd been talking about how the political things tied to this case, but he hadn't had actual dates. *She* did. "I think you're onto something here." She moved around Barn and added a few sticky notes with her own timeline, from the first discovery of paranormals being rounded up to the invasion of the elven town to the freeing of the paras in prison.

She stepped back, studying the board, her mind chugging through all the notes. She had a thumb drive from Dexx with information on DoDO. "I've got something you might like." She contacted Willow to get that information over to Barn.

As soon as she hung up, though, she had a horrible thought. What if people were listening in?

There were only so many aluminum hats she could wear in a day.

Before she and Barn had completed their new notes—because he was on his computer looking helpful stuff up or something. She didn't quite know. He was a loud typist. That's all she really got—the front door opened.

"Hello?" and a man called out. "Paige Whiskey?"

Paige looked over at Barn hopefully. "That could be someone else coming to join us." She turned to the door. "Be right with you."

Barn's face diffused a little.

"Barn, please." Paige wasn't delicate enough to side-step emotions well. "If you're right—and I think you are—then this is a much bigger case, and we're going to need more people."

He screwed on a happier smile and turned back to his computer. "Just don't sideline me like you already have for the past year."

She winced as she grabbed her happy yellow cup and cheered him with it. "I can't. You're the *only* person who knows my favorite color. Don't think I'll forget that."

His smile beamed with a genuine glow though he didn't look up from his screen.

Paige wasn't sure who'd answered her call, but she'd been hoping for the harpy. The male voice said it wasn't, but the harpy had been a really close addition to the team the last time. She had previous police experience and would be a valuable asset, but Paige'd decided to keep a tighter eye on Quinn instead. She still didn't quite agree with that decision. At the time, it'd been the right one, but the follow-through?

Quinn Winters hadn't been a super great addition to the team. And she'd disappeared. On her own? With someone else? No one knew.

As Paige entered the lobby, the smiling face of Toad Man greeted her.

Okay. That was totally the wrong thing to say, but...

Oh, geez. Just how desperate was she?

Joel Furse was a goblin. She didn't remember much about him during the interviews, but she'd written *no* in cursive, which was kind of code for her saying that he wasn't a *terrible* choice. He just— he was so short... and one of his front teeth literally held up his upper lip.

She screwed on a smile and walked toward him, offering her hand. "Mr. Furse."

His expression was hesitant. "I almost called back, but just came, you know, in case...." His voice was gruff.

In case she knew it was him and rescinded the offer. Yeah. Well, she was desperate. "I'm really glad you did." She really wasn't. "Tell me about your background again?"

He swung his hands behind him and took a deep breath. "I was an enforcer."

"For the goblins."

"Yeah." He stuck his hands in his pockets and frowned up at her, his words terse.

Which could just be how goblins talked. He sounded like he was mad all the time. "And why are you looking to work here?"

"Kicked out."

That was a red flag. "Why?"

He released a sigh. "Sided with humans too many times."

"Ah." She had no idea about goblin politics. "Well," she said, leading him to the back, "I'm still working on the budget. The team is out doing—" She didn't *really* know what. "Out. And we have a case. I don't know how long this position will be open. Could be temporary. Could be long term."

"Understood." His brow furrowed.

"Are you good with cases?" she asked, stepping into the conference room.

Barn glanced up, then back down to his screen, then up again, his dark eyes wide with horror.

Paige raised her eyebrow at him then gave him two thumbs up as she raised the corners of her lips.

He followed her smile, then pushed his computer aside and offered his hand. "Barn."

"Looks like," Joel grumbled and offered his hand. "Goblin."

Oh, goddess. "No, he's—" Deep breath. "His *name* is Barn." She turned a focused gaze on Barn. "This is Joel. He lacks tact."

Barn frowned and regained his seat. "Ah. Okay."

Paige wasn't certain what the hell she was supposed to do with this raggedy team of misfits, but she was going to *try* to get to the bottom of this mystery.

Because it looked like it was *exactly* what she'd already been working on before.

What in the glorious hell?

3

B eing back in the detective seat felt amazing! Even with a sneering goblin on her team. Though, to give Joel some credit, it seemed like he wasn't *trying* to sneer. It was just what that tooth did to his face.

"Okay," Paige said, taking a step back and leaning against the window wall to better view their case board. "I know you still have to go through the information, but what if DoDO is behind these attacks?"

Barn had contacted "a guy" who was running a report on missing persons, per Paige's request. They didn't have a lot to go on because they didn't have a ton of descriptors on the ghosts who had attacked their citizens. But she needed faces and names in order to gather real evidence.

The information she had was *beyond* useless. One case said the ghost smelled like roses. Another ghost looked old, like it had spent too much time tanning under a hot sun. It wasn't a lot to use.

Joel had put in a call for a medium he knew.

Paige had already put in a call to Leslie who was the best medium they had, but had been informed rather bluntly that

Paige had all the information Leslie had. The end. Have a lovely day.

Which left Paige at ground zero.

She'd also put in a call to Ripley who probably wouldn't be a super big help, but the bar owner was a death omen so it was possible she could offer some assistance.

The person who might be the best help yet, though, was Jack Scott, an FBI agent and a reaper. She was saving that call for lunch because she knew it would likely take a little longer as it typically did when she talked to Director Lovejoy.

"If someone up top is involved," Barn said, pulling his glasses off his face to clean them with his green t-shirt, "then, yeah, this would make a little more sense. The numbers are just too big."

The numbers of missing persons cases around the U.S. had gone up steeply in the past two months, ever since the President had signed the executive order forcing paranormals to register. "How many are paras?"

"Paras?" Barn asked with a piqued expression. "That's a new term."

Was it? "No different than calling you Barn."

Joel frowned. "Why a barn?"

Paige sighed. Goblins seemed to be very literal. "It's short for his name. Steve Barnsworth."

Joel just looked even more confused, but he didn't say anything else.

"I don't know," Barn said, putting his laptop aside. "There's no real way to tell because most didn't register."

"So there might be more cases we don't know about." Which was yet another thing that needed to be fixed. But who would do that? It was a big picture problem for government officials.

But how many of those *actually* cared?

"We need a plan of attack on this case." They needed

someone who could talk to ghosts and get information from them before hemorrhaged brains. They needed names and information but getting that from invisible people was a little challenging.

"Where are the bodies?" Joel asked.

That was another great question. "If they're not turning up, that means they're being hidden. So, chances are good it's not a single serial killer."

Barn's eyes widened. "Oofta."

Paige acknowledged that with her eyebrows. "Which leads to a big organization, and I'm thinking DoDO because… right now, that really fits the picture. So, let's look at motive. Why?"

"Why?" Joel shook his head, his goblin face folded in what was turning out to be a permanent expression of confusion.

"Why kill these people?" Paige wasn't sure what he didn't get. "Why would a group kill this many people?"

Barn tipped his screen back, the white page reflecting in his glasses. "Because they're paran—paras, and because they're trying to wipe them all out?"

"That's the easy answer if we *assume* they're paras." Paige wasn't certain she liked that term. "But we're detectives. I want to believe this is DoDO because that makes sense to *me*. But if we *only* look at it from that point, we might miss something."

"But these ghosts aren't normal," Barn said. "They're possessing people and sending them into comas. What would do that?"

Joel raised his pointy chin. "There are some people are able to use the soul."

At least he wasn't confused anymore. "For what?"

"Power."

That was something Paige had already run into in her

dealings with angels and demons. Was it possible they had yet another angel on their hands, but this one was trying to regain access to the gates of Heaven? After all, the gates were blocked, and it was harder for angels and demons to get through. "Who do you know of who uses them, and for what?"

"Goblins." Joel shrugged. "And for many things. Souls can power things for a long time."

"Like?"

He looked around, looking uncomfortable. "Like doors."

"Doors." Was getting information from him always going to be like this?

He swallowed hard and his tooth disappeared, allowing his upper lip to settle in place where it should. "Like your grocery doors."

They had automatic doors in –well, wherever goblins came from—that were powered by souls. "Human?"

"Meh." He shook his head, his large hands flailing a little. "Human usually, but it's not great. Human souls can be weak. Goblin is good. Elf is best."

"Elf?" Holy crap. Well, she'd hired a rusalka who were mythologically compelled to drown people. So... "Okay. So, yes. Batteries. They can be that. But what if it's something different?"

"Like?" Barn asked, his eyes narrowed.

Paige wasn't sure. But... "You read sci-fi."

Barn's expression grew thoughtful. "Are we thinking experimentation?"

"Might make sense."

Joel's expression widened as something clicked in place for him and his upper lip regained its perch on his tooth. "I need to go for today. I'll be back tomorrow at eight."

Uh, okay. "I'll have the paperwork ready for you to sign then."

He waved her off as he headed for the front door.

Barn was quiet a moment as he watched the goblin's retreating back. "He's a weird one."

"They're all a little weird." Paige grabbed her phone and shook it. "You got this?"

He nodded and disappeared into his computer.

Paige knew that look. It didn't matter what she showed him or mentioned, he wasn't disconnecting his eyes from that screen. Which was good. It gave her time to have a few conversations of her own.

First, she went around the town and checked in with people. She still wasn't like Leslie who was able to walk down the street and just know everyone's names. Paige felt pretty good if she remembered the first letter of a person's name, but she knew which face went with which job.

Her real intent was getting the general pulse of the town, basically. Yes, she had Willow and Leslie and Suzanne who could tell her that. They did a good job of keeping her sheltered, too. Wendy was great at keeping her updated on the school.

But there was also just something about mingling with people on her own.

They were getting comfortable.

That had to be a good sign.

They were making plans for the future, investing in different ways things could go. A good number had preparations for another blockade just in case.

And the population had been growing with a lot more paranormals flocking in. They weren't running out of residential space yet, since they could still find abandoned homes from the demon attacks.

But they were at the cusp of people versus resources, and that was going to be a problem.

So, Paige made a stop to see Suzanne, the mayor. She definitely needed to be seen as one of their own because she didn't want to get yelled at again for overstepping her bounds.

Suzanne was a little embarrassed she hadn't caught this imbalance, but Paige assured her it was okay. Frankly, the only reason Paige even realized it was because of this strategy game she played on her phone. She was building a city. There weren't battles, so yay for that. She ignored it for days on end then played it for a few minutes here and there as she had time.

But it showed her that a thriving, self-sustaining town needed a balance of people and the resources they could build.

Suzanne was all over it.

Next stop was Tuck. Paige made the walk up the hill in human form, but almost reconsidered when she'd made it halfway. The hill to the police department was steep and her human legs hadn't gotten a lot of exercise lately. Well, in the last ten years or so. She wasn't the type of person who worked out.

His bullpen had the normal yellow look to it. It was neat and orderly with several desks that were all empty. She didn't remember how many people he had in the precinct, but it seemed like it'd grown since this whole thing had started. Tuck was in his office, but his desk was covered in police files.

Okay. She really couldn't *ask* him for anything. Obviously.

He looked up at her when she came in, his white mustache raising on one side in a way that could have been a smile? It was hard to tell with that much hair covering his face. "You're not coming to complain, are you?"

She shook her head. "Just checking in on you."

"You've got a case. You should be working on that."

Yeah. She had one case. He had… twenty? "What's going on?"

He released a long breath and fell back into his worn leather chair. "Weird things, mostly, but nothing uncommon. We've got a bunch of newcomers. The locals are a bit on edge with all of it. They have something go missing and it don't matter that it went missing eight months ago. They noticed it now when their new neighbor who happens to be a shifter moved in, and now I've got a case."

"Oh." Paige took a seat opposite him, settling in for a good vent session.

"And the newbies?" He rubbed his tired eyes. "They're a ragin' bundle of nerves, each of them. They need work, is what they need. Something—anything—to keep their hands busy and them out of trouble."

"Well, Suzanne's working on that."

"She's a good mayor."

At least they had that. "She is."

He licked his lips and studied her. "You really come by to check on me?"

She rested her elbows on the arms of the chair and folded her hands over her abdomen. "Yup."

He sighed heavily. "Well, I'm fine." But he leaned forward, glanced at a file, then launched into a vent-storm that lasted another thirty minutes.

The man was frustrated and didn't know exactly what to do. He was still sheriff of the county and he had a lot of land to cover, but travel wasn't exactly free at the moment. They weren't being blockaded, but they couldn't exactly just leave if they wanted to. Even his officers were stopped out on the highway coming and going. He hadn't been told he couldn't do his job, but they had informed him he was being watched. Carefully.

"There're pockets of people all over. In the woods, by the

river. They're just away from towns because that's where the military are."

"Not the *actual* military," Paige said because that would be illegal.

He waived her off. "National Guard. Same thing."

Except it really wasn't. If the president was sending the military at the citizens of the U.S., then they were in big trouble and this "peace" they were living in would be gone. Probably for good because the paranormals—or even some of the humans who lived with their furry friends—wouldn't stand for that.

Civil war was a bad idea wrapped in a burrito of stupid.

"How's the new team?" Tuck asked.

She released a puff of frustration. "I managed to get a goblin. No one else answered the call."

"It's been a day."

True. "It'd been hours the last time."

"Well, but it's a different world this time."

Yeah. "Okay. Well, I gotta go."

"More'll come."

"I hope so." Paige stood. "Keep your head above the paperwork." Which, in her head, was a play on the *keep your head above water* phrase, but she wasn't sure if he got that.

"Keep your eye on your team. I don't want a new Dexx."

Paige's heart twisted a little at the mention of his name.

He winced apologetically but charged on. "This town can only handle one of those."

Paige understood what he meant and also compre-hended they didn't have time for mourning people who weren't dead. So, she turned and left. She had thought about driving to FBI headquarters, but if there were block-ades between Troutdale and the FBI building, she'd rather not send up flares. Besides, she'd walked up here. So, she'd fly.

But before she made it to the parking lot, Danny Miller found her.

"Hey," he said in surprise. "Uh, I didn't think I'd see you here."

Saying more than hi with people on the street was always weird because...what *were* you supposed to say to start? "Yeah. Just checking in with Tuck."

"Eh." Danny grumbled, then winced. "You wouldn't know when Dexx is scheduled to be back, would you?"

Her heart twisted a little, but not as much as it had a month ago. "Hopefully soon."

"'Kay."

The look on his face said he had something big. "What's going on?" She could at least ask, even if Dexx was the person he wanted.

"Missing persons." Danny winced. "I know you're not working on that anymore, but—"

Interesting. "I'm working on a missing persons case right now. Did you stop by Red Star?"

He gave her a baffled expression. "No."

"Okay. Well, um, Barn's there now. He's got information. Share what you have and maybe—I mean, we're short-staffed, so if you can help, great?"

"I'm a reporter."

"Exactly." She knew there was a fine line between investigating to share the news with the people and investigating to catch people. "We could use the help. Tuck's busy. Dexx's gone. I have a goblin."

Danny jerked in surprise.

She nodded with a sigh. "We could use the help."

"Well, I guess it couldn't hurt just to go down there and give what I have." He headed away from the station and toward Red Star.

Paige didn't wait any longer. She shifted into a bird and

flew to the FBI building not far away. She didn't take the direct route, though. She decided to see what Tuck was talking about.

Sure enough. There were check points along the way. Not just one, either. There were three along the highway from Portland to Troutdale, and there were several along the side streets that connected the two cities.

She even felt the presence of magick. She wasn't certain if they could detect her, but it did feel as though she'd slipped through at least two shields similar to the magick wards that protected Troutdale.

Not good.

She almost landed at the front doors to the FBI and walked in as a human from there, but she had a feeling. So, she landed on a patio on the same floor as Director Lovejoy's office. She didn't *sneak* in, but really, she did. Bypassing the guards meant illegal entry.

Lovejoy didn't appear to be *over*joyed to see her. "Paige, how nice to see you." Her face didn't reflect the words.

"Director. I came by to check in. See how things are going."

"There are red flags popping up all over the network," Director Lovejoy said after Paige had taken her seat. "Personnel are being flagged and removed for internal review."

That certainly wasn't good. "Are they being arrested? Disappearing?"

Lovejoy shook her blonde head. "They're home safe. For now. But it's clear that even with this 'peace,' the president is cleaning house."

Paige wished she could feel surprised, but she couldn't. She only felt relief that the agents weren't being shipped off to prison. "What about you?"

Lovejoy was a firebird with a soft red fire aura when Paige switched to shifter vision. She shrugged and bit her lip. "I'm safe for now, but how long will that last with people like you showing up at my door?"

"I flew in."

"Small favors." Lovejoy played with a pen on her desk. "I don't know how much longer I'm going to be effective here."

It felt like their entire world was dismantling. "Stay as long as you can."

Lovejoy cocked her eyebrow. "You *are* coming up with a plan, right?"

Paige understood the plan was for how to stop this government invasion. "Yeah, sure." No. Not really, but she had stopped asking why everyone was looking to her for answers. She'd finally figured that out. There were others who *could* do it, and maybe do it better.

But no one else *was* doing it.

"'Kay." Lovejoy's tone was hopeful, but her face said she understood what Paige hadn't said. There was no plan. This predicament was too big to handle or to get a grip on.

"I'll try to give you a heads up if something big happens." That was something she'd actually have to remember to do. Having Lovejoy there was imperative. "I could use Jack Scott's help."

Lovejoy shook her head. "I had to pull him out before he got flagged."

That made a little too much sense.

The director pulled out a card and handed it over. "Here's his number. Keep your head down. His too. The world's becoming a damn scary place."

Paige took the card. "Thanks for everything. I appreciate it more than you know." Then she went to the balcony, trying to be as inconspicuous as possible. Having a case was nice, but she had bigger fish to fry. She had to come up with a plan of attack. The president was playing nice.

For now. But what happened when she got the support to strike out again?

They had to be prepared and the only way to do that was to stop pretending this peace was going to hold. These ghosts could be the indication that it wasn't.

Yeah. It was time to get serious. Again.

4

But first, it was her night to cook, so she flew home, but not before she did a bigger sweep of the area to determine just how many check points there were and if people were being turned away.

The answers were quite a few and yes.

She didn't dare get close enough to tell what was being said because she didn't know what kind of magick detection devices they might have had. She needed to learn more about those screens she'd passed through. Were they wards? Was DoDO keeping tabs on her? How many were there? She decided to come back out with some of the pack later to determine just how big they were and what they might be.

She did manage to spot a few packs and tribes moving off-road. Some were on four-wheelers and side-by-sides. Others were traveling by paw or foot.

The Pegasus was there, which meant that Doe and the Utah pack were as well. If Doe was there, then who was protecting the desert region?

She'd have to ask Chuck. Again. Later because it was her turn to—yada, yada, yada.

Paige wondered where the twins were.

On our way home now, Rai's voice said crisply.

Okay. *How are you talking to me?*

Ember grunted. *You're shifted and you're using the pack bond, Mom. Duh.*

Duh? As if this was a thing they all used all the time? She added that to the list of things to ask about.

Her claws shifted to booted feet as soon as they touched the ground and she walked the last few feet to her back porch, waving for Margo to join her in the kitchen.

"It's not my night," Margo said, her hands raised as she moved to follow.

Paige shook her head and immediately went to see what kinds of ingredients they had on hand. Occasionally, thoughtful people would put out a package—a Whiskey-sized package—of meat to thaw on the counter so that people like her could just start there. This night, however, she wasn't that lucky. However, they had half of a leftover meatloaf from the night before—or two nights ago? She couldn't remember. She'd just use that. "I've got a question for you."

"Shoot." Margo went to the pantry and pulled out the bag of potatoes, heading toward the sink to wash them off.

"Do you—" Paige was about to sound real dumb. "Do you hear the voices of the pack when you're shifted?"

"Um." Margo tipped her head to the side, turning on the water, and thought about that. "Not qui—really. No. We communicate, but not with words."

"Ah."

"Why? Did you? Hear someone?"

"Um. Yes." Paige drew that last word out. "Ember and Rai."

"Oh. Well, that could make sense. They're your kids?"

"But they said its normal?"

Margo washed potatoes and set them to the side. "Maybe for them. We're still working out how they work."

That was a very true statement. "There's something else." She explained what she'd felt on her way to the FBI headquarters.

Margo was a bit relieved. "I was going to tell you about that, too. Garek and I noticed something on our patrols the other night. I meant to tell you."

Paige also found a wealth of veggies in the crisper that were about to go bad. Her specialty dish was shit-in-a-pot, which was usually just anything she could get her hands on thrown into the same pot. "There's been a lot going on."

Margo grunted and pulled out the spiralizer. "We need to do something as a pack, especially now that you and the kids are back."

Something with the pack. Oh, right. "That's something Dexx usually handles."

"You're right. But he's not here. So."

"Okay." Paige rubbed her right hand. She didn't know what she'd done to it, but it ached slightly. Getting old sucked. "Well, then we'll go check these things out after dinner." Paige knew Margo was giving her the you're-the-alpha talk. But she wasn't the alpha. Dexx was. It took a lot more to be an alpha than being a powerful person. Chuck showed her that. Doe did. Heck, for that matter, Kat did. Paige was a powerful witch and she had the ability to shift. And she'd given birth to two really amazingly powerful shifter witch kids. That was it.

There was a knock on the door.

Paige glanced over at Margo. "This is literally just crap in a pot."

Margo narrowed her eyes. "Still not my night."

Paige headed toward the door. "I'll take you off the calendar for next week." Because Paige was "technically" at home, she had become the scheduler for chores. Yeah. She sucked at it.

With food no longer in dire threat of being destroyed, Paige went to the door, wondering just who in the heck it could be.

It was a familiar face. Tall, tanned, sun-bleached dark hair in a slightly feminine high-and-tight pony tail. Pinched expression on a pixie face. This was the harpy who'd applied before and had almost made the Red Star Team. She was the one Paige had *wished* she'd hired instead of Quinn. "Detective Drake," Paige said with surprise.

"Scout. You said you were hiring." The harpy pushed her way through.

Technically, there were a few things Paige could have done to stop her, but she chose not to. Instead, she just closed the door behind the detective and followed her into the living room. "Would you care for something to drink?"

"Whiskey if you've got it."

Paige actually didn't know if they still had whiskey or *any* alcohol. They'd all been so busy and none of them were real drinkers. Of course, there was always the occasional glass of wine that she could now partake in since she was no longer pregnant and obviously not nursing. But she just hadn't remembered.

She went to the liquor cabinet and pulled out two glasses. "I thought you'd call."

"I decided to just come."

"From where?"

"New York." Scout took the offered glass and shot it back.

Okay. "That was a sipping whiskey." Was she in trouble?

"I'll sip the next one." Scout offered the glass for a refill.

Paige picked up the whiskey bottle with her right hand, but the ache intensified. So she filled Scout's glass with her left instead and just left the bottle out. She decided to take this to the kitchen. There'd been a reason a lot of the bigger conversations at Alma's house had happened while making food. "I'm making dinner. You can talk while we cook."

Scout frowned, then looked around in mild confusion. "There are a lot of scents."

"Probably so. There's a sma—medium-sized zoo in this house."

Margo had managed to spiral cut the potatoes and had put them in the two massive pans.

It was time to get information from the harpy. "What happened?" That was a rather out-of-left-field question. "At your old job. Why do you want to work here?"

Scout leaned up against the counter and set her whiskey beside her. "I make people uncomfortable."

That wasn't a selling point.

"I do, too," Margo said simply, grabbing a large onion. "Men mostly. It's why I don't work."

There was actually a lot about Margo that Paige didn't know. "What did you used to do before…" Coming to protect the Whiskey lands for free because Paige didn't actually pay her. Was that…was she… Crap. She needed to think about that.

"Before I became security and a babysitter?"

Paige probably wouldn't put it that way, but… "Yeah."

Bobby came running in from the front door with a wild laugh. "Mom, Mom, Mom! You won't *believe* what happened today."

Paige set down her stirring spoon and gave her son a one-armed hug. She wasn't going to get used to the fact that her toddler was now the size of a ten-year-old or that it had happened nearly overnight. "I'm in the middle of an interview, I think. So, ten words or less." Paige had discovered that part of Bobby's new personality was being a chatterbox.

He brushed his dirty blond hair out of his blazing blue eyes. "I aced the science experiment."

He'd only been ten for a matter of weeks, so they'd been pushing him through school, trying to get him caught up.

It was like he inhaled knowledge. There were a few subjects that tripped him up, like history. He kept getting it confused and Paige suspected it was because he was mixing up the past, present, and the future. How was she supposed to help him with that? She didn't know, but it was something she'd need to find an answer to.

Add it to the list.

"That's *great,*" she crowed while making her mental notes. She'd stayed up for the last two nights helping him. She enjoyed science. Science was cool, but it wasn't something she invested a lot of time in because…well, reality and bills and people and jobs and kids and… yeah.

Scout picked up her whiskey and sipped.

"I can take over," Bobby said, shucking his backpack, his grin still wild.

"It's my turn." Paige grabbed his head before he walked away and planted a kiss on it. "You did awesome."

"Thanks, Mom." He pecked her cheek. "Where's Lee?"

Paige winced. "I don't know?"

Bobby gave her a smile that was a little more grown up than it should have been, but then his eyes unfocused and gave off a slight golden glow. They snapped back into focus and he gave her a frog-like smile. "Upstairs. I'll go bug her."

"Dinner'll be ready in a few."

He frowned at the still raw potatoes. "Yeah, okay."

Scout watched the boy leave. "Zoo. Gotcha."

"You haven't seen anything. Stayin' for supper?"

"Really?"

Paige looked down at the whiskey glass, almost empty.

"Right. Uh, sure?"

"Great." Paige added some oil to the pans of potatoes and handed Scout the stirring spoon. "Look, I don't care if you make people feel uncomfortable. You'll be teaming up with a goblin. Trust me. People will be looking to you. What I want is your past experience. I've been running this team with one person. I need someone with any credible experience as a cop and a detective."

Scout frowned and pulled her head back as she tentatively stirred the top few potato strings. "Okay. What *is* the sitrep?"

"Scout, if you're going to cook the potatoes, you've gotta move them." Paige grabbed the spoon and showed the harpy before handing it back. "The situation's not great. The world is in upheaval already. The team I built is out on a mission. The gods know how they're doing. We've got a major ghost case."

"Ghosts?"

"Yeah." Paige grabbed the veggies, trying to figure out the best way to add them. Veggie stacking was something she was actually good at. Who knew? "It's paranormal for sure because our only clues are the ghosts, but it could be tied to DoDO. We think. We don't know. Seriously, the only clues we have right now are ghosts."

"Sounds like New York."

Paige seriously doubted that, but okay. "I don't know what I can pay you yet. The sheriff sent over the budget. I haven't had time to review it. And I don't know how permanent this is going to be."

"So, trial period." Scout blinked and nodded thoughtfully.

Which was a good sign. "Yeah. Look, if things go pear-shaped with the president, we might all be in jail or internment camps. Things could go well, and we'll still all be out of work, or things could go back to normal."

"Just how close are you to all that?"

It felt weird being with someone who didn't know. "Real

close. I'm the unofficial Secretary of Paranormal… I forget what."

"That sounds really official."

Scout's sarcasm was strong. "Well, it can only be assigned by the president, and I doubt she's gonna give that anytime soon. However, chances are good we won't ever see our old normal again, and I have no way of knowing what our new world will look like."

Scout pressed her glass to her lips, setting the spoon down. "Okay. I'm in."

A thread of relief ran through Paige. "Great. I might be taking off during the investigation—"

"For what?" Scout asked incredulously.

"To handle… Secretary stuff. I don't know. I'll try to stay as long as I can." The potatoes were starting to smell like they were ready to be seasoned. She grabbed a bunch of different seasonings and dumped them in until her nose said they were good. Starting with well-seasoned meatloaf had been a good idea. "If you can prove you can do your job, I'll assign you lead."

Shock filled Scout's face as she pulled away from the stove. "Lead?"

"Yeah." Wait. "Is that a problem?"

"No. It's just—" Scout opened her mouth and closed it a couple of times, her hands going wide then coming back to her body again. "I'm a harpy."

"I'm a bitch."

Margo snorted a laugh. "She is."

Scout blinked, a slight smile settling on her lips.

Paige held out the spoon. "You do your job and you do it well. *That's* what I care about. We've got ghosts putting people in comas and a president throwing people in jail for having teeth. I can handle the president. I need someone to handle the ghosts."

"Okay." Scout took the spoon and nodded some more, but with real acceptance and a hint of excitement. "Okay. You got a medium?"

The onions were starting to smell like they were burning. "Not one with time on her hands."

Paige went back to cutting veggies while fielding Scout's questions.

Margo continued to forage in the two refrigerators for leftovers that could be added. That was the other great thing about shit-in-a-pot. It got rid of leftovers that would have normally gone bad because people refused to eat them. However, going through the leftovers also helped all the people because cooking for big groups meant serving different people with different eating issues: likes, dislikes, allergies, diets. Shifters didn't have to worry about diets too much. Witches did, though. Magick didn't burn calories.

Paige almost wished she'd brought the case files home. It was enough she'd brought her computer. She'd have to seriously look at that budget.

The kids came down and emptied the cabinets of plates and the silverware drawer of the flatware. The pack and family came in and everyone sat at the large, u-shaped dinner table.

Leslie seemed happy as she joked with her husband, Tru, who seemed super stressed. But as he sat at the table eating, he began to unwind.

Nick and Mark had their heads together a lot of the night. Their adopted daughter, Kate, poked her head in occasionally, making her points with her finger which was curved slightly backward. Her elf hands were double-jointed.

Barn came over with Joel. Goblins ate like toddlers.

Ripley and Joe showed up just in time to shovel the remains in their gullets before doing dishes because it was their night.

Paige watched, focusing on all of them instead of just her kids for once. This was her pack. But where most shifters would just look at the *shifters* as being part of that pack, she saw them all. The witches, the kids, the goblin and the harpy and the human. They were her family—her found family. *That* meant pack to her.

Before they all dispersed, she called out. "Hey, would you all like to do something a little dangerous tonight?"

Leslie looked over at Kammy who was the only kid who hadn't grown in leaps and bounds, but only because they'd been able to stop the rapid growth before it had killed him. "What kind of dangerous?"

Paige took in a deep breath and stood. "DoDO set up some kind of magick detection system around Troutdale. I need to know what it is, how dangerous it might be, and what they're doing. Can they put us on lockdown with these? Will they harm shifters? Paras? Witches?"

"And you want us—" Scout said, gesturing to all of them, "—to risk our lives to find out."

"I do."

The harpy shrugged. "Okay. I'm in."

Paige split everyone up. Each shifter got a witch buddy and the two were to stick together. The way she saw it, this way they'd be able to handle just about anything that came their way.

Joel was teamed up with Nick and Margo. Not because Paige had assigned it that way, but because her brother had wanted to learn more about this particular goblin. "He's getting close to my sister and I want to know why."

That was really sweet of her baby brother. She might not have grown up with him, but she was enjoying getting to know him as an adult.

Paige separated the twins to go with others. They were witches and shifters, so they didn't have to team up with anyone in particular. Rai went with Ripley. The two were nearly inseparable anyway. Ember went with Scout and Tru.

Yeah, even the humans went on this one.

Barn was beyond tickled until he learned they'd be walking. "I didn't bring the right shoes."

"That can't be helped, Barn." Paige knew they had a lot of spare sets of clothes, but shoes weren't things they kept on hand. "Take your phone."

He glared through his coke-bottle glasses and didn't back down.

Bobby bounced around, excited to go along as well. He paired up with Leslie and Kammy. Paige had tried to keep Kammy at the house, but Leslie hadn't agreed. "He's staying with me."

Paige knew better than to get in between a momma and her cub.

Tyler called in his best friend, Toby, and those two slinked away with Clem and Alex. The bear, wolf, and hyena should be perfectly safe with a bard watching over them. What a weird world they lived in.

That left Paige, Leah, and Mandy together with Joe who had refused to let the three go without him. "Look, Rip can take care of herself. My ego can handle that. But let me at least pretend like I'm doing some good here."

Paige chuckled, but let the imposing grizzly shifter join their team. "We're looking for information," she told everyone. "Do not engage."

She got the affirmatives from everyone then they all headed out in different directions.

The true shifters took off their clothes. The shifter witches simply shifted.

The humans grumbled.

Paige chose an elephant so Leah could ride. It was Leah's favorite shape, though traversing the woods as an elephant wasn't easy. The pine trees weren't super forgiving.

She listened with her mind, trying to see whose thoughts she could hear, and who she could just get impressions from.

Kammy's voice underlaid all of them. Each voice she heard, each thought that entered her mind, held a tint of Kammy's tone, his soul-resonance.

I have wondered what a telepath would do for a pack, Cawli said as Paige, Leah, Mandy, and Joe made their way through the woods. He appeared beside her in small cat form.

Really. So what do you think?

Cawli sighed. *The shifter bond is different than the coven pledge. We give a little bit of ourselves away. That is what gives the pack greater strength.*

Paige didn't feel as though she'd really given herself to this pack, that she really belonged.

You do.

But what have I given them?

Cawli didn't answer immediately as he hunted for something hiding in a bush. He came up empty-mouthed. *What haven't you?*

Her attention. But before she could continue with that line of question, Mandy sent out a startled screech from Joe's back. *I found something!* "I found something!"

Well, at least the girl said what she thought. *What is it?*

"Aunt Paige?"

Speak with your mind.

"Uh." *Okay. I found something?* Mandy mentally whispered back.

The girl would shout with her voice, but whisper with her mind?

Paige cleared the trees and shifted into a fox.

Leah slid to her own feet. *What is that?* she asked also in a mind whisper.

It appeared they'd found what they were looking for. It was a black box with sickly white vines digging into the ground.

But what exactly was this?

And how was it going to be used against her family?

---

5

*C*an *anyone else see this?* Paige asked along the network, not sure who all was going to hear it.

Paige? Tru asked, his voice laced with confusion.

Kammy, was all Paige said.

There were a few grunts, though she was pretty sure none of them *truly* understood how it all worked.

Since Paige wasn't sure any of them knew what she was talking about, she offered more information. *I've got a black box over here with white vines going into the Earth. Anyone else see something similar?* How many could DoDO have planted? *If you find one, don't touch it.*

We've got something like it over here, Tru said. *Em just found it.*

Where you guys at?

Paige got a sense of location through their bond that was tied to how long it'd taken them to walk. It didn't make a ton of sense.

Just passed Eldora's, Tru said.

Blackman compound didn't belong to Eldora now that she was dead, but it was hard to train the brain to call it something else. She waited to hear back from the other teams and took the time to study the box in front of her, careful not to touch it.

Joe shifted to mostly human but kept fur over his private bits. He was strong enough in his shifting abilities that he could do that, something Paige had only seen other bear shifters do. "It smells…funny."

Cawli? Paige maintained her fox form and circled around it, looking at it through her fox vision which was actually really good, but not superb for this. She needed to see better.

Cawli took over and shifted them into an owl. With her large eyes, she was able to see even better. Just one more reason to love the owl. The vines disappeared into the earth, but with her owl eyes, she was able to see other smaller threads coming from each one, almost like roots. No, *just like roots.*

The conversation she'd had with Mario weeks ago came floating to her mind. Ley line magick. When she'd been forced to feed the wards when Dexx had slammed an angel into them almost a year ago, she'd accidentally touched one of those ley lines, something she wasn't supposed to be able to do.

Then, she'd been able to absorb the mage power thrown at her in the elven city and again in Kansas.

She wondered if she could do that now to find out more information on these boxes now.

Use the connection of the pack to keep you stable, Cawli said, stopping beside her in his natural form, more ethereal than solid.

Paige nodded and shifted into human form. "If something happens, get ready to knock me off," she told Joe.

"Off what?" he asked, perplexed.

"Her feet," Leah said, stabbing Paige with her glare. "I hope you know what you're doing."

She gave her daughter an of-course-I-do look but inwardly

hoped the same thing. Releasing a breath, she shook out her hands and called on her magick. The last time she'd touched the ley lines, she'd knocked out her magick and her shifting abilities for a few days. And she'd done it all on instinct. This time, she was doing it on purpose.

She did everything with her witch hands, not quite knowing how to do magick without them. Well, she could talk to the elements on her own, but her magick came with her inky black, door-magick hands.

She reached for the roots around the box, fearful of what might happen when she did. Would she be able touch it? Would she be attacked? She wouldn't know until she tried.

She gripped the box with her witch hands.

A blinding white light flared out around her.

Leah and Mandy shielded their faces with their hands.

Joe growled low and reverted to a bear.

The magick, though, screamed.

The Earth cried out, struggling, the feel of constriction bleeding into Paige. They begged to be free.

From what?

Captivity.

She felt the constriction around her neck as if she was being choked. Her arms felt heavy as if they were bound, fighting the pull of gravity.

The roots around the box pulsed with angry red light pushing from the earth.

That light beat in a rhythm and swelled in a dome. Well, almost. There were several of the domes and they all inter-connected, like soap bubbles bundled up together. With a red film the same color as the light.

With the visual came understanding of intent.

Mark. Maim. Murder.

When Paige looked down at herself, she saw that same red film covering her.

Marked.

And on her right hand—her real hand, not the magick one —she saw a wound of sorts, where the red film had found a weakness—a bug bite? A scratch?—and was leaching into her.

Maim.

She turned her gaze to Leah who was covered in the red film. Then Mandy and Joe.

Equally covered.

They'd all managed to slip through one of DoDO's barriers.

Mark. Maim. Murder.

She panicked, seeing her family and friends marked like her. How could she kill something not alive? She studied the light and the roots. She answered herself. Don't kill it, bring life back to it.

A peaceful calm settled over her as a sense of what needed to be done filled her. Kneeling where she stood, she grabbed two of the roots.

And fed them with the light and power of her soul, sending it through the ley lines, seeking each root of sickness, obliterating them. Not in massive explosions, but in the subtle leeching of light and life.

As the roots were eaten away, the Earth sighed and relaxed as if testing to feel freedom once again.

"Whoa!" Leah steadied herself with Paige's shoulder for a second. "Mom, what's happening?"

Paige pulled herself away from the ley line magick and shook. Hard. Like immersing with the elements, working with the ley magick was like disconnecting from humanity. As she slipped back into her own consciousness, she felt the earth shake. She knew what that was, though. "She's just glad to be free."

"What?" Mandy demanded.

"The Mother. She had cages on her. Forcing compulsion. She's… happy."

What's going on with your boxes? Paige asked the group, not sure if her words would be heard by anyone.

No one answered.

She shifted back into a fox and tried again.

This time, Margo answered. *It's…disappearing."*

Good. Paige watched through slitted fox eyes as the blinding light ate away at the roots around the box. Shifting back into a human, she stared at her daughter, niece, and packmate to watch the red film recede from them as the black box and the roots disappeared. With life or death, she couldn't tell. The domes overhead burbled away as if a corrosive agent devoured them.

The mark on her hand, though, remained. It didn't grow, but it didn't go away either.

She'd have to deal with that later.

After the domes and boxes were gone, Paige had everyone search a little more, but no one found any malicious magick. DoDO agents didn't pop out of nowhere.

Why? Because they had what they wanted?

Studying the mark on her, Paige was fairly certain that was the answer. So, what was this and how was she going to remove it?

The next morning, it wasn't better. The throb was still there, but now it ran up her arm. Checking it with her witch vision, she couldn't *see* any difference, but her body was certainly telling her it was there.

Cawli was concerned and showed it by disappearing. Again.

Cats. Is this what Dexx meant when he complained about Hattie?

Paige barely made it to Red Star and sat in the chair with

a puff of exhaled breath before Danny Miller called. "There's a riot in Denver."

Of course there was. "What am I supposed to do? That's way outside my jurisdiction."

"There's no one else to call. You're the only one doing anything about anything."

Paige was, frankly, having a hard time focusing on anything other than her hand. What was going on? Her magick didn't seem affected. She was still able to shift. "What's it about this time?"

"Paranormals. Of course. There's a group of people upset they can't travel, that flights have been canceled because of concerns some of them might be paranormals. They're tired of the precautions being put in place."

She stood, heading back out to the conference room. Habit took her to the office in the first place. "Like what?" Paige opened the office door with her left hand, fumbling with the knob and her laptop bag. She wasn't used to doing stuff with her off-hand.

"They're being told to stay home. Only go to the grocery store if needed. There's a curfew."

"A curfew?"

Danny sighed. "Some of the precautions aren't terrible. They're not arresting people. But the government did a pretty good job in scaring the crap out of normal folks. Their jobs are being affected. They're having a hard time paying their bills because of it."

"Humans are?" Paige was struggling to see what the issues were. "This is a war on paras. The president is having *us* arrested. Humans are doing just fine. We're not telling them they can't work."

"But some of the businesses have closed."

This wasn't making any sense. "Because why? We're contagious?"

"Because your lot owned some of those businesses."

"Oh." Fuck.

"Yeah."

Well, crap. "Let me make some calls." Because she was the only one who would.

Joel and Scout were in the conference room and it looked like they were working the case just fine without her. Barn was nowhere to be seen, but that just meant he was working somewhere else. The man was always working even when he didn't have a "real job."

Paige went to Dexx's office, taking a seat in her old chair.

She pulled up the news feed as soon as her computer booted up and got caught up on Denver. People were storming the capital with loaded guns. Who in their right minds would do that? If paras did that—Well, they already *knew* how the government would treat them. They'd been arrested for going to work and paying taxes like normal people.

How was it possible that things could be blowing up this hard this fast? This was the twenty-first century, after all.

She called Tuck, who had a different view on going to Denver. "Even if you use door magick and zip over there real fast like you do, they've got people waiting. Now, I'm not supposed to know, but we're a tight bunch and we look out for each other. Yeah. Things are real bad down there. They'll be looking for an 'invasion of force.'"

Paige groaned. She really couldn't fault them. The last two times she and her team had come in using door magick, she'd put the hurt on some bad people.

Her next call was to Chuck. "First, why is Doe in town? Everything okay in Utah?"

He grunted. "We have things to discuss here, and no. Things are not great. I've got it under control."

Perfect. "Have you heard anything from Nederland?" That

was the paranormal community just outside Denver. Well, it wasn't *just* outside Denver. It was tucked up in the hogbacks closer to Golden.

"Not a peep. You heard about Denver, I guess?"

She nodded then remembered he couldn't hear that. "Yeah. I was thinking of going."

"It's probably a good idea."

Direct contradiction to Tuck. "Do you have any advice for me?"

His tone said he didn't know why she'd called him, which was a little disheartening because she needed *someone* who was smarter than her. "You do remember you have a seat at the high alpha table." His soft, Mediterranean accent bit at her a little.

It only bit because she was so familiar with Leslie and her Texas drawl only deepened when she was trying to point out that Paige was being dumb. "Right. What should I do with that, though? They weren't effective the last time."

"Show them how to *be* effective."

Right. Be the leader of the most powerful paranormals of the United States. That should be easy. "How do I put out the call?"

"I'll make the arrangements."

"For after I get back."

He sighed at her. "Don't take a team. Go alone."

Why was he all of a sudden putting restrictions on her? He'd started out saying he was glad she was going. "With my kids."

"Just *one* of them."

She understood what he was saying. Her kids were powerhouses.

And one of them had very nearly killed her—

Which reminded her… she had a healer. That should

work on her hand. "Okay. One. Bye." She hung up and texted Leah. *I need Bobby. What class is he in?*

She didn't get a response back immediately, which she was glad of. Leah was supposed to be focused in class.

It gave her time to call Phoebe. "Hey," she said after the Blackman coven leader picked up. "I've got a question for you."

"You're about to start another war." Phoebe's words were blunt, but her tone was soft.

"No. But one's been started for us."

"I thought we were at peace."

"So did I. Just, hey. Are all the Blackmans home?"

"Uh." Phoebe stalled.

Paige's phone buzzed, letting her know she had a message. Probably Leah.

"No? I mean, yeah no. Why?"

"Because I'm afraid they might be captured and used. Word's out. We use door magick and DoDO knows Blackmans have the market on that. So, you might want to pull everyone in."

"They have lives, Paige."

"And this war won't care about that. Just… I want them to *keep* their lives." Paige pulled the phone away as another message came in. Both from Leah. She put the phone back to her ear. "Tell them to at the very least to be careful. I really think they're in danger."

"Okay. So, you don't want me to bring them in so you can add them to your arsenal."

Oh, she did. Phoebe had proven she was at the very least more trustworthy than her predecessor. "Yes, but I won't if you say no. Just, look, okay? Things might get ugly again and I don't know where it'll stop this time."

"Okay." Phoebe made a strangled noise. "I'll make some calls."

"Thanks. Have a good day." Paige hung up and opened Leah's messages.

He's not even in my school.

What's wrong? R U okay?

Paige rolled her eyes and texted back. *I'm fine. What school is he in?*

The response was quick. *Doesn't he call U MOM?*

YES. But Paige hadn't been the one to enroll him. Wendy was still putting him through tests and letting him sit in on classes.

OMG.

Paige doubted she was going to get much more than that from Leah. But then another message did come through.

It was a gif of a cat with big eyes and flashing pink letters that said, O-M-G with confetti.

Okay. That was fair, but Bobby might be the way to heal her hand.

She could wait until after work.

She worked on Dexx's least favorite job. Paperwork. She figured out the budget, and made Joel and Scout hard offers, printing them out and giving them over. Then she had to process them in. She even got Barn hired on, finally.

Hiring people was a pain in the ass.

By the time she was done with the paperwork, there wasn't time for her to butt into their investigation. So, she told them she'd be gone for a few days and that Scout was in charge.

Joel and Barn didn't even bat an eye. Well, Barn might have, but she couldn't see him with his face so close to the computer.

Paige found Bobby as soon as she made it home and asked him to heal her hand.

She held it out to him and his cool fingers moved her arm so he could see.

He just frowned at her. "Mom, there's nothing there to heal. You're fine."

"No. Bobs, it's right there." She pointed at the spot that hurt most. "It's a wound. It *hurts*."

"I can't see anything wrong with it."

Paige frowned and switched to witch vision. The wound wasn't getting better. Angry red veins reached up her arm. "You're sure you can't see it?"

Bobby nodded. "Yeah. I'll call Roxxie. See if she can see anything."

"Nah." Paige held up her hand. Roxxie was an angel and Bobby's protector, but with the angel gate partially separated from the earth, it was harder for her to move around. She didn't have a complete connection to Heaven anymore and she lived an hour away. "I've gotta go to Denver. Maybe when I come back."

"Okay." He grinned. "Be safe. I love you."

His kiss on her cheek felt like a punch to the gut. Her son was so used to her just leaving that he wasn't even broken up about it.

She worked out a few of the babysitting details with Margo and Leslie. They were used to taking over as well, so it was old hat to them. Leslie made changes to the chores calendar, and luckily that was the biggest issue.

The twins were nowhere to be found, but Paige could feel them. They were with their Uncle Nick and Cousin Kate. She sent them a *see ya later* through their bond and got one back in return.

Her twins were months old and she hadn't spent hardly any time with them at all. That casual return call was like a twist to her mom-soul.

She needed to do better. When would the world slow down so she could?

She found Leah at the dinner table pouring over her biology book. "Hey, Bean. Wanna take me to Denver?"

Leah brightened. "Seriously? I'd be out of school."

"Only for a day or two. I just need a ride."

Leah grinned and grabbed her bag by the garage door. "I'm ready when you are."

Paige reached down and grabbed her own go bag along with her laptop, then hooked Leah by the neck and pressed a kiss to her head. "Love you."

"Love you back. Where to?"

Paige gave her as much information about Nederland as she could. Leah used her unique ability to locate *where* to go and opened a door from their kitchen to downtown Nederland.

When Paige stepped out, she knew something was wrong. Very wrong.

Nederland was a ghost town.

6

N ederland was never quite bustling as a back-country, nearly forgotten, mountain town, but it certainly had never been *this* deserted. It was a small mountain town—a Colorado small mountain town. All the buildings looked like they'd been built during the Wild West days, even though one of the buildings was new. She didn't remember seeing it the last time she'd been there.

But the last time she'd been there, Dexx'd been bitten and she'd been chosen by Cawli. Oh, how times had changed.

"What are we doing here?" Leah asked, hitching her backpack a little higher.

Paige massaged her hand around the spot. It hurt like it was bruised and going through the door hadn't helped at all. "Well, I was going to borrow a car or get a ride into town."

"Yeah, but why didn't we just open a door to Denver?" Leah spun in a slow circle with a bored frown. "I thought this place'd be...cooler somehow."

Well, Paige had told her some pretty incredible stories about this place, that was for sure. A lot had happened there.

"It's the people who make it cool." Where had everyone gone? "See if you can find signs of leaving under duress."

"Uh, okay." Leah headed off down the literal wooden sidewalk, staying close enough to Paige that if anything happened, she'd be okay.

Paige also looked. The doors were locked. Peering inside the windows, everything looked fine.

But there were a lot of cars still left in the town.

They decided to venture away from downtown and into the more residential areas. A few streets jutted from the main street with long drives where the green pines, cottonwoods, and aspens obscured the view of the homes which were usually log cabin-esqe in nature. She was looking for cell reception because she knew she needed to call someone, or have Leah take them back home. But they'd made it here, so she wasn't going to just leave.

She managed to find cell coverage in one spot in the middle of the street. She had two bars. That should be enough. So, she called Dexx. It rang and rang and rang. If anyone could teach her how to hotwire a car, it would be that guy.

But he didn't answer.

She'd hoped. He'd managed to get her the thumb drive from DoDO, so she'd… It was dumb. She didn't have the full story, but she knew he was in trouble and that she…

She just wanted an emoji text conversation. She just wanted him to text her demanding a sandwich, knowing it would set her off because she wasn't the "get her man a sandwich" kind of woman. And he thought that was funny.

Only because he made better sandwiches anyway.

And he did.

She looked up to the great, blue sky and sighed. When was she getting her man back? She felt naked and alone without him.

But capable. She was very capable. Maybe not for the task at hand, but she was…yeah. Hotwire a car. Who else could she call?

Pushing down her worry about him and the developing situation and their kids and…everything, she tried Tuck.

"You want me to what again?" Sheriff Tuck asked pointedly.

She realized by that tone that calling him as a lifeline in this situation had been a bad idea. "I'd only be borrowing it."

"That's still theft."

"But only if the owners reported it as stolen. I'll leave a note."

He didn't answer.

"I'll call someone else."

"Please do." Tuck ended the call before Paige could.

Well, oops, but in her defense, Tuck had a lot of skills no one would think of because there were things he needed to sometimes do. He excelled in breaking *into* cars, for instance. Also, he liked old cars and was able to talk engines with Dexx for hours at a time, so it'd just seemed like a good fit.

But this *was* technically a crime.

Were the people of Nederland okay?

Chuck was her next call, but he didn't answer either.

She called Margo and Ripley—who gave her a trick to use on older trucks. Something about a solenoid and a screwdriver? Paige put that on the list of things to try out later when she had more than one bar to play a Youtube video on.

Desperate, she called Ollie because he was in charge of criminal activities as leader of the Eastwood Coven. Granted, his coven specialized in killing people, but he had to know someone who could hotwire a car for her.

He picked up after the second call and third text message. "Hey, Paige. I assume from the messages that it's urgent?"

"It is. I've got a bit of a situation. I need to hotwire a car and need someone who can help."

"And you called me." His tone was very dry.

"Well, if it makes you feel any better, I tried calling everyone else first, including Tuck."

"The sheriff?"

"Yes. You'd think he'd know."

Oliver paused for a moment. "Where are you?"

She sighed, realizing she wasn't acting her normal self. This was outside her wheelhouse. "Nederland. Everyone's gone. Leah and I are trying to see if we can find anyone left."

"You've got Lee with you?"

"Of course." His tone wasn't completely accusatory, but it didn't tell her she was making good decisions either. But why did she care what her half-brother, the crime leader thought?

Not having Dexx there was starting to wear her thin. She could see around the edges. Something like this should be easy with him around. He'd grounded and centered her. They'd snark about cars. He'd find an old clunker that was "perfect," and they'd be on their merry way.

She hoped he was safe.

"Where are you *exactly*?"

"I don't know. Down a road, looking at houses."

"I'll send a driver."

"What?" A taxi? All the way out there?

"I have drivers in every city. I'll call Bastian. He'll be by to pick you up. There's no cell coverage in Nederland."

"You're not kidding."

"He'll call you on Mom's amulet."

The amulet Merry had given her? "Uh, okay?" Paige wasn't certain how that was going to work.

"He'll find you. Try to get closer to actual town, though."

It'd become habit to take that amulet with her even

though she'd only used it once. So, that was one thing in her favor.

"And, Paige?"

"Yeah?" Who just had *drivers* in every city?

"Be careful."

"Yeah. Will do. Thanks."

"Any time."

This time, she was the one who disconnected. She didn't know how Bastian was going to be able to locate her and Leah, but she also knew she had a mystery to solve.

Too bad Sam lived so far away.

Wait. Leah could take them to Sam's cabin.

She felt a moment of panic before she found Leah around the corner of a tourist trap selling authentic tack and gear. "I've got an idea." The corners of her mouth pulled up in a grin.

"It's better than stealing a car, right?" Leah shook her head, arms out to her side.

Paige rolled her eyes. "If Dexx was here, that wouldn't have been the dumbest idea."

"If Dad was here, we'd be on our way to Denver by now."

Leah had a point. Also, it warmed Paige's heart to hear Leah call Dexx her dad, but it also made Paige realize that she really needed to tie that knot. "When I was here last time, there was this guy, Sam, and he was helpful. I'm wondering if he might have left us a clue of some kind."

"So, you want me to build a door to take us there?" It wasn't a question. More of a WTF statement.

"Yeah."

"But not to Denver."

Also, yeah. "Do you remember that time we busted into a prison and freed the prisoners using your magick?"

Leah winced and blinked into the high sun. She remembered that time vividly.

"And do you remember that time we used your magick to sneak into an elven city and we waged war on DoDO to save as many elves as we could?" The vision of the dead elven kids still haunted her. What an idiot she'd been to bring her own. And yet, here she was again with Leah in tow.

Leah lost her bluster and the tone. "Okay. Point. Where are we going?" Leah screwed her lips to the side and offered her hand.

Paige gave her as much location information as she could so Leah could open the door. Leah parted the air with a dark light, which Paige hadn't thought was a thing until she'd seen Leah's magick. The thin, jagged line parted and Sam's backyard came into view.

Stepping through, Paige winced as her hand gave off a dull shoot of pain. Whatever was going on with that would have to be dealt with soon. Did it hurt more than a few minutes ago?

The yard hadn't changed much. The growth from the forest still encroached on the cabin. It could use a new roof, and boards were missing from the porch now. A stone from the fire pit had fallen out and the blue lawn chair was accordioned up and lying on the ground beside it.

Was that a sign that things were bad or that Sam was old?

Keeping her magick on high alert, Paige moved forward. Everything was still and quiet.

The backdoor was unlocked. She hadn't expected it to be any other way. "Sam?" she called as she walked in. "It's Paige Whiskey. We met a few years ago. Sam?"

Leah followed practically on top of Paige's heals, stepping on the bottom of her shoe so it slipped off her heal a little.

"Lee," Paige growled, gesturing with one hand for the girl to give her a bit more space.

"Sorry," Leah whispered.

Paige walked into the kitchen. It was small but clean. The

dishes were stacked neatly beside the sink. Nothing seemed out of place. It looked like he'd planned for an extended visit.

But if that was the case, then people would have left of their own accord. Because of the trouble brewing locally? Or because they'd known they'd be taken?

No. If they'd known someone would be coming for them, they'd migrate away. Right?

Then, why were there so many cars around town?

"Mom," Leah said, her tone tinted with confusion. "Isn't this *yours?*"

Paige turned to see what her daughter was talking about and found a ring she'd liked to wear that had gone missing a few weeks prior. She hadn't thought anything of it because her stuff—especially her jewelry—went missing often. Because of her. Because of her daughters.

She walked to the table it was sitting on and picked it up. There was a folded piece of paper under it. Picking that up, she read it. "Got your invitation. On our way. Be safe. It's not what it appears. Sam."

What did that even mean? "Could you be a little less cryptic?"

"What does it say?" Leah asked, craning in to see.

Paige handed Leah the note.

The girl read it and whooped, backing away and beaming a grin at her. "It worked!"

"What do you mean?"

Leah danced a funny little jig in the middle of Sam's living room. "Well, we were talking—"

"We who?"

"Me and Rai and Ty and Toby and Kay-Kay and Burr and Bob-bo and Dee. You know, us." She smiled bright, still reveling in her plan's success.

Paige had no idea when Leah had assigned the Whiskey kids—and Toby—nicknames. Some of them were rather cute.

Kay-Kay had to be Kate. Burr was a fun name for Ember. Bob-Bo was Bobby, obviously. It took her a couple of seconds to realize Dee was Mandy. "Okay."

Leah's blue eyes lit on Paige. "Okay, so, we know these guys are going to come after you."

"What guys?" And why did it feel like she'd walked into the middle of an on-going conversation?

"I don't know. The extinct bird or something?"

"DoDO."

"Yeah. Them. Anyway, we figured they'd take a play out of just about every good book we've ever read. And the best one was to go after the people you've helped. Happens on *The Flash* all the time. So, we sent them messages."

"Messages." With her jewelry. And here Paige had thought her daughters were just being girls.

"Yup. We told them their lives were in jeopardy and to get to Troutdale."

Huh. That was… good thinking. Except… "I've helped a lot of people."

Leah clamped her lips shut and raised her eyebrows. "We know."

That meant a lot of people could be flocking to Troutdale. With the DoDO ley line wards Paige had been able to take down and the roadblocks and who knew what else. She had to message Chuck.

Her phone was in her hand and the text was being drafted when she realized that could be tracked. Crap.

She shifted to wolf form and sent out a tendril of thought. *Can anyone hear me?*

Rai's voice came through first. *Yeah, Mom. Is everything okay?*

Maybe. You know those messages you guys sent out?

You found out about that? Her tone was filled with excitement. *Did they work?*

Maybe. Paige was going to hold off her excitement until she got word that the people she'd helped hadn't inadvertently landed themselves into more trouble. *Tell Margo what you did. She'll know what we need to look out for. We just need to make sure everyone's okay as they come in.*

You mean those things from last night?

That and maybe things we didn't *find. I don't know, Rai. That's why I need her to look for more traps.*

We're on it.

Not you kids. They'd already done enough. They might have been successful, but there was a real possibility they weren't.

Rai paused. *Okaaaaay.*

Paige felt the disconnect as if her daughter had just hung up on her.

She was going to have a talk with her. Granted, Paige had no real idea how to parent the twins. If they'd grown at *normal* speed, she might have had a chance. But her teenaged daughter was literally *months* old. So, just how hard could Paige come down on her?

Paige shifted back into human form.

"Mom," Leah said as if she'd been trying to get Paige's attention for a while. "The thingy's glowing."

Paige sighed and looked down at the amulet. "Our ride's here. Can you take us back to downtown?"

Leah opened a door with an angst-filled eye roll and shoulder slump, and as Paige stepped through, her hand throbbed with *extreme* prejudice.

What was that and how was it hurting her? She worked her hand, waiting for the pain to subside a bit. The sharp pain dulled to a throb.

A tall man in a nice, black suit stood beside a limo.

Oliver had to be kidding her. A *limo?*

Leah's eyes lit up. *"This* is our ride?"

Paige bit her lips and offered a smash-lipped smile at the driver. "Denver PD, please."

"Of course," Bastian said, opening the door for them.

Paige listened to Leah run on about how cool it was to sit in a limo and how this was a totally better idea than hot-wiring a car. But Paige wasn't listening.

She was worried about her hand. The throbbing had spread.

She wasn't a moron. She knew that something was going on here, something she needed to handle quickly. And she also had a strong feeling that this growing mark had something to do with her using door magick because each time it throbbed, each time she went through a door, the mark grew. It now went halfway across her chest in glowing red veins that only she could see.

Getting to the Denver police department wasn't easy because the streets were *filled* with protestors. They were tying up traffic all over downtown. Paige was glad she wasn't the one driving.

At least the pain backed off to a high irritation.

When Bastian finally did get them there, she and Leah hopped out and Paige did her level best to stay out of sight of the people milling by and the media. She was there to try to help, not create a media circus.

Once inside, many who saw her stopped and stared. She knew a few of them from the short time she worked there. It was unnerving for them to watch her with those looks of awe and a fear. Others came across angry and resentful.

She tucked Leah close and headed to her old boss's office.

Chief Gormon met her at his office door, shaking his head, his hand on his gun. "That's some nerve, Whiskey."

"Just came by to see if you need help, chief."

"Not from your kind, we don't." He shifted from foot to foot but kept his hand ready at his side.

"Maybe invite me in and let's talk." She held her hands up and open. No weapons.

Chief Gormon glanced around the bullpen for a moment, then turned a stony, cold stare at her. "Get in here and close the door behind you."

Leah's eyes were wide. "Do I go in?"

"Would you rather stay out here on your own?" Paige asked under her breath.

Leah scurried through the door and took the furthest seat.

Paige closed the door behind her and released a long breath. "Looking good, chief."

"Cut the bullshit, Whiskey." Gormon stomped to his side of the desk and sat down heavily. "You here to make this worse? You and your new partner?"

Paige glanced at Leah. "No, she's— I wasn't the one who made this situation in the first place."

Gormon rolled his head back and slammed his right hand on the desk.

Leah jumped.

Paige kept her reaction to herself, keeping her face blank.

"You tellin' me you didn't damn near blow up Troutdale?"

"No, I did not." Keep it simple. He would hear the truth.

"You tellin' me the videos we're seeing all over the news are false?"

"No, I was there."

"Then how the hell is it you didn't blow this up?"

Paige sat down and crossed her knees. "*We* saved the world from a demon who unleashed a rather large army of demons. Your *world* was about to be *erased* and we saved that. What you saw is the battle that was so *damned big*," she said, allowing her anger to show through the cracks in her walls of reserve, "we couldn't *hide* the whole damned thing. What you're seeing now is *your people* overreacting. Now, then. How would you like me to assist you?"

Gormon stared at her hard for a long moment.

The door opened behind Paige, and closed again. Someone stood there, quietly waiting.

Paige resolutely kept Gorman locked with her eyes.

"I don't have to deal with you. I threw you out of my city once. Take it as a permanent invitation to stay away." He gave her a very satisfied look and shrugged.

Leah frowned in disbelief.

"You're *their* problem." He smiled. "Good riddance."

Paige turned to see who had entered.

And came face to face with Quinn Winters.

7

Paige closed her mouth. Quinn Winters? But she was—

Quinn walked in front of Paige, blocking Gorman. She wore a business suit that would have looked at home in a major merger.

"Chief Gormon," Quinn Winters said with a pleasant enough smile as she offered her hand. "DoDO appreciates your assistance."

Gorman took her hand. "Of course," he said, looking a bit flustered as he released her hand and retook his seat. "Anything I can do."

Paige had hired Quinn Winters to work at Red Star when she'd first opened the paranormal police department in Troutdale. Though, the reason she'd hired Quinn—with no police experience—instead of Scout—the police detective *with* experience—had been because Quinn had been assigned to teach Tyler how to use his bardic voice.

Quinn was a siren with a troubled past and no one in the Whiskey household had trusted her. But a few months into her stay, Quinn had disappeared in the middle of an investigation when the team was being framed for murder. There'd been evidence of foul play, but they'd had no leads.

And Paige now knew why.

She'd left to work for the enemy. Had she staged the scene in her house?

Quinn turned to Paige and gave her a polite but stiff smile, her bright green eyes flashing a warning. "Ms. Whiskey, if you and your daughter would please follow me."

What did that "message" mean? That she wasn't supposed to know Quinn? That she wasn't supposed to start a magick fight in the Denver PD? Paige stood, ready with magick to defend herself. "What's going on?"

Quinn offered her hand. "Agent Winters."

Paige narrowed her eyes and kept her immediate taunts to herself, taking Quinn's hand. So, she wasn't supposed to know who Quinn was. Peculiar. "Secretary Whiskey." She was just throwing out the title. She knew it wasn't real, but she also didn't want to introduce herself as a plain-old, civilian…like, Witch Whiskey? That wasn't nearly as cool.

Quinn turned Paige's gripped hand slightly, bringing the red mark that only Paige seemed to be able to see into the light. She raised a dark eyebrow and tipped her head toward the door before releasing Paige's hand.

Okay. What the *hell* was going on?

"I assure you," Quinn said, her tone soft yet firm, "no harm will come to you or your daughter. We simply intend on getting you back home safe and sound."

"And when you get there, stay there," Chief Gormon said stiffly, resituating in his seat. "Where you belong, trash."

Paige held back the urge to throat punch him.

Quinn's lips tightened around the corners and her eyes went hard for a moment before she turned her smile back up a notch or two as she sing-songed, "Mr. Gormon, thank you *so much* for your assistance."

A drunk smile overcame his round face.

Paige kept her mouth shut with the little title slip—because it'd felt good— but she also wondered at the goal behind the siren's song. She'd been lulling Gorman, obviously. But why? Without questioning Quinn just yet, Paige guided Leah out of the room. As soon as Gormon's door closed behind Quinn, Paige opened her mouth. "What's going—"

Quinn raised her hand, cutting Paige off. "Not here," she said quietly then briskly led the way through the bullpen.

The officers there were doing a good job of pretending to work.

Not that Paige cared too much. When she'd worked there, she'd been an outsider. She hadn't known why at the time, but now she did. Gormon had known about her magick and the troubles she would collect, and he'd done his best to keep "his" people away from her.

Quinn hustled them to the hallway, then to the elevator.

This seemed like a good place. "When are you going to tell me what's going on?" Paige asked as soon as the doors closed.

"When it's safe," Quinn said, her voice hushed. "Cameras. Eyes and ears. Just wait."

Something Paige wasn't particularly good at, but she'd give it a try.

Leah kept her mouth shut as they walked out of the elevator and toward the back door.

"How are you intending to get us 'home'?" Paige asked, allowing a thread of doubt enter her tone.

"Not with your portals, if that's what you're asking," Quinn said, holding the door open for them.

"What's this mark?" Paige asked on the other side, pretty sure there weren't cameras with audio recording out there.

There were, however, people.

"Keep your heads down," Quinn said harshly. "The people here don't want you around."

Well, the protests were *because* of them. So, yeah. Probably.

However, Paige couldn't tell *where* Quinn was *trying* to herd them. The parking lot was pretty big. There were a lot of cars, most of which were marked.

Paige's sole intent had been to show up and *do* something about this, so she wasn't just going to be shuffled off and silenced. Giving Leah a bare glance, she headed toward the crowd.

"Pai-Ms. Whiskey," Quinn called after her.

Paige called on the air to helpfully amplify her voice. She didn't *know* if it would work, but she had to try. "Hey, guys!"

The people closest to her looked confused until one, then a couple, then a few more realized who was speaking.

Paige found a dumpster and hopped up, grateful yet again for her spry shifter legs. She raised her hands to get the attention of the people there.

She… got the attention of a few, but the chant, "Get them out! Get them out!" pulled quite a few more faces.

"What are you afraid of?" Paige shouted to the crowd.

No one responded, but the chant was growing in volume.

How was Paige supposed to help if the herd refused to listen? Her alpha will snarled around the knot of frustration and downright anger festering inside her and ripped out through the people.

The crowd went quiet then.

A baby cried and was shushed.

Paige had her audience. She tried it again. "*What* are you afraid of?" she growled to the crowd.

"You," a woman yelled.

"Really?" Paige asked, holding her arms out on either side of her. "I'm a person. Same as you."

"You've got powers." A pretty woman with a heavy over-coat flicked fingers at her.

"That guy's stronger than you." Paige pointed randomly at a tall man. "Are you scared of him?"

"We want our rights back," a man shouted. The crowd parted and he stepped forward, carrying an assault rifle, the barrel pointed down, the rifle strapped over his chest.

Paige's power could do many things. Stopping bullets wasn't one of them. "You think *I've* stripped your rights away?"

"Haven't you?" he demanded.

The crowd cheered around him.

"We can't go to the store—"

This was getting dumb. "The grocery stores are still open."

"We've got a curfew."

Paige didn't know why that was. "Ask your city officials, not me."

"And our kids aren't allowed back in school."

"And you think that's because of us," Paige said.

The crowd of people nodded and agreed. Not everyone did. A few simply stood there.

"Well, let me tell you what it *really* looks to have your right stripped away from you."

She asked the air to amplify her words even louder so everyone could hear, or as many as possible. "We're not allowed to leave our *town*. Some aren't allowed to leave their *home*. They're not *allowed* to get groceries. They're not allowed to *gather in groups* like this. Their safety is threatened. They're being told they need to register. They won't be allowed to *vote*. They'll be allowed to work, I'm sure, you'd call it a 'fair' wage, considering, but it'll be tantamount to *slavery*. And you want to complain because you can't go to the mall and buy pants at midnight? And you're telling me this while waiving your rifle in a crowd of human civilians when paras who were caught had *all* their weapons taken from them? I've got stories of shifters who aren't allowed kitchen knives."

That didn't even phase the man. "I have my rights as a born American."

"Texan, right here," Paige growled.

The man advanced. "But your rights shouldn't affect mine. You're forcing the government to give you *special* rights that hurts the rest of us."

"How does allowing us to get back to normal, allowing us to get back to work and school and paying taxes and voting, affect you? How does allowing us to be *people* strip you of your right to be a person?"

He didn't have anything immediate to say, though his lips were moving.

Paige shook her head and turned to the rest of the crowd. "Allowing people to breathe the air beside you doesn't make you less of a person. But it does—"

"Bring back our freedom!" someone yelled.

Then the world rocked. A wall of sound blanked her vision.

Paige rolled onto her back, dazed, not quite sure what had just happened. Her ears rang. Dull sounds clunked in her ears. Muffled voices made it through the ringing.

She picked herself up off the ground, pushing something away. A car door. She put her hand down to push herself up and pulled it away again as she realized she'd set it on someone's shoe.

A shoe with a severed foot.

A bomb. Someone had set off a bomb in the middle of the crowd. Who would do that?

Someone grabbed her arm and dragged her up and backward.

Paige swept her hands out, trying to find Leah, trying to call on the earth to heal those around her, on water to quell the fires.

In the confused requests, something obeyed.

The sun went dark as a large cloud grew above them and floodgates dumped rain on them.

Paige pulled away from the hand—Quinn's hand—and studied the damp scene, the rain flattening her hair into her eyes. She was drenched.

As were the people in the street.

It was pure chaos. People ran. Some stumbled. A few knelt beside prone bodies.

The ringing in Paige's ears cleared just enough for her to hear the screams and the cries. The ringing was preferrable.

"Mom!"

Leah's voice.

"Mom!"

Hands grabbed her again. When Paige turned, she saw Leah unharmed but scared.

"We've gotta get out of here," Leah yelled over the ringing, tugging on her mother's arm.

Paige's instincts told her she had to stay. She had to help.

The look in Quinn's eyes said she didn't have that kind of time. Quinn took Leah's other arm and dragged them both down the street toward LoDo, though Lower Downtown didn't seem to be any safer.

The people on the streets weren't interested in Paige or Leah. They were concerned with their own safety or with getting a better view. Several were trying to assist.

"What happened?" Paige asked, limping forward to keep pace with Quinn.

The siren shook her head but kept moving.

A loud crack splintered through the chaotic scene.

Paige stopped, searching for the source of the sound.

Where it had come from? Were they being attacked by angels? Demons? Was this another bomb? Had something run into a building?

Quinn yanked on Leah who tugged on Paige, and they continued their trek toward LoDo. She stopped and looked up.

The building in front of them let out a ghastly breath and heaved slightly.

Paige pulled against Leah's arm, pulling the girl close and sheltering her with an arm as she watched in horror. A building in lower downtown Denver slid to the ground in a lump of rubble, screams and cries following.

What in the *hell* was going on?

Quinn shook her head and plowed forward as a wave of air and dust rolled over them. She continued to push upstream through the rush of people fleeing from the collapsed building.

Were they seriously heading in *that* direction? What the *fuck* had taken the building down?

As Paige studied the scene, however, she didn't see angels or demons or magick or creatures.

She just saw mundane destruction which meant only one thing. This wasn't the work of paranormals.

The chaos on the street was too loud for Paige to hear Quinn, though her lips moved. Paige couldn't even hear Leah and the girl ran right beside her. But the three of them didn't let go of one another. They were crammed into a herd of people, pressed together like cattle in a chute.

A woman latched onto Paige, shoving her phone in Paige's face. "—do something?"

Paige wasn't sure how the woman's phone was working in the deluge of rain. "I'll try."

"Who—what?"

Paige looked at the woman and growled, "Humans."

Then, she turned away and let Quinn and Leah lead her away.

Eventually, the people thinned out in a wide ring around the collapsed building.

"Over here," Quinn said, then took them toward a door just to the side of the pile of rubble in LoDo.

As they drew closer, a chunk of concrete the size of a VW bug moved.

Paige rushed toward it, thinking it might be a survivor.

A stone goblin with wings rose, shaking off the rubble like a dog, flinging muddy cement dirt and rainwater all around him. A chunk of concrete and rebar whizzed by her ear.

Paige stopped, her hands out.

Quinn slapped her arm down.

"Roc," Quinn cried, skirting around the marble monster. "It's me."

The thing growled low, but settled on his front feet again, folding his wings to him. He released a loud cry to the sky.

Other marble forms answered.

Paige stared around in amazement as she watched gargoyles crawl up the sides of tall buildings and reform into statues once they'd gotten to the top. "Did they do this?" Paige asked quietly.

The look on Quinn's face told Paige she was being stupid. "I need the door, Roc." Quinn disappeared through the broken doorway that didn't look stable anymore.

Roc shook his head and followed. "It will open as it always does," he said in a big, booming voice.

Leah looked over at Paige, her blue eyes wide.

Paige shook her head and shrugged. Quinn, she wasn't sure she could trust, but gargoyles? Weren't they guardians or something? If they even really existed?

She had to hope so.

Paige led the way through the door.

Paige stayed away from Roc's slashing tail, and reached behind her for Leah's hand, which slid into hers eagerly, the smaller fingers squeezing tight. Paige made sure to keep them both away from Roc's tail, which was harder than it should have been. He walked agonizingly slow. Eventually, they stopped in a large antechamber of some sort.

When Paige and Leah caught up to her, Quinn glanced at Paige. "This is the old city," she said quickly. "It's mostly hidden, so few people know about it."

"DoDO obviously does."

Quinn shook her head then looked at Roc. "Door."

The gargoyle gave a heavy breath and sat on his haunches, raising his front clawed hands.

A door appeared in the middle of the room, but it wasn't like Leah and Paige's door magic. It also wasn't like DoDO's portals. She couldn't see through to the other side for one thing. This was just a purple blob that made a warbling sound as an underground wind kicked dust into her sopping wet face.

Great. It was going to be caked with mud.

"Just go. I'll explain on the other side." Quinn leapt through, a slight *weorp* sound showcasing her passing.

Leah looked at Paige. "Mom?"

Did they have a choice?

Yeah. They could stay. But what would be waiting for them? DoDO had *known* Paige was there in Denver. They'd sent Quinn. A building—the building above a secret room and a secret door guarded by gargoyles—had been demolished.

That couldn't have been a coincidence. Could it?

Paige nodded and gestured for Leah to jump through.

She did with another *weorp* sound.

When Paige followed, she half expected that stabbing

feeling she got when she used door magic, but this passage was gentle and easy. It literally felt like walking through a normal door. She stumbled into a desk then moved aside as another larger *weorp* sound filled the rather small room.

Roc came through the portal and it closed behind him. He looked to Quinn and sighed heavily. "We have been compromised."

Quinn quirked her lips and nodded. "I figured that." She turned to Paige and studied her for a long minute.

Judging her. Waiting. Watching?

Paige returned the assessment.

For over a year, she and Dexx had wondered what had happened to her. Had she been kidnapped?

It looked like she'd gotten a better job offer. She looked good. Well-fitted suit. Professionally done hair and nails. Whatever she'd done, she'd done well for herself.

"We need to talk," Quinn said quietly. "You're in a lot of danger and you just sped up a war I've been trying to stop."

8

Paige stepped through the dark portal into light.

Okay, first things first. Roc had dumped them in the middle of downtown Troutdale. Right in front of Leslie's soap and wine store.

That was good—because Leslie could take care of Leah—and bad, but mostly bad.

People started coming out of their shops to see the new commotion. Leslie beat a few of them to the front as Paige ignored just about everyone else. "What the hell happened? The news is saying you attacked Denver."

Of course they were. "Find a real news channel. Get me Danny. Where's Willow?" Also, Paige's hand was really hurting now, but it was more than that. Her heart was starting to trip in her chest. "There were real people in those streets with phones. We need as much of that video as we can get. Where's Tru and Barn?" What about Leah? Paige needed to take a minute and make sure daughter was *okay*.

Leslie nodded almost continuously as she scribbled a text to someone.

But she was one person and Paige had a sea of them wanting to help.

So, she chose individuals and assigned them to the things she needed done, ignoring the fact that she was wet and covered in drying mud and that her right hand *hurt* and that her heart was tripping somersaults in her chest.

And if she couldn't find a goddamned *minute* to be a goddamned *mom* to her own goddamned *daughter*… her sister could.

Fuck! When would the fucking world just fucking *stop?* For *one* god…damned…

Shit. That had been… hard. She just needed a minute.

Quinn stared at everyone like she'd been sucked onto an alien spaceship.

Willow pushed her way through the crowd, her phone in one hand, her tablet in the other. "I've got Danny. He's working to find the real news."

"I've got Tru," Leslie shouted above the crowd, shoving Leah at Mandy. "Him and Barn are seein' what the hell they can get."

"We've *got* to get the real story out there," Paige told Willow and Leslie.

"You," Leslie said, leaning in, "need a shower." She then grabbed Leah and pushed her toward the shop.

Willow took charge of the crowd, shouting them back to their shops.

Quinn took a step up, ready to speak.

Tuck and Suzanne rolled in.

"Paige," the mayor said, her blue eyes wide, her round face set in an expression of deep anxiety. "What did I tell you about breaking anything?"

Nothing, actually, but Paige knew what the mayor was saying. "Not me. Someone else attacked."

Suzanne tipped her head to the side and winced. "Were

you at least able to save anyone? That would be a good headline."

If only. Paige licked her lips and shook her head, meeting Tuck's gaze. She blinked, her eyelids caked and heavy. "No. We all ran. They blew up a building."

His eyes held her gaze with a weight of understanding. He nodded and led the way back up the hill. "We got showers. Come on."

Leah was firmly ensconced with family. Paige knew that they'd find a shower for her, probably at home where she belonged.

Paige didn't have that kind of time, though.

Quinn led Suzanne away, back toward the mayor's building, talking quietly.

Paige should have cared more, but she didn't. She took the shower, changed into someone else's sweat clothes, and sat in Tuck's office with the door closed in a kind of numb shock.

Tuck said nothing as he watched her. Finally, he opened a drawer, pulled out two glasses and a bottle of amber liquid and poured. He handed one over to her, still saying nothing.

There was nothing *to* say. Paige took what he offered and swirled the glass, trying to make sense of what she'd seen—no. What she'd experienced.

Parts that had been people just *moments* before. Had that leg belonged to the man who'd refused to listen to her, who had just repeated the same statement he'd come to the rally with? Had the broken body she'd stumbled over belonged to the woman who'd just wanted her "freedom" back? Where was the baby who'd cried after Paige had silenced the crowd?

She wanted to sob. She wanted to rail and scream and shout and beg for change.

But too much had happened. The battle in the Elven city. The one in Kansas.

The battle in her own damned town.

The fear she'd had to put a lid on when her babies had started growing much too fast.

The terror when she realized her own children were endangering the life of her nephew.

The loneliness of her empty bed and the acknowledgement that her partner was somewhere else fighting for his life. And might not return.

The reality of realizing she might have to *choose* between her children and her family, or the world.

Paige let the un-sipped glass sit in her lap as the numbness grew.

She knew this was a good thing—the numbness. For now. It gave her the room to *think*, which was necessary.

But if she didn't watch it, she might stop caring. She'd seen it with others.

The *world* couldn't *afford* for her to stop caring. Because she was the *only* one who cared *enough* to *act*.

Paige took in a deep breath and blinked her gaze at the amber liquid still in her glass.

Tuck dropped his gaze and sipped more of his.

"I've got a lot of work to do," Paige said, finally getting up, so incredibly thankful that Tuck understood that even though he might not be able to guide her anymore she still needed… a safe space.

Tuck took her glass back. "You don't want to finish this?"

She did and she didn't. A year ago, she would have shot that back and plowed forward. But the game she played now was so damned tight, she couldn't afford to be buzzed when making decisions. When she made mistakes now, people paid the price. Heavily. "No. But thank you." And she still had to figure out if she'd made a mistake in Denver, or if she'd just been in the wrong place at the wrong time.

Tuck nodded.

The president or DoDO must have *known* she would likely show up in Denver to help the situation and had planned to destroy her with the bombs.

He set the glass down, his mustache and beard fanning out as he smashed his lips together. "You bet."

Her mistake might have been in being predictable.

With her soul propped back up for now, Paige stepped into the bullpen and found Leah talking quietly to Ashley and Mandy, visibly shaken. Why weren't they home?

Mandy looked up at her as Paige came to them. "Mom wanted to make sure you knew where she was," the girl said before anything was even asked.

Good thinking. Probably. Paige gripped Leah's shoulder and forced the girl to look her in the eye. "Go home. Get rest. Cry buckets and buckets. But when you're done, be ready to fight. Because whoever is responsible..." Paige stopped herself. She *couldn't* finish that sentence. She *couldn't* be one woman against the world anymore.

Leah licked her lips, sucking them in as tears filled her red-rimmed eyes. She nodded, paused, nodded again and walked with Ashley and Mandy out of the precinct.

Paige swallowed hard, hating her reality, and closed her eyes for one moment.

What did she need to do first?

Get answers.

Where was Quinn?

Paige didn't wait. She leapt into the air and shifted into an owl. She just wanted...

Silence.

She headed toward town, but the silence called to her. So, she allowed the air currents to carry her higher into the sky, her wings eventually just gliding on the air as she soared, the sun slicing against her feathers, the silence filling her soul with strength.

But eventually, she had to get back to her duties. So, she tipped her wings to the mayor's office and landed on her tiny balcony, stepping inside through the window.

Suzanne startled but didn't yell at Paige this time. She just put her hand to her big bosom and took in a deep breath. "We've got work to do."

She ran Paige through the things everyone was set to do and the information streaming in so far.

The real story *was* getting out. Not as fast as the media spin, however.

People on the ground were sharing their videos and their experiences. There had been a moment of coverage blackout, but someone had managed to get through. Paige had a feeling it was Tru or Barn, their two tech geniuses.

One guy who looked burly with a beard and a rifle strung across his chest had managed to catch part of the explosion.

Several men and women in DoDO assault gear had waded through the streets with backpacks. They'd set the packs down but soon they'd been forgotten.

Another person caught one of those very same packs going off as Paige had been talking to the crowd.

The video was horrific.

Paige swallowed her sick soul back into a tiny box before it could vomit any sort of emotion that would weaken her resolve or her mind. "Keep this out in front of people."

Suzanne went uncharacteristically solemn. "This is really... bad."

It certainly was and Paige was starting to wonder how much more of this "bad" stuff she could witness before it started affecting her. It already was. She knew that. But... until it affected her in the wrong ways.

She turned to Quinn. "Roof."

Quinn shook her head. "Basement." She led the way.

Paige didn't even react. She just followed until they were

both safely hidden away in a small, quiet room in the middle of the basement. "I need answers."

Quinn nodded, looking around as if trying to figure out where to start. "I'm not working with DoDO. I'm trying to take it down from the inside."

Paige pushed down her rising anger at that last sentence. Take it down?

"Dexx was okay the last time I saved him."

Saved him?

"We've tried monitoring his movements, but he fell off the grid. I should be back looking for traces of him right now."

"Okay." Paige let that word be a questioning statement but didn't want to interrupt. However, she *wanted* information on Dexx. Not at the cost of helping others, but... yeah. Maybe for one tiny moment, she *did* want *her* man to trump the importance of the rest of the fucking world.

But she kept her mouth shut and listened.

Quinn narrowed her eyes and shifted uneasily. "They've still got ways of listening in on you here. You took out a lot of them, but the domes can listen in."

Paige made a mental note to talk to their wards about trying to find a way to defeat that.

The siren bit her lip, looking away. "Okay, so the war you're fighting isn't about government. The president isn't your villain. Cardinal Bussemi is way up the chain and that's who Dexx is trying to take out right now."

Okay. This was news. Actually, it was really big fucking news. She was cursing a lot in her head. Yeah. Yeah. She was... still really shaken. "Who is this guy to Dexx?"

Quinn's eyebrows shot up then returned to normal. "They... knew each other."

What?

The siren held up a hand. "I don't know all the details.

Bussemi is ancient, was one of the first people to have magick. And he's *very* powerful. Also, Dexx is working on his hundredth life or something. Dexx was around when everything first started. Somehow, Dexx found a way to reincarnate and Bussemi made a demon deal for long life. I know. It's way out there."

Paige didn't quite understand what that had to do with anything.

"Bussemi *created* DoDO to control the power of the paranormals. He did that when the Catholic church was born. Some theorize he's behind the church being formed as well, but..." Quinn shook her head and waved that thought off. "He's been using DoDO and the church to control the world for centuries."

"*That's* our enemy?" And ancient... evil? So, she *was* fighting demons. Worse? She was fighting something worse than demons?

Quinn nodded, her lips shut.

Paige had more questions. "And if Dexx wins against Bussemi?" Did that mean she'd win? That the president would back down? That the unrest in their society would dry up and disappear? Or was this a genie they couldn't put back in the bottle?

"DoDO would be seriously damaged." Quinn moved around the room. "I'm not alone, but there aren't many of us and we don't know who we can trust. We're looking for anyone who's working with Bussemi, who might have attachments to him. We're trying to destabilize DoDO so that *when* Bussemi *does* go down, the entire organization topples with him."

That sounded like a great plan. "Your tone tells me you're not sure Dexx will succeed."

Quinn released a long breath, her shoulders slumping. "I

—" She jutted her jaw to the side before straightening. "Dexx isn't doing great. He's not himself."

Well, that was exactly what Paige needed to hear.

Quinn clamped her lips shut and looked away before she continued. "Bussemi got his hands on Dexx and did a real number on him. Now he's not—you know, how he was before? He was cocky, didn't think? But now he's hurt on the inside. I have no idea how to fix him."

Dexx was hurt. Paige's heart twisted, not knowing what to do. "If Bussemi's the real problem, then I should go help Dexx."

"Yeah, I thought about that, too. But no." Quinn studied the wall behind Paige's head. "We've been studying you through your mark." She gestured to Paige's hand. "You're what Bussemi needs. You're able to—" Quinn cut herself off and shook her head. "Yeah. You need to stay as far away from that man as you can because if he gets his hands on you, he *might* win and then he'll be unstoppable."

"Why?"

"Because of what you do with the ley magick."

Was Paige about to finally get some damned answers? "And what's that?"

Quinn licked her lips and took a step forward. "You feed it. Cleanse it."

Paige didn't understand.

"Okay, so…" Quinn pulled her head back and paced away. "You know the mages do ley line magick?"

"Yes."

"Well, they *take* that energy and they never give it back. And it sits. Kind of like dirty dishes, still there but unusable."

That's also what they'd done to the ancients. They'd captured them and stripped them of energy, sending the powerful shifter spirits into hiding.

"Earth's been drained. Everyone can feel it. But you?"

Quinn stopped and turned to Paige, her eyes alight with something Paige had never thought to see on the siren's somber face. Hope. "You bring the energy back, clean it, strengthen it."

Paige recalled the times she'd managed to take the damage the mages had given. She'd absorbed that energy somehow and it'd unleashed inside her.

But where had it gone?

"You're leaching it and don't even realize it," Quinn said. "That's the reason the mark is affecting you the way it is. I'm here to remove it."

"You made the red skim and boxes— the… bubbles?" That didn't make sense.

"No." Quinn took something out of her pocket and offered it to Paige. "That was something— someone else, but I did piggyback the magick with the help of a friend. We thought we could use you to help us take Bussemi down."

Paige took it. Half pen and half crystal, she felt magick in it, but the energy was too foreign to pin down.

"He's very powerful."

Paige felt stuck. "Dexx is in trouble, isn't he?"

Quinn nodded. "I did what I could to help."

"Thank you," Paige whispered, then pushed her worry for her almost-husband to the back of her mind. "What else did you learn?"

"I'll try to explain it. Here goes." Quinn explained in a long and roundabout way that every time Paige took the expended ley line magick, she reconverted it using her abilities. The culmination of everything she was made that possible. She had door magick and she tapped into the dimensions. She had Whiskey life magick which tapped into the very Earth herself. She manipulated *all* the primal elements and not just one or two of them. Her shifter made a conduit of sorts, and the end result of the power was a clean ley line magick.

All of those things were needed to convert the ley line magick the mages fed her.

And, without her even knowing what she was doing, she was sloughing that off around her, filtered and rejuvenated.

Quinn's expression filled with excitement. "The crops in this area are set to produce twice what they normally do. The water's cleaner, with an eighty-two percent drop in contagions. The air inside your wards has thirty-six percent fewer pollutants."

Should Paige be upset with how much information Quinn had been able to glean? "We haven't been driving."

Quinn shook her head. "We believe as the energy is sloughing off you, it's scrubbing the environment around you before returning to the ley lines."

That was neat but... "How am I returning it?"

"Right now?" Quinn raised her eyebrows and pinched them together. "You're doing that every time you go through one of your doors."

So, her natural ability was giving her a solution because the door sliced between dimensions and spaces. Somehow, that had to inadvertently connect to the ley magick. "And this mark?"

"It—" Quinn interrupted herself. "Okay, it didn't react the way we thought it would. But your magick doesn't work the way we guessed. So, I'll fix that if you're ready."

Paige nodded slowly. "I am."

"And we apologize." Quinn said as she stepped up and took the crystal pen from her. "We really were just trying to see if you could help us help you." Quinn met Paige's eyes, searching. "This fight is worth it."

Paige realized in that moment that she'd really misjudged Quinn two years ago. "What do I do?"

Quinn pressed the crystal against the mark and chanted under her breath. She did *not* sing.

Pain shot through Paige as the red veins receded and sucked into the crystal. Paige had to give it a three-count before she could do much more than fight not to scream.

When the pain was over—or at least working on becoming a memory—Quinn winced at her. "I have a favor to ask."

"What?" Exactly *what* kind of favor could they want now? Make a million doors and walk through them all?

"Can I re-mark you?"

"You wanna what?" The first mark had been excruciating.

Quinn held up her hands. "We're still working to figure out how this works—how your power and abilities do what they do. So, if you're willing, I'll re-mark you and study you as you continue to work magick. You don't need to do anything special."

Paige's immediate reply was no. "I need reports. Regular, concise, and transparent."

Quinn nodded and reached into her pocket, removing an electronic device. "This is double-encrypted so no one—okay, very few people—should be able to hack into it."

Taking it, Paige still had to decide if this was what she wanted. She needed to know what was going on with her abilities. She knew that. But... "How do I know I can trust you?"

The siren thought about that then she looked around for a moment. Then Quinn took out a knife and sliced her arm, offering the blade to Paige.

She narrowed her eyes and took it. "What are we doing?"

"It's a trick I learned from a friend. I'll bind myself to you."

"If I die, you die?"

"Not like that. But... you will be able to affect me. You

will be able to call me. You will be able to get a general idea of what I'm doing."

That sounded a lot like a pack bond. "Reciprocal?"

Quinn nodded.

Paige didn't think about it much further after that. She sliced her arm and waited.

"Hold your magick. Just hold it, but don't do anything with it." Quinn raised her voice and sang, her song thrumming through Paige, making her feel better and more in control.

Which was odd and she wasn't certain she was a hundred percent okay with this, but she needed answers.

Quinn finished, and lowered her arm.

Paige dropped hers. A thin trail of blood seeped down her wrist. "And no one else will have access to this information?"

"*Only* trusted people. We're being very careful."

Yeah, well, she'd better. "And this war you're trying to keep the lid on?"

Quinn shook her head and grabbed something out of her pocket—a handkerchief? Who still had those?—and bound her arm. "Don't draw attention to yourself."

"It's going to be hard to do that as the Secretary of Paranormal Affairs."

"Yeah." Quinn flexed her hand on the cut arm. "Well, just try not to use your magick on camera. If Bussemi sees you—"

"There are videos of me taking down an army of demons."

"With Dexx beside you. He thinks that was Dexx and we're keeping him focused that way."

Really? "And what happened in Kansas and in the Elven city?"

"About that. Don't do that again."

Paige would give it her best. She held up the phone. "This gets to you?"

Quinn nodded. "I'll send the information we have so far."

She pulled out another crystal pen, but this one was a garnet color. "You're sure?"

"No." But Paige gave the siren her left arm. "Will this hurt?"

The siren shrugged. "Hopefully not? I didn't make it." She touched the crystal to Paige's skin and sang at it.

The crystal flared then a prickling tingled along Paige's arm as if it had fallen asleep and was being awakened again.

Quinn pulled out another device that looked a lot like the one she'd given Paige and smiled. "We're set." She put it away. "I've got to go."

Paige had one more question for Quinn. "Did DoDO send you to Denver?"

The siren shook her head. "But it *was* a trap. They *knew* you'd show up because of who you are. Focus more on fulfilling the role of a Cabinet Secretary."

"I don't actually have that position yet."

"Yeah, well, some of us need you to be. So, put your focus there."

"Thanks." Paige took a moment to assess Quinn in a much different light.

Quinn nodded then left the room. "And remember, they're watching you from everywhere."

That was the next thing Paige needed to fix.

9

The first thing Paige had to do was to talk to the wards. She went the tree in the middle of the park in town and communed with it. It was like talking to a child who struggled to listen. But eventually, their wards flared and a bubble-soap scum slithered away from its surface.

Paige just had to hope that they hadn't been able to glean a lot. She hadn't even thought about protecting what they said or did after they'd combed through the town, removing devices.

After the ward agreed to keep an eye out for invading technology or magicks, Paige went home, changed her clothes really quick, and headed back to the mayor's office.

Before she made it, though, Scout stopped on the street corner, looking up at her as she winged in, and waved at her.

That was a little odd. Paige didn't know of anyone who could tell her apart from any other bird in the sky, unless she chose something like a pterodactyl. Which would be the size of an eagle. Bummer.

Paige shifted as her feet touched the ground and only stumbled a little. She was getting the knack of this. Finally.

Scout gave her a brief smile. "Talk or point?"

"Point." Paige didn't have time for small talk and she didn't think that was a skill Scout even had.

Relief spread over the harpy's pixie-like face. "I want Rocco."

Rocco? Did she mean the gargoyle? "Uh, okay? Why?"

Scout tipped her head to the side. "He used to be a detective back in the day. 'Course, that was before I was born, but he's got the skills. We could use the help."

Paige shrugged. "Offer him the job. I'll draw up the paperwork if he agrees."

"Great." Scout looked pleasantly surprised.

Paige doubted she was taken seriously often. She remembered being a woman in the field. "How's Joel working out?"

"Meh." Scout shrugged with a don't-worry-about-it wave of her hand. "You just gotta know what you're workin' with. He's got his uses."

"As long as he *is* useful."

"Yeah. Not real strong in the thinking department, but in others. Sure."

"We're not allowed to break things like faces and towns."

Scout looked at Paige like she'd lost her mind. "He's a goblin, not a troll."

"Okay." Paige didn't know what the difference between the two were, but that was fine. "Request approved."

"Thanks." Scout turned about face and walked off.

Paige continued across the street to the mayor's office. She'd get the update on the case shortly, but for now, she had Paige-sized business to attend to. Like what she was going to do about these riots, and if it was just Denver or if it was everywhere.

The answer was everywhere. In most of the major cities—

except Alaska and Hawaii because her level of problems hadn't affected anyone there yet—there were curfews, and more than a few stores had closed down.

But the cities were still getting their supplies. People were just taking precautions in the wake of finding out that some people had sharp teeth behind their sharper tongues.

Someone was enflaming public opinion, and it wasn't the president this time. It also didn't look like it was DoDO. At least, not that they could tell.

Without a focus, Paige didn't know how to attack this one.

So, she decided to show the world what *should* be rioted and how Troutdale was dealing with the response.

So, Mark the Cameraman and his growing crew were on a mission to livestream life in Troutdale without supplies and how they'd been able to innovate without basic things like electricity or gas for their cars.

"This'll blow back," Suzanne said.

"Oh, I know." Paige was starting to get an uncomfortable familiarity with the cruelty of mankind. Her phone buzzed in her pocket, so she fished it out. "You're the best at turning stories around. What do you suggest?"

Suzanne's brow scrunched. "Well..."

Paige looked down at the caller ID and raised her eyebrows in surprise. The White House was calling her. "Suzanne, I gotta take this."

The mayor waved her off. "Let me work *my* kind of magic."

"Please do." Paige stepped out of Suzanne's office, ducking into the conference room and closing the door to answer the phone. "Paige Whiskey."

"Ms. Whiskey," the president said, her tone dry. "I'm extending an invitation for conversation again."

"Of course, Madame President." Paige hoped it would go better than the last two times.

"Leave your children at home this time," the president said with a sigh. "There will be no need for theatrics."

"You're offering enough of those as it is," Paige said with a smile. "Time and place."

The president transferred her to someone who offered her the details on her arrival. No appearing in the Oval Office—that was strictly forbidden—but she was allowed to appear in a conference room of the Eisenhower Executive Office Building, which Paige thought was a little odd. Those offices were used for a lot of different high-ranking politicians. At least, that's what she'd been able to gather on her own.

But she also knew that was where the Cabinet members were allowed to have offices. And if the president was seriously considering giving her the Secretary position…well then.

She messaged Leah and told her the news and asked if she was ready to go again or if she needed to sit this one out.

After a minute, Leah responded. *sad face emoji* *I can't go this time. Don't be mad.*

Paige immediately replied. *I will never be mad at you for knowing your limits. I love you.*

Love you back, came the reply along with a string of heart and silly face emojis.

Leah knew how much Paige hated when her phone just blew up like Dexx would do, so she kept all the emojis in one message and sent them all at once.

She called Phoebe to get a ride to D.C.

The Blackwood witch said she'd get someone up there as soon as possible.

Paige went to Willow's make-shift office. "Hey. Just checking in to see how everything's going."

"Considering everything, it's going. How about you?"

"The president called. I'll be heading out as soon as I get a ride there."

"Did you want me to go with you?" Willow asked, her tone hesitant as if she didn't know if she was *allowed* to tag along to Washington D.C.

The woman was saving her life by being her assistant. So, yeah, she could invite herself along. "I don't know what we're walking into."

Willow nodded, her fingers working on gathering papers. "But if I went, I could make a few contacts. Names. Faces. Job titles. Phone numbers and email addresses."

That would be amazing. "How soon can you be ready?"

"How long are we staying?"

Paige shrugged. "I'm bringing a Blackwood with me, so I'm guessing just a couple of hours."

"Then I'll be ready in a few minutes."

What a relief. "You got it."

Paige had enough to keep her busy in the twenty-eight minutes it took for their ride to show up.

Derrick Blackwood knocked on her door and beamed a grin at her. "Hey, sis."

Paige was going to have to just invite them over some time and get to know them. She got up and followed him out of the conference room, then took lead to gather Willow. "I met Angela." Derrick's daughter and her niece. "Nice kid."

"Thanks," he said proudly. "Where to?"

As she entered Willow's office, she gave him the address, which included the room number.

He waggled his eyebrows. "Got it. Just us three, then?"

Paige nodded.

Willow smiled and pulled a backpack over her shoulders. "Ready."

Derrick adjusted his black business pants and opened a door.

Paige probably should have gone home one more time and put on better clothes instead of whatever was on top of the clean pile, but she didn't want to beat around the bush and she didn't want the invitation to expire. Too many things could happen in this arena in a very short period of time.

They were greeted by Naomi Wright and a small team of other people.

Secret Service waited in the hallway.

Willow didn't ask permission. She sank her teeth into information gathering and coordinating. Naomi's people were whizzing around as she made contacts and memorized faces. The woman was worth her weight in gold.

"Derrick, I think you should stay behind with Willow. This is a *big* pond."

His expression stated he'd expected as much, and he pulled out a paperback book from his back pocket. "Came prepared."

Paige chuckled as she followed Naomi and two secret service agents out the door. "How are Todd and Ginny?"

"They're doing great." Naomi walked close to Paige, chummy-like. "How're Rai and Ember?"

"Fifteen."

"What?" Naomi asked incredulously.

During the drive, Paige filled her in on what was going on with the twins.

"That is…" Naomi shook her head, pressing her pink skirt down with her thumbs. "Wow. How are you still sane?"

"Is this sane?" Paige asked as the White House came into sight. "Okay. What can I expect?"

"Honestly?" Naomi leaned over to look through the window. "No one knows. Not even the chief of staff, and he's tried to gauge what she's planning to better prepare us all. Maybe she'll give you the assignment of Secretary. Maybe she won't. She's the only one who can, though."

"And it's really a thing? She can just make a new position?"

"You think the country was founded with fifteen Secretaries? No."

But would she?

Getting cleared through security was a little easier this time. There wasn't even a mention of the collar, though she'd been informed there were devices in place in case she chose to use her magick. She was told to leave her phone behind, which she was okay with. She was armed with everything she needed.

Paige walked into the Oval Office without even a hint of the fear and anxiety she'd had earlier. The numbness was something she could use as a shield.

The president rose from her chair behind her desk, a frown marring her brow. "Ms. Whiskey."

"Madam President." Paige offered her hand, and after a brief handshake, they sat on opposite couches. "You wanted to talk."

"Indeed." The president crossed her ankles and folded her hands on her bright red pencil skirt. "I need you to stop with these horrendous activities."

"Which ones are those?" Paige, without her emotions clouding her judgement, was able to deduce that the president was trying to get her on the defensive over Denver. But Paige wanted it spelled out plainly so there'd be no "interpretation" error.

"You cannot go into a peaceful riot and blow it up to quiet it."

Paige watched the other woman, carefully studying her micro-expressions. "I have video proof it wasn't me. It was DoDO."

"It most certainly—" The president raised her hands then

slapped them back onto her thighs. "It was not me. I am not your villain here, Ms. Whiskey."

"I know."

The president stopped, her expression going still.

"Our enemy wants to make a mockery out of you and wants to provoke you into starting a war with us. He's playing on your every fear and moving me around like a chess piece, moving from one altercation to the next."

The president frowned. "Do you know who it is?"

Paige did but she didn't know if she could trust the president with the information. She wanted to believe that the woman wasn't a part of this, but... what if she was? "I'm looking into it."

"How?"

"I have someone on the inside," Paige said quietly, holding the president's gaze.

The woman flinched. "Who?"

"My husband," Paige said evenly, waiting for the president to slip. "Dexx."

The president shook her head. "That's—they would never allow him into their organization. He's a shifter, isn't he?"

She seemed sincerely in the dark. "Madame President, DoDO came into my town and kidnapped my husband while you and I were negotiating."

"What?" All pretenses slipped away from the president's face. "I don't understand. I thought you had your wards up."

"I did. But they found a way around them."

"They assured me there *was no way* around your wards, that you'd in effect made yourself an enemy of the Union." The president tapped her lips with a finger.

"No, ma'am." If the president was going to be honest, then Paige was going to be as well. "They found a way around it, but I haven't been able to get the full story from Dexx."

"Then…" The president's tone changed. She uncrossed her legs, leaning her elbows on her knees. "How are you getting information?"

"Carefully. I can tell you they stripped him of his memories. I'm guessing they tortured him." Paige shrugged, wondering if she was even going to get *her* Dexx back at the end of all this. She didn't care. As long as she got some form of him. "He's… recovered a bit, and he's getting me the information he can."

"And you know for a certainty that we're both being played."

"How about you and I share notes the way *we* know them and find out."

For the next hour, the President of the United States and Paige hashed out the details of what went down in the Elven city, in Kansas, and at the various detention facilities.

"They *are* playing us," the president whispered.

"Yes," Paige muttered back.

The reports they'd given the president had started with false information. Then, the tac team that had gone in had only shown their unit being attacked as they'd invaded people's homes without a warrant and without reason. After the people were killed, more violence followed until more DoDO units had to be called.

"I authorized the additional manpower," the president said.

Paige swallowed hard. It was one thing to go through this knowing your villain was a fucking asshole. It was something else realizing that the person you'd *seen* as your villain actually *felt* the repercussions of her actions. "Madame President—"

"Dawn."

Okay. Now, she was on first-name basis with the president. Cool. Cool-cool. Things could be going worse. "Dawn, there were kids killed in the elven city. And we had no right or reason to be there. Toddlers. Babies."

Dawn raised her chin, her eyes rimming pink. She clasped her hands together and propped up her chin. "And you didn't bomb Denver."

"No, ma'am. I did not." Paige was swept with a hopeful relief as the president seemed to actually take her words at face value.

"And you have proof."

"I do."

Dawn met Paige's gaze. "Show me."

"I don't have my phone."

Dawn ducked her head for a moment then stood up, going to her desk. She pulled out a drawer and brought out a business card. "This is a secure email. Send it there."

"It can't be tracked and erased. I've got multiple copies." Paige took the card.

Dawn narrowed her eyes. "Is that a threat?"

"No, but your team has been erasing all our evidence, our videos, our tweets, our posts."

Dawn closed her eyes. "Operation Silence." She shook her head and sank back onto the couch. Opening her eyes, she clasped her knees. "I authorized that as well."

This was certainly not the way Paige thought this conversation was going to go. "Madam—Dawn, we need to eliminate DoDO in the United States."

"I can see your point, even agree, but it won't be that easy. Their connections run deep. Deeper than mine."

"How so?"

Dawn stared at something behind Paige's head. "I— I don't know who I can trust to get more information. Who I can trust in my administration."

"I..." Paige took in a deep breath and held it. "I might have an idea of where to start."

"How?"

"I can't share too much, but there are people in our government who are fighting to keep you in control."

"They're trying to impeach me."

"You're trying to tell me they didn't have a good reason?"

Dawn opened her mouth then closed it, sitting back in her seat, looking older than when Paige had first entered the room. "Do you know how big this job is?"

Paige leaned back on the couch, mirroring the president, and nodded, exhausted. "We've got an entire paranormal nation out there scared as hell and they're looking to me to help them. And they come up with questions and problems and I have no idea how to help them. I don't have the resources they need."

Dawn chuffed slightly. "Like what?"

"Like..." Where should she start? "Internet. Getting the truth out there because everyone's freaking out that they've gotta stay in the house after dark when we're not even allowed to go to a grocery store *for supplies*. Insulin. Drugs. How are we supposed to get that when we don't *have any money*? Electricity. We've got food going —had food going bad. We had to find a solution to that. Gas for the cars because, strangely, not everyone can shift."

"But violence?"

"In town? Are you fucking kidding me? We're trying to stay alive and the only we're doing that is as a town. Together."

"But..." Dawn shook her head. "The people of different cultures? Religions?"

"Dawn, I wish you could see how we've come together. We've got wolves boarding with cats. We've got witches going to school with porcupines. We've got humans learning about shifters. We've got—" Okay. She shouldn't say this one out loud— "—shifters practicing their shift in school." Why couldn't she keep her mouth shut?

"But they're naked when they're human."

"Yeah. Had that problem dropped at my doorstep too." Paige shook her head. "We're coming together and teaching people to be *decent human beings* instead of..." She gestured wildly with her hand and let it fall. "Douchebags."

They sat in silence for a long moment.

Finally, Dawn let her head fall back. "I don't know what to do."

Paige didn't either. "This guy—he's high in the DoDO chain of command. Can you break off from DoDO?"

Dawn shook her head. "They seem to be too well lobbied."

Paige didn't *quite* know what that meant, but guessed it meant he had backers in high places. "Well, you and I could... try to flush him out."

"How?" A light lit Dawn's blue-green eyes.

"I don't know. But I *do* know I need to be *here* more often."

"So, you're proposing I make you Secretary of Paranormal Relations."

"If that's what it takes." Paige nodded.

Dawn sighed heavily. "I brought you here to tell you to your face that I wasn't giving it to you. That the people who orchestrated that could take their will and shove it. No one forces me to do something I don't want to do."

Paige had kinda figured.

"Tell me why I should give this position to you."

Shaking her head, Paige sat up, leaning her elbows on her knees, and gave the president a very frank look. "Because I'm the one stepping up to help. I'm the one who's taken the beating, who's fought to protect them—the paranormals and the humans." Paige pressed a finger to her lips for a moment, then released the words that had to be said out loud. "Because we're on the brink of civil war and I don't want that in our country."

Dawn nodded, sitting up as well. "Okay. You've got the job if you want it." She pulled something off the table between them and held it out to Paige. "That's your commission scroll. You got your votes already. All that's left is swearing you in."

The rest of the hour was kind of a blur. The president put her mask of presidency back on and called people in. Paige was sworn in before witnesses. "I don't want a big thing on the news, Madam Secretary," Dawn said tersely.

"I will need to tell people, Madam President," Paige sniped back because once the masks went back on, that lull of common decency that had been in place had slipped away.

But what was left was something... better almost. They had an understanding.

Then, Naomi shuttled Paige back to the Eisenhower Executive Office Building where Paige was shown her suite of offices. *Not* in the basement, surprisingly. She was told the protocols for this, that, and the other thing. Her door magick was allowed in x, y, and z room. Yada, yada. Staff yada, yada.

There was a lot of yada, yada.

It really happened super fast.

Then Naomi "kidnapped" Paige for lunch.

They went to a nice place, not somewhere Paige would have chosen.

"It's private," Naomi said, putting the green napkin in her lap. "We have a lot to discuss."

And, apparently, they did.

The congressmen and women who had helped her before, the ones who had rigged the vote to make her a Cabinet member, also wanted to impeach the president. As a matter of fact, the vote for the impeachment hearing was scheduled for the very next day.

"I don't think that's a good idea," Paige said.

"Why not?" Naomi asked, startled. She smiled up at the waiter as he brought their salads then left. She leaned forward. "You think she *wanted* to give you that position?"

"She wasn't going to." Paige didn't want to know how much someone was going to be paying for this slab of lettuce with a single tomato. "We need to check and balance her, but I don't know that impeachment is the way to go."

"Well, it doesn't matter," Naomi said. "You don't get a vote."

Thank goodness.

"But you might be called on as a witness."

Paige picked up her fork then set it down on the plate, looking to Naomi in exasperation. "I'm not a politician."

Naomi gave her a wolfish grin. "Great. Because that's exactly what we need. Now, dig in. I've got a lot to catch you up on."

Paige stepped through the doorway with Derick hours later, but Willow stayed behind to get things situated.

Willow had Derrick's number and he told her that if he couldn't get her, he'd find someone who could.

They left Willow still looking a bit shell-shocked by a few things, but frankly so was Paige.

She'd sat Willow down and told her to let her know if things got too big or too much or if she wanted out.

"I don't want out," Willow said emphatically. "I want this opportunity."

Paige chuckled. "Okay, but if the job starts feeling like a noose, you tell me."

"I will."

"No." Paige understood the hunger shining on Willow's face. "You won't. You want to prove you can do this and I'm telling you, you've already shown me you can." Paige didn't want another woman to fall on her face trying to make it in a world she was told constantly she couldn't advance in. "So, don't think of asking for help as a failure because it's not."

"Okay." The look on Willow's face said she didn't believe her and that she could take on the world, thank you very much.

She would, though. Paige knew that like she knew the sun would come up in the morning.

Paige went home to spend some time with the kids.

Leah still wasn't herself yet. Paige wasn't expecting her to just bounce back. She was a Whiskey, but that didn't mean that she didn't feel.

So, Paige went to the large attic that she and Mandy and Rai shared, and crawled onto Leah's canopy bed. It wasn't a perfect bed because it'd been built by Dexx and Paige in their spare time. Dexx was great with cars. Paige was great with paperwork. Neither of them excelled in woodworking, but they'd gotten it rigged together. Mostly.

Leah was trying to keep it together, and Paige realized it was because Leah thought Paige needed her to be strong. "We don't gotta be strong all the time, Bean." So, Paige hugged her close and let the emotions drain out of her. A year ago, she wouldn't have considered that. A year ago, she was still working under the assumption that a parent couldn't show weakness because failing parents lost their kids.

But now? No one was coming to take her kids and the only thing she had to do was to prepare for the shit storm their world was becoming.

So, they cried together and Mandy and Rai joined them, not even knowing what they were crying about. But they could feel the pain, and so they'd wanted to share the burden.

At bedtime, Paige went through and collected *her* kids. Leslie and Tru were having bedtime rituals their own way, sequestering themselves in Leslie and Tru's room. Living in a big house with lots of people could still feel like being in an empty house. There were still plenty of ways for people to hide.

Paige decided to hide in the girls' room. If Mandy wasn't there, anyway, it was the biggest room in the house. So, she gathered Leah, Bobby, Rai and Ember together to play a quiet game of UNO on the floor. Paige was about to call it a night when a blue mist invaded the room to her right.

Paige scrambled to her feet, reaching out with her mind and calling lightning. What had gotten in through the wards?

Cawli had no answers.

The kids scrambled to their feet, their faces set in determination.

The cloud solidified into a woman. She looked elemental with her long hair flowing as though she was under water. Her dress appeared to have been partially eaten but still somehow beautiful with underwater flora growing on it.

What was this? "Identify yourself," Paige said clearly.

The woman tipped her head to the side, her dark hair billowing for a moment. "You are the Paige and the Paige children." Her voice rang out like a symphony of tiny bells. "The Dexx has gained favor with us."

Puzzle pieces were *trying* to connect. "You know where Dexx is?"

"Yes," the woman said with a smile that didn't look entirely happy. It almost looked a little feral. "The Dexx has asked for you."

"Okay." Paige wasn't certain what was going on, but this didn't *feel* like a DoDO trap. This felt… like something else. "What are you?"

"We guard over our child," the water woman said. "And the Dexx has protected our child. We have granted a boon."

Boons were good. Right? Paige relaxed.

The kids followed, glancing up at her in question.

"Can you take us to him?"

"Yes," the water woman said. "Please do not try to…" The woman paused as if searching for the words as she glanced at Paige and Leah. "Lead."

That was the only warning Paige had before she and the kids were enveloped in blue mist. Paige couldn't see anything or sense anything.

But when the mist receded, she found herself crammed in a small bathroom with her four kids.

Something moved on the other side of the door.

What the…

Paige motioned for the kids to stay where they were as she cracked the door open and peered out.

The room looked like a dumpy hotel room that Dexx preferred. She liked clean and convenient. He liked cheap and cheesy.

"*Damn* it," Dexx swore, surveying the room. "I got screwed again."

A wealth of emotions erupted in Paige's chest. "By who?" She stepped out of the bathroom and into the room, devouring Dexx with her eyes and *trying* to concentrate on the room to see if there were any traps. "And you better have a good excuse for being gone so long."

Dexx spun at Paige's voice. His brilliant green eyes widened. "Pea?"

Relief cascaded around her like a waterfall. It was really him.

"Pea, is that really you?"

"Is that really *you*?"

"You're not an undead blue lady trying to get me to drop my drawers, are you?"

Paige had no idea what he was talking about, but she figured it was probably some movie reference she didn't understand. "No. It's just me."

He made a guttural noise that made her insides twist,

then came to her in two long strides, wrapping her in a fierce hug.

It was *really* tight. Her ribs felt like they were about to pop. She tapped him on the shoulder, trying to make sounds of distress.

He pulled away. "Is it really you? Like *really, really*?"

She was standing right in front of him. What else did he want? But moreover, what had he endured?

"Nine hells, it *has* to be. I missed you so much." His fingers tangled in her hair and he squeezed her again, but not as hard this time.

She reveled in the feel of his arms around her until her hair and neck got wet. She pulled back and took in the sight of her big, alpha male with tears in his eyes, his face crumpled in joy and sorrow and fear and happiness.

She cupped his prickly cheek and just absorbed him, giving him what she could to fuel him, taking from him what she needed to keep herself tall. Then she wrapped her arms around him again, holding him to her as he held her up. She breathed deeply, taking in his scent as tears streamed from her own eyes.

So much had happened. Without him by her side. Without him giving her a hard time. Without him adding to her to-do list.

She missed the fuck out of him.

He stepped away and sniffed big. "How?"

How the hell was Paige supposed to know? "You come up with the weirdest friends." She had to tell the kids it was safe. "Come on out."

Leah poked her head through the doorway, an incredulous expression on her face. "Is that you, Daddy Dexx?"

Dexx's breath caught in his chest and his face lit up like a light. "Me in the flesh. Most of it anyway."

"Dad." Leah ran out of the bathroom and into Dexx's

arms, sobbing and babbling until he squeezed too hard. She mumbled something Paige couldn't quite understand.

Dexx released her, pulling back but not away. "Sorry, Little Leah. I've been missing you."

That hit Paige in the feels real hard.

Rai tentatively stepped out of the bathroom followed by Bobby and Ember. "Dad?"

Dexx looked around in confusion. "Huh? You channeling someone?"

"Dad?" Ember asked, tipping his head to the side.

Paige had no idea how to even explain this one to Dexx. "Babe."

Dexx turned to the kids and his mouth dropped open. He put Leah down and looked at Paige. "There something I should know?"

"Um, yeah." But *how?* "First, let me introduce you to your kids." She walked over and set her hand on each child as she introduced them. "Bobby."

Dexx's eyes bulged. "What? You're shittin' me. I'm dreaming or holodecking or something."

Paige wished she understood half of what he said. "This is Rai and this is Ember."

Dexx said something else she didn't understand about Heaven and Hell and... He was babbling in a non-coherent, trying to be funny in a who-understands-him-anyway kind of way.

She held her hands up and explained what had happened in twenty words or less. Or more. It could have been more.

It hurt her heart a little that Rai was so reserved. Bobby was all over Dexx, injecting himself into the conversation where he could, giving Dexx helpful information on things that didn't matter much. She tried to get him to talk about what he was doing in school, but that, apparently, wasn't nearly as exciting as dirt.

The temperature in the room dropped.

Paige raised her attention to determine if this was a threat. "Are we safe?"

The water woman appeared in between the two beds. "The Dexx can have them for a time only. The Dexx people must go from this place, and the Dexx must go from this place."

Were they safe? "Who is that?"

Dexx shrugged. "She's the 'currents' Rainbow is always talking to." He turned his attention to the water woman. "Okay. Message received. How long do we have?"

The water woman turned to Paige. "We can tie back the strings of fate for a short time. The Dexx has his to meet and cannot be helped by the Paige. The Paige must dance to the unseen a while yet before reunion. But we made this place for the Dexx and the Dexx people. It is small, but there will be no danger."

"Pea, this is Blue Lady."

The Blue Lady tipped her head to the side again, a starfish raising its arm in her hair. "The Dexx has our favor. We have granted a boon unto him. This was The Dexx second choice."

Paige raised an eyebrow. "*Second* choice?"

Dexx's eyebrows shot up in alarm. "Pah. Yes, because my first choice would have made this possible on my own but in the real, real world."

Paige chuckled and turned her attention back to the Blue Lady. "Thank you. We'll try to use our time wisely."

The Blue Lady shook her head. "We doubt that."

Wow. Ow.

Dexx raised his brows at Paige. "The kids can go out and play?"

"No harm shall befall the Dexx people in this protected place." The Blue Lady's eyes glowed silver and the curtains behind them billowed.

"Excellent. Because I'd like to give Pea a proper hello."

They'd just seen each other for the first time in months and he wanted to—yeah. Okay. She did too.

"Ew, gross." Leah looked at Paige incredulously, her blue eyes filled with a little hurt. "Are *all* boys like this?"

Paige understood. They had limited time and Leah wanted as much dad time as she could get. "It won't be long, Bean."

"Hey," Dexx said, a little hurt.

She gave him a look that tried to convey that there were other people to consider other than him and his small brain.

His expression said he didn't get the message.

It took a bit to make sure the kids really were okay outside the room, but once Paige was satisfied—it was a big playground with literally no other kids around. It looked as though the Blue Lady had created this space out of a white room—she kicked *all* the kids out and had some *quick* adult time with her almost-husband.

When they were done, though, Paige needed explanations and adult conversation before the kids came back. "You owe me some explanations, man kitty."

"You got it. You see, Mario came to see me—"

Paige shook her head. They didn't have time for the long version. "Five words or less, babe. You've got kids who want to spend time with you and twins you need to bond with."

It took a lot more than five words, but he filled in the blanks, telling a story very similar to the one Quinn had shared with her. Every part of her wanted to stop what they were doing and join the fight with him. She'd never seen Dexx this... off. He wasn't himself. The only thing Paige wanted was to protect him, save him, be there beside him as he took on this threat.

He'd already told her no a dozen times.

"And you never passed a phone?" She needed to *get* just

how bad he was. "Couldn't pick one up and send a message, at least?"

"Babe." He tucked a strand of her hair behind her ear. "I knew this conversation had to be had in person."

"So that brings me to the next thing." If she couldn't rescue her man, maybe she could rescue his team. "*Where's* Red Star? I was told you *took* Rainbow, Frey, and Tarik."

"They're safe. Close by. We're okay."

Good. Paige closed her eyes, wanting to fill him in on everything going on with her, but… he was facing a powerful evil who had been his brother several millennia ago, so telling him she was now a Cabinet member of their government seemed… small.

That's how messed up the situation was.

She got up to get dressed.

"And the kids?" he asked, following her. He paused to take her in as she dressed.

Oh, she'd missed that, too. Feeling appreciated by the man she loved. She dressed slower to revel in the feeling of it, but… kids.

"They're doing okay," she answered, tucking her shirt into her jeans. "They're healthy. Their spirit animals seem to be stabilized. They're *powerful*. They need their alpha to train them."

A shadow crossed Dexx's eyes as he nodded.

Paige understood that shadow more than he could realize. They'd both suffered a few hardships over the past two months. She closed the distance and ran her thumb over his eyebrow, capturing his gaze in hers and holding it.

She didn't say anything, though. She just shoveled as much love as she could muster toward him.

He clunked his forehead to hers and breathed, sharing breath and warmth for a moment.

Paige stepped closer to him and tucked her head under his

chin, listening to his heartbeat as she curled around his still-bare chest. She'd ask about the new tattoos later, when they had time to waste.

They didn't. They never seemed to.

And that was really starting to wear Paige out.

"Come on, hot stuff," she said, pulling away. "Get dressed. I think your kids want some dad time." Before he was taken from them.

Again.

1 1

Paige was happy to watch Dexx interact with the kids. Yeah, okay, not all of them were his. But the way he treated them? Interacted with them? Claimed them? No one would ever know.

The only one who was reserved was Rai, which Paige found a little odd. As a baby, she'd been the outgoing one. She'd been the one everyone had gravitated to.

But now? Pre-teen Rai? She treated strangers better than she treated Dexx.

Eventually, Bobby, Rai, and Ember crashed out on the bed, leaving Paige, Dexx, and Leah to catch up.

Dexx sat with Paige at the table while Leah, lying on the bed, propped her head on her hands and crossed her ankles in the air.

Paige was done waiting. "Okay, babe. Spill." Because if this was just him being himself, but galivanting across the world in order to prove a point, she was going to sucker punch him in the throat.

Dexx kicked back against the wall, almost sideways in his chair. "There's a lot to tell you."

There'd better be. Okay. So, yes. She knew there was a lot going on. She'd received a few updates and she had the thumb drive with information from DoDO which… it hadn't been helpful *yet,* but she was hopeful it would be.

"So, I guess," he started, darting his eyes toward the window then to the door, "we could start with the fact that something really old is attacking me and I'm trying to keep him away from you."

Something was off about Dexx. What was it?

Leah's eyes widened. "Older than *Mom?*

"Hey!" That was rude.

Dexx's lips rose in a smile, but his eyes winced, the crow's feet deepening around his eyes. "Older than civilization. Not this body, of course, but my soul, my mind, and my magick."

There was *something* going on with him. Paige'd noticed it earlier, but she hadn't said anything about it. Okay. To herself inside her own head. "You don't have magick." Paige sat up. "You collect magickal weapons and when you tattoo, that works great."

"I've *always* been a shifter." He let his head fall back against the wall with a soft thud. "This life needed a bit of help. I'm rethinking a lot of my old thoughts."

What in the hell was he talking about?

His Adam's apple bobbed as he swallowed. "I have been reborn I don't know how many times, and I'm able to do that with the help of a *kadu,* something I created in my first lifetime with my magick. Each lifetime, I'm a shifter. I only bond with Hattie. I don't know much more than that, other than I usually know more. But when I was born this time?" His hand flopped in his lap.

Why did it look like her man was… tired? Off? Beat up? How much had it taken for him to *learn* this information?

"Okay, let's go back to the magick part. What sort of magick do you have? Those *koodu* things—"

"*Kadu.*"

Okay. Still didn't mean anything to her. "—keep your soul tied to them. I get that part, but how are you *magickal*?"

"That's a really good question. I don't know. The cardinal... Bussemi, he's supposed to be my brother, I guess. It's so complicated I'm having a hard time sorting it all out."

"You have another brother?" Leah's eyebrows wrinkled.

"I only have the one. In this life. But in the first one, I had one too?"

"I don't get it." Leah shifted her eyes to Paige. "You have a brother now, and you have a brother from the time of the dinosaurs, and Hattie is your shifter spirit, but she got stuck and so you didn't have magick *or* a shifter spirit this go 'round?"

"You still haven't got to the magickal part," Paige said, *trying* to keep up. "I've tested you. My witch ball never registered you as more than a shifter."

"I guess somehow I lost some of it. Maybe all of it. Alma told me I was magick borne, but she never told me anything else. Like, how did she even knew about it? Then, Bussemi comes along and..."

"What aren't you telling me about him?" Paige leaned forward across the table and took Dexx's hands in hers. "Every time you say his name, you wince a little."

"I do not." Dexx tried to pull his hands back but couldn't.

She had them in a vice grip. "You do. I've been a cop for a long time, and I've seen a lot of battered wife symptoms."

"Name *one.*"

"Fear of your abuser."

"You think I'm scared?" Dexx almost blew out his cheeks to scoff. He didn't.

"So, you deserved what you got?"

"No." Dexx shot Leah a glance. "I can't beat this guy. He's always three steps ahead. All of us together couldn't beat that guy."

"But now you have knowledge. What's that thing you always say? Knowing is most of the way there, or something?"

"Now you know. And knowing is half the battle. It's from… never mind. I read you loud and clear. It's just that he's had time to prepare. Time to get where he wants and now he's there. World domination. He's made DoDO legitimate in Britain, and who knows what he's done in other places? He's big time, and I don't know what to do."

Leah got off the bed and hugged Dexx. She didn't say anything.

Paige rubbed his hand with a finger.

"And this spell or ward or whatever he put on me is going to kill me if I don't break it or remove it. I can't shift, I can't even talk to Hattie and there's so much he's done to…" A haunted look entered his green eyes as he looked away. "I can't… I just can't."

Paige just *couldn't* carry Dexx's problems on top of her own. She had to build him back up so he could handle this. "Dexx, even without your shift or… magick, you're strong. You *know* what to do. Get back to that and then work from there."

He grunted.

Paige stared at the top of Leah's head. "Regain your confidence. But not too far. You don't want to be cocky or arrogant—"

"I've *never* been cocky —"

"Really. Then come home. Please."

He shook his head. "I can't. Not yet. I've gotta take care of this guy. I can't bring him home. And I gotta fix what he did to me."

Paige didn't know where to start.

Dexx released a long breath through his pursed lips. "I have to finish this. He's too dangerous to you, the kids? I have to lift the curse first, then I can come home."

Well, he knew what he had to do and it wasn't like she could really argue with him.

"Cardinal Bussemi. He's a bad, bad guy."

Paige gripped his hands a little tighter for a second. "You find him and beat him or find a way to escape him. Those are your options."

"I'm…" He gave a ghost of a chuckle. "I'm tired. I've been chased, and chased, and chased, and I haven't had a break in I don't know long time."

So? Like *she* wasn't tired? "That's your life now. We have enemies everywhere. Even back home." She stood and pulled Dexx into a hug.

Leah wrapped her arms around them both.

The hard part, though, was getting the update from Dexx about what he'd had to face on his own. He'd been beaten. Bad. And the Dexx sitting beside her… wasn't *her* Dexx. He was in there somewhere. She could see that. He was just buried behind trauma and about a year's worth of abuse.

"I don't know how long I was there. But he kept me chained. Beat me while I healed. Broke bones, internal organs. For months. He just wanted to torture me. Over and over he broke me just to watch me heal enough to beat me more." He looked haggard. "I don't know if I can face him."

Judging by his PTSD micro-reactions, she'd wager he'd been tormented for about a year.

Tortured… for about a *year*.

Guilt ripped through her, clawing at her. How many times had she cried herself to sleep, *mad* at him for not being there?

Well, twice. However, now? Staring at him? She just felt

bitterly selfish. She'd been in over her head. Sure. But he'd been…

Broken.

Paige didn't know when they'd fallen asleep, but she felt the heat leave the bed. She groaned and rolled over, her hand reaching behind her to touch Dexx.

She sat up all bleary-eyed and mussed up hair. Her lip snarled when she saw Dexx was awake and talking to the Blue Lady.

"Hurry, coffee." Dexx motioned to the kitchenette.

The Blue Lady stared at Paige.

Paige stared back. What was going on here? "I hope you don't think you're taking him away again. He's coming home with me."

"The Dexx will take an action. We have granted him a boon."

Kindergartners talked better than that. "I don't care if you gave him an elephant, he's coming home with us."

"She didn't mean an animal, Pea. She meant—" Dexx held his hands up. He usually did that when he wanted to retreat to the coffee maker.

"I know what she meant." Paige wasn't an idiot. She wasn't allowing Dexx to slip through her fingers again. "And I know what I meant. You're coming home with us." She slipped from under the covers, bringing out her witch hands.

"Pea, put those away. I think I have to do this. Besides, what about facing or fleeing Bussemi?"

How in the *hell* had he known she pulled out her witch hands? She didn't *really* believe he was magickal until then. "I changed my mind. I finally had a warm bed, and I forgot I liked it." She held her hands steady, ready to use them if she needed.

"Coffee?" Dexx sounded scared.

"The Dexx will take the action. The Dexx people will return to away. No harm shall come to them."

"Pea, I know you don't like this, but I need something from you. I need you to hide the *kadu*. I can't know where they are, so you have to hide them. Could you do that for me?"

"The what?" He must have been talking about the rocks in the backpack.

"The Dexx will champion our child. Our child will action with the Dexx. The people of the Dexx will return away."

Dexx stepped in front of Paige with his hands raised, but still no coffee. "Okay. Listen. This could have been a lot of things. But the Blue Lady chose to do the right thing here and actually let us have some time together. I say we trust her. Hide the *kadu*. I'll come back when I can, then all this can be put behind us. Yes?"

The currents turned to the bathroom. "Our child will be with the Dexx."

"Knock, knock?" Rainbow's voice was soft and questioning..

Rainbow?

Paige's eyes lit up. "Is that you?"

She rushed by Dexx to give Rainbow a hug.

When she stepped back, Rainbow motioned to the woman standing in front of Dexx.

"I see you met the currents. They're so nice, don't you think?"

"Um." Paige wasn't sure how to answer. She had said she was taking Dexx away again.

Dexx waved a hand between them. "Pea, I'm thinking the Blue Lady could be running low on patience. I love you, and I'll have Rainbow to protect me."

The room flashed blue.

P aige stood, staring at her bedroom door in stunned silence.

The kids were awake and facing the door just like Paige. None of them spoke for a good long moment.

Then chaos erupted.

"Where'd he go?" Rai demanded fiercely.

"I'm hungry," Ember said, turning in a slow circle as if trying to figure out where food would be.

"Mom," Leah said, her voice a mere whisper, her blue eyes filled with fear and desperation.

Paige grabbed her by the shoulders and drew her in, hugging her close.

Bobby took in a deep breath and flexed his hands several times like he was getting ready to lift weights. "He's going to be okay." He rolled his shoulders like shaking off a coat.

Paige hadn't seen him that serious ever. "Are you okay, Bobs?"

When he looked up at her, his eyes glowed gold. "I see the first of the greatest. At his right hand, the devil, and his left hand, the lesser monster. I see the greater monster that brings the dark that consumes. As he walks, he leaves no stone unturned in the darkness. I see the one that follows the greater monster and the greater evil. His tongue is like fire, and his words are destruction."

Paige took a knee next to Bobby, not really excited about this new development in his magick. "What are you saying?"

He took a breath and turned to the outside door and pointed. "The world shakes and there is gnashing of teeth. The low will be high and the high will be low. Brother will stand against brother and father against son. The lesser mother fights the greater daughter, and the greater daughter breaks herself. Beware the councilor, I see him laugh and he is greater evil. I see the angels stand to fight but they cannot. They cry out for help and none shall come. The angels of the Earth will rise and fight in their number against the rise of the greater evil. And he will be called brother."

Leah gathered Ember and Rai. She stepped back from Bobby, wide-eyed and slack jawed.

Why hadn't God installed an easier code to break? If He really wanted anyone to know what his prophets said?

"I look and I see light coming from his right hand and darkness in his left. He will cover the light with the dark, and the angels of the Earth strike at him. I hear him say, 'Who is worthy to fight me? Who is worthy to slay the greater evil?' And none will answer, and then the lion will come with fire and lightning and bright darkness to slay the greater evil. And the earth will shake and there will be gnashing of teeth, for the end has come."

Bobby's eyes returned to normal and he fell to a knee. He stood back up looking at the rest of them.

Great. That had just been a prophecy and Paige no idea how to interpret any of it. "Is there anything else you can tell us?" Like... names? Dates? Times? Actual details instead of *gnashing teeth?*

"I— it's all foggy. It's clear, and then it fades. Like a dream but I saw things. I can't make any sense of it."

"Okay, then." Paige looked out the big sliding glass window, not quite sure what to do with her God's prophet son—and who said he was God's prophet? She seriously doubted He had any care in the world about Dexx or paranormal kind. "Let's see what day it is and what I need to explain now."

Leslie was downstairs, making pancakes for her kids. She looked up from her coffee cup, the spatula in her other hand. "You're up early."

Ember burst into the kitchen and grabbed another mixing bowl. His movements were mechanical at first, then he relaxed and became more natural.

Leslie set about getting the mix out. "You're also lookin' awake." She slid a coffee cup to Paige and narrowed her eyes as she pulled out the brightly colored measuring cups and handed them to Rai who joined them. "What happened? Is the world on fire again?"

Leslie didn't appear to be upset or worried. That had to mean they hadn't been gone long. "What day is it?"

"Tuesday," Leslie said carefully as she tapped the rim of the cup.

Paige took it and sipped. Normally, coffee would have soothed her soul, but after the night with Dexx and Bobby spouting a prophecy that made little sense, the coffee wouldn't work.

Rai got the water, poured it into the bowl, then slammed the glass measuring cup on the counter.

Leah breathed heavily as she walked to the island, pressing her hands to the countertop, struggling to keep it together.

Leslie put her coffee cup down, concern crashing onto her face. "What happened?"

Paige carefully put down her cup.

Just the look on her sister's face, the realization that something *had* happened, and that Paige *wasn't* okay, flipped a switch in Paige and the tears started flowing, sobs wracking her body.

Leslie moved around the island and kids, and wrapped her sister in a tight hug, muttering words Paige couldn't understand.

Leah released a choking sob and joined them.

Then they were dog-piled by Rai, Mandy, and Tyler.

Kamden just stood by Ember, watching in confusion.

Paige had to be strong for so many people, her kids included. But she just couldn't anymore. "They broke him, Les," she whispered.

"Who?" Leslie asked just as quietly.

"Dexx. They broke him." Paige's heart twisted just saying his name out loud and fresh tears started all over again.

Leah started babbling, but she was crying so hard, none of her words made any sense.

Rai tried, but she was so angry, her words were clipped and, strangely, not all in English.

Leslie pulled back a little, surveying everyone. "I'm gonna need *someone* to tell me what in the tar hill is going on here."

Ember filled her and his cousins in on what had happened as he and Bobby made breakfast for everyone. Bobby worked on drinks—Paige wasn't the only coffee drinker—and Ember made a feast of pancakes.

Leslie frowned as he brought another platter over to the dining table, the first batch still cooling where he'd left it. "I don't understand the tears. You got to see him. He's good. He's alive."

Paige shook her head, closing her eyes as she gripped her untouched cup of coffee. When she opened them again, she knew —she *knew* she shouldn't be saying this in front of the kids. But… why should she hide this from them? Who knew if they'd suffer another amazing growth spurt the next day, the next week? They might be adults in a day or a year or ten. She didn't know. And what happened if they were faced with a similar—

Situation? When would they *ever* be faced with something like this?

She buttoned up her overriding emotions, turning off the tears, leaving only the numbness. "He was tortured for over a year."

"How? He's only been gone for a couple of months."

Paige shook her head and swallowed. "There's someone there who knows how to manipulate time." She glanced at Bobby. "Like with…" Bobby's mother. She didn't want to say that out loud. Heather had been tortured for days while a djinn had tried to get Bobby's location out of her. He'd been in the next room, hiding under the bed, barely a few days old, as his mother had been brutally murdered. But she'd saved his life.

Leslie's eyes widened and her lips rounded.

Paige was grateful her sister didn't need reminding. "That brother Em told you about from Dexx's first lifetime?"

Leslie nodded.

"He's the leader of DoDO."

Leslie's frown deepened.

"He's been searching for Dexx for centuries, trying to kill him? Take his life or magick or something? Dexx doesn't quite know. But—" Paige gestured to the kitchen, not sure what she was implying.

Leslie fell back in her chair. "So, he's the reason for this whole mess."

Paige nodded, staring at the pancakes. She knew she needed to eat, but her stomach was filled with sorrow and angst. There was no room for cakes.

"The president?" Leslie shook her head, her confusion fusing with frustration.

"A pawn. Dexx didn't say, but if this guy is as smart as he claims, Dexx is the reason DoDO came to the U.S. This guy, Bussemi or whatever, came looking for him."

"And the war on paranormals?" Leslie asked incredulously. She reached over and grabbed three pancakes. "Look, if you're not gonna to eat, I am. These are better hot."

Ember and Bobby were the only two eating.

The other kids were taking their cues from the adults.

Paige shoved aside her sorrow for a moment and grabbed a pancake, tearing off a piece and shoving it in her mouth without butter or syrup.

"You're so gross," Leslie said like she did every time.

Paige hadn't diverted her attention from Leslie's question. "I think Bussemi's war on us was one way to flush Dexx out."

Leah grabbed a pancake and paused as she smeared butter over it, her face filled with horror.

Leslie glanced at her and motioned for the girl to continue eating. "Just how powerful do you think this man is?"

"Enough to control two powerful nations." Paige lifted her face to the ceiling, biting back the feeling of crushing overwhelmingness. She shook it off and shoved another bite of pancake into her mouth. "We're on the brink of war. He just declared it on England—or whatever they call their country. UK?"

Leah paused with a bite partway to her mouth. "That's a collection of countries. Like how the U.S. is to Oregon."

Paige nodded, kicking herself for being so dumb about so many things. Just how sheltered had her life been? A part of her wanted to crawl back to *that* life.

"But that's what happened at the Parliament the other day?"

The other week? "Yeah. He was trying to keep Bussemi from taking over on the spot."

"And did he win?" Leslie stopped with her cup halfway to her lips. "It didn't look like he won."

Paige wasn't sure which *he* she was referring to. "They voted unanimously *against* paranormals. The initial bill or whatever they'd originally been voting on had been small compared to what they're creating now."

Leslie set her cup back on the table. "So, this guy is winning."

Paige nodded.

"Okay." Leslie gestured to their table full of kids. "Then what can we do about it?"

Nothing and that's what pissed Paige off. "I want to find Dexx and fight beside him."

"Me, too," Rai growled.

"Then," Leslie said as if preparing to ask the dumb question. "Why aren't we?"

Paige stared at Rai then Ember before raising her gaze to her sister.

It took Leslie a minute, then her eyes flared. "Well, that changes a few things."

It did. Paige wouldn't be able to take them into harm's way anymore. Not that that had been a great idea to begin with. She knew that. She wasn't entirely stupid. But it meant that *every* situation from here on out was dire.

D.C. wasn't safe. The trip to an outside grocery store wasn't safe. *More* protections needed to be put in place around Troutdale. And when Paige wasn't there, *everyone* needed to be on high alert.

Because if that man got his hands on her kids, the world would never be the same again.

Leslie growled low, and Robin, her griffin, shone through a bit, her green eyes turning orange.

"He's the reason the ancients hid," Paige told him. "He's the reason the *Vaada Bhoomi* was created in the first place."

Robin blinked and Leslie's green eyes came back into focus. "Well, that scared the shit out of him. It hasn't been this quiet in my head in a good long while."

"One of the first visions the ancients showed me was of some wizard or mage or something stripping Robin of his energy. So, yeah. I bet he's pretty scared."

"I want to fight," Rai whispered fiercely, holding her fork in a chokehold.

Paige understood the sentiment, but her two-month old tweenager had a lot to learn about life. "You'll stay here and protect our town. Protect your family. Not just us. But everyone here."

Rai raised her gaze, lightning shooting off in blue arcs.

"You'll protect your pack and your coven."

Rai ground her teeth, her jaw clenching.

Leslie met Paige's gaze and narrowed her green eyes before turning her attention back to the platter of pancakes. "Well, if you guys ain't eatin', I'll put some of these in baggies and send them with you. You're gonna be hungry at some point and then you'll crash and burn and throw tantrums of a kind that might destroy our tiny town before Captain Evil gets a chance to." With that, she got up, carrying the two heaping platters.

Ember and Bobby snatched a few more pancakes before they left.

Paige rose and went to the kitchen with her sister.

Leslie set the platters down and touched Paige's arm, not saying anything or moving to offer more.

It was what Paige needed. "He's *broken*, Les. And I'm not there to help him."

Leslie closed her eyes for a moment then opened them,

her eyes bright with tears as she stared at the coffee pot. "He'll make it through. He always does."

Paige wasn't so sure. "The fight he usually has—I don't know what Bussemi did to him, but..." She didn't know where that thought was leading. She only knew the churning in her heart was making it hard to make sense of words. "He did a good job of breaking my man. And the only thing I can think is that I was *so mad* at him for leaving me when *I* needed him most? And that entire time—that *entire time*—he'd needed *me*." New sobs threatened to take over. "He *needed* me and I did nothing."

"You didn't know."

"But I could have done more. I could have searched harder."

"The world was ending, Pea," Leslie said softly, her tone firm. "You made a call."

"And it was the wrong one."

"Was it?" Leslie turned Paige toward her and cupped her face, bringing her forehead down, almost touching hers. "You knew how strong he was, how powerful. When push came to shove, you bet your chips on him."

And she shouldn't have. She should have been fighting harder to help him.

Leslie shook Paige's head, getting her attention back. "And he's alive. He was tortured for a year, you said?" She let Paige's face go and crossed her arms.

Paige didn't *know* that for certain. "His memories were stripped, but just gauging from his reactions to stimulus and based on my experience in the field, yeah. I think he was probably tortured for about a year. Could have been more."

Leslie smiled at her. "Think about it, Pea. He withstood that. And they took his memories? They tried to strip him of all the things *they* thought made him strong."

And they'd succeeded.

Leslie gave a snort then growled low in her throat. "And he escaped. Not only that, but he managed to fight that bastard back. In a foreign country."

That was all true. Paige wrapped that knowledge around her heart, trying to bolster it back up again.

"So, yeah. He's broken, baby girl." Leslie's hands went back to Paige's neck. "But he's far from down. Maybe he just had to be broken down so he could rise up stronger this time. You ever think of that?"

Hope flickered in Paige's soul again. She just had to keep focusing on that. She let her forehead fall to Leslie's. "Thank you," she whispered around tears. She couldn't speak again for a few beats. She sniffled and beat back her tears. "I needed that."

Leslie nodded, fighting her own tears. "Look," she whispered. She opened her mouth, blinked furiously, then tried again. "I can't do what you can." She pulled away to look Paige in the eye. "Okay? I can't fight a world. I can't save towns and people."

Paige doubted she could either.

"But the people need you. Not just paranormals. Humans too. We need our life back. So, you focus on that and you *keep believin'* in Dexx. *That's* what he needs. He's not some damned damsel. And neither are you."

Paige breathed in Leslie's conviction. "Okay."

"Now, you take another damned pancake and you shove it in your damned mouth and eat it before you have a meltdown that breaks the world as we know it." Leslie choked and tears she couldn't beat back filled her eyes.

Paige wrapped her sister in her arms and held her as Leslie's own sobs overwhelmed her.

Leslie pulled back after a bit and sniffed delicately, wiping at her eyes. "I hate feeling so damned helpless."

"You're not." She was one of the strongest women Paige knew.

"But the only damned thing I can offer are pancakes?"

That wasn't the only thing. Leslie was the glue that kept their family together. "And soaps. Don't forget that."

Leslie snorted and a slip of snot shot out. She grabbed a paper towel and blew her nose, turning away from Paige.

"I wouldn't be able to take on this kind of problem if I didn't have you," Paige said quietly. She couldn't have Leslie falling down. "The only reason I'm doing this is *not* because I'm the strongest."

"Well, you're pretty damned strong." Leslie grabbed the box of baggies, her voice thick.

"Not as much as you."

Leslie rolled her eyes and started shoving pancakes into bags and sealing them.

Paige stopped her. "I'm doing this because no one else is. And they're not because they don't have someone like you, a partner who has their back, who can keep their family and loved-ones safe if all hell breaks loose. I go out there *knowing* that if I fail, *you'll* still be able to keep us safe."

Leslie's gaze latched onto Paige's.

"They don't have that. You're the reason we're going to win, Les. Not me."

Leslie nodded and looked away, drawing in a deep breath. "Okay. Well, then, eat your damned pancake. There's a spell in there for fortitude."

Paige picked one up and stared at it. "Really?"

"No!" Leslie gave her a look like she was an idiot and filled more bags. "It's loaded with eggs and flour and water. Now, eat and get out of my damned kitchen."

Paige gave her sister one last hug.

Leslie held on tightly, the two of them clinging to each

other as if they were the only lifelines they had in a maelstrom of terror.

Then they broke apart, shoved their worry and angst and fear and sorrow and tears aside, and threw pancakes in sandwich baggies at their kids, shuffling everyone off to school like it was any other Tuesday.

By the time Paige made it to Red Star, she felt a little more like herself. A bit better, actually, because she was still riding the high of having seen Dexx. She walked in with a handful of recyclable coffee cups filled with lattes from the shop on the corner. She'd have to rethink that because she couldn't get those *every* time. She handed off the drinks to her new team and asked for updates.

The information being pulled off the thumb drive was... well, there was a lot there, but applying that to what they knew was taking considerable time. It wasn't that the information wasn't fitting together. It really was. The ghosts and DoDO *were tied* together. The question was how.

But Scout was on it. She was leading this raggedy team of misfits well, and that's what Paige needed. She gave the harpy a few things to keep her eye on, a few rules not to forget, then she went on to do what she needed to.

She was the Secretary of Paranormal Affairs and she needed to do paranormal...stuff.

What was she supposed to do?

When she made it to the mayor's building, things were... different. Suzanne was keeping office on the ground floor and was surrounded by people. She looked like she was flustered and enjoying herself at the same time.

Before Paige had a chance to say anything, however, Willow came through and swept her down the hall and to the elevator. "Thanks for not flying in like you normally do. I've got a lot to catch you up on."

Mainly, her staff. Because…she had staff now. And quite a bit of it.

As Secretary, she had eighteen people and was informed she needed to hire at least two more, if not more as her needs grew. She also had a direct line to the president but was cautioned against using it. "Use the Chief of Staff when you can," Willow said. "Ruben's a real stickler for not skirting him. His job is to make sure the president can do hers. So…" Willow double-shrugged with a head twitch as if that explained everything.

It kinda did.

But it was going to take quite a while to learn everyone's names. First and foremost, she needed to get a message to the president. Willow said she'd let Ruben know.

But before they got too far, Paige had been extended an invitation to New Orleans. "The Voudon have invited you." Willow didn't sound too sure about it. "It was quite myste-rious and sounds a little dark. I don't know if you should go."

She'd have to. The Voudon were a part of the paranormal world and just because Paige didn't know much about them didn't mean she had to be afraid. After all, the world was afraid of shifters for having teeth.

How bad could a little voodoo be?

P aige left all of the kids behind this time, especially now that she knew the dangers. Derrick, who was officially her number one "gate witch," questioned how smart a move that was. But she didn't have time for that.

"You don't trust me?" he asked, a little pissed.

Trying to build a sibling relationship with a total stranger was...difficult. "No, it's just..." She watched the door he'd cut open. A view of an occult shop beckoned on the other side. "A lot's happened and... You know what?" She really needed someone to talk to who wasn't emotionally tied to her. "I love gumbo. Let's find a place to go after the meeting or whatever and I'll fill you in."

A frown flickered over his wide face, then he ran his tongue along his teeth and smiled with a nod. "Sounds good." He then stepped through his door.

One would think she'd have experienced building a relationship like this because she'd done it with Nick who'd been raised by their mother in a different state.

Except Nick was so busy with his firm and with being a

new dad and being with Mark—Nick's Mark—and she'd had her time tied up with near-constant world-ending doom and new kids and...

Yeah. They were going to have to put the whole world on pause so they could be human beings together in the same room for a minute.

They walked through the door, and Paige rubbed her arm where Quinn put the mark.

How much ley line magick did each trip through a door revitalize? How much ley line magick was there?

Another question for a time when it could be answered.

The shop was amazing and Paige's little witch heart wanted to go crazy, buying as much stuff as her thinly-lined pockets could carry home. But she hadn't had money in a crazy amount of time. Their loan payment hadn't been put on hold, and her other bills were still due. She'd had to dig into her meager savings to cover everything.

She was broke.

But there were *so many things* that just called out to her. She felt like a starved woman at a buffet.

Which...wait. This was an occult store in the middle of a paranormal war. How in the heck were they still open? And not being persecuted? Yeah. She had a few questions.

No one immediately greeted her, and she was okay with that. It gave her and Derrick a few minutes to look around and get a feel for the people in the place.

Paige also got a sense of Derrick's sense of humor which was a little dark and Dexx-esquely immature. She realized how inappropriate his chicken feet jokes were, but they were making huge inroads on her growing anxiety.

Finally, a woman with long, flowing black hair and a short black skirt with fishnet stockings and biker boots walked up to her with a big smile. "How can I help you today?"

Paige was beginning to think she'd gotten the wrong address. "I'm Paige Whiskey? I was asked if I could come?"

"Oh!" Understanding scattered across the woman's face as a broom joined them, walking on two feet made of bristles. "Right. We kinda thought you'd be sending a message lettin' us know when you'd be showin' up, you know? But you're here." She clapped her hands then noticed the broom. Her eyes widened as she looked at Paige then around the store. "What did I tell you about showing yourself?"

The broom wobbled as if he was talking.

The woman rolled her bright teal eyes and spun on her heel, heading toward the back. "Well, if you're going to make a nuisance of yourself, go tell Mama she arrived."

The broom bounced like a happy puppy then flew off.

The woman reached for and saved two candles that fell as the broom zoomed out.

Paige caught a third, staring after the…flying *broom* in stupefied wonder. Things were really different here.

"Don't mind Whomper." The woman sighed as she put the candles back. "I charged my broom as a kid, thinking, 'Oh, what a neat idea! Give my broom a personality.' And, yeah, sure it was. For a minute. Now, it's like having a dog." She thought about that for a second. "With a stick for a tail."

Paige whuffed a chuckle and shared a glance with Derrick.

He grinned, but kept his mouth shut.

"Well, I'm Wynonna Hunt," the woman said, offering her black-lace finger-gloved hand. "I own and run this shop. And this—" she said with a brightening smile as she saw something behind Paige. "—is my lovely Veronica."

A tall black woman sashayed to Wynonna's side and wrapped an arm around her shoulders, beaming a welcome smile at Paige. "We're so glad you could join us." Her tone was laced with surprise.

"Thanks for extending the invitation." Maybe she *should*

have sent word. She'd make a note to do that in the future. "I forget to forewarn people we can just, you know, drop in."

Veronica laughed throatily. "Well, we had been warned. But seein' it with your own eyes... Yeah, it's a sight."

"I just saw a broom walk. So, back at ya."

They all shared a chuckle.

Paige wasn't certain if this was just a formality because she was Secretary now or if this was something more important, but she wasn't going to ask in the middle of a public shop. "Is there some place we can talk that's more private?"

Veronica tipped her head to the side. "Of course." She rubbed noses with Wynonna. "Mind the front?"

"It's *my* store." Wynonna pushed to her tiptoes and gave Veronica a brief kiss before disappearing to the front. "Don't use the mushroom tea. It's a bad batch."

Veronica mouthed, "It's not," to Paige.

"I saw that."

"No, she didn't," Veronica mouthed.

"Yeah. I did."

Whomper peaked out from around a shelving unit and waved his handle.

Veronica's entire face glared at him as she shook a joking fist at Wynonna's back. "I hate it when you do that."

Wynonna laughed maniacally.

"This way." Veronica gestured for Paige and Derrick to follow but pointed a dangerous finger at the broom. "You, stay here."

"I feel like," Derrick said in a whisper only Paige could hear, "we stepped into a different world."

"Same."

The back was a *lot* like Leslie's place, except it was bigger, older, and darker. This place looked and smelled like it'd been in use for centuries. There was a good chance it had been.

Several women were stationed around the room, sitting on whatever was available: upturned buckets, stools, boxes.

Veronica gestured wildly at the room. "Make yourselves comfortable. Would you like something to drink?"

"Something that isn't mushroom tea?" Paige asked, not sure what the joke was.

Laughing, Veronica walked to the fridge toward the back. "We have sweet tea."

Paige kept her gag-face to herself. She was in the south, after all. "Water?"

A lithe black woman sat serenely to Paige's left, a yellow piece of material wrapped around and threaded through her hair. She oozed power.

She is indeed very powerful, Cawli said, walking through the backdoor.

That was a surprise. *I didn't expect to see you here.*

And miss this opportunity? Cawli curled up at her feet. *I have been trying to gain an audience with her for centuries.*

Interesting.

The woman in the yellow—Paige had to own her whiteness. She made eye contact and pointed to the woman's head. "What is that called?"

The woman smiled. "A *dhuku.*"

It represents many things depending on how it is tied, Cawli offered helpfully.

"Well, it's lovely."

"Thank you." The woman took in a deep breath. "You may call me Mama Gee."

Paige had the distinct impression that wasn't her real name. "Thank you for the invitation." She looked around, more than a little nervous. She felt her whiteness sitting in this room of proud black women and didn't want to come off like a complete ass. "Your invitation didn't say what you wanted to discuss."

"And yet you came anyway?" Mama Gee asked with a ghost of a giggle.

Okay. When she said it like that— "I was told the Voudon had requested my presence and I decided it might not be wise to piss off a voodoo priestess." She clamped her lips shut, not sure what else to say.

Several of the women around the room laughed.

One didn't.

I get the impression she does not like you.

So did Paige.

"Well," Mama Gee said, clasping her hands around her knee and rocking back slightly. "We wanted to meet the great leader of the paranormal world and to see if she was going to write us into the bottom of history like so many before her."

Okay. So, this was that moment in Paige's life she had hoped to avoid. She *knew* she was white and sheltered. She was starting to realize she was privileged for all that she'd struggled. Like, her life was far from easy. But the one thing she was *really* starting to understand was that the *world* had been built *against* people who weren't her. Okay. Aside from the witch part and the shifter part and the—yeah, all of that. *She* wasn't a witch *and* non-white.

That was also not something she'd actually thought about. "I've just been focusing on not getting our world destroyed. I haven't had a chance to… figure out how to…" Not sound like a complete asshole.

Veronica smiled and ducked her head, handing Paige a glass of ice water. "We *did* notice."

"But we wanted ta see," the bodacious woman by the back door said with a grimace, "if we could trust you, child." Her accent was deep, but understandable.

If you could win their support… Cawli's voice trailed off. *Do you have any idea the importance of this meeting?*

No. "That seems fair." Paige took a sip of water, trying to

buy herself some time. She didn't know why she kept walking into situations before thinking them through. At some point, she was going to have to learn to prepare. Child? "What do you need from me? An update? Um… a talk about…" What did other politicians do in situations like this? "…views?"

The women looked to each other and eventually nodded.

"Okay." Paige could do that. Of course, she wasn't sure what information was secret and what could be openly discussed, but as she hadn't been given her clearance yet—which, apparently, was a really big issue that had a lot of people upset—so she had to assume that nothing she knew was top secret.

Well, on the government side. There was information *she* knew on *her* side of things that were. And, come to think of it, she needed a vetting process of her own. Who could she trust? Who would gain *her* top secret clearance?

What kind of world had she stepped into?

"Well, let's see. We could start with DoDO?"

Mama Gee nodded. "Start where you wish, child."

She invested time just talking to them, sharing news and information about what was going on and what she had managed to do. She kept her information about the president on the down-low, but she warned them about the effects of the collars and how they didn't affect her witch abilities. In time, everyone's body language was more relaxed, including the woman by the door.

Child, indeed.

Cawli was actually purring.

It was time to get serious. "I have a few questions."

Mama Gee nodded with a soft smile. "As do we."

Start with the obvious. "How are you still operational?"

And not being taken? Cawli said, raising his head and flicking his ethereal whiskers.

That too. "There's a war out there. We're on lockdown. I've got reports of paranormals being grabbed off the streets, and here you are practicing openly. Do you have protections that could help others?"

Veronica narrowed her eyes but sighed. "We're New Orleans," she said evenly as if that was the answer to the universe.

And, okay. It kinda was. "So, *that* is helping. Tourism?"

It's more than that, kitten.

One day, Paige hoped that cat would finally fill her in on a few things.

Mama Gee ran her hand along her chin. "Since everything has started, our business has grown. People come here expecting what you have shown the world."

"Leslie's has too, but she can't get supplies." Because the money had been frozen. "But you can?"

"We are not Troutdale, child," the woman at the door said. "Predominately white and Protestant." She waved her hand in a shooing gesture. We've got a real culture here and *that is* what is keepin' us open."

Paige didn't think Troutdale was *Protestant* by any stretch of the imagination. But it was something she'd look into— what that meant—at a later date.

She means restrictive, Cawli offered.

Oh. But the tourism aspect was also something she'd have to run past Suzanne.

"Question for you." Mama Gee stabbed Paige with her dark gaze. "What's goin' on with the ghosts?"

Paige felt a little trapped by the woman. "Ghosts?" What were the chances that their ghost problem was the same as hers?

"Spirits been inhabitin' people," said the woman with the high-pitched voice. "Then, they've been sendin' 'em straight to the morgue. Dead in the brain."

Interesting.

That could be connected. "I've got a case we're working on right now, but our ghosts are sending people into comas."

Mama Gee narrowed her eyes. "Comas?"

Paige nodded and handed Derrick her phone, unlocking it. "Can you message Barn and tell him to extend his search parameters here. And while he's at it, he might as well look everywhere." She wasn't sure if this was new information for Barn who had a tendency of thinking outside the Coke-bottle box anyway, but it was safer not to assume.

"We believe," Veronica said carefully, "that inhuman acts are being performed."

"Inhuman?"

"Torture."

"Oh. Well that's our take on it, too." But the way the woman who said that gave Paige the impression her source was different. "How'd *you* conclude that?"

Veronica opened her mouth, a frown marring her brow. She then closed it, her expression saying she was putting pieces to together. "A source."

It looked to Paige like the woman was trying to determine if she was able to reveal who that was. "I'd like to meet this source."

"I'll ask." But her gaze said she was already pretty sure of the answer.

Mama Gee waved them to silence.

Someone comes.

Paige clamped her mouth shut and waited.

Wynonna stepped through the door with a smile. "Lunchtime lockdown. Best be goin'."

Mama Gee nodded and waited as the women rose to their feet.

Paige didn't. There was something in Mama Gee's gaze that made her feel she needed to stay.

"Paige?" Derrick offered his hand to help her up.

She blew out her cheeks, making a decision. She dismissed Derrick in a very little-sister-kind-of-way. "Can I have a minute?"

Derrick considered for a moment, but finally nodded and left.

Once the room was cleared, Mama Gee stood and walked sedately to the sink by the back refrigerator. "There is a base nearby," she said softly. "It is my belief the people in danger are there."

Hmm, Cawli said, rising to his feet. *I will go check it out.*

You can do that?

He didn't say anything else. He just dissipated.

That was good information. Paige joined her, rinsing her glass out. "I'll check it out."

Mama Gee nodded once, then pursed her lips. "Where are you staying tonight?"

"Well, I'd—" Actually, she hadn't thought about it. "I've got door magick. So, I was gonna go home. Be with my kids."

"Can I invite you to stay the evening?" Mama Gee asked carefully.

Was there more to this than met the eye? "As long as I'm not putting my foot in it, yeah. I'd love to."

The woman smiled and stepped back. "Most excellent. Wy'll give you the address for your door. Enjoy your evening."

And like that, Paige was also dismissed.

Why did she get the feeling there was more going on than she realized?

14

So, lunchtime lockdown just meant that everyone had to *get* to the place they were *going* to eat as quickly as possible because agents would be patrolling the area. They didn't have any authority or jurisdiction, but they were able to make trouble.

Paige wanted Cajun really bad. So, she opened a search screen and looked for places to eat nearby. She found a likely spot and she and Derrick went for lunch. They had their lunch date and caught up a little.

The conversation was a little awkward at first, but once they found they really did have a lot in common, she relaxed.

Derrick did, too.

Paige had this feeling that the Blackwood witches were like cult members thanks to the way Eldora presented them to her, but she shook off that misconception and filled her in on the real goings-on.

They were just as dysfunctional as everyone else.

And that made Paige feel a whole bunch better.

They didn't talk about anything important. No real talk about family or beliefs or sharing stories of growing up. They talked about world events and weather and showed each other their warped takes on the world.

They were building a relationship, but it would take time. This was just one step in a long line of steps.

When they'd left to meet the Voudon, they hadn't really made plans to stay overnight. The door magick was just so convenient, they didn't need to. But before accepting Mama Gee's additional invitation—which, how was that going to work to be out at night after the city-wide curfew?—Paige and Derrick needed to spend time with their own families.

Derrick dropped Paige at her house. "Give me a few hours. M' wife'll want some time, and then there's the kids."

Paige pulled a face. "Same. But with Leslie and the kids."

He nodded, turning to leave. "I'll meet you here with a door." He grinned. "And thanks for lunch. That was nice."

It really had been.

Paige went to the house to grab her go bag and spend time with her kids before bed. The joys of magick. And she was *really* grateful to Quinn for dealing with that mark on her hand, which... she still wasn't *entirely* comfortable with someone monitoring all of her information, but she needed answers. And with everything else on her plate, she couldn't *deal* with the "Can I trust her?" debate.

The answer was yes followed by, *I'll deal with the fallout later. Hopefully, when my plate isn't so buried.*

Paige went to the kitchen to grab some travel snacks after putting the kids to bed finally, and caught Leslie pouring her nightcap of wine. They'd had a really heartfelt moment earlier, something that didn't happen often though it seemed like it should. When people lived together, there was this assumption that you were really close when, in fact, you could practically be strangers living in the same house. "You gonna be okay?"

"Oh, yeah." Leslie raised her copper cup in salute.

"Reading a good book and going to bed curled up to a man I was mad at this morning and now I just intend to be grateful the skinny bastard's snoring in my ear."

Paige chuckled. "I don't know I'd be grateful for *that*."

"You will," Leslie said softly on her way out of the kitchen. She touched Paige's arm on her way by. "I love you, Pea."

"Love you back," Paige returned quietly, taking that little morsel and stowing it away in her heart for later.

By the time she made it to the front door, she was greeted by two faces she'd almost sworn she'd put to bed earlier: Leah and Rai.

Leah straightened herself and pushed her long, blonde hair over her shoulder with her chin held high. "We're going with you."

"No. You're not." Paige had made her point quite clear. Children's safety first and foremost.

Rai's eyes danced with blue lightening for a moment, then she smiled. "Okay." And she stepped aside.

Oh, that sneaky little— "You're not coming."

Rai shrugged, her smile turning cockeyed. "Okay."

Was that little brat taking a note out of Paige's book? This was distinctly unfair. She hadn't had a *chance* to *use* those tactics against her. "You're going to just come on your own."

Rai's smile straightened as her posture tipped, her weight sliding to one side as she cocked a hip.

Paige rued the day she'd brought *her* spawn into this world. Not once. Not twice. But three times. What a... "Fine. But if you die, it's on you." It wasn't. It'd be firmly on her, but she pushed down the thread of terror threatening to tiptoe inside and blossom. The danger was *probably* low.

Derrick was on the porch with another young girl who looked a lot like him. He took in the sight of Leah and Rai and beamed a grin. "We had the same idea."

They weren't going to the circus. "There could be danger."

"Lilly," Leah screeched with excitement and attack-hugged the girl.

The three girls talked so fast on top of each other, Paige had no idea what any of them were even saying.

"And there might not be," Derrick said with a shrug. He opened a door that took them to New Orleans then walked through.

Paige prayed to the goddess that things would work out just fine and followed.

The address they'd been given actually dropped them in an old cemetery, which, if Paige was going to spend any time in New Orleans, she'd *wanted* to enjoy some prime cemetery time. She'd seen pictures but walking the pathways and viewing them online weren't the same. Especially at night. It was midnight, so the timing was perfect.

Even though Paige *hated* ghosts, she *loved* cemeteries.

The girls, who'd gone quiet for a split moment, started chatting excitedly to each other again.

Well, they were entertained and letting everyone know they'd arrived.

Derrick surveyed the area with narrowed eyes as the door closed behind Paige with a whispering whoosh. "I'm confused."

He wasn't alone. Paige switched to witch vision to see if there was anything else.

A bright, violet light lit a trail to her left.

"I think we're supposed to go this way."

Derrick just narrowed his eyes in the darkness. "Lead on."

Paige wasn't sure what Derrick, Lilly, Rai, and Leah could see because there was no light. The only way Paige could see anything was thanks to her shifter abilities and the witch light guiding them.

She led them along a slightly broken pathway through the maze of crypts. She wanted to stop and look at them, but she wasn't sure what she'd be able to notice, really. She wasn't Leslie, the medium.

There *were* strange symbols glowing in several locations, and that *was* something Paige could make out. Some of them looked like they were rune-based, similar to the case that had started everything. She recognized a few of the runes, but they'd been spliced together in ways that didn't quite make sense to her.

Veronica stepped out from behind a large crypt with a welcoming smile and a lit candle. "We weren't sure when you'd arrive."

"I was trying to tuck the kids into bed." Paige shrugged then gestured to the three kids *with* them.

Veronica threw her head back and laughed. "Welcome." She swept her arm wide, turning to walk away. "We wanted to welcome you properly."

As Paige stepped into a small clearing between crypts, she was hit with a wave of power. It wasn't terrible or chaotic. It was just power. Several women filled the small space, along with one man. They were doing things that made Paige's witchy heart *squee* a little. A pair chanted while another shredded herbs into a bottle. Another used a stick to carve symbols into the dirt.

She wasn't the type of witch who needed ceremony, but she was a voyeur. When she saw practitioners using it, she liked to watch.

It didn't look like there was any real organization to their activities. It was as if there wasn't one ruling doctrine. Everyone seemed to be doing their own thing, working their magicks their own way, using the tools that made sense to them without worry or regulation.

"Wy," Veronica called with a smile that left her front teeth propped at the back of her bottom lip in an oddly endearing way.

Wynonna raised her head, a gust of wind billowing her hair out of her face.

Whomper leapt up, dancing on his bristle feet, and jogged over.

Leah screeched.

Paige chuckled. She'd forgotten to warn her about a walking broom. Earlier that day had been the first time *Paige* had ever seen anything like it in her life.

Rai's face lit with excitement as she led the way toward Whomper.

The broom was like a puppy meeting people for the first time.

Wy shook her head. "Be nice. And Whomper, no whomping."

Paige recalled the *Dora the Explorer* phrase of "Swiper, no swiping," and it made her like the other witch a little more. "Does that actually work?"

Wynonna shook her head. "If only. So, call me Wy."

Why not? Paige laughed inside her head, feeling lighter than she had in…weeks, months? Years?

Maybe that power that had washed over her had been more than just *power*.

Veronica tucked a strand of Wy's hair behind her ear with a loving smile, then turned to Paige.

Something hid in those dark eyes that Paige couldn't quite place. A sadness? A knowledge? She didn't get a lot of time to dig into it, though.

"We invite you into our power circle," Veronica said, her words ringing with something more than just words, something more than just power.

Paige realized this *meant* something. "What?"

Wy stepped forward, grabbing Paige's gaze then her

shoulders. Something reached out from her teal blue eyes and latched onto Paige's soul. "It means," she said quietly with a power unlike anything Paige had ever felt before, "that if you pass, you will *never* be alone again."

The ache of those words rang like a bell in a wide chamber of Paige's soul. She took in a deep breath, swallowed, and released it. "And if I fail?"

Wy shrugged. "You'll still be you, but…" She released Paige and took a step back, gesturing to the people in the small area with a cocky grin. "Without us."

This was certainly *not* what Paige had expected. "Well, I, um, probably shouldn't have brought the kids if this was a te—"

Wy waved her off. "They probably felt the pull. If they answered, be assured, they're meant to be here."

Paige wasn't comforted by that, but at the same time, the weight of her responsibilities, of the sorrow and angst and hurt and loss—it just wasn't there to *add* to her discomfort. She was *free* to review this without the burden of all the emotional *baggage* of her past.

She was free to simply experience this as herself.

"Lilly," Derek barked.

Paige turned to the girls and the broom.

Lilly was kneeling at Whomper's feet, playing with his bristles. "I'm trying to figure this out."

Wy gathered Paige and led her away. "He doesn't bite," Wy called over her shoulder. "But he hits like a stick." She leaned closer to Paige. "He's made of alder. Oops."

Paige didn't quite know what that meant. She wasn't really up on all her witchiness.

Wy smiled and stepped away. "Witch warrior wood." She waggled her eyebrows.

Veronica clapped her hands. "Witches, let's raise our voices."

Paige didn't know what to do, but several of the other witches stepped up, raising their faces to the sky, and sang. Some used words she understood, but most seemed to just be bringing notes together. The man brought out a drum, starting slow at first.

A few of the women broke away and began to dance, throwing themselves into the song.

Paige just stood there feeling completely out of place. She could *feel* the power rise and it was intoxicating. But she wasn't a singer and she *wasn't* a dancer.

Lilly's smile grew bigger as she continued to watch until her voice joined theirs.

Leah had been watching in confusion until that moment. Then, it was like something hit her. She blinked rapidly, biting her lip nervously. She met Paige's gaze, her bottom lips sliding to the side still within her teeth's embrace. She shifted her weight evenly then raised her face to the stars and sang.

Something pulled at Paige, the sound of her daughter's voice, releasing her soul to the heavens. It was so pure and so simple. No words. Just notes.

But it was more than that. Those notes were filled with emotion. Emotions she hadn't been able to vocalize before. They rolled over Paige, bringing tears to her eyes, with her unspoken emotions.

Rai's voice joined in next, filled with anger and resentment and frustration. And youth.

This young woman Paige didn't know. She hadn't had time to form into a person yet. Not really. She hadn't earned experiences that would shape her character.

She'd been born with one.

Derrick frowned and joined the drummer. Not all the witches were singers or dancers.

A few drums and other instruments sat behind the circle

and were eventually picked up, each person layering the song with their soul.

It wasn't so dissimilar from her wards.

Even knowing this, though, Paige's voice was silent and her hands were still. This moment was just so beautiful, but she was… afraid to dip into her soul.

Wy took her hands and dragged her closer to the center with a smile. "Magick," she said, her words piercing the voices, "is more than just power. It's an expression of who we are."

And there it was. Her fear. Paige had made some terrible choices in the recent past. What if she sent her soul out there and she was rejected by these seemingly amazing women?

Wy tipped her head to the side and licked her lips. Taking in a deep breath, she released it with song.

A song that sang of a fear so great, she'd run away instead of fighting. She sang of the loss only a mother could experience, of having lost her child. But her loss was more than that, twisted with guilt. She'd *abandoned* her daughter.

Paige thought for a moment that Wy was singing *Paige's* song until she realized… Wy was giving *her* soul song.

A song filled with travel and experiences. Of love and loss, but always that fear that she could never truly go back home, to face a daughter she didn't know, who should hate her for everything Wy wasn't.

Paige turned to her own daughters who were now dancing and laughing with their cousin.

Wy's song changed slightly, offering acceptance.

Paige flicked a tear she hadn't even realized had escaped from her cheek and took in a deep breath. She had the singing voice of a crow.

But she closed her eyes.

And released her soul.

She sang of the loss of her partner and best friend, of

being angry and alone, of the guilt of having learned of just how bad his situation was—and still being mad at him. She sang of the sheer terror she refused to allow herself to feel of the threat she now knew dominated over them, something so much larger and bigger than demons and angels and politics.

She sang of the bone quaking fear that she'd doomed her children to terrible deaths by inviting powers she hadn't fully understood into their world. Of being overwhelmed and in over her head, and how she was afraid she was making bad choices with bad information.

Her notes soured with her frustration at herself for being… not *enough* for what the world needed from her. With her need to be *more,* and the fear she'd find the end of her abilities and the world would be thrown into a turmoil she couldn't protect or shield them from.

Her soul wept for the comfort of ignorance but roared with the refusal to accept its protections again. It clawed toward the stars as the crescent moon rose, pushing to be better, *more,* not for herself. Not for her children.

But for the world. For the people around her. For the people who were struggling every single second of every single day to just … survive, much less trying to be *nice* and *good* while doing so.

As her soul found an end to her silent screams, her ears opened to the surrounding silence. Hers was the only voice raised to the sky. And it wasn't a song. It wasn't a sob or a scream or a roar.

It was a battle cry.

She choked it off, her throat raw, and sagged forward, resting her hands on her knees. What had she just done? What had she just released?

Wy's biker boots and fishnets came into view as she lightly touched Paige's shoulder.

Paige tried to stand, but she couldn't. The weight that had

been lifted when she'd stepped into this space was back and it was heavy. Tears splashed onto the cobbled and moss-covered square at her feet. She took in one ragged breath then another, unable to think past the barrage of emotions her cry had released.

Wy's fingers dug into her shoulder, lifting her up.

Releasing a jagged breath, Paige straightened, facing the witches around her.

They didn't offer comfort.

They reached out to her…

And offered their strength.

Paige woke up the next morning in a studio apartment filled with Bohemian things that showcased creativity and spunk. The high rafters were bare but filled with decorations of hanging stars and moons and other occult symbols of protection and wellbeing.

She pushed herself out of the bed, wondering if the night before had just been a really weird dream.

Her throat told her otherwise. It was raw and sore still.

She stumbled barefoot to the kitchen and prepared coffee, taking note of Leah and Rai curled around Lilly in a large, purple beanbag chair, and Derrick draped half-on the leather, heavily patched couch.

A rainbow-colored cat hopped onto the counter and rubbed himself against Paige's chin.

She smiled and croaked at him what she'd intended as words, but they came out the sounds of a bullfrog.

The cat headbutted her chin then hopped down, disappearing.

Cawli appeared in the other cat's place, looking around, his cat face upset. *I found the base.*

She nodded, not ready to speak. She looked to see where the rainbow-colored cat had gone off to but saw nothing. *What did you learn?*

It is indeed a base and it is something we need to take care of.

And the torture?

I could not get in everywhere. It is warded against our kind.

"Spirit animals?" Her voice croaked out, but she understood herself. That seemed unheard of.

Cawli nodded.

Except that Dexx's enemy, Bussemi, knew about spirit animals. "I'll figure something out." She couldn't go in the way she had at the prison, not while she was *trying* to make peace. But maybe she could take the matter to the president.

The door opened and Wy stepped in like a fresh breeze. Her fishnets had been replaced by black tights with holes in them. Her biker boots were the same, but this skirt was fuller and sashayed with every step. Her green shirt had a slogan Paige couldn't quite read, but she figured it would probably be something snarky. Wy smiled at Paige and set a heavy bag of groceries on the counter. "You're up. That's great."

Paige opened her mouth and croaked again, then frowned and grabbed her cup of coffee to wet her throat.

"Oh." Wy grabbed the cup out of Paige's hands and went to work building something else.

Cawli trotted to end of the kitchen counter. *Don't do anything stupid, kitten.*

Whatever, cat.

He flicked his bushy tail and disappeared.

Wy handed a mug to Paige. "Try that."

Sipping the sweet concoction of lemon water, honey, and some sort of tea, Paige's throat felt a little better.

Wy put the groceries away while she sipped. "Sleep well?"

Paige had. "I didn't mean to kick you out of your bed."

Wy chuckled. "I spend most nights at Vee's, anyway. So, it's fine. These old walls enjoyed the company, I'm sure."

Just the walls? It suddenly registered to Paige that she'd seen a *rainbow-colored* cat. "I, um, met your cat."

Whomper peered into the large window at the foot of the couch and knocked.

Wy went to let him in. "I don't have a cat."

"Uh." Well, okay then. Maybe she'd just imagined it? She didn't *think* so, but... this place wasn't like what she was used to. She could talk to a broom. So... "My mistake then."

Wy shrugged, closing the window behind her broom. "It might be a stray, but I doubt it'll stay long. Don't—Whomper, seriously. No. Leave 'em alone."

The broom sagged as he shuffled away from the sleeping girls.

Wy clapped her hands quietly and looked over at Paige. "You need to get dressed and ready. Whomper'll watch the kids and your brother. The coven wants to convene."

Oh. Just the sound of those words made Paige cringe a little on the inside. "Something to be worried about?" Her girls had better stay safe. But after last night, local danger seemed less likely.

Wy shook her head as if to say she didn't know. "Get dressed then come downstairs. The store is *hoppin'* today. I'm busier'n shit." She disappeared out the same door she'd arrived in.

Paige made quick work of getting dressed and finished her tea. By the time it was done, her throat felt a little better, though not a hundred percent. She finished her standard breakfast routine with a quick shot of coffee.

The kids and Derrick were all still super passed out. Whomper paced impatiently in the kitchen for them.

"They'll be up soon," Paige told the broom, feeling like she was talking to a kid.

Whomper just turned toward her and shook himself as if telling her she didn't know what she was talking about.

She chuckled, glancing around to see if she could get one more glimpse of the rainbow- colored cat. Out of the corner of her eye, she thought she spied a bit of blue, however, it disappeared so quickly, she wasn't certain she had seen it at all. This place was certainly different.

She just had to hope she hadn't messed things up the night before.

Paige made her way down a set of rickety stairs that reminded her of the staircase leading to the attic in Alma's Texas house. It dumped into the back room of the occult shop where she was greeted by no one.

She made her way into the shop itself only to discover that Wynonna hadn't been lying. The shop was crammed with customers.

Wynonna broke away from a group of young people and approached Paige with a smile. "Just head over to the coffee shop." She hooked a thumb behind her. "Everyone is waiting for you there."

Paige had seen a show about a spunky demon fighting girl, and this gal was really only missing the tight jeans and the big pistol strapped to her thigh. Paige had a hard time not liking her, but she also wasn't sure about the whole situation. "Is this normal?" Paige was certain that if Leslie could get this level of business on a daily basis, she'd be swimming in money and wouldn't be wondering about the success of her shop every month.

Wynonna shook her head with a frown. "Something tells me that this has something to do with what we released last night."

That sent a thrill of fear down Paige's spine. "What was that?"

"Knowledge." Wynonna stepped away from her and called

over her shoulder, "Sometimes, people just know things and don't know how. And now they're here to protect themselves. Go. Go, go, go, go."

Obviously dismissed, Paige stepped out of the shop and onto the busy New Orleans street. She didn't know the area, but the storefronts were exactly as she had seen them in movies and in pictures. She wanted to stroll up and down the streets and sightsee. She wanted to enjoy this feeling of old time magic, as if she could just reach out and touch memories in a non-scary way.

On these streets, she was greeted by shifters who were partially shifted. No one screamed or ran away.

The obvious tourists in their shorts and matching shirts would simply ooh and awe at the spectacles and take pictures.

Paige wasn't certain this was exactly what she wanted Troutdale to become. However, if they could find a way to survive the coming changes to their society by opening themselves up as a paranormal tourist attraction, they might have a better chance of survival. That was something she needed to at least consider.

She watched the locals as she crossed the street. Being a tourist attraction was something that the people who lived here just took for granted. Maybe not quite that simple, but it was in their mannerisms and the way they walked, the way they talked. The way they dressed and carried themselves. If this was something they chose to do, the citizens of Troutdale would have to learn how to become performers.

However, as she had witnessed, it also gave them the freedom to be themselves in a way they had never experienced before.

Mama Gee and Veronica sat at one of the bistro tables on the patio outside the coffee shop. Veronica waved to Paige and gestured for her to go order her drink and come back.

The drinks were all named with cute nods to the occult. She ordered the zombie voodoo latte which would "bring her back to life." She was never one to turn down an overabundance of coffee. However, this particular drink sounded very similar to others she had ordered around the world. In the west, these were often times called *grizzlers,* coffee with shots of espresso added to them. She knew from personal experience just how well these worked.

She went to the outside patio, not quite sure if she was braced and ready for the conversation she was about to have. She didn't know which way it was going to go. She didn't know what she even wanted to get from it.

Having an agenda for some of these conversations might be something she needed to get better at.

Veronica Rose and gave her a hug before offering her the empty seat. "You look like you survived the evening well enough."

Paige's reception was certainly a relief. "I need to be heading back today." She needed to know if she had met their expectations and if there was anything else that needed to be said. "Do you have the location of that installation nearby? I could have my team look into it and see if we can put a stop to whatever they're doing."

Mama Gee nodded and leaned forward, her expression serious. "We can handle our own ghosts. That was only the thing to draw you here. You did what you needed to with the song last night."

Paige swallowed hard, but she couldn't quite let the ghost issue go. "We *do* have an open investigation on the ghosts. So if there is anything you learn, please pass it on to my team."

Mama Gee gave a brief nod then flicked her fingers as if to tell Paige to let it go. "I needed to know if our kind would be left behind yet again."

Paige wasn't certain if the woman was referring to paranormals of this region in general or witches. Or if this was a conversation about race. And if this was a question of race, was Paige the right person with whom to even have that conversation? The thought made her uncomfortable. "And what did you learn?"

Mama Gee licked her lips and leaned back in her seat. "My child, I found you not lacking of a challenging soul."

Paige felt the tremor beneath those words, the emotion that empowered them. This was more than just simple word choice. There was experience and history shaping each syllable as the witch uttered them.

"I try. Alma always said I was a challenge."

"And if we bring you new challenges, issues we face, I need to know we will be heard."

Page didn't know what the full weight of that would have meant until after she'd screamed her own silence into an empty night. But that had been *her* silence. She had never carried the silent voice of another.

"I don't know that I'm the right person for this." And she didn't. She was realizing just how much bigger her world was. The song her soul had sung the night before about how she missed her ignorance but didn't want to take it back was still true after she had awakened. Now, faced with the reality of the knowledge in front of her, she felt insignificant. Too small. "You'll be heard, trust me, but I'm not certain I have the experience to help you correctly."

Mama Gee nodded and ran her fingers up and down her paper coffee cup. "That is enough for me."

"If I were to tell you that some of our people have gone missing around our neighborhood," Veronica said carefully, all welcome and warm smiles gone from her sharp face, "what would you tell me?"

Paige wasn't certain what her jurisdiction was, but this was common ground for her. She knew how to handle missing persons. "I would tell you that sounds exactly like DoDO's MO. We've got a case file open right now with people who are disappearing all over the country. I'm willing to bet that this has something to do with them and your ghosts."

Veronica frowned and leaned forward. "Tell me more."

Paige leaned forward as well and breathed in the heady aroma of her overly strong coffee. "My theory is that paranormals are being taken off the street. And I believe that DoDO is experimenting on them. We have intel from within the organization and what we've been able to determine is that they're trying to strip the gifts from paranormals and hand them to people of their choosing. But of course, I don't know this for certain. I'd need more information."

Veronica dropped her hands and met Paige's gaze. "And what if I were to tell you that some of the people who disappeared weren't paranormal? What if I said they were simply black?"

Did that fit into the puzzle?

Yes and no. Even though Paige and those she surrounded herself with didn't openly talk about the divides that racism had carved into their society, she instinctively knew that if her theory was right, DoDO needed people to experiment on that were worth sacrificing. That wouldn't mean just black, though.

"They still might be attached to this case. And if not? Then at the very least we'll be able to provide another set of eyes to look at your cases. They might be able to figure out something previously missed."

Veronica nodded and leaned back in her chair.

Mama Gee rubbed her hands together, her gaze distant. "The president is being investigated for impeachment."

A day or two ago, that statement would have made Paige very excited. But not now.

Hope lit Mama Gee's eyes. "If that is the case, we could put an end to this war."

"If the president was our real enemy," Paige said carefully, "then I would agree. But she isn't. There are people in play right now and changing out the top leadership may not do enough."

Mama Gee traced a pattern on the tabletop. "If we were to give you a weapon to use in our government, would you use it?"

Probably not, but Paige needed to know what she was offering. "*For* or *against* the government?"

Veronica opened her palm on the table. "Wynonna is a karmic witch. She can give you a spell to place in the building where they work. In the White House. In the buildings of Congress. It isn't necessarily a weapon. It is simply a method to reflect their own karmic energy back upon them, to help them grow and be better people as they guide us into the next era. Is this something you could do?"

Paige's an initial negative response changed minutely. Karma was something totally different. That was energy earned.

It was the return of the spell. It was the first law of everything she did. Whatever she put out there would be returned threefold.

"Yes." Her voice was quiet, and she wasn't certain if she could when it actually came down to it, but if this was a way to keep politics fair, she had to try. This might be the way to pave a better path not just for paranormals, but for everyone.

Imagine if people had to bear the responsibilities of the consequences to their own actions. Imagine what that world would be.

She did in that moment, and she realized that if the people of her society were forced to face the monsters they created, to face themselves, their world might very well be a better place.

Veronica nodded then reached in her purse with her other hand and pulled out a piece of paper with a rune spell marked on it in sharpie. "Just press this into any wall you want to mark, and it will transfer over."

Paige took it then rose to her feet. It was time for her to leave. "I can only promise to try to do my best for everyone. I'm not promising to please everyone or that everyone will be happy with what I do or choose."

Mama Gee rose beside her, standing tall and proud, her brown *dhuku* rising above her head like a sovereign crown. "That is the only thing we can ask."

Armed with a spell Paige wasn't certain she could deploy, she walked across the street to collect her children and head home. She needed to talk to the president. If the president was being impeached, then there was a very real chance that everything she was attempting to do right now would be undone by her successor.

She had far too many promises she had to keep.

After gathering the kids and her brother, Paige barely made it through Derrick's door to the Whiskey house Mandy ran down the stairs, breathless. "We found the cat."

Cat?

Paige turned to Derrick before getting to the bottom of whatever act issue they might have. "Thanks for everything. I mean it."

"You're welcome." He gave her a half smile. "I think you'd better... we'll see you later." He and his daughter went through the door back to the Blackman compound.

Paige turned around to face the excited teens.

They didn't *have* a cat. Not because Paige forbid it, but because Leslie did. For very adult reasons like responsibility, cleaning, care, that sort of thing. "What?"

Kate waved her off as she stopped beside Mandy, her violet gaze on Leah, her elf ears twitching with excitement. "Come on. Let's go."

Paige wasn't sure what was going on. "Hold on a sec. They need to set their stuff down, get settled—"

Leah's face split with a grin. She dumped her bag on the ground and it disappeared through a door she opened in the floor. "Love you, Mom. Be back!"

Be back? "Wait! Are you making trouble?"

Kate stopped and shook her head, her mouth open.

Mandy gave Paige a *very* cheeky grin. "It's just kid stuff. Seriously."

Which meant they *were* making trouble. Crap. But it was probably just kid-related kind of trouble.

Rai gave Paige a tight smile and followed the other three girls who all shuffled down the hallway to the kitchen.

Paige shook her head as she headed upstairs to her bedroom to change out her go bag. She called for Bobby and Ember but didn't get an answer. She even put out the telepathic call with Kamden's help, then shifted to send the call along the pack link and received silence.

Well, maybe everyone else was busy.

Paige checked her phone before she figured out what to do next and discovered eight texts from Willow and twenty-six voicemails from Suzanne. That was a bit excessive. They were all a bit vague. Willow had tried calling but hadn't left a voicemail because Suzanne had managed to take up her entire mailbox.

Though none of them made any sense.

Paige went to her bedroom balcony, shoving the karma spell into her pocket, and leapt, shifting into an owl and flying into town.

When she touched down on the balcony to what was now her office, a flying woman with eagle feet attacked her from above. Paige let out a screech and scrambled to get out of the way.

Scout transformed from a harpy into a human, breathless and visibly upset. "We're being attacked and overrun by ghosts *right now*."

"What?"

The harpy's shoulders sagged. She took in a deep breath and tried again. "Ghosts are sending all kinds of people into comas. We've had thirty-three go into the hospital just today. There're probably more. It feels like a fuckin' war out there. What do I do?"

What could she do? "Protecting them isn't your concern or your priority." Which was the hardest thing for Paige to remember as a detective. "You figure out who's behind this and stop that. Did you find anything out from New Orleans like I'd asked?"

Scout raked her fingers through her short blonde hair. "Yeah. There are *too many* connections. Also, what Barn's found. Deep Throat shit. I'm tellin' you."

Paige wasn't certain what, if anything, Scout was telling her. "Slow down. Explain."

What she and the Red Star team had discovered with the revised search parameters was that the ghosts weren't just hitting Troutdale. They weren't even the hardest hit. They were, however, the only city where those attacked by the ghosts were going into comas. All the other victims were dying.

Like in New Orleans.

But each of these epicenters were in cities near DoDO bases.

"I didn't even know we had a base here." How many other things about DoDO had been hidden from Paige?

Apparently, there was one located over by the FBI head-quarters between Troutdale and Portland. But thanks to the information Dexx had been able to secret out of DoDO, they now had a network of all the DoDO headquarters and safehouses. They had also been able to determine where paranormals were still being held.

"They're being tortured," Scout said, slamming her fist into Paige's hand-me-down desk.

The woman had a bit of a temper, to be sure.

"Tortured until their abilities are milked from them. It's *vile* and disgusting."

Paige remembered Dexx and his inability to shift or even connect with Hattie. Was that what had happened to him? Had he been able to survive only because of what he was? Some long forgotten mage or wizard or whatever from before Arthurian days? "What hard evidence do we have?"

"Not a lot. Almost nothing. We have a few grainy videos with people dressed up just like those clowns dragging people into vans. Is it enough?"

"There *might* be enough to take this to the president and have DoDO dissolved or removed from U.S. lands at the very least."

"We think your wards are what protected the people here," Scout said, calming down.

Paige agreed. It was the *only* thing that was different. "And the towns *with* wards?"

Scout shook her head, her lips pushed out in confusion. "There are no other towns."

There had to be. Paige had requested they do that days ago. "I'll look into that. *And* I'll see what I can do about stopping this once for all."

"What do I do?" Scout bared her teeth. "We do. What do *we* do?"

Paige had a suspicion that Scout had finally found the place she truly belonged. "Remember you're a detective." She licked her lips, grabbing a sticky note to jot down her priorities. "The last team forgot that and got themselves taken away and are now fugitives." World fugitives. The reality of that mess still hadn't quite sunk in yet. "So, close cases. You know who's behind this. Give me a copy of all the evidence so I can take care of the rest. Then, as Tuck hands you more cases, deal with them."

"But the comas?"

"Are being handled by doctors. Did you ever find a medium?"

Scout nodded, biting her lips. "Comin' in shortly, but she might get held up on the highway. Lots of people getting turned away lately."

"In the past couple of days?" Paige needed a sense of where they were.

"Yeah." Scout thumped the back of one of the brown chairs in front of Paige's borrowed desk, looking a bit less flustered. "You really got this."

She'd give it her best try. This was new territory for her. "Yup."

"Okay." Scout held up her hands, fingers splayed, and headed for the door. "Thanks, boss."

"I'm not your boss," Paige called. "Tuck is."

"Not what he says," Scout shouted over her shoulder as she left the door open.

Willow burst through, looking flustered. "When did you get in?"

"Just now," Paige said, taking a seat on the couch and inviting Willow to join her. "What's going on? Suzanne's messages didn't make any sense."

Willow stood in front of Paige's desk visibly agitated. "Dexx and Red Star are on arrest-on-sight orders and flyers are going up all over town by DoDO agents. Apparently, no one can find them. They fell off the radar."

Paige wasn't about to tell her amazing assistant that she'd seen Dexx.

"More than that, though," Willow held out a piece of paper to Paige, "you've been subpoenaed."

"For what?"

"The impeachment trial," Willow said with a mix of anxiety and relief. "I was supposed to tell you as soon as you arrived."

"Okay. Well, you did." Paige wasn't certain what she was going to do about that. She didn't want to help get this president impeached. At least, not yet. It was possible Dawn would change her mind, do a complete three-sixty on her opinion of paranormals, and be the big enemy again.

Paige had to have faith, she had to believe that people could be *good*.

"And," Willow said, rolling her eyes as she resituated her top-spiraled notebook in her lap, "Leroy wants to start you on a grassroots movement."

"A what? Wait." Paige didn't even know who this person was. "Who?"

"Your PR person," Willow explained. "You've got about twenty or so people working for you now? Maybe more. You *need* more."

"Okay." That was great on one hand, but just one more thing to manage on the other. "What does he think I'm going to do with this?" And what the hell *was* a grassroots movement?

Basically, Leroy wanted her to tour the U.S. and talk to other paranormals every day for a few weeks to get a feel for their needs.

"That's actually not a terrible idea." She was supposed to be the Secretary of Paranormal Relations, not Troutdale. "Does he have an agenda in mind?"

Willow nodded, her expression dry. "You didn't want to see your kids ever again, did you?"

Damn it. "Tell him I need family time incorporated into whatever grassroots whatever he has planned." Paige needed to also get in to see the president. "You don't happen to have

Ruben's number, do you? I need to get in to see the president."

"Before the hearing?" Willow asked, an expression of you-might-want-to-rethink-that all over her face.

"Okay. Well, who else should I talk to about the DoDO installations and the paranormals still being held and tortured until their souls flee and kill people?"

Willow narrowed her eyes and thought about that. "You should try Dr. Ivan Rivera."

Paige shook her head, remembering briefly the name, but not why.

"He's the Secretary of Defense."

Right. Right. Because…yeah. She was a Secretary too, which meant… What in all the hells was she thinking trying to play in this field? She swallowed her self-doubt and brought out her confident face with a settling sigh. "Okay. Get me his number."

Willow frowned at her like she'd lost her damned mind. "I'll call his people and have him call you."

That was really a thing? Huh. "Okay. What else?"

"Well, uh, hmm." Willow flipped her notebook closed and clicked her pen. "You haven't seen Dexx, have you?"

"Nope." The lie came easily, but she really hadn't seen Dexx… in a day? So, who knew where the man was by now?

"Okay because, I mean, really. If you did and you hid him, you'd be up for extradition charges."

This was getting really close to home and very real. "I know." She *didn't* know how the international laws affected her husband or what the processes were for that. "I will make sure the authorities find him as quickly as possible so they can all work together to clean up this mess."

Willow's expression went flat, but her eyes pinched with worry as she stared at the desk. "He's in some real trouble. The kind you might not be able to get him out of."

Paige closed her eyes for a moment and released a long breath. "Yeah," she said, opening her eyes again. "I know."

"Okay. Well, um, okay." Willow got to her feet. "The first thing you need to do is get ready for D.C. I think they're putting you up for a bit. Though, you need consider getting an apartment there."

"With *my* salary?" Which barely paid the bills when money was coming in. "No. I'll just do what I've been doing."

Willow looked at her like Paige was confused. "You make two hundred thousand a year now."

"Huh?" Paige was certain she'd heard wrong.

"Yeah." Willow's eyebrows shot up as she nodded. "You can afford it."

It didn't *quite* register just what Willow had said. She'd heard the number, but it didn't connect with Paige *or* her life at all. Two hundred thousand dollars a year? Doing fast-maths, that was seventeen thousand a month.

Paige shook her head. That was some hard talks she could have later, like once she realized what taxes would be and… yeah, stuff. Like, of that seventeen thousand, would she only see ten? Or…Yeah. Math wasn't her best subject and budgets were even worse. So, she decided to just leave that for another matter and called Derrick for a ride.

He said he'd be available the next day and that worked for Paige who had more than her fair share to deal with.

But she'd no sooner gotten off the phone with her brother when she received a phone call from the Secretary of Defense.

"When do you plan to arrive?" he growled over the phone.

"Well, hello, Ivan. If you want to rephrase that, I'll let you. Because… I have magick." Paige said, immediately going on the offensive. He wanted to play who could be a bigger bag of dicks, she could play. He might have armies at his disposal or whatever, but she'd faced the demons from Hell.

He sighed. "Hello, Ms. Whiskey."

"Paige."

"Of course. It's been a long day. When are you coming in?"

"Tomorrow."

"Did you clear that with Ruben?"

Did she know she needed to? "I've got information for you."

"About what?"

"DoDO and some prisoners they haven't rele—"

"Paige," Ivan said loudly, then continued in a much more pleasant voice. "Don't you think you should come in now? My wife's making lasagna. Come over to my place. I'll give you a good home-cooked meal."

She didn't understand fully what was going on, but she distinctly got the sense he'd told her to shut up. "I love a good lasagna."

"You're not vegetarian, are you?"

"I'm half cat."

"Ah, right." His laugh was forced. "Seven?"

"Sure."

Her office phone buzzed as soon as she was off her cell phone. "Hey, I know you're busy," Willow said, turning in her chair to look at Paige through the office door. "It's Ruben."

The chief of staff. Paige was going to have to get all these names straight fast. She picked up the phone. "Whiskey." Damn it. Paige. She needed to get used to answering the phone as Paige.

"Yeah," Ruben said nonplussed. "When you coming in? You've been subpoenaed."

"I heard."

"Good. When?"

"Originally, I thought tomorrow." But she had a lasagna date for that evening, so…

"Not soon enough."

Okay. She was gathering that. "It's just an impeachment hearing." She didn't remember much from the other impeachment hearing that'd happened in her lifetime. She'd been in school at that time, but it'd taken forever and had been excruciatingly boring. "What's the rush?"

"The rush is that your people are in *life threatening* conditions because of the sitting president," Ruben said harshly in a tone that felt like finger quotes. "I thought you'd be thrilled."

No. Crap. "Okay. If I come in now, can you see me right away? There's information I need to share with you."

"That's going to get my president impeached?"

No. Yes? Paige didn't know. "That's going to save her job."

He growled. "I'll give them clearance for you to arrive at my office. Check in with Pearl and do *not* just barge into my office with your damned magic."

"Yes, sir."

"It's going to take me a minute, so get over here, and go through the paperwork I put on your desk. You're behind."

Great. She couldn't wait. Paige hung up. Now, she just needed a ride.

She called Leah, thinking she'd like to play doorman, but the girl wasn't picking up her phone. Odd.

Derrick had said the next day, which meant he was trying to spend time with *his* kids and Paige was going to respect that. She left a message with Leslie that she had to leave for D.C. maybe for the evening and to please watch the kids. Then she called Phoebe looking for a ride.

Paige *could* technically open the door herself. If she was

better at it. But she wasn't and she didn't want to risk pissing people off in Washington where real things like security clearance and the like was an issue.

Which reminded her. She needed to get a list of likely doormen and get them cleared. Her list was so long.

She shot Willow an instant message asking her to do that as Phoebe picked up.

"Hello, Paige. What can your servant class of relatives do for you now?"

Ouch. "Shit. Sorry. I'll add you into the budget."

Phoebe sighed heavily into the phone. "I'll send someone in a few moments. We won't work for free forever."

If Paige couldn't get it on the staff budget, she *should* be able to pay it from the *two hundred thousand dollars* she'd be receiving just to work.

Did that come with vacation pay?

What about maternity leave? Because… yeah. She wasn't planning on getting pregnant any time soon, but not getting maternity time for her babies who were now tweens was *still* a pain she was feeling and she doubted she'd get over it any time soon.

Before she was ready, her ride showed up. She told Willow to coordinate with Suzanne about what was going on and to assure the mayor that Paige was on it.

Willow grimaced.

Paige held up her hands in surrender. "I might need you. I'll message you if I do."

"We're getting a team together to follow anyway," Willow said. "I need a pay raise."

Yeah. Since she was currently getting paid the same amount of nothing Paige was, she understood that. "I'll make that happen. No. You draw up the paperwork to *make* that happen. We have a budget, right?"

"We do."

"Great. Just make sure we're under that. I'll need that for review."

"Yup."

Derrick smiled at Paige from the door. "Hey, sis."

Oh, fuck. "I thought you were taking the night off."

"Tried."

Paige felt a twinge of guilt.

He shrugged and chucked his chin in her direction. "Hanging out with you is fun, though."

She just hoped it wasn't more "fun" than either of them could handle.

Because it felt like her life was starting to explode yet again.

Paige didn't have time for a lot of small talk with her brother. It wasn't her strong suit, and she was a bit nervous to talk with the chief of staff. Even reminding herself that she'd faced off with demons and angels weren't helping her nerves.

She was met with some security guy who checked her and Derrick out and informed her that "this type of thing" wasn't going to get passed regularly and "not to get used to it."

She just smiled and waited for Ruben to open the door.

Eventually, the secretary's—Pearl's—phone buzzed to tell Paige to go in.

Taking in a deep breath, Paige opened the door and closed it behind her.

The office was pretty big and looked lived-in, but not in a the-kids-can't-do-anything-by-themselves kind of way. Just in a I-live-eat-sleep-and-breathe-in-this-place kind of way.

Ruben glanced up, his wire-rimmed glasses perched on the end of his nose. He returned his attention to the document folder in his hands. "Get better dressed, Whiskey."

Paige rounded her eyes. "When that salary comes in, sure. Until then?" She wasn't taking the bait. "I need to get—"

He brushed aside whatever she was going to say and set his document down, taking his glasses off and tossing them on his desk. "First of all, hire someone who actually knows how our world works. Willa—Willow's her name?"

Paige nodded.

He nodded back, but his steel grey eyes were pinched. "Nice enough woman. Not a damned clue on how things operate here." He picked up a folder and handed it to her. "Resumes of all the people you *should* be hiring."

She took it and claimed a seat opposite him. "Okay. But I'm keeping Willow."

"Whatever. Experience is what you need. Next." He pointed at the folder again and raised his eyebrows. "Your budget. You've got enough in there for a staff of twenty. Pay people creatively and you could make it twenty-two. There's a list of positions you need to fill pronto."

"Okay." She realized she should be feeling overwhelmed, but this was actually making her feel better. Finally, someone who knew what the fuck she needed to do. "Clearance for myself and my staff, specifically my door managers."

He rolled his eyes and sat back in his seat. "Never thought I'd see *that* on a budget. But yes. Get me a list of names and we'll get started."

"Mine?" Because the man didn't seem the type to mince words with. When *she* said five words or less, she *generally* was requesting this kind of bullet-trajectory conversation. But it took a lot to keep up with.

"Held up. You piss off anyone off I need to know about?"

"Depends," she said, not really thinking about the consequences, mainly because she wasn't *sure* what those would even be. "Your office bugged?"

Ruben went quiet. He glanced at the door behind and to

his left, then studied her hard, leaning forward. "You said you had information."

She didn't know if she could *trust* Ruben. She didn't know *who* she could trust. So, she screwed on her detective mask and watched him as she spoke. "You hear of an organization called DoDO?"

He narrowed his eyes and picked up his glasses, folding his hands around them. "Continue."

She *could* tread carefully, but she didn't know how. Tact had *never* been her strong suit. "They're the ones behind the paranormal attacks. They've infiltrated our government. They—"

"How can you be sure?" he asked quietly.

"Because," she said just as quietly, "their friends in high places are a little *too* high to think otherwise. I have *proof* of a lot of things. Bases, illegal experiments leading to the murder of innocent civilians."

"Paranormal or human?"

Paranormals *were* human. "Both." She wasn't going to hang herself on that thread just yet. Other battles had to be won first.

"You tell Ivan this?"

"I started to," she said carefully. "And he interrupted me to invite me to dinner."

"Lasagna or teriyaki?"

She'd been right. It was code. "Lasagna."

Ruben nodded, thought about that for a minute, and then picked up his phone, punching in three numbers and then waited. "Yeah. Hey, I hear Lisa made lasagna." He nodded, glancing at Paige. "You bet. I'll be there." He hung up.

It looked like she'd stumbled onto a secret group. Like book club but with politics and high stakes. She just needed some James Bond music playing in the background.

"Let's talk about the impeachment schedule. Anyone fill you in about that yet?"

She shook her head unable to read anything from the man that set off any alarms. He legitimately came off as a guy just trying to do the right thing. It was hard to find anything to dislike about him.

Well, aside from his gruff manner, tone, and word choice. He was the old school, baby boomer, white man type whose tough exterior made him look a lot tougher than he probably was. Now, that all *sounded* bad, but she'd dealt with more than her share of this alpha type as a detective. She understood they were highly valuable. She just had to "speak their language" in order to maintain their respect. It wasn't just her word choice, or her tone, or what information she shared or how. She'd be graded on her actions and her emotional responses as well.

Finally, a social game she could play.

She was on schedule to be interviewed the next day. "I can't tell you what to say, but just be warned. You will be sworn in."

She was a cop. She understood what being under oath meant.

"And you can be impeached."

Well, that was news. "Is there a way to stop or pause these hearings?"

He studied her, his tongue at the roof of his mouth, leaving his lips curled awkwardly. He shook himself. "Why would you want that?"

She closed her eyes and released a tight breath. "We'll discuss it later over lasagna."

Ruben jutted his chin to the side for a moment and rose. "How does your damned door thingy work?"

Leading the way out of his office, Paige introduced him to

Derrick. When Pearl had given them the address, Derrick opened the door and she led the way through.

They stepped onto a rather impressive lawn. The house looked like it'd been built in the sixties but had received a few make-overs. She was only familiar with this because occasionally she helped Leslie research renovation ideas. Their house was new and had been, literally, built for them, but after having moved in, there were a few things they both wanted updated.

Ruben led them to the front door and rang the doorbell.

It was a little weird to be back in the land of doorbell ringing.

Though, no. They still did that in Troutdale. She was just used to everyone coming in through her backdoor without invitation.

A blonde-haired woman greeted them with a smile. "Hi, I'm Lisa. You must be Paige."

They exchanged introductions and pleasantries and then Ruben turned to Derrick and sighed heavily. "We're going to have a conversation you're not cleared for. Can you..." He flicked his head to the side and then widened his eyes, his chin low.

Derrick smiled with a I-got-the-hint flare and turned to Paige. "Message me when you're ready."

"Yeah." She gave him a one-armed hug, not quite feeling comfortable with the show yet. But she had to start somewhere. He was her brother, not some damned stranger.

He tucked her in and pressed a kiss to the top of her head. "Stay safe."

"Will do."

He let her go, looking around. "And don't break the house."

Before she could tell him to shut up, he opened a door and disappeared.

Lisa showed them to the dining room table. "Ivan'll be down in a minute." She then disappeared toward the back.

Food was already on the table, and it wasn't lasagna.

Ruben grabbed a plate and helped himself. "I hope you like Indian."

Paige loved it but finding a good Indian place in Troutdale was hard. "What's going on here?"

"Well, for one thing, you're not cleared to have this conversation either. But I made a call and got you your clearance. Whoever you pissed off," he said, dishing up an orange sauce onto his rice, "wanted you embarrassed. You weren't cleared to enter your own office. Now, your staff? Well, I'll still have to work on that, but you're cleared for you job at the very least."

They then went over the finer details of what that clearance meant. What she could and could not tell to whom and when.

"This isn't like Hollywood where you 'accidentally' tell the right person the right thing for the right reason and you're forgiven. You do that here and you're in jail for the rest of your life."

Paige nodded. Shit was getting real.

But the food was amazing.

Dr. Ivan Rivera was a portly black man who was going grey at the temples. He had a slightly less burly personality than Ruben did, which was nice.

When they all had their dinner plated and were well into eating, Ivan turned to Ruben and nodded.

Ruben pulled out a pen and clicked it, setting it down beside his plate. He then looked to Paige. "If you have something that'll keep the magic prying eyes out, do it now."

Well, that was a surprise. She frowned, but then called on the air to help her keep prying ears out.

It buzzed and chittered excitedly as it skittered around the house.

A few slight sizzles and puffs of smoke followed.

Ruben and Ivan didn't even seem fazed.

This could go a lot better than she thought. "So, we can talk now?"

Ivan glanced at Ruben again as if asking if he still thought this was a good idea.

Ruben lifted one shoulder in a shrug. "Shouldn't waste it." He gestured with his full fork, still chewing.

Ivan straightened over his plate and met Paige's gaze. "What can you tell us about DoDO?"

She spent the next hour filling them in on everything she knew about the organization, including how they they'd kidnapped Dexx and tortured him for a year.

"They have several bases around the Lower Forty-Eight," she said, rubbing her belly and wishing she hadn't eaten so much. "They still have several paranormals captive and I have evidence that they're torturing them to death."

"And you have proof of this?"

Paige nodded. "I have what my team has compiled for you. But it's more than that. When these paranormals die, they're becoming ghosts, inhabiting people, and killing them."

Ivan's expression said something had just made sense.

Ruben just looked confused.

She backed up and filled him in on the rest of the ghost case.

"So, they're—DoDO, you mean, is taking paranomral abilities," Ruben said slowly as if still digesting it all, "to give to other people."

"Yes." He wasn't dumb. He was just faced with things that didn't necessarily make a lot of sense to his mundane mind.

"And these people are killing others after they're dead."

Again, yes. "We think, based on what we have, that the process is so traumatic, it's driving them to insanity."

"And this proof you have?" Ivan asked.

This was the part Paige already knew might get them into trouble. "Was illegally obtained by my husband as he attempted to escape DoDO custody."

"After he'd been kidnapped," Ruben said, his grey eyes narrowed.

"He's a hard man to break," Paige said with a small amount of pride. "Though they tried. They tortured him for about a year, stripping away his memories. They were trying to use him."

"A year?" Ivan leaned forward, his expression confused. "I thought he was only gone for a couple months."

"He was. But you're dealing with demons who have the ability to warp time. My son's mother was tortured for about a week while Bobby was in the bedroom for a couple of hours hiding under the bed."

"Whoa."

Yeah. It was time they understood that in this arena, she was the one with the experience.

Ruben flicked his eyebrows up. "And the Parliament?"

"Was my husband trying to stop the leader of DoDO from taking over their government."

Ivan took in a harsh breath. "That was a bit explosive."

He wasn't wrong. "Unfortunately, that's Dexx. He doesn't do anything small. However, as you can now see, he shouldn't be extradited to England. *They* illegally took him, tortured him, and he was just doing his absolute best to make sure the world was safe."

Ruben glanced over at Ivan who shrugged.

"Please. I'm not asking as a wife—" Or almost wife. "I'm

asking as someone who is doing everything she can to protect her nation."

Ivan nodded. "The extradition process will be starting soon. You don't know where he is, do you?"

"I knew where he was." And she hoped he wasn't there anymore.

"Okay." Ivan let his head fall back against his chair, staring up at the ceiling. "He needs to remain hidden for a bit longer until we can make the proper arrangements."

A swell of relief washed over her.

"I'm going to take your information," Ivan said, raising head to look at her. "My team will review it and we'll use what we can to assist his negotiations for release."

"Okay." That was… great. Did she really believe it would work that easily? No. But this was at the very least a step in the right direction.

"And we will also," Ivan continued, "be looking into these bases and the torture you say you have proof on. We'll be gathering the kind of intel we can bring to the president."

"Good." Because she'd told Scout not to worry about that. "This is out of my team's league."

"Indeed it is. We're also going to need to redefine what your team deals with."

"I'm looking for someone who can run that role." Department? What she needed was someone with excellent intelligence gathering experience. Someone who used to be in the FBI or CIA. The only two people she could think of were Director Lovejoy and Special Agent Jack Scott. But she knew she couldn't lay this out on Jack. He was a reaper and so his hands were full. But Lovejoy?

That woman was doing everything in her power to keep her job.

"I'll see if there's anyone I can think of to help you out there," Ruben said, rubbing his face. "Is this everything?" He looked pointedly from Ivan to Paige. "I've had about as much of this I can stomach for one night."

Ivan nodded.

Paige did too. This was a lot more productive than she'd hoped. "Can I call you a door?" She pulled out her phone.

Ruben glared as he finished his Scotch.

She messaged Derrick and waited for his reply.

"You're not what I expected," Ivan said quietly. "I thought you'd be more… piss and vinegar."

She was going to take that compliment. "I thought you'd be more asshole than elbow." That was a play on metaphors she wasn't sure he'd pick up on, but elbow grease was a metaphor for hard work. Goddess bless, she hoped he understood that.

His grin said he did.

The doorbell rang, heralding Derrick's arrival.

Paige stood up. "So, what's the difference between lasagna and teriyaki?"

Ruben stood with her. "Whose house we meet up at. I may need you to swing by my place and do that thing you did?" He glanced over at one of the houseplants where a puff of smoke had emanated from after she'd sent the air to search and destroy.

She grinned. "Yeah. I could do that."

For the first time since she'd arrived, it felt like she was finally making inroads.

She couldn't fuck this up. For Dexx. For paranormals.

For the world. She had to get this right.

1 8

Paige spent the night sleeping on the couch in her office. That wasn't going to work for long. One night? Sure. But she needed to be able to return home and until Ivan could clear Dexx, that was off the table.

So, the next morning she committed herself to busywork to pass the time filing out all the paperwork that accompanied having a staff. She also looked for someone who could fill in for intelligence gathering like Ivan wanted, but she and Ruben were struggling a little on that front. He had several people who would be great in the position, but very few who were willing to accept it.

Going through these motions reminded Paige that she truly did have enemies in high places. What she needed was something to buy her way into their good graces. She didn't have money. Goddess knew that, even with her new salary she still hadn't seen. Also, she had no doubt she was talking about people who would laugh at how small her "great new salary" even was. No. She needed something else.

Convenience.

And she had that. Quick travel from D.C. to wherever

they wanted or needed to go in the world. If she could bring that as a bargaining chip, she might be able to bribe her way in.

She called Phoebe and pitched her idea.

Phoebe's tone definitely had a chill in it. "We're not chauffeurs. Don't make me spell it out for you."

Paige felt better about Phoebe because Eldora would have been all over this like butter on toast just for the political possibilities. "I know. I do, but I'm trying to build inroads here and if we can show them that letting us be open with our abilities isn't always bad, this could help smooth a few things over."

"We'll be their lackies."

"Until they grow dependent on us," Paige said, only then realizing how cold this thought was. "And then we won't be able to be erased."

Phoebe groaned. "I hate this."

But she wasn't saying no. "Shoot me a number for expenses and who you think might be best for security, and I can put that on a fast track."

Phoebe sighed. "Fine. I'll get you the information, but I'm going to charge high."

"Do it." They talked a bit longer, but Paige's growing stack of paperwork—would Willow just leave her desk *alone?*—was starting to really give her anxiety.

She was given word that her appointment with the impeachment hearing had been pushed back, but hadn't been given a new date. She was just told to stay in D.C. and not to go home.

Crap. She guessed she and that couch were going to get real cozy. She'd searched for hotels and apartments in the area, but after about thirty-two seconds, she'd abandoned the idea. Her salary was great, but it was still a "future" salary because there were zero dollars in her bank account.

Not quite true. She had a few dollars left. She could buy a Happy Meal in a McDonalds located outside the immediate area.

Goddess bless, she was so poor.

Paige returned her attention to the list of positions Ruben thought she should fill. She would *not* have thought to have *that* many positions just for PR. He wanted her to have a media person who just handled her social media accounts—which she'd ignored for the most part. She'd *used* them to get the word out the one time, but before and after that? No.

She was strongly advised *not* to fire her speech writer, which she wanted to. Arrow—Aaron. Yeah. Aaron. That was his name. He was nice and all, but he just didn't *get* the message she needed to put across. She was thinking of replacing him with this Maisy person who was also a speech writer. But there were a lot of things that couldn't be seen on a resume. Paige needed to call all of these people and ask them to come in for interviews.

The longer Paige waited for her new impeachment hearing schedule the more her stomach twisted in knots. All the mundane paperwork in the world wasn't going to help with that.

Paige sat down with Willow, going over the resumes and getting her thoughts on who to call. They reviewed the budget and a few other logistical and wildly boring—okay, it should have been boring but Paige loved them—details.

Then Willow handed her the types of things *Paige* needed to be handling.

People from around the country were contacting her but didn't want to give her all their information. They were still afraid of coming out into the public, of being flagged. That was something she'd have to talk to... Ivan? She'd ask Ruben and see what he thought.

He would just remind her that he'd told her to replace

Willow with someone who knew those answers. Paige didn't want to have that conversation. Willow had been a life saver in Troutdale, but they were both in way over their heads in D.C.

Fuck. If she was going to make headway on this new pile of work, she *needed* someone with experience to point her in the right direction. So, she grabbed Willow in one of her eighty trips into Paige's office. "Hey, what would you say if we hired someone in a position *like* yours but who knew the ropes better? Knew the people here better?"

"Yes," Willow said with relief, drooping into a chair. "Please. For the love of God."

Really? That was…easy?

"Okay, yes." Willow waved generically with her hand and straightened. "I know I basically *told* you to hire me and, for the smaller stuff, I would have been okay. But this?" Willow's eyes were wide. "Do I *want* to do this? Make this my career? Yeah. But we need someone in this position who knows what they're doing. So, yes. Hire someone. Now. Today. Yesterday." She slow blinked through an exhausted sigh. "Please."

Paige didn't want Willow to wake up one morning and regret this decision. "But someone who isn't afraid or unwilling to work *with* you because…" Paige didn't feel right just hiring someone to take Willow's place after all the *free hours* the woman had invested into the position. How was Paige going to pay that back? Through the budget or through her extra funds? She realized that a personal salary wasn't *extra funds,* but that big of a salary? Yes. It was. "Loyalty means a lot to me."

Willow nodded and took in a deep breath that straightened her back and shoulders. "And I appreciate that. I really do. But there's too much riding on you doing this right." She pointed to the stack of folders with paranormals wanting to talk. "They need this too much. Maybe we all do."

Paige opened her mouth then closed it. Her heart needed to say something, but her brain said it was dumb. No. She needed to *be* dumb if that's what she was. "Maybe if we show everyone how to accept paranormals, they'll figure out how to accept everyone else."

Willow blinked a few times but nodded. "That rarely works, but sure. Yeah."

The phone rang and Willow grabbed it before Paige could. "Secretary Whiskey's office." She gave Paige angry face for reaching for the phone. "Yes, let me see if she's available."

Paige shot the angry face back. What was the woman doing? Oh. Running interference. She had smarts.

Willow held the phone to her chest as she danced in place, then handed the phone to Paige.

One day, that move might save her. "Paige here."

Ruben controlled his gruff voice. "Have you taken a look at the resumes I sent you?"

He didn't believe in slacking. "We're scheduling interviews now."

"Good. Good. Glad to see we have someone who knows how to move."

From a male boomer, that was a huge compliment.

"The president wants to talk to you."

Oh. "I thought that wasn't a good idea."

"It's not, but we serve at the pleasure, so..." He let that thought slide.

That did kinda remind her that she hadn't *earned* this position. It *could* be taken away. "When."

"Now. Get your door—Derrick and get up here."

"Okay." Paige hung up, wondering where her brother had gone.

Willow stood with her.

"Got to talk with the pres. Hold the fort down?"

Willow nodded and Paige headed for the door.

There were a lot of security protocols that had to be followed for Derrick to use a door from the Eisenhower Building to the White House, and she was reminded that most people just took the tunnels connecting the two buildings. She said she'd use that next time.

Derrick just smirked.

She stepped into Pearl's office—Ruben's administrative assistant— and was greeted with a warm smile. The woman seemed a bit uptight, but she also never actually stopped working. Her hands were always busy, and her eyes were always focused on something else *while* she spoke to those in the room with her. But she was nice.

Ruben opened the door personally without even meeting Paige's gaze. He was reading something in his hands. "Names of the ones you're interested in."

Was he *reading* out loud what was in his hand? No. Probably not. Then… Paige scrambled to catch up. He had to be back on the staff thing. That man was like a steel trap. "When I get them through the interview process, I'll tell you."

He grunted. "Most of these people will live here."

She was pretty sure he'd meant that these people would be working night and day for her, which sounded a lot like slavery or servitude. "Well, one of the boons of working for me is that they won't have to. They could save a little money and live somewhere nicer and less expensive."

He looked up finally and narrowed his eyes at her on his way to the back door of his office. "I don't like where this is headed."

But how could he not? "I'm working the details through the proper channels to offer certain people the use of door magick." This wasn't a dumb idea. "As an invitation."

"Or a bribe." He tipped his head to the side as if to say he wasn't completely opposed to it and put his hand on the doorknob. "That'll be something, I guess." He opened the door. "Madam President," he said as he walked into the Oval Office. "Secretary Whiskey."

Dawn said something Paige couldn't quite make out because she wasn't *using* her shifter hearing, but the president rose from behind the desk, leaving her glasses behind, and greeted Paige with a smile and a handshake.

Well, this was a different greeting than she'd had before.

With the pleasantries aside and coffee in hand, Dawn's warmer expression faded away. "I need to bring you up to speed on the Dexx situation now that you've got clearance."

Paige hated that she needed *clearance* to hear about her husband-to-be. She waited.

"He's made a few enemies with DoDO and we've been informed to bring him in, no matter the cost."

Paige had had a conversation with Ruben and Ivan about getting a negotiation together for Dexx's release, to eliminate the need for extradition, but she didn't know what their process was or what information they'd shared with the president. Or if Dawn was setting her up to see what Paige would share with *her* that she already knew. Politics was a horrible battleground. "You need to know who the real bad guy is here and there's some information I need to share with you before the hearing." Which she still had a lot of questions about.

Dawn frowned. "I'm intrigued."

"I can't reveal my sources, but..." Paige brought the president up to speed about who Bussemi was—but not his relation to Dexx because Paige didn't want anyone to know just *how powerful* Dexx might actually be—his involvement with DoDO, and the depths the cardinal was willing to go to. Including what appeared to be a demon deal with a *bahlrok*, something Paige was *still* trying to wrap her head around.

Dawn had stopped moving or reacting a few minutes

before Paige stopped talking, giving Paige the impression that this wasn't a test.

"So, I was played," Dawn said finally.

"Like a fiddle," Paige answered quietly.

They sat in silence for a while longer.

But this place moved so quickly and so much had to be done in a short amount of time, Paige didn't think they could just honor a moment of silence. "That doesn't mean you have to continue to be played."

Dawn nodded slowly, her blue eyes unfocused.

"I need to know if you intend to continue your war on paranormals."

"Because if I do, it'll change your testimony?"

It would certainly flavor how she phrased things. "I'll still be under oath." And there was a lot of damaging information she could say.

Dawn shook herself and met Paige's gaze. "I need to know that paranormals will be made to answer to the law."

"Absolutely." Paige would raise the priority of that issue closer to the top. "I still need to save paranormals from captivity, though."

"We've released them all."

"That's what you've been told." Paige then launched into filling the president in on what DoDO was doing to the paranormals still trapped inside their facilities and what those ghosts were doing when they escaped.

"How do we fight that?" Dawn demanded harshly. "Fight ghosts?"

"Well, second, you get some necromancers, mediums, and reapers in there and take care of those. Clean up the mess so the ghosts don't continue to do damage."

Dawn looked away incredulously, as if trying to wrap her head around the knowledge that a faith-system was now reality. "And the first?"

That should be a no brainer. "Stop DoDO."

"And how do we do that?"

"Let me just remind you that you're the President of the United States of America." And then Paige had to hope Dawn could figure out a way after that because Paige had *no idea* what Dawn could even do. Paige had always had this impression that people in high office were above the law because it certainly looked and felt like it when the boot was always on *her* neck. But now that she was here, she realized they just had *different* laws they had to follow as well as the other laws of the lower people. And sometimes, one trumped the other.

And *that* made things very foggy.

Dawn nodded. "So, you're handing this off."

Technically, she already had, but if Ivan was getting pressure from the top as well, it'd be harder for him to ignore. Paige licked her lips and set down her coffee cup on the table. "I have to. That's a club only you can swing. My team is really struggling with this, though. They're your first line of defense on this situation and they have *no way* of dealing with it."

Dawn nodded again, setting her cup down as well. "You can't talk to Dexx. You're going to want to, but if you do, you will be breaking the law unless you turn him in."

"Understood." But would that stop her?

"He's state-side. We know that."

How did the president know more about her husband's location than Paige did?

"And we're closing in on his location."

That made Paige feel a thread of fear. "How are you tracking him? I'd like to be kept in the loop on this one. He *is* a paranormal. And an American."

Dawn shrugged. "I guess." She took in a deep breath. "Ivan is putting together a meeting where the parties can come together to try and find a peaceful solution."

Well, at least he was a man of his word. "That doesn't involve Dexx's arrest? Or his team?"

"I can't promise that, but if we can get the players in the same room and if certain things could come to light, we might have the power to get your husband and his team back safely without threat of extradition. Maybe they'll never be able to leave the states? I don't know. I'll have the Secretary of State draft up a few proposals or ideas. She's very good at this."

She? Paige's head buzzed with all the names and faces and titles and things she needed to know. It was like cramming for a test while taking it. "Shouldn't I be a part of this as Secretary of Paranormal Affairs?" Or relations. She really needed to figure out what her damned title was and keep it straight in her head. What was wrong with her?

"With your husband?" Dawn shook her head. "Conflict of interest and I don't want to put you in a position where you're going to be *that* tempted to break the law. I need you in this position, Paige." She stood. "Don't mess that up."

Paige hated the idea of trusting Dexx's wellbeing to someone else. "You'll protect him?" And trusting a woman who'd been an enemy just days before? Yeah. That wasn't helping either.

"As best I can."

That had to be enough. Paige stood. "Well, I guess I'll do what I can to keep you as a sitting president."

"I appreciate that. I don't think…" Dawn bit her lip and turned her gaze down. "I don't think Dick has your best interests in mind."

Who was Dick? Oh, right. The vice president, who would step into Dawn's position if she was kicked out of office. "What do you mean?"

"I don't know. He's been a little upset that I've changed my stance on paranormals. He really didn't like the fact I'd given you the Secretary position. So, watch your back. You have enemies in Washington."

Paige already knew that. "Thank you, Madam President." And she meant that.

"Thanks for coming in." Dawn dismissed her with a brief handshake.

It didn't take Paige long to get back to her office and when she did, she was almost immediately attacked by Willow, Aaron, and one other person Paige just couldn't remember. She couldn't even recall what his position was. She was on information overload. "What? For the love of craps."

"You can't say that," Aaron said.

"Leroy has something," Willow said on top of the speech writer, "that you should probably consider."

That didn't sound good. Paige turned to the guy she couldn't remember as they continued through the open bullpen—for lack of a better word because Paige didn't know what else to call it—and to her office. "What?" Leroy. Leroy. Leroy. But what did he do?

His dark eyes lit up with excitement. "I got you on *Live with Jazzi Hesh.*"

Oh. He was her PR person. Was this a radio show or something?

"It's a late night talk show," Willow filled in.

That would be why Paige hadn't heard of it. She didn't have time for late night shows. "Okay? Is this legal?" Was there any way she could get out of it?

"Legal?" Leroy said, his excitement raising his volume. "This is amazing. I've been *trying* to get people on the *Jazzi Hesh* show and she won't take anyone. But you? *She* came to *me.*"

"Well, I guess I need to figure out who she is."

"YouTube," Willow offered at Paige's door.

Great. Yes. Paige gripped her office door. "Anything else?"

"Only," Aaron said, his hazel eyes wide, "that if you *do* do this, we need to go over talking points."

Not just that. There was a lot she wasn't sure how to say because…

Being the first spokesperson for paranormal kind was intimidating as hell.

She shut them all out of her office and phoned Ruben.

"What?" he asked.

"*Jazzi Hesh* show. Yes or no."

He thought about that for a second. "Yes."

That was a little surprising. "You're sure?"

"Yeah. Happens all the time, but most politicians are boring, so it doesn't matter. You, on the other hand, are very exciting. They'll eat you alive."

And… solve his Paige Whiskey problem? Because she kinda got the impression he was offering her to the wolves. "Uh." She'd *thought* they'd been growing a friendship. Work-ship? Bonding. She thought they were bonding.

"Look," he said frankly. "Don't speak above their clearance. Don't smear the president if you're really trying to help her stay in office. And just, you know, be the speaker of paranormal, you know, people and whatever. Don't be an ass."

"Ah." Okay. "Thanks. And when am I supposed to be in court?"

"Still working on that." He hung up.

He was *really* a crammer-talker.

She called Willow and told her to set up the interview.

Willow sounded terrified and excited.

It was time to check out the YouTube videos, which… Paige had a bunch of other things to do instead, so it felt a little like cheating on the job.

But it was a good idea because this woman was… brutal.

Paige was so fucked.

T he window of getting onto Jazzi's show was *tight*. Paige was hopeful for about one second that it meant she was off the hook, but that hope was dashed as soon as she was told she was going on air that night.

There were a lot of rules and papers she had to sign. No magick on the show. The show was live, so she had to be clear of what she was saying because there was no editing and no way to control the narrative.

Those were the two big ones.

She also had to show up two hours early for hair and make-up. And the people working the back were aghast at what she wore.

With new hair, actual make-up, and a new outfit she could keep "on the house" because she "obviously" needed it, she was ready. She also had the number of a "great fashionista" who could help her with her "optics issue." She needed to *appear* like she should be in charge of paranormal people across the nation.

Yeah. That wasn't demeaning. At all. A shirt didn't define whether or not she knew how to do her job.

Aaron tried coaching her on a bunch of things she could and shouldn't say, but they were all very... guy. Paige didn't know how else to put it. Her speech writer, the person whose job was to keep her sounding smart, had no damned clue what it meant to be a working mother in this world. She still didn't know if Maisy was going to be any better—Okay. How could she remember the name of a woman she hadn't even met and struggled with her PR guy's name?— and maybe she wouldn't hire the woman, but Paige had to find a mouthpiece controller who had at least a little something in common with her.

Finally, it was time to head to the stage. People gave her more helpful tips. People with headsets barked orders at her.

She'd rather go into battle with demons. Her heart was racing. She could barely comprehend what the hell people were even saying. She was going to fuck this up.

Her name was called, and she was *pushed* onto the stage as the music played loudly to her left. She vaguely recalled her directions on what to do once she got on stage, waving to the people clapping even though she couldn't *see* them through the blaring lights. She made her way passed the desk were Jazzi was stationed—she hadn't gotten up to greet Paige— and to one of the three blue chairs on the other side.

Finally, things calmed down a bit. Paige turned to the host and realized in that moment that Jazzi had *every* intention of flaying her *alive*.

Okay. Time to get the game face on. Paige'd battled *demons*. She could take on one woman with an over-obsessive love affair with lipstick.

"Madam Secretary," Jazzi Hesh started, glancing at the audience. "It's a pleasure to meet you. I'm so glad you could make it."

Paige realized that every micro-reaction was going to be read under a microscope. "Paige. And thanks for having me on."

Jazzi smiled like a shark smelling blood. "Paige. What's it like being Secretary?"

"Well, it's a lot like anything else." Only bigger. "It's just that I have a lot more balls to juggle than before. Why don't you ask the questions you really wanted to ask?" Because if she was smelling blood, it was time to make the waters *bloody*.

Jazzi's green eyes lit with the pleasure of the challenge. "You came up out of nowhere. Can you tell us a little bit about that?"

Like what? "I didn't come out of nowhere, I can tell you that. We were just normal people living normal lives—"

"Normal." Jazzi scoffed.

"Yeah. Normal." Paige leaned in as if telling the host a secret. "You want to know where witches buy their supplies?"

Jazzi glanced at the audience and craned her neck in. "Where?"

Paige looked toward the lights, finally able to make out a few bodies. "The grocery store," she whispered.

The audience laughed.

Jazzi appraised Paige for a moment as the laughter calmed down, her smile relaxing a little. "What's it like to be someone everyone's terrified of?"

"Terrifying."

Jazzi's darkened eyebrows shot up.

"No, seriously. Like…" It was time to loosen them up. "You don't realize what it's like being the outsider. Growing up? I was just like everyone else, but I had this really cool hobby I kept in my basement. Kinda like being a model builder, you know? You keep that hidden because if anyone found out about your level of geekery, you'd be done for. That was just my life, but I couldn't invite kids over because Grandma openly practiced."

"So, you had witchy things in your house everywhere?"

"You mean like cinnamon? Yeah." Paige laughed, knowing what *they* thought was witchy.

The audience made a few noises of grunts and exclamations. One woman with a raucous guffaw laughed.

"Yeah. I guess people think we use a lot of pentagrams and candles. Chicken feet?"

A couple of people clapped at that.

Paige shook her head. "Not really a thing." At least not for the Whiskeys.

A few people moaned. Guffaw Girl laughed.

Paige rubbed her ear, settling into it. Jazzi was starting to loosen up too, going a little less for the juglar—though, what would that look like? This could actually turn into a real interview. "But, you know, we did have a few things. Like, Grandma had a broom hung over her door and witch balls hung in the windows. And there were bottles filled with herbs she'd collected, and stuff like that. I mean, it wasn't *Practical Magic,* but it was, you know, stuff."

Jazzi leaned back in her chair. "So, you're telling me you had a normal childhood."

"Yeah." Paige grinned, trying to imagine what others must think. "I went to school. I got into fights. There was one fight—" What story could she even *tell* in this moment? What had she lived through that would be a story worth telling? "—with, um, my best friend, actually. Heather. And, uh, she was so mad at me, she couldn't *talk* to me, so we passed notes to each other using other kids. You remember that? Before cell phones?"

A couple of people in the audience shouted back, or spoke up, but she couldn't pull anything individual from them.

That was both helpful and a little frustrating. It was like talking to the ocean.

"Yeah. The 'coded messages' we sent to each other were like chess moves." Paige rolled her eyes. "We thought we were so cool. Like, I think about that now and just cringe."

Jazzi ducked her head. "I think we all have a few of those stories, but what about growing up as a witch? That had to be different. Right?"

"Kinda, I guess." It really had been, but she needed to make people feel like she was *like them*. "But it was like—" How to *do* that though. "Okay, you know how we all went to school and had homework after?"

The audience agreed with grunts and mumblings.

"Well, it was like that, but with *more* homework. And we didn't *get* summers. Summers were working to gather things and dry herbs and—" How had Paige forgotten all this. "And baking. We did a *lot* of baking."

Jazzi nodded, her green eyes narrowed. "Okay, folks. After these messages, we'll be right back with Secretary Whiskey."

Someone Paige hadn't seen waved his arms, and the audience chatter reduced to a slight buzz as they talked.

"Okay," Jazzi said, leaning forward. "As nice and apple pie as all this is, I need some real meat."

Paige shrugged and shook her head. "What are you trying to do? Stir up hate for us?"

Jazzi pulled a face. "No. But I want to get the truth out there."

"Like what?" Paige asked quietly. "That we're being rounded up like criminals? That people are afraid to go to the work because they don't know if their baby sitter who's been super safe for three years might suddenly have extra teeth?"

"Yeah," Jazzi said and leaned in. "Exactly like that."

Paige leaned forward as well, giving that woman a good alpha growl, but nothing more. "There's already enough fearmongering out there. Be better." She then sat back and ignored whatever else Jazzi was trying to bait with.

Eventually, the cameramen waved and the set went quiet again.

"And we're back," Jazzi said after the clapping ended, "with Secretary Paige Whiskey. So, what *is* it like going into battle?"

Oh. Heart to the dagger. "Terrifying." Paige released a short breath, realizing she had to stop using that word and trying to figure out what else to say. "You never know what you're going to face. The people attacking us? They're not following any rules of society. They're outside the *law*. They attack and the only thing you can do is *not die*."

"What does that look like?"

Bloodshed. Dead children laying on the ground. But Paige couldn't tell them that. She shook her head. "There's a reason we don't take the public into war. You don't want to see what I've seen."

"Or do what you've done?"

Or that.

The corner of Jazzi's lip rose. "We've got a clip of you fighting, actually. Let's take a look."

It was video taken from someone's phone in Kansas. Paige knew that what she'd done there could be seen as excessive, but the clip stopped before they got to that part. It was a short clip. Lots of chaos. A shaky hand. The person recording had been scared. It'd been really loud.

And Paige had been center stage, stalking forward on rubble, and had been throwing magick at a black-clad army, talking into a camera.

The studio was silent after the clip.

"Imagine," Paige said, not knowing what to do or say here, "facing down a force intent on killing you. You don't have to ask. You can *see* the dead bodies around you. You don't know if the people are paranormal or just normal people. You don't know if they were on their way to grab a cup of coffee or to pick up their kids at school. You don't have *time* to ask those questions. You *only* know that someone is out there killing these people."

Jazzi frowned and picked up a blue square of paper.

Paige wasn't done. "But *everyone else* can just pick up a phone and call for help. You can call for the police." As an ex-cop, she *wasn't* going to talk about police brutality because the people didn't understand what an officer had to face, either, and she needed to limit her see-through-my-eyes stories to the paranormal for the moment. "*You* can call the government. Senators, mayors, people. You can call *people* and they'll come. The situation might suck at the moment, but someone will come and make reparations. Justice will be served."

"And that's not the case here?"

Paige hadn't even had a chance to consider *that*. "No. Do you know how many people died that day in Lawrence?"

Jazzi nodded and glanced at her card. "Almost two thousand."

It'd been more than that. It had to be. "Those are just the ones being counted because the organization in charge of that is controlling the information." A red flag flew in her head. She was steering dangerously close to information she couldn't share. "So, how do you know it was *only* almost two thousand?"

"Do you know it was more?" Jazzi asked quietly.

Paige shook her head, wishing she did. "How would we be able to know when the people who *could* find out were forced into hiding?" She rubbed her head and ran her fingers through her hair, which was almost a mistake because there was *product* in it now. "When I'm on the battlefield—when I'm on the streets of our cities and towns—I don't *know* I'm safe. I *only* know I'm alone."

"But you're not, are you?" The set in Jazzi's shoulders said she was ready to pounce. "There are thousands of your kind."

"Who are all in hiding because being born is now against the law." Paige showed her own sharkish grin.

Jazzi sat back with a frown.

Paige wasn't going to give the ground she'd gained. She opened her mouth to say something else.

Jazzi looked toward the audience and held up a hand. "I've just been informed we're continuing without a commercial break."

Oh, crap. Not good. Right?

"So, do you think that we as Americans are inherently evil?" Jazzi asked after the crowd's muted response.

"Are we? Why is that even a question?" That was one thought-road Paige refused to travel. "No. I don't think anyone is."

The audience clapped.

"But I will say that there's something to be said about comfortable ignorance." Paige scratched her head, a bit uncomfortable and wishing she didn't have *quite* so much crap in her hair. "You know, I have to admit, but before this all happened, I knew very little about our government or our society. You know, like, I'm white. I didn't know what it meant to be black or brown or something not white. I knew what being a woman was."

She raised a fist of solidarity as a few people clapped. "I mean, I was a cop and then a detective, so I saw a lot. I did, but I didn't really *understand* how a systemic society and our government worked. I didn't know—like, I was dumb. But when you're forced into the outside, when your privilege is stripped away, you get a real *insider's* view, and it changes a lot. It changes how I react to things and think about things."

The audience made a few noises.

Jazzi's gaze went out of focus again.

"And I remember thinking to myself just the other day that life would be so much simpler if I was just dumb *again,* you know? Like, if I could just go back to the life of living for myself and my family and only thinking about what was right and good for them, but…" She shrugged. "If I did *that,* then, I think I *would be* evil. And I think that…" Oh, fuck. How to phrase it. "It's so hard to learn what's needed in society. People can *tell* you, but how do you *know?* You've really gotta be able to put yourself in someone else's shoes, and I think *we* think we do that. Until we're forced in someone else's shoes and we can't put ours back on again. There *are* evil people in this world, those who refuse to see beyond themselves. But most of the time, it's just people who haven't been able to figure out how to see a world outside of their own."

The audience clapped. A few people whistled and Guffaw Girl hooted. She had a unique voice.

"Do you think religion plays into that?" Jazzi asked.

"I'd be dumb to not think that," Paige said with a laugh. "Like, hello. Salem."

Jazzi chuckled, relaxing around the shoulders. "Can you tell by how a person reacts to you what their religion is?"

"Generally? Yes." But this was a slippery slope. "You've got the people who are like, 'Yeah, okay. Cool. You got teeth. God can't talk to me specifically, so if you say you're not evil, I'll believe you. Just keep your teeth to yourself. Unless I ask for it.'" Paige wiggled her eyebrows to the audience suggestively, putting a dirty spin on it.

They laughed and cat called, this time with a lot more enthusiasm than before.

She didn't want to steer the conversation down the next road, but it had to be talked about. "But in some areas, people are like, 'Bitch, please. God talks directly to me. He fills my fear-raging heart. I am empowered by the grace of God to hate you with every fiber in my being.' It's enlightening and a little terrifying. Like, I wish that religion was better for making people just better people, but it's like—you know. We were driven out of our homes hundreds of years ago to avoid this divide among us and we're still tilling it, sowing its seeds and showing the world that we learned…nothing."

"Oof, that's harsh."

Too harsh? "I'm a witch. What did you expect?"

Jazzi and the audience laughed.

"What's it like raising kids in this, though?"

Paige's leg suddenly itched and she reached down to scratch it. "That. Oh, blessed Mother. Wow. Uh, challenging. Like, you know what it's like to have a baby—in the privacy of a room *without* national TV cameras on you?"

The audience laughed.

If she couldn't find the humor… "And raising a baby is tough. It's really hard. But you can put that baby in a seat or a crib and strap them down in a car seat and buy yourself a little time to deal with other things. But when that baby—or two of them because we need to up the crazy—shifts into something with four legs or, worse, wings? All bets are off."

Jazzi snorted. "I bet."

"No. You don't understand. The couch has claw marks on it because one of the kids rolled *off* it." Should she have said that? "All of our lamps are duct taped back together because Rai liked to fly and destroy them. Like…" She flared her eyes at the audience. "Whole new levels of insanity. Like, I *knew* I'd struggle to sleep before, but then…" She shook her head. Then she just kept shaking it as the audience took the cue to respond.

Jazzi waited for quiet. "You looked terrified when you first got here."

"Fuck, yeah, I was." Wait. Hadn't she been informed she couldn't curse. "You're vicious."

Jazzi beamed a smile and blushed a little. "Thank you, I think."

"You're welcome?" Paige turned to the audience. "You guys don't understand. I fight demons and men in black, right? Like, demons. The things that make you go 'Oh, God! I swear I'll be good.' And I'm like the Terminator or something, just throwing down and taking them on without really much thought. Go in. Don't die. Save the world. Those are the three things I gotta do, but this? My assistant was like, 'No, dude. Seriously'—She doesn't say, dude. I don't know why I said that, but—'You've gotta be careful with this one because she will eat you alive.'"

The audience clapped and hooted and hollered.

"Right?" Paige said to them with a grin. "And then she added, '*With her words.*'"

The laughter doubled.

Paige bit her bottom lip and shook her head until she had the space to talk. "I mean, come on. I don't have a fireball for that."

The audience exploded with even more laughter.

Jazzi did too. "I never thought of myself as being able to intimidate someone *like you.*"

"Now you get it," Paige said to more laughter.

"Would you do a magic, I don't know, trick?" Jazzi asked as the audience quieted.

But then they got excited and started clapping.

Uh, no. Paige *couldn't*.

"You don't call it a trick, though, right?"

"No," Paige said, trying to figure out how to handle this one. "Do you call *walking* a trick?"

"Well," Jazzi said with a more relaxed smile. "It depends on how much I've had to drink."

Paige chuckled along with the audience. "Okay. That's valid. Yeah. But, uh. No? I signed a paper saying I wouldn't do that."

"Perform magic?"

Paige could tell by the expression on Jazzi's face that someone was talking in her ear. "Yeah. I was told 'no' rather forcefully. They frown on magick use in D.C. too. It's so weird."

A man in a headset came onto the stage, approaching Paige and muttered, "You're cleared for something small. Don't destroy anything."

Right. Right. But could she *take* his word for it? Or did she need another piece of paper covering her butt? She needed someone in legal on her team.

"How about fire?" Jazzi asked. "I saw someone in one of your videos throw fire. Can you?"

Oh, crap no. "The kind of fire I call would break your building." Which was probably the wrong thing to say. "My niece could. But yeah, no. My fire is magma." Paige looked to the audience, waiting for them to catch on. "Yeah. I summon fire and everyone'd be like, 'Put it back! Hell isn't welcome here!'"

Jazzi grinned and shook her head. "That's crazy. So, what about something else?"

"I could shift." That *technically* wasn't magick. It was *shift-ing*. She stood. "Okay. What do you want me to shift into? Just throw some stuff out there and I'll..." This couldn't go bad, right? Though it did feel a little like a circus. "I'll do what I can."

The audience shouted several things, and for the first time since she made it on stage, Paige could finally make out individuals.

Guffaw Girl wanted a t-rex.

Nothing could go wrong there.

Jazzi helped Paige collect the requests. After about a minute, the host looked up with a look that said she was excited and nervous. "So, what do you want to do? We've got red panda, armadillo, crocodile, elephant, and dinosaur."

A few more were thrown out there.

"Uh," Paige was a little nervous.

I say, Cawli said calmly in her head, *we show them what you can do.*

But the rafters. An elephant and a t-rex would bust those.

We don't have to be full-sized.

Right.

Paige gave the host a nervous grin. "Okay. Here goes. Ready?"

The audience shouted they were.

She then ripped through the shifts in quick succession, pausing long enough to pose or roar or—in the case of the t-rex, strangled-chicken-squawk—and ended with the red panda, standing tall and fuzzy, with her short, stubby paws in the air.

Everyone laughed and clapped.

Jazzi got up and joined Paige up front. "That was *amazing* and that's all the time we have. Thanks for joining us, Secretary... Panda?"

Paige shifted into human with a laugh and took the host's hand. "Thanks for inviting me. This was a lot more fun than I'd expected."

"Same." Jazzi turned to the audience. "I hope you enjoyed it. Until tomorrow, folks! Have a great night!"

Music from the live band blocked out anything else, the lights cuts down a bit, and confetti floated through the air.

Blessed Mother, she'd survived.

Fuuuuuuuuck.

P aige spent the next day unwinding by interviewing a lot of people for *work*, which was a much more relaxing kind of interview. Well, that and complete a lot of paperwork, which included changing the name of her office from Paranormal Affairs to Paranormal Relations. It just seemed to fit better.

After running through three interviews—Maisy being one of them—she had compiled her notes and realized that... she needed a bigger pool of people to choose from.

Her cell phone rang after the door closed on the third interviewee. Paige read the caller ID and answered, confused. "Lovejoy," Paige said, letting her tone fill with shock. "I thought you didn't want to raise any flags."

"I didn't, but I was let go anyway. I'm just leaving now." She sighed as a plane flew over. "I heard you were looking for people."

"I am." Was this convenience? Or had Ruben and Ivan done some careful maneuvering to make this happen for her, and if that was the case, then how had they known about

Lovejoy? "Go to the Blackmans and see if you can get a door over. Or I can send Derrick?"

"Depends on who has clearance," Lovejoy said with no uncertainty in her voice.

"Right." Paige still had to learn how to tread those waters. "Where are you? I'll send Derrick."

She got the particulars and gave that information to her brother. "Are you getting any time with your kids?"

"You really think I'm just sitting around her reading magazines all day?" he asked incredulously. "No. I go home. Spend time with the family. And when you call, I come."

Paige winced. "That sounds… demeaning."

He shook his head and shrugged. "I'm doing my part to help you make this place safer *for* my kids. So, yeah. I'm good with it. Where do you need me to go?"

After giving him the information and watching him leave, Paige pulled Aaron into her office.

He went full-stride into an attack. "You didn't even *listen* to a word I said out there, did you?"

She was rethinking her solution to her Aaron situation.

He spent a good five minutes telling her he knew what he was talking about, about who all he had experience in writing speeches for, and on and on.

"Hey," Paige barked, sending out a little alpha will.

He frowned but took a seat. "I'm trying to help you."

But was he? Or was he feeding his own ego? Sometimes, it was hard to tell. "The talking points you gave me didn't address anything important *or* the questions she asked."

"She was told not to ask those questions."

"But she did." Because sometimes, people did things because they felt right at the time. "And the interview went well."

Aaron's eyes widened as she shrugged. "If you listen to Leroy."

"Who is in charge of these things. We're—" she turned to Willow as she walked through the door, "—'trending well,' and whatever, so I think we did good."

Willow nodded.

Aaron frowned. "No. You did good."

Paige was having a hard time seeing his point.

"I heard you interviewed another speech writer," he finally said, bursting like a grouse from the bushes. "Maisy Molina comes off as great, but she's young, inexperienced—"

"And female," Paige said bluntly.

"You can't use my maleness against me. There are laws against that."

Technically, Paige was *pretty* sure the laws were to protect people who actually got discriminated *against*. "What I'm saying is that she gets a few of the issues I have to face, some of the situations I'll be thrown into, better than you can because of your maleness."

"Like what?"

"Like..." Paige cleared her throat. "If you'd understood the situation a bit more, you would have realized Jazzi would have been hungry for a story because she has to work harder to stand out."

He shook his head, deflated. "I just want to do a good job."

Paige had *hoped* Maisy would have been the fit she was looking for, but after completing the interview, she wasn't sure.

Willow was, though. According to her, Maisy was *out*.

"Then, *do* a better job. Talk to women. Ask them what they face and then show them you're listening. Pay attention. Walk around as a woman for a day or two."

"What?" He shook his head. "How, why would I—"

She nodded. "Look, if you tell people it's an experiment, those around you will either make *more* fun of you—which will help you understand—or they'll support you—which will help you get information and maybe stories. But outside of work? You'll get a real good look at the kinds of things I can't even explain. Like…" Like what could she even say? "Like, go for a jog in the morning with your headphones blaring in both ears dressed like a woman and see how that works for you."

He narrowed his eyes, looking a bit confused.

Her phone buzzed with a message. She was getting a lot of those.

"You're not firing me?"

"I want to." They *could* look for another speechwriter, but they may not have time. "With the president possibly getting impeached, I don't know how long I'll keep this job."

"They wouldn't *fire you*," Aaron said indignantly. "They *need* you."

"If Dick can even be talked into keeping my position, you think he'll keep me?" Paige was *only* going off what Dawn had told her.

Aaron frowned, his expression serious.

But that hammered home the fact that the conjecture might actually have merit. She really might *not* have this job long. "I can't afford to mess up."

"Well, you did pretty well without me."

"This time." She pressed her finger into the conference table. "But what about the *next* time? I might not be as lucky."

His dark eyes widened. "Okay. Okay. I'll do better. And, I guess, I'm coming as a woman for a… week." His tone said he couldn't *believe* he was saying that.

She couldn't really, either. She wasn't *sure* it was a great idea, but if he was going to run with it, she'd support him. She looked at her phone. Leah needed to talk to her. "You good?"

He nodded, biting both his lips.

"Great." Paige stood, gesturing with her phone. "My kids."

"Tell them hi for me," Willow said with a smile, gathering her stuff and leaving the room.

When Paige had the room to herself, she called her daughter.

"Mom!" Leah sounded out of breath.

"Bean." This couldn't be good.

"Okay. So… I did a thing and you need to come home."

"Is the house still standing?" Because when it came to the kinds of *things* her kids could do, that was a fair question.

"Yes."

"And the town?"

"Is still good. Mom, please? I just…I need your help and Aunt Les is…she told me to call you."

"Oh." Well, if Leslie had told Leah to call, it *must* be serious. Or Leslie was just over it. "I'll be there as soon as I can."

She messaged Derrick and asked when he'd be ready to doorway back to D.C. so she could catch a lift home.

Damn. It. Shit was fucking insane.

He sent a message back that he and Lovejoy had five more minutes.

She had enough time to use the restroom and get something to drink. The morning and afternoon following the interview with Jazzi had been hectic.

Derrick opened a door in the "lobby" in the roped off section exclusively for his use with Directo—ex-FIB Director Stef Lovejoy.

He looked at Paige with an exasperated expression. "Leah just called me."

"Um, yeah," Paige said, holding off on greeting Lovejoy. "I was going to ask—"

"Yeah. If you're ready, I am."

His tone said she might actually be in trouble. That... wasn't good. What did he know that she didn't? "I need a few minutes. Then we leave."

Derrick sat and pulled a magazine from the table.

Paige led Lovejoy—Stef now that she wasn't the director anymore—into the conference room and shut the door.

The other door opened and Willow joined them.

Paige introduced Willow to Stef and offered drinks from the pitcher of water on the table, then they sat.

"You need a job," Paige said. "And I need someone who can help with intelligence, fact-gathering and management, and security. Also, paranormal law enforcement because we need regulations so we can bring everyone under the same umbrella."

Lovejo—Stef narrowed her amber eyes. "Okay. And my background won't be an issue?"

"Were you forced to register?" Because Paige was really curious as to why she'd been let go.

Stef angrily clamped her lips shut and shook her head. "I failed my clearance because it was discovered I was paranormal and didn't claim it."

That might be a hurdle she'd have to go over. But Paige was willing to try anyway. "I'll talk to Ruben. You want the job?"

Stef nodded thoughtfully. "Pay?"

"I've gotta go, but Willow can go over all that." Paige turned to her assistant. "Run this through Ruben. Tell him she feared for her life and that's the reason she didn't reveal it. It's a true story and if he doesn't buy it, I'll remind him by telling him a few truths he won't like."

Willow gave Paige a look that said she wasn't going to enjoy that conversation but that she'd do it.

Paige found Derrick who was pacing outside in the hall-way, the magazine open and forgotten on the table.

He didn't say anything, just opened a door and grabbed her arm, dragging her through.

They dropped into the Whiskey backyard.

"Uh." Paige wasn't sure what the huge rush was.

Mandy stepped through the back door. "Upstairs."

"Why—"

Mandy just grabbed her arm and led her through the house.

People sat on the couch but Mandy pulled on her so hard she didn't have time to see who.

They continued up the stairs and down the hall to her room.

Rainbow, Ethel, and a man she didn't know were in the hall.

"What the hell?" Paige tried to pull back but Mandy had a firm grip and tugged again.

They got to her room and all her kids and Kate sat on the bed watching someone sleep.

Dexx.

She forgot all the things she'd promised the president she wouldn't do in that instant. She went to him, holding him close to her in the comfort of *their home* for a long moment.

She pulled back and lit into the kids. "What happened? I was worried for your lives calling me like that. What's he doing here? Here of all places? Do you have *any* idea what's going on?"

Leah shrugged, shaking her head. "We had to do something. Haven't you told us to think, and do what we need to?"

"That's not what I meant. It's—" What she wanted to say was that it was for *her* to do. Were the kids growing up too fast? She'd missed so much.

Paige fished Dexx's hand from beneath the covers and held it. He was warm and— "Wait. Is he hurt?"

No one answered.

She looked around the room.

Leah shrugged.

"We were fighting." Rainbow shuffled into the room. She didn't look like Rainbow at all. No smiles, and the bright light in her eyes was almost gone.

Leah wrung her hands. "Sorry, Mom, we found a way to bring him back and—"

"You *what?!*"

Rainbow looked over at Ethel for help. "DoDO chased us absolutely *everywhere*, and then we went into another world. That was right after we saw you."

Ethel picked it up, nodding hopefully with her hands wide. "We left Dexx and Rainbow in Morocco."

Morocco? What the…

"We didn't have a choice. They were everywhere—DoDO. We couldn't wait any more. Then we thought we were free, but then the djinn came."

"Right, right," Rainbow said. "We saw a lost city. I think it was Atlantis. I think we time-traveled, and Mario got blasted—"

Ethel chuckled. "That was good. But then we lost the trial, but Dexx killed one of them."

Good?

Rainbow groaned. "They shoved us in the fight ring."

So, not good. None of it really made sense. "Stop." Paige had enough. "Everyone, leave. Kids, take everyone and get them something to eat."

Leah gestured to Rainbow, "But we already—"

"Go." Paige really didn't know what she was feeling right at that moment, but it was a lot.

Red Star filtered out first. Leah was the last to leave. She had tears in her eyes and shot daggers at Paige.

She couldn't let her go like that. "Bean."

Leah stopped, her hand on the door.

"You did really good. I'm mad at him. Not you." Much.

Leah gave her a slight smile. "Don't be too mad, 'kay?"

"Promise." Not to kill him.

Leah left and closed the door behind her.

Paige heard the click of the door and turned to Dexx. What the hell was she supposed to do with him? Did he have any idea what she'd been up against?

No. He didn't. But he'd fought off DoDO and gladiator trials. So…

He stirred.

She wanted to touch him but wasn't sure if she'd stroke him out of love or punch him out of frustration because both were warring inside her. "Dexx."

"Hey, babe." He turned and looked at her.

She sank onto the bed. "Hey. So, uh, everyone tried to fill me in but… yeah. I'm just really confused. Where were you?"

"Just… a lot of places. I know I should have texted or called. I just—" He bit off what he was about to say and looked away.

That told Paige a lot more than any of the crazy words she'd just heard had. "Do I need to care about any of the stuff you did? Like, is this a mess I need to clean up? Does this affect you being arrested—well, I mean, soonly arrested for what you did in England?"

He shrugged. "Not this latest thing, no. The demon trial? I don't think they'll ask politely if they can *arrest* me. It's just one more amazing thing I've had to deal with."

And *he* wanted to complain? Her head was still spinning form the sheer amount of information she was trying to keep straight. "What was the gladiator ring thing? I assume that's why you're…" She gestured to his bruised appearance.

He nodded. "That was our sentence."

"Do I need to know?"

He shrugged. "Nah."

That wasn't a very Dexx-like response. "And the girls saved you."

He nodded again.

"And you're safe?"

"I am. We are now. I promise."

He looked... exhausted. But she didn't care. "Do you have *any idea* what I've been going through? Now that you're *safe* and *home*?"

He turned over in the bed, finally looking at her. The look on his face said he wasn't ready for this conversation.

Paige *couldn't care*. She didn't have much time. It was time finally to fill him in on what was going on with her because he was about to go into *her* kind of battle and when *he* did, he was going to fuck *everything* to smithereens. "Did you know I'm the Secretary of Paranormal Relations?"

He shook his head and the expression on his face just asked why he should care. "No. Congrats? I'm really excited for you?"

Wow. So, what? Because she hadn't been tortured for a year, hadn't been put through a demon trial, or thrown into a gladiator ring, her problems didn't matter? That was... so manly of him. She turned away from him and clamped her pressed hands between her knees. "Tell me about what happened to you."

He didn't answer immediately, then he brought his legs up and swiveled around so he could sit next to her. He stared at the wall, clamping his mouth shut.

That should have been a warning that something was wrong, but a part of her didn't care how much he'd gone through, because, damn it, she'd gone through a lot too. However, she really needed him to understand that his next battle was serious and not something he could just punch or claw his way out of.

But this Dexx didn't even look like the kind of person who'd try to claw his way out of a fight.

He raised his eyebrows, but his lips remained closed.

She needed to shut up and listen to him. She knew that, but she also just needed *her partner and equal* to not fuck up the delicate balance she had going on. Because if he did? He'd be in prison. Their kids would lose their dad. She *might* lose her position.

She licked her lips and pulled herself back from her high-emotion bluff. When he shut down like this, his ears stopped working.

Releasing a breath, she hunched forward and leaned against him. "What's going on with you?"

"Too much to list. Be specific."

"I—" Paige said, releasing her head in frustration, "I've got a very delicate situation and you're not listening. So, what's going on that broke your ears? Because…." Damn it! She needed Dexx. Fuck!

He ground his teeth, his green eyes flashing. "I lost Hattie."

Well, that would be pretty earth-shattering. "How?"

"I fucked up." His voice cracked a little and he cleared his throat. "I had help. It might even have worked. I'll never know. In the end, I charged ahead, and I thought I could wiggle through. She was hanging by a thread and I swung the sword anyway."

"None of that made any sense."

He raked his hand through his hair. "We were separated as soon as I crossed the barrier to the time before."

The Vaada Bhoomi, where the spirit animals lived when they weren't bonded to humans.

"That's where the currents sent me and Rainbow. Mah'se tried to kick us out, but Hattie wouldn't let him. We, uh, me and Rainbow, and… Hattie—" He swallowed hard. "—we decided to go. Mah'se couldn't be left out or whatever. We found my past life. A huge city, down there under the ocean. Big as Denver. Maybe, I don't know. But they had the right idea. He almost made it work."

"Who? You saw people there?"

"My past life. He almost had a place that all the paras could live. Free from the fears of mundanes. Then Bussemi came—"

"How did *he* get there?" Paige's eyes were wide.

"He didn't call himself that— it was weird. It was more of an interactive memory, I guess? He— my past life me—was kind of a douche actually. But his vision was so close. Just think how different our world would be if we had a place all our own. Where we could let the rest of the world burn and be safe behind our walls."

"That wouldn't work. A place like that would draw the wrong sorts of attention." Paige shook her head.

"It would if it just popped into being right now, but if the world grew up knowing? Babe, you *know* we'd be on the first plane out."

"No. We would stay. We would help the mundanes from—"

"They have always been afraid of change. Afraid of something different. Easily swayed into violence, prejudice."

Paige inhaled and took his hand again. "Let's table that argument. So then what?"

"He gave me a crystal, and... And Mario attacked, and the memory blew up."

"How did Mario get there?" Paige shook her head again, this time in disbelief.

"I don't freaking know. He just was. We escaped and found the desert. We were going to the library and some djinn got in the way. They were pretty cool at first, then we found out Red Star was on trial and... lost. Got put into the magickal gladiator fights. Pretty sure Frey wants to kill me. I killed her horse, I think. Then pow, Leah pops through a door goes all John Connor and black out. That was my day, how was yours?"

Well, he *had* gone through some stuff.

"Bottom line? I discovered my magick. But to get it—to save us—I sacrificed my connection to Hattie." He closed his eyes and took in a breath. "I think I made the wrong call."

"Look," she said, not sure if she could even trust him to go into the negotiations at all. Maybe she'd send Lovejoy as a proxy and forgo the whole thing. "Daw—the president is going to help us get DoDO out of the country."

Dexx's eyes turned solemn as he met her gaze.

"She's setting up negotiations to discuss you and team's extradition. Meaning, we're talking about sending you guys back to England to stand trial. And if you go, I can't protect you."

"For what again?"

"What you did in Parliament."

"That was—oh. Right." He dropped his head and let it hang. "I'm just so tired."

Ah, fuck. She grabbed the lower half of her face, digging her fingertips into her under-jaw before she let her head fall. What was she supposed to do? How was she going to save this? What did she have?

Paige would come up with a Plan B. She had to. But what?

She'd intended to stay longer, but this was a situation she *had* to handle right away. She couldn't wait. She didn't have time for cuddles and loves and hugs.

Rising, she cupped his face and pecked a kiss on his cheek. She met his green gaze, not seeing Hattie at all. "I've gotta go, but I love you."

"I love you, too." His voice was low and trembled slightly.

Only slightly. The man was barely keeping it together.

Damn it!

She straightened and bit her lips. "Tell the kids I love them?"

He nodded and stood. "Always."

How was she going to help him? Her mind raced. She had to talk to Ruben or…

Merry.

That one wasn't a *great* idea, but it was better than nothing. "Don't break the world, 'kay?"

He nodded, though there was no laughter in his face. At all.

Shit.

Pissed as hell about this situation and that she couldn't be there for the man she loved, she turned away and went in search of Derrick.

It was time to talk to a blood witch about a deal.

Paige shut the door behind her and leaned her head against it for a minute. Dexx would have to find his way through this. He would have help because she'd see to that.

Derrick informed her he was spending time with his family and that she could take Leah who had also been given clearance, though not super high clearance. Paige might have to walk from one appointment to the next because Leah wasn't cleared to open a door to the White House. She was too young.

That made sense.

So, Paige went in search of Leah who was a bundle of excitement over what she'd done. "I saved him! Well, we did. We saved him!"

"Yup." Paige didn't want to rain on her parade. Leah'd done something pretty incredible by saving Dexx and Red Star. She wasn't going to diminish that. But she didn't need to give her daughter high praise for it either because it was *still* a mess Paige was going to have to try and clean up. So, instead, Paige just gave Leah two thumbs up and continued out the door. "Sorry. Gotta run. The world's still on fire."

Bobby gave her a twisted frowny face on his way from the living room to the stairs leading to the second floor.

Right. Right. She grabbed his head and gave it a kiss, then ran to the kitchen where she'd left Leah and gave her a kiss and a hug, too. "You did good." Even though Paige was currently in a lot of trouble if anyone found about this.

"Thank you," Leah said, beaming up at her mom. "Go save the world."

Paige just had to make sure *no one* found out about Leah's involvement or that Paige had seen Dexx and hadn't turned him in.

Paige grabbed Derrick who hadn't made it home yet. "Merry's."

"So…" He shook his head, looking at her expectantly.

She widened her eyes and gave him a I-understand-what-you're-asking-but-I'm-still-ignoring-you look and nodded. "So… Merry's."

He grunted and opened a door. "I'm stopping to see my kids. Text me when you're done."

"You got it." Paige stepped through and knocked on Merry's door.

Merry Eastwood sipped a sherry as she listened to Paige prattle on.

"So, there you go. Dexx needs the kind of help I don't think I can help. I've got what few contacts I have putting a meeting together, but I have no idea if they have the power to pull a save. Can you help?"

Rubbing her temple, Merry tapped the foot of her crossed leg. "You never have small problems, do you?"

Paige took a sip of the sherry, letting the liquid burn its way to her stomach. This was her second glass. "He's going to fuck this up." And by "this," Paige meant the negotiations.

Though, for totally different reasons than she normally had to plan for. Normally, he'd be half-cocked. The Dexx she'd just left was the *exact opposite* of that. Like… she didn't even know how to plan for that.

"You're certain about this."

"Oh, yeah." Paige released a long breath, closing her eyes. She realized this was not the person she needed to be confiding in like this, but she had to tell someone, and all of her confiding people were busy. "He's had it rough."

"So have you."

Paige was a little touched that Merry had admitted that. "You're not lying." But Dexx was at his limits. That was evident. "I need a solution to these negotiations that brings him and his team home."

"Okay. What do you want to have happen?"

Paige opened her eyes and leaned forward, resting her elbows on her knees. "First, I want Dexx and his team released, no jail time, no extradition process."

"That's going to be hard to do. They attacked Parliament." But Merry raised her chin as if considering how to spin it.

"They attacked an invading army and a demon." Paige wasn't sure they could actually sell that, but she'd give a try. "And Parliament just happened to get in the way."

Merry slid her gaze over to Paige, calculating.

There were times when the woman seemed like she was turning a new leaf and being…well, not good, but decent, and then there were times like this when Paige realized that Merry was going to get the upper hand. And it might be serious.

"And?"

Right. "And I want DoDO to leave the U.S."

"I'll see what I can do about Dexx." Merry shook her head. "I don't know if I know the right people who can remove DoDO from our borders. We've been working on that for a while."

"Well, I'm pulling strings on my end, too, but I'm really new and the strings are really old."

Merry's expression said she understood.

"I need you *in* the negotiations. Or someone powerful you know who could… I don't know. There are stories of rich people getting stuff like this fixed. Whatever that means. Do you have that ability?"

Merry's dark smile grew sideways like Maleficent's. "It would be my pleasure."

This wasn't going to end well. "How much is this going to cost me?"

Merry shrugged. "What's a little blood?"

Paige had no idea. "Whatever. Just… don't make this worse than it already is." She finished her drink. "You'll keep me informed on how things go?"

"Of course." Merry smiled and stood in her pencil skirt.

Yeah. Maybe Paige should also send Lovejoy—Stef. Blessed Mother. Stef—in with them as well. Paige still didn't know where this extradition negotiation meeting was going to take place or if Dawn could even pull it off. But if it did happen, Paige needed at least one person she could trust.

She texted Derrick for a ride back to the Eisenhower Building and her office.

He was very congenial as he showed up, cut a door, and then closed it behind her.

Yeah. Paige could really get used to that.

Her office suite was abuzz with people, getting more desks and offices ready for the new people arriving over the next few days or weeks.

Security stopped her. "Madam Secretary."

"Um, yeah." Paige wasn't certain why she was being stopped if they knew who she was.

"You still need to check in with us when you come by portal."

Well, at least he was professional about it. "I went over these protocols the other day."

"They've been updated. If you'll just follow me."

Paige invested a minute to talk to him about creating a system that would work for them both and then she gave him Derrick's number as the person to talk to about finalizing the procedure. She then texted Derrick to give him the heads up on her way to her office.

The woman the president had asked to babysit Paige and the twins the first time they'd been in town walked through her door not long after Paige had sat down. She'd just managed to turn her computer on. Well, wake it up, really. "Naomi," Paige said with a smile.

With a smile, Naomi tugged on her blue blazer, a strand of dark hair falling forward as she ducked her head. "I was wondering if I could talk to you."

Paige wasn't certain what she could do for the…crap. She didn't even remember Naomi's title. Oh, right. The Office of Faith-based and Neighborhood Partnerships. "Are your kids okay?"

"Yeah, yeah." Naomi waved her off. "Do you have a place to stay?"

"Oddly, no." She really wasn't looking forward to another night on the couch. "I'd never planned on staying here, not with door magick at my disposal, but with the impeachment and everything, they want me to stay in D.C. No overnights at home for a bit."

"Ah. Well, okay." Naomi spread out her hands. "I've got a spare room. I'd be happy to have you stay with me."

That would actually be… "Awesome. Thank you so much."

"Yeah, but, um, I…" Naomi played with her fingers. "You

know what? I'm just gonna come right out and say it. I want to work for you."

"Oh." That…in what manner? "Why?"

"Well, I work great as a liaison. I'm also sure you'll get people from around the country, dignitaries from around the world with different cultures, religions, and practices, and I could help them. Help you help them."

Paige wanted to say that was unlikely, but she was so new to this, she had no idea. And Ruben had actually put something like that on her list. "That doesn't tell me why you want to come over here."

Naomi smiled grimly. "I want to help, and I don't feel like I do that in my current position."

That worked for Paige. "Okay. Well, uh, I think I'll need your resume before I can make it official. Talk to Willow about the particulars. When could you start?"

Naomi grinned, shaking her head in surprise. "Um, right away." She released a chuckle. "That's it? Really?"

"I worked with you all ready, remember? I basically interviewed you for a week and a half." That's how long it'd been. Right? All the days blended together.

"Okay. Thanks."

Paige's office phone rang. She waved Naomi out. "You'll do great. Thank you."

Naomi left and closed the door behind her. Her smile was the last thing Paige saw.

That was nice. She picked up the phone. "Whiskey." Damn it. How the hell was she supposed to answer the phone?

"What's this I hear about a convicted felon being invited to the extradition negotiation?" Ruben demanded.

Paige didn't know how *he* knew. She hadn't filed any of the paperwork. "Do you have me bugged?"

"No. But Merry Eastwood has some *very* high connections." He shifted something around in the background and grunted. "Are you *sure* you can trust her."

"No. I put her in jail for multiple murders."

"And then you got her out of jail."

"Yeah. To commit multiple murders in a war with demons." Which didn't sound great. "She's got a job skill."

"And you're thinking she'll be able to kill this cardinal guy and take care of our issue?"

"No." But when he *put* it that way. Was that something she could do? "She's a good moderator."

He grunted. "And Lovejoy? You want me to reinstate her clearance after it was revoked?"

"Yes." There wasn't enough time in the day for all these conversations. "It shouldn't have been revoked in the first place."

He grunted.

Did that grunt meant *he'd* been the one to fire her so Paige could hire her? Or did it mean he agreed with her? Or did he just have gas?

"She didn't tell her supervisors about her change in status."

"Because her status hadn't changed. She was born this way. You don't have to go in and tell your boss you're black after a law outlaws it."

Ruben paused. "Don't ever say anything like that again. It's crass."

"That doesn't make it any less true." And Paige needed to cut through attitudes and mindsets with something because this whole situation was so painfully similar to other things in life, it was hard to admit that they were all too… unable to find a viable solution. "Look at her track record as a director. That should speak for itself."

"It does," he grumbled. "Fine. Could you choose more people without questionable backgrounds in the future?"

"Sure. Hey, before you hang up?"

He sighed. Again. "Yeah?"

"Do I need to talk to the Secretary of State?"

He paused before he answered. "Why the *hell* do you need to talk to Salma?"

Paige was making a mental note on the name. No. She rummaged through her drawer and pulled out a pen, scribbling it on a sticky note. "Because of the extradition negotiations. I could offer some—"

"No. Absolutely not."

So, yes. She absolutely should. "Okay." Got it.

He groaned. "Don't do it, Paige."

"Okay. You said no." She just had to see if she could "accidentally" stumble into the woman and she now had someone on her staff who could help her accidentally do that on purpose. Paige hung up this time, then smiled at the phone.

The *mountain* of cases of paranormals who needed help moaned at her like the groans of the walking dead.

Leah came in, bored but nervous.

"Hey, Bean," Paige said, barely looking up. Then she realized Leah was standing in her office. "What are you doing here?"

"Derrick and I needed to talk to Eric—"

"Who?"

"Security guy. Anyway, I saw Naomi and she asked if I'd stay and I was just wondering..." Leah bit her lip and gestured with her entire body for the lead in.

"You want to hang out with Toby and—" Oh, crap. She forgot the girl's name. She only remembered Toby's because she had two of those.

"Ginny," Leah said helpful.

"Yeah." Paige snapped her finger and pointed. "Her. You want to hang out."

"Well, yes?"

"And what about school?"

"My teachers are already planning to video chat me in because of the door thing." Leah beamed a shrugging grin.

Paige did like the idea of actually having one of her kids there. It didn't look like she was going to get attacked for once, so that was a plus. "Sure."

"Cool," Leah said, her blue eyes lighting up. "Am I gonna be responsible for security?"

"In a way, yes?" Paige realized this was yet another mom fail moment. "It will be mostly Derrick. But when it's you and me, I need you to be able to handle that… stuff. Learn the protocols. Check in with the right people and don't, you know, get me in trouble."

"I got a book of protocols and they're giving me a test in two days."

"Oh, well." Interesting. Had Derrick had to pass a test? "You'll be fine. I need to go take care of something. Can you…" Paige *really* needed to get to that stack of people in need. It didn't look like she'd have time soon enough, though. She wasn't certain if this was something she could even hand off to her daughter. An adult might say no based on the fact that Leah was still a teenager. But a mom might realize that Leah might have to learn things she wouldn't otherwise if she was sheltered all the time.

No. No. The judgey helicopter moms would tell her that the only place her child belonged was at home. So, uh, yeah. There was that.

Paige snorted and rested her hand on the stack of folders. "Okay. You need to know that what you learn in here, you can't act on."

Leah's eyes rounded. "Okay."

"You can't share *anything* about these except with me and Willow. You got that?"

"Okay, Mom." Leah's mouth rounded with determination while her eyes lit with excitement.

Paige picked up the stack. "These are people and paranormal groups who are reaching out to our office. They want to talk, to discuss their future. A few have issues going on right now that need to be addressed. And none of them are talking or sharing where they're even located."

"Uh, okay?"

"So," Paige said, getting to her feet and trying to remember which room she needed to go to next, "you go through them and tell me which ones need my attention first. Or what kind of attention they need."

"Based on?"

"Needs. Their needs. Right now, that's the only parameters I have." Paige shrugged. "That might change later. But you'll know as you go through them."

"Yeah, okay." Leah sank down in the corner chair and turned on the lamp.

Paige walked over to her and pressed a kiss on top of Leah's head. "Love you, bean."

"Yeah, okay." She tipped her head to Paige.

Leah was immersed.

Paige took the elevator up to the roof. She needed to take a short flight to the Congressional Office Building. She set down on the steps outside and shifted to human before walking in. What would life look like in a year when people could just shift and walk, run, or fly to work if they wanted?

Okay. Maybe ten years. One was a little *too* soon.

Congresswoman Jacobs was in session when Paige arrived and Rachel—admin assistant Rachel, not Paige's mother—reminded her that if she wanted to talk to the congresswoman, it would be best if Willow scheduled an appointment.

Right. Right-right-right.

She made the rounds and finally found one of her three co-conspirators in her office: Congresswoman Hernandez.

"Secretary Whiskey," the congresswoman said with a smiling frown. "What an honor to see you."

Paige closed the door. "Let's cut the titles."

The congresswoman nodded. "They're cumbersome. Jardena."

"Paige." She took a seat. "I've got a slight problem."

Jardena grimaced and folded her hands on her desk. "And what's that?"

Trying to figure out exactly how to phrase it, Paige bit her lips. "I need to keep President Flynn in office."

"You want to *what?*" Jardena set her palms on her desk and leaned forward, nearly coming out of her chair.

Okay, well, that was a bit of an extreme reaction from a congresswoman. "Hear me out."

Jardena batted her baleful brown eyes, her lips tight as if to say she'd better hurry.

Paige just had to make this sound really impressive. "I've discovered the people behind what's really going on."

"Okay. And?"

"And… the president was played."

"And so were a lot of other presidents, but they didn't authorize the killings of hundreds of their own people."

When she put it that way… "Right? But she's an ally now."

"And when did this *miracle* happen?" Jardena demanded, raising her hands and letting them fall to the desk.

"A couple of days ago?" Had it only been that long? Or longer? She couldn't remember.

"And for a couple of days, you've been *working with* the president?"

"I got the post, didn't I?"

Jardena closed her eyes. "She—what did she get you to agree to in order to get it?"

"Nothing."

With a sigh, Jardena opened her dark eyes and stared hard at Paige. "We pressured her into giving you that position because American people were dying on the streets."

"Yes."

"And that case *helped build* the impeachment case we have —a case you're going to testify in, I might add. And you're our star witness."

Which wasn't exactly what Paige wanted to hear at the moment. "Yes."

"Why should we allow a murderer to remain in power?" Jardena gripped her fingers together, her fingertips and knuckles going white.

That was a slightly loaded question, and it was imperative Paige get the answer right. "Because Dawn is going to help us take down the real bad guy here."

"The bad guy?"

"DoDO. And the man who not only started it but is running it."

Jardena shook her head primly. "That organization was built hundreds of years ago."

Paige waited for that information to set in then said quietly, "I know."

"Wait. You—" Jardena raised her chin, pulling her lips in. Then she shook her head. "No. The answer is no. President Flynn—" She emphasized the name hard as if to remind Paige not to slip again. "—authorized murder on her own people on her *own soil*. She's not fit to serve, especially if what you say is true and she's been duped."

But what if Vice President Dick Walton took her place and only made things worse?

"I realize you're nervous," Jardena said tightly. "But your people are freed. The next step is to give them rights."

"They had rights before."

Jardena ignored her. "And then we'll fight the next battle, and then the next one. But *not* with *this* president."

Fuck. Paige sighed. She was going to have to figure out something else then because in order for Dawn to help her take DoDO down—which was what they were going to need—she needed Dawn, President Flynn, to remain *in office*.

"I'll see you tomorrow at the hearing."

Damn it. Damn it all to hell.

2 2

To say that Paige wasn't ready for this hearing was putting it mildly. She *tried* to make it seem like it was any other day as she called her kids—individually—and did paperwork. She hired five more people to fill positions she hoped would still be available when they reported for work in two weeks.

She called Leslie, Tuck, and Chuck. She checked in with Suzanne who said it was weird to be called by her, and to please stop because she thought the world was on fire. Again. Paige even called Merry who told her to politely fuck off and to not destroy the world more than they already had.

The moment of her testimony finally arrived. She was informed they were following less "formal" proceedings, whatever that meant. She was introduced to a lawyer who would sit behind her. Because she could get arrested? She didn't even fully understand just how much trouble she could be in, or how much she could be liable for. She was an officer of the law, so she knew this could very well blow back on her.

And, unfortunately, the more she thought about what

Jardena had said about the lives lost and how Dawn had to be held accountable, the more Paige agreed.

How had everything gotten so sideways?

Because she'd seen the human side of President Dawn Flynn, and it had affected her. Who was to say that wasn't exactly what the president had hoped for?

Paige was shown into a large room with lines of long desks and microphones. She took a seat and was talked through how things would work. How long she had to speak, how she had to turn on her microphone to be heard. Just— there were a lot of things to remember and she was freaking out so she was undoubtedly going to forget something.

Congresswoman Jardena Hernandez turned on her microphone when everything was cleared—it took a long time to get to that point—and looked at Paige with a slight smile, her dark eyes offering strength as if understanding fully what Paige was feeling. "Thank you for taking the time to speak with us, Secretary Whiskey."

Paige inclined her head because her microphone was off.

"We're going to forego opening statements and just go into the questioning to save time. We're all very busy and we want this to go as smoothly as possible."

Being as Paige hadn't *prepared* opening remarks, this was good by her. As long as she had a chance to say what needed to be said.

Which was what exactly?

That waging war on the paranormal people—or any people of the United States—should be deemed unlawful. And that it shouldn't take the threat of secession or civil war to make that point.

But she worried that she hadn't prepared enough for this moment. Maybe instead of calling people, she should have been organizing her mental notes. But, no. No. She was Paige Whiskey. She might not be able to use magick in *this* battle, but she *was* prepared for this. She *had* the knowledge. She *wasn't* twisting the story. And the *only* thing she really needed to be perfectly clear about during these proceedings was that citizens shouldn't need to fear their government. The end.

The congresswoman folded her hands in front of her and smiled. "Secretary Whiskey, can you please tell us what led to the decision to arrive as you did in the elven city, Nythlebelle."

Paige tried to ignore the fact that there were a lot of faces she didn't know staring at her, or that there were cameras up everywhere. She focused on Jardena, one of her only allies—though, how much of an ally the woman was she had yet to determine—and proceeded like it was any other deposition. She reached over and turned on her microphone. "Thank you for having me." She *had* invested *some* time into researching a *little*. "If I may be allowed, congresswoman, to take you back to what led up to this."

Jardena nodded and gestured with her hand for Paige to continue.

Each exchange was timed, and Paige had to watch the clock to make sure she didn't run over. Okay. So, not a long story. "I'd just gotten back from our first trip to Washington D.C. and meeting with the president. We'd—my children and I—had been put in collars to suppress our abilities, which is dangerous for those around us."

"How are the collars dangerous?" Jardena asked.

Paige gripped her fingers hard.

Calm down, kitten, Cawli purred in her head.

I don't know if I'm smart enough for this.

You do not have to be smart. You are simply speaking the truth.

But Paige knew how truth could be used against her. She pulled the karma spell out of her pocket and pressed it against the desktop. "It's a little like building a dam, except that in this case, the power builds until it explodes outward.

DoDO—the Department of Delicate Operations—knew this when they offered the collars. I came across their experiments in Alaska a few months prior."

"Experiments?" Jardena asked in surprise. "You mean human trials?"

As long as paranormals were being labeled as humans. "Yes. And in these trials, DoDO was sanctioned to 'clean up' when their collared shifters exploded."

"What do you mean?"

"I mean, they hunted these shifters down and killed them."

Jardena nodded and wrote something down.

Had Paige made her point well enough? "When we got back to Troutdale, we were in lockdown. Our entire town was shut off from the world. We couldn't get supplies. Food, prescription drugs, the things we needed. Our electricity was shut off. Our social media accounts were being stripped and wiped."

A few of the people there acted like she wasn't even talking.

Jardena looked aghast as if this was news to her. "I just want to go back a moment to the collars. Is it true that your daughter, who was only days old at the time, was injured by this collar?"

Paige cleared her throat, realizing that with every word out of her mouth, this was going badly for the president. "DoDO knew what they were doing when they put those collars on my babies. In Alaska, we'd uncovered their intent. They put the collars on shifters to repress the shifter spirit until they burst out rather explosively. believe that's what they intended with my children."

"And yourself."

"Yes. I believe they wanted a reason to kill us."

Licking her lips, Jardena glanced at the people beside her who didn't seem to be paying attention. "And was she hurt?"

Time to lay the truth out there. "I was afraid she would be, but by the nature of her shifter spirit, she was not."

Jardena frowned. "Please explain."

Paige didn't want the world to know a lot about her children. "Her shifter spirit can control electricity, so she short-circuited the collar."

"Oh." The congresswoman blinked and wrote a few more notes. "And being cut off when you got home, your social media profiles were erased. So, you were cut off from the world."

"Yes. We were being wiped from existence."

"And you couldn't get your story out."

"We found ways. But to get back to your question, congresswoman, we were trying to determine what to do next to make sure everyone had what they needed—" Paige didn't want to tell the world they'd been strategizing for war. "—and that's when the elf queen arrived, telling us their city was under attack." Paige closed her eyes as the visions of that day played over in her head. "The destruction was devastating. Their city was—" She licked her lips and opened her eyes again. "There was so much destruction. So many dead. It was a war zone."

"And the president authorized this attack."

"I don't know who authorized the attack, congresswoman. What I *know* is that DoDO was there. Not American soldiers. Not our militaries. DoDO field agents. And I believe they're the ones who provided the intel for this mission, whatever it was. DoDO has led a centuries-old mission to annihilate paranormals across the world. This wasn't new to them. This was just another day at the office."

"And you believe that *they* are responsible."

"I believe we've invited a cancer into how we run our government."

"And do you believe the president invited that?"

"I don't know who invited it. I do, however, have proof of DoDO's actions. I have proof of their illegal operations. And I believe an investigation needs to be spearheaded into their practices, and that they need to be removed from American soil."

"And the president?"

Paige took in a deep breath and expelled it. "I can tell you as a factual witness the horrors and atrocities paranormal people have been forced to endure." She was running out of time. "I can give you details on the battles we fought in a city so outside our jurisdiction, it's not even in our dimension. We had no business being in that elven city. And as far as I know, *we* weren't. DoDO was. I can give you evidence and proof of the atrocities performed by DoDO in Lawrence, Kansas, and what they did to us in Troutdale. And that *was* on American soil. I can give you proof of what they were doing to the illegally detained paranormals incarcerated around the states." Here was one topic she didn't *quite* have the proof of *yet*, but she was close. "I am gathering proof of what they're doing to paranormals *right now* in DoDO facilities here in the states which has led to the deaths of hundreds of paranormals in those facilities, but also to humans in the surrounding areas."

"The congresswoman is out of time," the chief justice said.

"Understood," Jardena said, raising her voice in the microphone. "But I would like to ask about this new development."

He shook his head, then frowned and nodded. "As would I. Would Secretary Whiskey care to embellish?"

Her detective muscle-memory kicked in—her decade-honed skills and training—and she pushed aside her terror. "We're still investigating and people in the chain of command have been informed of this situation. It's still developing. However, not all paranormals have been released as promised. Some are still being held in DoDO facilities around the U.S. There are also many strange cases of people dying for no scientifically explainable reason other than 'severe terror' attacks. Their hearts are stopping. However, my team and I have been investigating it, and we've determined that these individuals—people around these bases—are being attacked by the ghosts of the paranormals being held, tortured, and killed at these facilities. It is our *belief* that the ghosts are trying to get a message out."

"And what do you believe they're trying to say?" Chief Justice Jordan asked.

She honestly didn't know. "No one's been able to understand or receive their message, but I believe they're trying to get people to know they're there and that they're in trouble."

Paige was alternately interrogated by and lectured to over the course of the next hour. Some people used their time to grandstand and flout their ideas and opinions, of which Paige wasn't allowed to really speak because a question hadn't been asked of her.

Until Congressman Weaver got his time. "Secretary Whiskey, I just wanted to discuss this 'strict lockdown' you said had been placed on your town. You were still able to leave, were you not?"

That was a tricky line to travel. "No. The *people of Troutdale* were stopped on the roads and surrounding areas by DoDO agents who redirected them back to town."

"But weren't you able to save this elven city?" He chuckled. "Which, by the way, has no tax record."

"Because it's not located in the U.S." Was he really that

dumb, or was he using ignorance as a weapon? "It's located in another dimension."

He snorted. "That's not possible."

"Neither is magick, according to some, and yet I'm able to practice it, defend the defenseless with it."

"But they're not really defenseless, are they?" Congressman Weaver said with a smug smile. "In your own words, 'they're animals. Wild animals.' And we all know *they're* not defenseless."

"Even a wild animal is defenseless to an atom bomb." But Paige didn't want to tread down the path of the other paranormal types. She didn't want to out those who were better able to hide just yet. It wasn't *safe* for everyone to come out. "They're not indestructible nor are they bullet proof when they live in a society that—"

"They attack people for the sake—" Congressman Weaver said over her.

Paige ignored him and continued. "—imprisons them for defending—"

"—of their own personal—"

"—themselves and their families," Paige finished.

"—interests," Congressman Weaver completed with a victorious look.

This wasn't about what was said or recorded. He was grandstanding for the cameras, and the only thing that would be remembered was *that look* on his face in that moment.

Paige smiled and nodded. "What are people supposed to do when they're not allowed to defend themselves, when *defense* is against the law? When *protecting yourself* is against the law?"

"That's not what we're talking about here. They have teeth—"

"As do you."

He stopped and smiled tightly, letting the smile slide into

a look of disdain. "You attacked a federal prison and freed the inmates there. Was that defense?"

Paige bowed her head, trying to figure out how to phrase this because she had to make it clear that her actions weren't *right* but that they weren't *wrong* and they most definitely shouldn't be replicated. "False imprisonment requires a defense." But not all of them, so this was a dangerous road.

He snorted. "But how do you know?"

"It's my *job* to know."

"It wasn't at the time."

"I am still an officer of the law." And that was…mostly true. She'd given up her badge, but she still helped run Red Star. Barely. "But it is true that we invaded that prison." She pressed her palm over the karma sigil under her palm and hoped she was doing the right thing. "But was it wrong? I knew that if I went through the legal chains, our voices wouldn't be heard because our *voices* had been stripped. Our rights had been stripped. We had no recourse."

He opened his mouth to speak.

Paige wasn't done. "So, when you strip a people of their basic rights, when you make them outlaws by their very existence, you thrust them outside the laws you govern by. You make them *all* criminals. So, when they defend themselves, every action they would take is against the law. So, we would have been wrong no matter what. I did what I needed to do by the only laws that applied to us at that time. Morality. Moral code. That's all we had to defend ourselves with. And it's the one thing that seems to be lacking in yours."

Congressman Weaver pulled his lips back and pressed his front teeth together for a moment, his time running out. "So, you admit to breaking the law."

"I admit not having any to follow as we had been stripped of our citizenship and our lawful rights that had been granted to us by birth."

Congressman Weaver pursed his lips with a snarl. "I yield my time."

Jardena leaned forward. "If I might ask a question?"

Chief Justice Jordan shook his head. "You may but it might be stricken from the record."

She nodded. "Secretary Whiskey, do you think the president stripped you of your *most basic* rights as a citizen?"

Fuck. Paige couldn't blame this one on DoDO. Damn it. She pressed the button to her microphone and leaned in to hammer the nail into the president's coffin. "Yes."

The room erupted into chaos.

23

After her testimony in front of Congress, the only thing Paige really wanted was to crawl back to the hole she'd sprung from and do what she did best: fight demons and angels.

However, reports were still coming in about how paranormals all over the nation were being segregated, fired, refused medical treatment, and various other things. Paige couldn't just go home even if she wanted to. There was too much to do to ensure everyone was okay.

But she *really* wished she had a magick fireball that could fix all of this. Her *magick* was what made Paige special. Not this.

And yet here she was.

The states were still rolling out votes for secession, which surprised Paige a little. She thought that'd been taken off the table with everything she was doing, but...no. That threat was still imminent and she'd been "granted" a meeting with the Secretary of State to discuss how that would be disastrous for *everyone*, having that big a shift in world power.

Yeah. Paige *got* that. She really did. But what the hell was *she* supposed to do about it? She was spending too much time trying to help draft legislation to protect the rights of paranormals and trying to dig up evidence to drown DoDO and…

The list was longer than she was powerful, and that was saying a lot.

The good news was that the magnifying glass was finally on DoDO and there were a lot of people calling into question the validity of their presence on U.S. soil. The claims were that because paranormals had existed outside the boundaries of law, they'd been well within their rights to come and deal with them.

So, Paige was trying to expedite a few "laws" that would protect paranormals across the states. That, of course, wasn't super easy. It required some pretty long nights. She practically slept at the office for the next couple of days, paying scant attention to the impeachment hearings or anything else. She did get reports on that and on the secession votes.

The ghost attacks had dwindled, though, so there was *at least* that. Shining the light on the DoDO installations had managed to curb whatever they'd been doing.

Of course, she'd had to turn over all the evidence in her possession to the intelligence agencies who then took over the investigation. Lovejoy—who preferred being called Lovejoy, thank the goddess—was staying on top of those tasks and enjoying the shit out of her new job. Paige had never seen anyone so happy to be pissed off all the time.

But with all that going on, the media had taken to questioning her testimony at the impeachment hearing, demanding to know if she really cared about the paranormal people or if the president had paid her off somehow.

She'd tried to get a message out to the people using Leroy, her main PR person, but that wasn't enough.

So, she had Aaron help her draft up a speech so she could address the media herself.

He sat at his desk in a sky-blue pencil skirt with a matching jacket. His feet were encased in matching blue pumps and his short, yet wavy brown hair was done up in a rather neat pixie-like cut.

He looked up at her with pain in his brown eyes. "I'm learning my lesson. When will this be over?"

"When you feel you're done." Paige crossed her arms over her chest and perched on the edge of his desk. "Though, I have to ask. You look great. Did you get help?"

"Yes." He rolled his eyes. "My neighbors across the street are drag queens." He opened his mouth to say more, but closed it and tossed his head instead.

"Well, you look great."

"No." He held up a finger. "Yesterday, I came in wearing a skirt and all the guys refused to shut up about my legs."

Paige looked down at them and had no idea why. The man had well-shaped calves.

"I hadn't shaved. Shaved. They shame women for not shaving their legs? Seriously? So, I shaved my legs last night. So, today, I'm being harassed for not wearing mascara."

Cringing, she hid her laugh. "Yeah. You *do* look *really* tired."

"I hate this—seriously. Is this how you're treated?"

"Well, probably not. I mean, you're a man dressing as a woman and you're sticking out like a sore thumb. But…" She couldn't finish as her laugh took over. "Has it opened your eyes at all?"

"Yes!"

"Then, I think you learned a lesson."

"Thank God." Aaron reached down and yanked off a pump. "These things are torture."

"That's why I don't wear them. Also, I can't run in them."

He grunted. "What did you need?"

"I need a speech."

"Oh, good. I was hoping you were thinking that. Here's my first draft." He dug around in his backpack and handed her some sheets of paper.

She took what he offered. "How do you even know—"

"You've got to get in front of this." He massaged his aching foot as she read what he wrote.

The speech was…good.

Giving it wasn't. She still didn't like getting up in front of people and talking, but it was getting easier, as much as she hated to admit that. She went to the press room and went on record to state that in a hearing, she could only provide the evidence she was witness to and that's what she did, and that she intended to not only seek justice for paranormals, but to ensure that they were protected like their mundane neighbors.

She was very careful not to call mundanes human because it was time people started thinking of paranormals as being human as well.

However, by the time she got to the end, she felt better for having given the speech. She was still barraged by questions, some smart, some pointed and stupid. She did her best and then made a hasty retreat.

Leah sat in Paige's office afterward, with the folders in piles, but her shoulders were dejected and slumped.

Paige went up to her and hip bumped her arm. "What's up, Bean?"

"Nothin'. It's just… Dad's… not Dad."

Paige pushed some of the folders aside and sat on the edge of the coffee table. "I hadn't realized you'd gone back."

"Of course I have. He's my dad."

Paige scratched her neck. "I'm going to pretend I didn't hear that you know where he is," she said quietly so only Leah could hear, "because I'll go to jail if they know that I know where he is."

"Oh." Leah let her head fall, her lone braid falling forward. She pulled her head up, rolling it around, her neck popping and cracking.

"That is so gross."

"Mom." Leah pulled a face and then scooted closer. "He —" She growled and tried again. "He won't get out of the garage."

"Well, at least he's working on a car?"

"No." Leah let her gaze dash around the room as she shook her head. "He's just *sitting* in Jackie."

Jackie was Dexx's first love, his 1970 Dodge Challenger. She'd been demolished in one of his cases and he was building her back up. Basically, the car was taking up an entire bay semi-permanently.

"I don't know how to help him." Paige rested her elbows on her knees and brought her hands together. He'd now been home for almost a week, hiding out and healing. She didn't know how much longer she could stall to buy him time to... be ready for the one meeting that would decide not only his fate, but the fates of his team, of his family. She was a little upset with him. She hadn't been given a week to be a new mother, but he could take a week to bolster himself for a meeting? After being tortured for a year? Geezus, she was a terrible person. "I know I need to be there for him. He went through some really tough stuff."

"But he's *Dad*."

Paige didn't quite know what that word meant, but yeah. "He'll pull through."

"Mandy, Ginny, Kate, and I are – and Lilly if she can because Derrick—" Leah rolled her eyes. "Whatever. Anyway, we've got a plan? Maybe?"

"And you've cleared this with Naomi?"

"Yeah." Leah's look said no. "I mean, okay. I'll ask her."

"Oh, dear goddess." Paige held her hands out clawed toward her daughter. "I love you so much."

"Hey, thanks. So, these cases."

Leah then launched into how they were all separated and how she and Willow were coming up with a game plan to get them in front of the people who could actually help. The girl actually had this under control.

Nine days after being awarded the Secretary post, Dawn pulled Paige into the Oval Office to inform her that she had taken the evidence Paige had provided and was taking care of the DoDO installations. There was significant red tape due to "jurisdiction."

That infuriated Paige to no end. "DoDO shouldn't *have* jurisdiction on American soil. They're a foreign policing entity who should have no rights."

"I know," Dawn said, lightly punching the couch arm, a look of I'm-so-fucked on her face. "Your testimony really did a number on my ratings."

Paige didn't give a shit about ratings. "I only told the truth." It was the only thing she *could* do.

Dawn nodded her gaze distant. "I'm going to take care of as much of this as I can before I'm removed from office."

So, she was already admitting defeat. Great.

"Walton isn't going to support you."

Paige didn't miss the fact that Dawn had just called her vice president by his surname.

"You need to understand that. He's not an ally."

"Will I keep the appointment, though?"

Making a tsking sound, Dawn shook her head then winced. "Probably not."

Then, Paige needed to make sure that every second counted. "And the laws we're putting into effect now?"

"Nothing has been passed by Congress. Executive orders aren't laws."

Well, then, Paige just needed to make sure she was careful. But how? Even after taking online classes, she didn't know very much.

Dawn blinked into the silence, pensive, then stood. "I'll send you the name of a few lawyers who should be able to help."

They actually *had* quite a few who were doing a good job. "Thanks."

"And go home," Dawn said when she made it to her desk. "Spend some time with your kids. Be a mom."

Except that every moment she spent with her kids were moments that took away from protecting… everyone, *including* her kids. "'Kay. Keep your head up."

"You too." The president sat down.

Paige left, stepping into Ruben's office.

He didn't look up, didn't grunt at her. He'd been giving her the silent treatment ever since her testimony two days ago.

Which wasn't good since he was a pretty influential person in her constricted circle of power.

She made it back to her office suite and was met by Willow, Leroy, and Aaron who was now wearing a sweat suit.

"Are those your workout clothes?" Paige asked.

Aaron waved her off.

"You have a movie offer," Leroy said with excitement. "And I think you should take it."

That wasn't likely to happen. She liked the idea of good PR, but a movie? That sounded invasive. She turned her attention to Willow. "Let's pack this up and head home for a day or two."

Willow nodded and handed her a cup of coffee.

Leroy's face fell.

Aaron gave him a look that said he'd told him so.

Paige accepted the coffee, even understanding it was in

the afternoon, a time when she *should* be saying no, but she had too much to accomplish and too little time.

"We heard that the extradition negotiations have been scheduled," Willow said carefully. "And a location has been decided on. For Mr. Colt."

Oh, crap. Dexx. *Could* she go home if Dexx was there?

It still irked her a little that he hadn't texted much. He had a new phone, but it was the same number and she doubted he'd forgotten to put her in his contacts. Which meant he was really busy or really depressed.

"That's good," Paige said out loud, then turned to Leroy. "And I'm not ignoring you or saying no outright. It's just a lot to take in."

"I know," he said, his eyes wide with renewed excitement.

She still didn't think it was good idea or that it would even happen. Why would they want to make a movie about her? "Give me the details and I'll look it over."

"Great." He gave Aaron a smug I-told-*you*-so look and broke away from the pack as Paige led the way to her office.

Aaron shook his head. "You may want to revisit your message."

Paige didn't really have the energy to think about "her message." She'd been as clear about it as she could be and it hadn't changed. "Talk to the social media people and Leroy and have *him* come to me with a game plan. Remember, he's PR." She needed everyone staying in their own corners.

Aaron sulked but walked back to his desk in his comfortable sneakers, obviously reveling.

Paige walked into her office with Willow still on her heels. "Where's Leah? I need to know—" Shit. She didn't know if her office was bugged or if she should say anything out loud.

Willow shook her head. "You're safe." She clapped her hands together and wrung them. "Leah's pretty upset. When I said they had a place to put him, I meant not there."

Not at home. Okay. Thank goodness. Paige'd be so happy when all of this was over, and she could just...spend time with him. They really needed to get married. For reals. "'Kay. Give everyone their orders for a few days and let's go home."

"Phoebe is letting us borrow a couple of door witches. We have a protocol for requesting transport. Honestly? Things are starting to feel... normal again."

That was nice. "And you? Are you feeling better about your job?"

Willow gave her an are-you-kidding-me laugh and shut it off with strict sobriety. "No."

Paige chuckled. "Me either."

She was just tying up loose ends and getting ready to head back to the house when Derrick walked through the door. "Where's Leah?"

"School." Derrick smiled, his eyes a little dull. "She had a lot of fun with Naomi and the kids. Lilly did, too. So, that was nice."

"Lilly was here?" Wow. How much was going on in the world—*her* world—when she didn't even notice that? Or that her own daughter had gone home.

"You were busy."

"Do you know if their 'mission' was successful?"

Clicking his tongue, Derrick gave her an exasperated look. "Well, if you mean did they get him out of the car? Yes."

She gave him a look that said she wanted more information.

He raised his chin and ignored her. "Are you ready?"

Paige read that he was unhappy about something, but she really had a *lot* on her plate. She didn't *want* to volunteer to take more. However, as she walked by her brother, she asked, "What's wrong?"

He flattened his lips and shook his head. "Not a thing, sis."

Oookay. So, it was definitely something. "Well, if you aren't going to spill, I'm not going to pry."

His lips flatlined, then he turned away and opened a door.

Willow and a couple of others opted to go with her, grabbing their backpacks and joining them.

"We don't have rooms," Paige said quietly as she leaned toward Willow's ears.

Willow winced and tipped her head to the side. "We don't? Hmm."

Paige wasn't sure what exactly *that* was all about, but she led the way through the door her brother opened and stepped onto the Whiskey driveway.

Only to discover some new construction taking place at the end of the driveway.

Everyone with her shuffled in that direction.

Willow smiled apologetically. "I cleared it with Leslie first."

"Oh, good." Because Paige would be getting an earful if she hadn't. She turned and headed for the house.

Leslie was in the living room and was pulling herself off the couch, setting the TV remote down. "We need to talk."

Oh, fuck. "Hey, Les. Nice to see you, too."

"Your new world is *invading* our safe space."

Wait. Hadn't Willow *cleared* it through Leslie? "They asked."

"What was I supposed to do? Say no?"

Paige dumped her bags by the china cabinet on her way to the kitchen. "If it was a problem, yes." She was going to need wine for this.

"Well, I didn't think I could."

Okay. Paige would task Willow about finding somewhere else to house her… small army of assistants.

Leslie slammed herself into a kitchen chair. "When did our lives become this game of politics?"

Paige wasn't aware that Leslie's was. She grabbed a cup and brewed some coffee instead. It was going to be a long day. Like all of them had been lately.

"Paige."

She turned with a sigh.

Leslie got up and walked to her, taking her hands and searching her eyes. "This isn't you. This isn't us."

Oh, Paige knew. She understood that. "I can't back out. I can't stand down."

"This isn't your fight."

"It isn't *anyone's* fight because it's *all of our* fight."

"But…" Leslie licked her lips then growled, looking away, frustration and anger flaring over her face as she paced. "I can't join you. I can't *help* you. There aren't any spells for this. No magick for this."

"I know," Paige whispered and sat against the kitchen sink, water soaking into the seat of her pants. Leslie had just hammered in her frustration with her statement. "I know."

"If this was an enemy we could fight?" Leslie threw her arms out to either side. "I could help rally the troops. We could work with our wards."

Wards. "Remind me to talk to Billie again."

Leslie nodded. "But even that, reminding you of things, you've got people to help with that. So, what do I do?"

Paige closed her eyes. For the past…nine days—longer than that. She'd been Secretary for nine days. For over two weeks, she'd been running from one fire to the next, talking to person after person who were all smarter than her, coordinating things she barely understood.

And she hadn't *used* magick once. Well, she'd applied that karma sigil in a few places around D.C. and she hoped like hell *that* didn't backfire on her. But other than that, the *Paige Whiskey* super power hadn't been applied at all.

Your superpower, Cawli said with a soft growl, *has never been your power.*

Liar, Paige said inside her head. *You're the one who reminded me just how long it'd taken to craft my line. So, don't feed me that line of bullshit.*

He sighed. *That's* not *why I chose you.*

Paige met her sister's gaze, just green, no Robin-orange. "Our world is changing." That was the reality of it.

And it was… a *hard* reality.

Yeah, okay, so she'd been *living* this reality. They all had, but when they were so busy dealing with the day-to-day, it was easy to overlook just how far they'd traveled from "normal." The days of hiding who and what they were were gone. Erased. They'd *never* be able to go back to that. They had freedoms now.

Kind of. Freedoms that had cost them a lot.

"What you said in the hearing…" Leslie leaned against the kitchen counter and folded her arms over her chest. "I hate this. I hate all this."

Paige did too.

"We lost—" Leslie's face folded in consternation. "We haven't. Have we? Lost our rights?"

Technically speaking? Yes. That was why Paige was scrambling so damned hard to get law *into* effect to not only boot DoDO from their world, but to also give paranormals some legs to stand on. "A lot's going to change." If she could keep her job long enough to bring that change.

Leslie was still a long moment, then she released a short puff of breath, looking away. "When will we be able to just go back to being witches?"

Well, Leslie would be able to soon.

But Paige?

She'd gotten a taste of what it felt like to make real difference, to offer real change for a voiceless people, and…

She didn't know if she could just let that go. "I don't know."

"You're not a politician, Pea," Leslie said quiet. "You're a witch. You're a shifter. And you're a mother, and a sister, and a…" She jutted her chin out, turning her face to the back door for a moment. She turned back around, her emotions under control. "I was never asked if I wanted to be a part of this. I…Yeah, you said the only reason *you* were able to take this on was because you had me. Well, you never asked *me* if I *wanted* to *be* that rock for you."

It was time to get Leslie off her pity-horse. "No one asked me either." She pushed off the counter and faced her sister, pulling on her alpha will a little to remind Leslie what a warrior she was. "But people just kept dying. And those we care about just kept falling. And people around us just kept *losing*. So, if you're trying to tell me that you're the type of person who can stand by while all that goes on because *politics isn't your game,* then let me know now. Right now."

Leslie ground her jaw and her fiery gaze latched onto Paige's.

"That's what I thought. Stop *whining* and help me *fight* this. Not just for us, this time, Les. Not just the Whiskeys, or the Blackma—Troutdale. Not just *us."* Paige swallowed hard. "We're fighting for *everyone* now."

Releasing a strangled breath, Leslie growled low. "And if we're not big enough for it?"

Paige shook her head. "Then we ignite a fire in everyone we touch so we're not fighting alone. *That* is the power of politics."

They were silent for a long moment.

Then, Leslie shook out her fingers and relaxed. "If you think that's the power of politics, you've been investing your time in the wrong places, Pea. Because…" She shook her head. "You should be getting paid *bank."*

"Oh." Paige beamed a grin, shaking her head in disbelief. "I am."

Leslie frowned hard as she slapped Paige in the shoulder. "Then, I need a pay raise."

That brought on a whole new onslaught of thoughts. That was a *really big* pay increase for Paige. One she didn't need.

But there was a slew of people who did. So… what exactly was she going to do with that?

Hmm. Neat question, but a battle for a different day. For now, she just needed to be reminded what it felt like to be human.

2 4

Paige spent the next day with the kids at home. She called up Wendy and asked what she needed to do at the school since she hadn't taken a turn in a while.

"It might be good to teach the kids a little bit about Civics," the Troutdale superintendent said. "Especially since you're in government now."

Paige had really been hoping to teach something along the lines of magick or shifting or... "Sure." She just had to make sure that whatever she came up with *for* the class was right because Paige *knew* she wasn't obeying all the laws and rules of government. Her very existence was breaking more than a few of the standards of structure.

The classes went kinda well. Paige left her first class feeling smart, and by the end of the day, the kids were outsmarting her. So, she wasn't entirely positive it'd been an overall good experience for everyone.

Dawn sent another text message update on DoDO to include the fact that Dexx's location had been "confirmed" and that he was safe and unharmed.

So, that was one worry off of Paige's plate. Kinda.

But as soon as she got out of her last class of the day and stepped onto the sidewalk leading into downtown Troutdale, she was hit with another piece of news.

Video evidence had been released to the public of what she'd done in the final moments of the Lawrence battle, calling up fire from the Earth and setting the DoDO leader ablaze.

Yeah. That... hadn't been great and wasn't being super well received. She had a new name now as the #FireKiller. That wasn't really accurate, and Paige wasn't certain how well that was going to hurt her. But she'd ended the battle in Lawrence a little...decisively. Paige'd been afraid of that going public with good reason, and having it go out now wasn't great. But that also meant that DoDO was starting to feel the heat. So, that was *good*.

Lovejoy texted and said she wanted to meet up. Paige wanted a coffee, so they made a date to meet at the coffee shop two shops down from Leslie's soap shop. "One of your coma patients has awakened," she said as they stood, waiting for their drinks.

The small shop was a little busy and probably not the best place for this conversation, but everyone knew about the coma patients. It wasn't top secret information. "Is she—he—"

"He," Lovejoy said as she grabbed her drink with a smile.

"Okay?" Paige's drink was also set on the counter and she retrieved it, then led the way outside to the patio. "Cognitive abilities? Impaired? Functioning? Damage?"

"He's fine." Lovejoy found a table with an umbrella. "Scout's interviewing him for information. He remembered a few things from his possession, so this is good."

"The kinds of things we can use?" Paige moved her chair so the bright afternoon sun was blocked and sat.

Lovejoy nodded. "I'm compiling the information in a

report and will have it on your desk later today. Or tomorrow."

"It's time sensitive." Paige smiled at a woman pushing a stroller... with a dog in it. Was Troutdale getting weirder? Or had this always been normal?

"And he just woke up from a coma."

Right. The world was on fire, but the man had *literally* just awakened. "Thanks. How's Scout doing?"

The street bustled with pedestrian activity. The people she saw seemed happy, content. They were going about their normal day-to-day as if the world *wasn't* on fire.

Well, maybe Paige was doing something good. Wouldn't that be neat?

"Remarkably well." Lovejoy snorted and frowned at something she saw across the street, but then shook her head looked away. "When you told me about your new team, I'd been really skeptical but..." She quirked her lips down and shrugged.

Paige was glad, but her mind raced about the video which could have serious repercussions. She had to get on top of the "narrative." She couldn't put the "genie back in the bottle" as it were, but she could make sure people understood the reality of that moment. Had it been overkill? Part of Paige said yes. Part of her said no. DoDO had invaded an American city, had been killing people, and she'd needed to stop it.

But had she really needed to do it by setting their leader on fire as her small and outnumbered team had retreated?

That hadn't been her *intent* at the time, but that had been the *second* time she'd had a disastrous encounter with the man. She wasn't entirely certain she'd been wrong. He'd killed innocents.

"You did good," Lovejoy said not realizing Paige wasn't even following their conversation fully.

Paige looked over at Lovejoy, pulling her head out of her side-tracking worry. "There's something I need you to spearhead."

"What? Red Star? Dexx'll be—" Lovejoy stopped herself, her expression pained. "I'm not taking over leadership of Red Star."

Yeah. Dexx was in a world of trouble Paige *still* struggled to really *grasp*. This wasn't something he could just swagger away from with a Dexx-smile and a charismatic wink. He might *never* be back. And the team might not either. That was a reality Paige didn't want to face.

"No," Paige said, pushing all the chaotic emotions and thoughts that rode that fear-road aside. "I mean teams *like* Red Star. We need them everywhere. In all the major cities, with smaller ones in the smaller communities. We need a Red Star for the nation."

Lovejoy nodded, pushing her drink with a ghost of a smile. "Oh. Well, I've been giving that some thought, too. I've got some ideas."

Thank goodness. "Draft them into a plan and let's get it started."

Leroy came barreling down the street, breathless. "There you are. Oh." He ran his hand over his dark hair and waved awkwardly at the barista who was cleaning the tables. "Hey, Tilly."

The woman blushed and waved back but didn't say anything.

Aw. How pukingly cute. "Leroy," Paige said, grabbing his attention back. "Tell me you have a plan to use social media to fix all this."

He rubbed his eyes then nodded with a slight smile. "Kinda—no. An interview."

Another one? Well, the first one hadn't gone terribly.

"Your house," he finished triumphantly.

Bad idea. "No."

"Hear me out." He raised his hands. "Invite people in. Let them see you're not this raging monster they're making you out to be."

"They're making me out to be a monster?" She *knew* they were and didn't know why she'd even asked the question out loud.

"You set a guy on fire."

The weight of that moment wasn't something she could *make light* of. "Inviting them into my home isn't going to make me seem less like a monster, Leroy. Just about every serial killer out there had a 'normal' home life."

"Not all of them," Lovejoy said, shaking her head with a pained wince. "Not... not most of them, actually."

Paige willed the woman to stop. "We need to clear this with the..." Family? Coven? Pack? What did she even call it? "Fam." Sure. Because that *could be* a pack and a coven and... extended people.

"Yes." Though the look on Leroy's face said it hadn't been easy.

"So, you already talked to Leslie?"

"Yeah." His tone was pained as if she'd beat him.

Well, she might have, though with her sharp tongue.

"And I've got people set and ready...now."

What? "Now?"

He nodded eagerly. "Well, I mean, they're setting up *right now* right now. But, yeah. Right now. We've *got* to get your narrative out there and it can't wait."

She wanted to reach out and throttle him a little. Paige looked down at her coffee. There were many things she could take with her into a shift, but a cup of coffee wasn't one of them. "I need a ride."

"Sweet!" Leroy clapped his hands and leapt forward, and then nearly ran right into a woman.

"Gods bless! Leroy!"

"Sorry," he mumbled, but he was focused on his sky-blue hatchback, cleaning a bunch of trash out of the front seat and throwing it into the back.

"Should I ask how you have a car here?" He'd literally been living in Washington D.C. just two days before.

He looked up from the passenger seat, leaning over the driver's seat. "Figured we'd be spending a lot of time here and I can't shift and fly around like you. So… this seemed like a good idea."

It was. "And you bought it this messy?"

He didn't answer, but went to work continuing to shove trash into the back.

Lovejoy stopped beside the car and gave Paige a good-luck look. "I'll get the plan together, and that report."

"Great. The work we do now, the paths we pave, will be important in the future."

"Yeah," Lovejoy agreed. "But just remember that what we do now might actually be effected by what we've done in the past."

Like setting enemy combatants on fire in the middle of a magick fight. "Yup." That could really backfire in her face.

Leroy was a ball of chatter on the drive to the Whiskey house. He was just as nervous as she was, which wasn't helping at all.

When she arrived, her kids were standing around like they had no idea what to do with their hands. Kate was looking like a trapped animal, her elf ears on proud display. Mandy descended the stairs with fabulous hair and winning lipstick, which—Paige was a little on the fence about that. She didn't think girls needed to be wearing make-up, but her background relationship with lipstick—and particularly mascara and how it could literally change a conversation— was different than others.

Leslie was in the kitchen sulk-baking.

The make-up artist grabbed Paige almost as soon as she stepped through the door and started "fixing" her face. There was nothing *wrong* with Paige's face. But she was "starting to show her age," according to this artist, and needed to take better care of herself. Cameras added ten years to a woman's face and that could take "points" away from her.

Paige wasn't going to call *this* woman for anything after this.

Leroy introduced her to the interviewer, Harry. He seemed like a nice enough guy. He was local and was excited to be making a name for himself, but he was nervous about taking on a story this big. "It might be bigger than me."

Chuckling, Paige had to agree. "Welcome to my world."

There were a few different cameras. Leroy's plan was to have a few crews around the grounds, videoing different things. Paige thought that was a great idea. Except, "Make sure we don't get naked shifters on camera," she mumbled to Leslie.

Her green eyes went wide and she scuttled out the back door.

Finally, everyone was settled. The lighting had been "opted" in the living room with the rather kinda clean dining room as the backdrop. Paige had really gotten a view of how "not as perfectly clean as it could be" they lived. But there was a small army of mess makers who weren't great at cleaning up after themselves.

They started the interview and got through the pleasantries as quickly as possible.

"So, let's talk about the elephant in the room," Harry started, crossing his leg toward her as he clenched his hands nervously.

Paige tried to project calm so he would. "The video."

He nodded. "The video. Why do you think it was released now?"

That seemed obvious. "I struck hard. DoDO's fighting back."

"You think it was Do—" He laughed. "Okay. Is it weird to call them DoDO? It sounds weird."

Paige shrugged, shaking her head wryly. "At first, we made a lot of jokes about it. But now… Well, the things they're doing are horrific enough that it isn't funny anymore."

"Right, what makes you think DoDO—" He put extra emphasis on that word. "—is the one who released the video?"

"Because they were the only other ones *with* it. And if you look, that was a body cam." Paige raised her eyebrows. "They were the only people *I* saw in uniform there. So, the only one with a body camera."

"That's interesting. So, they're like a paranormal law enforcement unit."

"Not really." Paige needed to make sure that was clear. "*Red Star* is a paranormal law enforcement unit attached to the sheriff's department. We answer to the county and to our state. DoDO doesn't enforce the laws of our country. They answer to no one. There are no trials. They're a foreign military unit. They come in. They combat. They take prisoners. But there are no rules with them."

"So, you think your testimony at the hearing hurt them."

"I do." Paige had to hope anyway. "The ghost attacks have decreased since then. We've even had someone wake up."

"Wake up? I thought—a victim?"

"Oh, yeah. Um, right. Well, the people who were attacked here by the ghosts were sent into a coma."

"You don't think that was information people needed to know?" Harry asked, uncrossing his legs. "You said people were being *killed* by these ghosts and now you're saying a few lived?"

Right because *both* answers *couldn't* be right. "When I was testifying, I was under a time limit. I got the most important information out as quickly as I could. At least, I tried. But yes. Some lived. We *think* the reason the ghosts didn't *kill* humans here is because of our wards."

She explained what a ward was and what they did without giving important information away like how they worked.

"So, yes. I'm glad DoDO is feeling the pressure, and if the worst thing they can do is show a video where I successfully stood up to them and defended American people against them, then I think I'm okay."

"But they're saying you're a monster," Harry said.

"They were saying that before." And a *few* people had been on social media and news outlets. "I'm a witch and in a lot of circles, that's still a bad word."

"You're not concerned?"

"Oh. I am." Paige sank back into her couch, trying not to get too comfortable.

A kid shot down the hallway. "Hey, Mrs. W!"

Paige shook her head. Now? "Flush the toilet this time," she called. The last *three* times, that kid *hadn't* flushed. She didn't know who he was or who he belonged to, but she'd appreciate a little toilet decency.

"Okay!" The boy stomped up the stairs.

They really needed a downstairs toilet. She turned her attention back to Harry. "I hadn't really fully grasped what war was before this. How ugly it can get. How horrible it can become. And I didn't know how far I could go."

"Well," Harry said, pulling the tendons in his neck up in an exaggerated grimace, "I'd say pretty far."

"Yeah." Paige tried to recall the level of horror that had led to that moment, but so many things were blurring together, one horror stacked on top of another. "They'd cut that city off from the outside world digitally. The people inside—paranormals and mundanes alike—couldn't get messages in or out."

"But they got a message to you."

"Not digitally." She'd leave it that. She wasn't going to tell the world about her dryad communications network. "And everything I tried to stop this guy both in the elven city and in Kansas…" She shook her head. "Nothing worked. The magick he threw at me should have killed me instantly. Instead, I… sent it back."

"So, it was like instant karma."

"Kinda. I guess. There are reasons we don't see videos of what happens in combat. Why those things don't make it to the news."

Harry nodded, thinking. "It's weird that the war is here."

That's what Paige had thought too until her eyes had been ripped open. "But is it *really* that weird? I mean, here, yes. But in other areas of this same nation there *are* battles on the streets as the voiceless fight to be heard. This isn't new. I just make it seem bigger because I use magick. But in a year or two, when magick is an everyday word, it won't seem that big."

"So, you think there'll be more of *this?*" He motioned generically with his hand.

"Setting a person on fire in combat in order to save thousands of lives? No. But seeing magick performed regularly? Maybe." But that did make her question things. What if this newfound freedom *did* lead to things she couldn't control or foresee?

What if this kind of battle *did* become commonplace?

"People are going to get sick of war eventually." Paige had to believe it. "And when they do, we'll find our peace."

Harry nodded. "Did you want to take me on a tour of your place?"

Not really, but she got up to show him around.

But the questions he'd asked and the thoughts they'd provoked had her questioning the direction she and the other paranormal leaders and government mundanes who were helping her were taking.

Not their intent.

But their direction.

Were they doing the right thing? She had to hope so because she didn't want to live in a world where fighting to save thousands of innocent lives was a bad thing.

Paige agreed to let the interview-slash-expose whatever move to the backyard. Harry said backyard interviews played well with viewers.

Half the town had to be out there. Not for anything horrible. There wasn't any rioting. It was just another Whiskey potluck. Paige saw a lot of familiar faces, people who had been over at potlucks before a few times.

One guy showed up with a big red cooler and opened the lid to a chorus of excitement from a few of the guys there.

Was that a beer cooler? She wasn't certain getting drunk on an interview was a great idea.

But the guy reached in and brought out a package of hotdogs.

Meat Mike. She'd heard about how he always somehow made sure there were things to barbeque. He was a hunter who socialized with other hunters. There weren't always hotdogs, though. It was usually venison or moose or something else he'd hunted. He'd brought bear one time and that hadn't been appreciated, so he'd stopped bringing that.

"Is this normal?" Harry asked.

Paige had a battery pack microphone, so she didn't really have to worry about what was said or at what volume. "Yeah. After Sven invaded—the demon that started all of this?"

Harry nodded.

"The town just started gathering here. I was worried. We couldn't hide who we were anymore. People, when they're afraid, are brutal. We've seen that throughout history, no matter how it's rewritten. And there were a few people scared."

Wendy looked over at them and waved, a glass of water in her hand as she talked to a couple of other parents.

She waved back as the woman headed their way. Paige wanted to hear how well her Civics class had gone over with the kids because she was a little worried that her last class had schooled *her* instead of the other way around. "I don't know. It started off as potlucks because we didn't have enough food for everyone to make their own. And it just... stuck. I didn't realize we'd be having one tonight though. It doesn't happen *all* the time. I also have no idea how people decide it's potluck slash barbeque night. I just go to find the kids and am sometimes surprised that there's food."

"Well, this certainly feels great."

"I can't..." She shook her head as pride swelled in her. It wasn't that she felt she could take ownership of what all these people had chosen to do by coming together. It was more the fact that she was just happy to be a part of it. "They proved to me that people *can* be amazing and that they're worth fighting for. Not just paranormals. Everyone."

"Is that *really* an obstacle course?" Harry asked, pointing to the walls and rope bridges and... the actual, honest to goodness obstacle course.

"Yeah."

Harry's eyes nearly bugged out of his head with excitement. "Can anyone go on it?"

"Yeah. Absolutely. Just try not to break yourself." Paige disengaged from Harry and joined Wendy. "Hey, so any word on Civics classes?"

Wendy laughed, the cloud-filtered sunlight laying a fine sheen on her darker skin, adding a kind of shimmer to her. "You did well. You wouldn't believe how excited they are to know you."

"It's really exciting to know me, too." Paige rolled her eyes and shook her head with a chuckle. "It's… otherworldly and weird and…" She frowned, guiding Wendy toward the obstacle course. "I don't think it's really sank in yet."

"I can only imagine."

"Hey, so…" Paige had so many thought-threads she was following that she hadn't even had a chance to write down yet. "Okay, so you know how we integrated here? Our schools? Paranormals and non-magickals? We need a better name for that."

"Yeah. And yeah." Wendy tossed her head to the side in a little *but-what?* kind of dance.

Mundanes was a word, but was that copyrighted? Trademarked? Could they even use it? "I need someone who can spearhead that on a national level."

Wendy gave Paige a deadpan look. "You're not asking me to do that, are you?"

"Why wouldn't I?" Paige stopped Wendy and turned to face her more directly. "Think about it. The nation needs someone who already knows *some* of the pitfalls, *some* of the obstacles they're going to face. I mean, look at what you've already accomplished. You've done a lot here."

"But I had help."

Paige took in a deep breath and held it, her mind running the hamster wheel. "I could hire you on as a liaison to education or something. I'm making everything up as I go, so I don't even know if that's a thing, but I know we need it."

Wendy frowned, glancing at the cameras before ignoring them again. "But I'm not paranormal."

"I didn't realize that was a prerequisite." Paige didn't know if they *needed* paranormals to run all things paranormal. Wendy had— "You've proven that you're capable of meeting the needs of people you don't fully understand. *That* means more, I think. I could *find* someone who's paranormal to fill the position. Maybe. But would they have *your* track record? No."

"I've only had a few months experience at this."

"And those months are more than anyone else has." Probably. "Look, Wendy, you..." How could Paige get this across to the woman in a way that made her feel capable of taking on the task? "You have a gift that isn't magick. When you're given a problem, you don't just quit. You face it. And when you fail, you don't just give up. You get up and look at it from a different perspective. And if that fails, you find someone with the perspective you need. You have the temerity to find the right answers and that *is* magickal."

Wendy's deadpan expression went flat then resigned. "I hate you."

Paige grinned. "I've gotta figure out what I need to do to even make this 'great idea' something tangible, so you have time to think about it, you could draft up some of your potential needs?"

"It's—this is huge, Paige."

Oh, if she only knew. "Welcome to my world." She turned and continued to the obstacle course, looking for Leslie. "We'll forge a good path for everyone. I feel confident."

"I'm glad someone does." Wendy ambled away.

Harry jogged to catch up. "Is that normal?"

"I feel like you're just going to keep asking me that every time something new pops up. Yes, Harry." Paige spotted her sister by the rope wall with Kamden. "This is all normal."

On her way to Leslie, Paige was stopped by several people who asked how things were going. Paige stepped outside of her own worries and focused on where their questions were coming from. This was her time to connect with…

…the people she now served. Though, technically, she served the president. She hadn't been voted in. She wasn't serving the people.

But…she really was.

They asked about supplies and school closures, job opportunity openings, travel restrictions. One lady wanted to go see her son and his wife before their baby was born but still lacked the clearance to leave Troutdale.

Doctor appointments. Visiting grandparents in nursing homes outside Troutdale. Playdates. Clubs and recreation. There was a kid who wanted to get back to Portland because she was learning to play the bagpipe and her band was there.

Veterans who needed to see their doctors or get medicines or visit support groups. Adults going through vocational school so they could get better jobs. People who needed to apply for food stamps if that was even a thing because there was no money flowing in, and thankfully the Whiskeys threw these potlucks, but they didn't do this every night.

So. Many. Things. To. Do.

The owner of one of the grocery stores stopped her to discuss the next supply run. He needed groceries, but he was really looking for fresh produce.

Eventually, he turned the conversation in a different direction. "Why aren't you going after the president anymore?"

"Going after her where?" Paige asked. She knew the answer to the question, but she needed to understand why he was concerned. And she needed it to be obvious to the public watching the interview.

"Your testimony. You really focused it on this secret organization. Is that even real? Or are they like the Illuminati?"

Paige snorted. "I think *they* think they're like that. But no. They're just another organization. And..." She licked her lips and took in a deep breath, remembering she *was* being recorded. That was...soooooooooo weird. Paige nodded gravely. "I had a very frank conversation with President Flynn about the reality of the situation and the gravity of her actions and she showed me she truly gave a shit. She became a human being."

"But after she killed so many of your kind?"

Yeah. There was still that. "I know. I don't know if she's salvageable. I don't know if she's..." What were the right words here? "If she can come back from that. I don't. But I do know that DoDO is evil and they're our real enemy. Was she played? I don't know. Are they making the situation worse? Yeah. Should she get off?" Paige didn't think so. "I just need to be able to do my job to make our nation strong together, and she's on board with making that happen."

The man turned the conversation away and they talked briefly about his son who was in college and how classes were starting back up again for mundanes.

She hadn't realized they'd been stopped.

She needed time with her kids, so she ditched the microphone, excused herself from Harry, and went to spend some quality time with them.

Which was a little weird with all the cameras still following everyone around. One camera crew had taken a particular interest in the twins and Rai was doing her best to ditch them.

Ember didn't seem to mind as much, so he led the crew around the obstacle course and challenged them to use it.

"I hate this. What if I..." Rai didn't finish that sentence.

"You'll be fine, Rai-Rai," Paige said, cupping her daughter's cheek and giving her the same pet name Leah'd given the girl. It fit. For now. "You're learning, changing, growing, adapting." She pressed a kiss to the girl's head. "Just don't kill me without Bobby around."

Rai snorted and rolled her eyes.

"Hey, Rai," Tyler shouted, his voice just at that point where things didn't explode but loud enough so he could be heard. "Red flag, blue flag. You game?"

Rai gave Paige one last glare, then spun, shifting into a bird and launching herself to her cousin.

Red flag, blue flag was like capture-the-flag? Kinda. But the kids had added a few more rules as more people joined and they'd discovered limitations were needed. When it'd just been the Whiskey kids, it'd been one thing. But with mundanes—and there were quite a few of them—it was completely another.

Paige was one of the many referees out on the course. The participants involved shifters, one of the dryad kids Paige didn't know, Lilly, Kate, and a bunch of humans. They all had to step in from time to time to help get kids out of the rigging or off of high places. It wasn't *safe*. Like—it *was*. The course had thick sand to lessen the impact of a fall. However, the obstacles weren't "playground" material. She was just *waiting* to hear about that.

Eventually, the red flag was captured and the blue team lost. But the kids were starting to make up some new game, each of them throwing out new rules and getting upset.

So, Paige found a ball and threw it into the mix, more to see what they'd do with it.

One of the kids—Ashley, Leah's best friend who was also a horse shifter—picked it up, holding it over her head victoriously, then shouted something to the other kids. They quickly gathered around, shouted a few rules that actually made sense, then took off on a new game.

One that seemed a bit less dangerous.

Paige's stomach reminded her she still hadn't eaten, so

she wandered off in the direction of the good-smelling smoke. She found Leslie at one of the grills, a cast iron casserole dish on the fire. "What are you making?"

"Roasted potatoes." Leslie chucked her chin toward the big grill. "They've got burgers and hotdogs."

Paige's stomach rumbled painfully.

"Is this our new normal?" Leslie asked, frustrated. "Every time you do something questionable, we get invaded with reporters? Or you have to go on TV and have another interview?"

Paige had no idea. "I hope not. Look, I'm sorry." And she was. She'd known this job would be hard. But... "I didn't realize the real impact this would have on everyone."

"Yeah, well, I don't think we did either." Leslie moved a big bucket of potatoes closer between the two of them. "Start peeling."

No matter what, Paige knew that she could be brought back down to Earth by her big sister. She grabbed a peeler and went to work.

Those who were staying for dinner helped. They either got tables out, or brought out chairs they had in their vehicles, or...food appeared out of nowhere. It wasn't really nowhere. It obviously had to come from somewhere.

Plates were put out—reusable, not paper. They needed supplies to be able to throw things away or burn.

By the time dinner was about to be served—well, the kids were already making their way through the line—Harry came over with a grin on his face and his laptop. "We're still recording, but I thought you might like to see what we're editing."

"That fast?" Paige was more than a little shocked.

He shrugged, embarrassed. "We're small. It's basically just my sister and I and, well, a few friends." He gestured to the camera crew still milling around. "We, you know, we have big dreams."

"Good."

Harry found an empty spot at one of the tables and sat down, offering the laptop to her. "Tell me what you think."

Paige sat down and watched what had been spliced together and edited. It was… good. And it very well might be what she needed to change the story. She looked up at Harry. "Do you think it's enough?" she asked quietly.

Harry's expression pinched as he shrugged deeply. "I know *you* wanted something specific, but *I* just wanted to get the truth out there. And I think I got that."

Well, if he was really going to run with what he'd shown her—which, he didn't *have* to show her anything. She wasn't *paying* for this story—then she could go to bed feeling a little relieved. "This war sucks."

Harry nodded, his lips pushed out with a breath that he released like a popped balloon. "Yeah. It really does."

Paige gestured to the food. "Make sure all your people get something to eat."

He shook his head. "I know you want me to stop asking, but…is this *normal?*"

Her chuckle turned into a laugh as she realized it was. "Yeah."

"Well, I guess I could hope *this* becomes a thing. Feels like a long time ago when I was a kid."

"Same." But it was time to search for her kids and make sure they were all feeding themselves.

After doing a head check—to include her nieces and nephews—she discovered they all were huddled together with several other kids, eating and talking loudly to one another. As she drew closer, she caught phrases that intrigued her.

She found Leah and sank onto the grass beside her. "What's going on?"

"A revolution," Leah said with excitement. She turned to her mom. "A thought revolution."

Uh. "Okay?"

"I want—a few of us want to talk to other communities and talk to the people our age."

Paige wasn't sure about the logistics. "And do what?"

"We're the next generation, Mom. Think about it. This is what *your* generation is doing. You're reshaping the world the generation before you handed over. We want to do that *before* it gets this far. We want to change things before it gets to war."

In theory, there shouldn't be need of another war. "How exactly are you going to do that?"

Leah beamed a grin, then moved aside so Paige could squeeze into the circle with them as they brainstormed wild ideas of meaningful change.

It was…intoxicating. Their ideas weren't all going to work, but the fervor with which they expressed them was refreshing. And by the time they were all called to do dishes, Paige had more than a few workable ideas of her own. She went and grabbed three burgers and a hotdog because she still hadn't eaten yet and chowed down, her mind racing with excitement.

Willow came up to her, her expression grim.

Oh no. Paige bottled her excitement and put a cap on it so it wouldn't escape, putting it aside for later. "What happened?"

Sitting, Willow leaned her head back, her shoulders slouched forward. "She was impeached."

"What?" Paige already understood what Willow had *said*. She just didn't *understand* what would come after.

Willow nodded and trailed the tip of her tongue along her bottom lip before letting her head fall forward.

Did Paige still have a job? She needed to refresh herself on the procedures of impeachment, but…

She also needed to remember that this wasn't about Paige *keeping* her job. The *people* who had been *murdered* under President Flynn's orders needed justice.

But Paige'd have a hard time providing structure to a nation of people if she couldn't *keep* her job. She had to hope those karma spells were helping.

The news was a double-edged sword. She rubbed her eyes and kept her cool fingers on her cheeks. "Okay."

"It's what you wanted."

"Yeah. It was." But that was before she'd started making real change in a world that needed it. Now, she wanted more. Paige raked her finger along her bottom lip.

The president's impeachment could put her in a real sticky situation if she didn't watch herself.

Now that the impeachment trial was over, Paige had a whole new list of things to do, one that she could have been doing a better job of drawing up beforehand. She *had been* mentally preparing herself, so she wasn't going to kick herself too hard. She was learning and not slowly. She just had a *lot* to learn in a short amount of time.

Paige had headed over to her Whiskey office building early the next morning after checking on all of her kids and telling their sleepy bodies where she'd be.

The offices were a work in progress and construction was still going on all around them. She was lucky to have an office with mostly finished walls? Her desk had started out as a white folding table and was replaced by a big wooden desk that had been "picked up from Marketplace," whatever that was. It was so newly old, it still had stuff in the drawers from the previous owners.

By mid-morning, Paige's windows were sealed—though still no blinds which was going to be an issue if she wanted to keep her eyes and still work on her computer—and rough drywall was up on all of her walls, though the ceiling was still open.

Willow's office was right next to hers and wasn't nearly as far along. She still had framed walls, and no window, and Willow's desk was still a folding table and chair.

But Paige wasn't going to complain. This was still better than trying to do this at the dining room table or in the cramped office space downtown.

Though, they could take this to D.C. They had an entire office suite there.

But Paige wanted to stay home for a bit, be closer to her kids. And the Blackman witches seemed to feel better about staying in *this* office suite rather than the one in D.C. It was probably because Derrick and Leah were still the only two fully cleared to be there.

Paige knocked on the two by four doorframe of Willow's office. "Hey, it's time to call Ishamil. Get him in here."

Willow didn't even look up from her computer screen. "He asked for two weeks to tide things over with Jardena."

"I know." And Paige felt a little bad. She did. "We don't have that kind of time."

Willow put her hand on her cell phone. "I'll see what I can do."

"Thanks."

Paige walked down the hallway and into the "common" area. It was crowded with construction workers and ladders and power tools and people talking.

Her people were ensconced in hastily put-together offices. She quickly touched base with all of them, still not remembering all of their names. She wasn't certain it was good idea to *learn* their names if she wasn't going to be able to *keep* them.

Ismail showed up three hours later, carrying a backpack and looking intrigued. His dark beard was neatly trimmed and his dark hair was folded over nicely. He seemed to be going for a more casual look in his jeans and boots, but they looked brand new.

She walked out to greet him as Bonnie Blackman closed the magick door and headed to the newly arrived couch. "I'm glad you could make it on such short notice."

He tipped his head and walked beside her as they headed toward hallway leading to their offices. It was more than that. There were small apartments upstairs with offices and conference rooms below. They were smaller, but it was a little nicer than the suite they had in D.C. just in the sense that everyone had their own privacy if they wanted. "Jardena was understanding."

"Good. I need a meeting with Vice President Walton." There was one thing she knew. Walton wasn't acting president just yet. Dawn had been impeached, but she was still in office. Paige'd had to look at that up.

"That won't be easy," Ismail said around two ladders semi-blocking their way.

"I'm aware," she said. "Willow's getting the runaround, which is why I asked you in early."

"Understood."

She gestured to the office right next to hers. The studs were up, but no drywall had been installed on anything other than the exterior wall. A black folding table and an office chair sat there ready for him, though the floor was covered with dust and buckets and tools still. "This is yours. Set up. Get comfortable. There's an apartment upstairs with your name on it." Though, she hadn't had a chance to go up to see just how far along they were yet. If they were only this far along on the offices...

Maybe Paige should take them all back to D.C. until these were further along.

"Really." His expression widened with surprise. "This... is going up fast. Unless you were planning it?"

She shook her head. "I didn't even know they were working on it. But the packs can build pretty fast. There's a lot of unemployed people right now." She didn't even know where the materials had come from. "Get me that meeting. Location isn't an issue. We just need coordinates or an address so we can focus a door."

"What about... floors?" Ismail stepped into his office and took a look around.

"We'll need to know that too. If it's questionable, we usually show up outside." Paige had no idea what would happen if they opened a door in the middle of floors. "Just get me a location."

"Yup. Will do." He gave her a two-finger salute.

She poked her head through the framed wall across the hall where Willow's office was. "Ismail's here."

"I see," Willow said distractedly. "I'll get him settled."

"Sounds good. And you're still good with this?"

"To get an on-the-job trainer?" Willow asked, giving Paige her full attention. "You bet you're a—butt."

Paige snorted, not quite sure what Willow meant by that, and headed to her own office at the end of the hall and between both Ishmail's and Willow's.

She settled in behind her new-to-her desk and hoped she'd be able to keep this position long enough to at least paint the walls and put in real furniture. Well, and pay the salaries of her newly hired staff for at least a month?

Paige knew she had a choice to make and she needed the information to make it. Should she back President Flynn, or could she see if Vice President Walton would be an ally? Congress still had to vote the impeached president out of office. Dawn could win that vote and keep the office, though Paige hadn't heard of a sitting impeached president before.

Her interoffice phone buzzed and Ismail's voice came over the speaker. "I got your meeting. How's now sound?"

"Great." Actually. "Where?"

"Here. I sent…Bonnie, is her name, I think? To get him. That's okay, right?"

It was as long as secret service was okay with it. "Next time, clear it with Lovejoy first."

"Right. Yup. That's my next stop."

Well, if he was going to handle it, that left her with more time to gather her faculties, information, and strategy.

Her top priority was to keep this position.

Her second priority was to ensure she'd be able to maintain the power to make the changes necessary to help paranormals.

Her third priority was to make sure the government she was now helping was worth fighting for.

She didn't want to teeter on that third line, she couldn't forget that her people—paranormals—were *ready* to go to war. Just because she'd managed to find a peaceful solution didn't meant the fuel for war had evaporated.

Two men showed up with two black leather couches. Things were coming together.

An hour later, Lovejoy and a handful of secret service agents cleared the suite and Vice President Walton stepped into Paige's office.

She was in mid-sentence on an idea she had for an education bill—of which she had no power to draft. That wasn't her position and she realized she was working outside her scope a little. But there was a lot of work that had to be done, and it had to start somewhere.

Once she'd gotten the brunt of her thought down, she sent it to Willow and cc'd Ismail with a note telling him she knew this wasn't the way it was supposed to be done. She asked Willow to make her sound less moronic and asked

Ismail to find the right channels to make it or something similar happen.

Then she turned to Vice President Dick Walton with a smile and joined him on one of the black, leather couches. "Thank you so much for seeing me on such short notice."

"Well," he said with a pleasant enough smile, "I thought it prudent to visit the person who made this happen."

She didn't have to ask what he meant. He knew it was highly likely he was about to become president. "I need to know if you and I can work together."

"I certainly hope so." He leaned back, crossing one leg over the other, then wrapped his folded hands around the crossed knee. "You've opened a whole new world of possibilities for us, Secretary Whiskey."

So, no dropping the titles. That was a subtle cue. "You're not wrong, Mister Vice President, but I need to know what you intend to do with it."

"What should I intend?"

Paige turned an eagle eye on him. "We need to disband DoDO's U.S. operations."

He shook his head, his expression still pleasant. "I'm afraid that won't be easy."

There is something about this man that makes me edgy, Cawli said.

Same. Paige raised her chin. "I understand that, but with the evidence I've already turned over—"

"That was illegally obtained."

"It was taken by a prisoner. It's legal."

He grunted, then let his knee drop as he released it. "They have friends in high places, people with money and influence. Do you have a plan to take them out?"

She didn't, mostly because she didn't understand how *that world* worked. In hers, evidence was all that was needed. Well, and luck. And people with clean intentions. But when a person could pay their path outside the law... "I'll find one."

He nodded. "You do that, Madam Secretary." He looked down at the hand he'd set on the seat cushion beside him. "And the changes you're drafting? The things you want to change?"

Cawli sat up in Paige's mind, slinking forward as if hunting prey.

Paige watched him carefully as well. "Yes?"

Walton thought about that for a moment then blinked a smile toward her. "They're good. They'll make a lasting change."

But he didn't say it was a change they needed. "I agree. Our people need this—these actions to be implemented as quickly as possible."

"Of course." Walton stood and brushed off his pants before straightening fully. "But do try to remember that government moves slowly. It's a giant, with many wheels and cogs to manage."

And many ways for progress to be stopped. It *felt* as though Paige had her answer. "Of course."

Paige saw him out then picked up her phone, closing the door to her office behind her. She dialed Ruben.

"What?" he demanded.

"I need to speak to the president."

"Yeah, well, she wants to speak to you too. Get up here."

Paige went out in search of Bonnie and arranged a door to Pearl's office. The admin looked up and waved Paige into Ruben's office.

Ruben didn't even look up. He just growled at her and waived her through.

"I'm sorry," Paige said quietly on her way by him.

He just grunted and gestured again.

Paige let herself into the Oval Office.

Dawn stood and met her at the couches. "We don't have a lot of time. Walton is ratifying the votes needed to remove me from office."

Crap. "So, not on your side."

Dawn shook her head and raised a finger from her lap. "I've got more information on DoDO installations. They *haven't* released anyone yet. We've been watching them from the satellite feeds."

"They have their own form of door magick," Paige said with a wince. "Your satellites wouldn't pick anything like that up. There's no need for trucks when you have doors."

Dawn narrowed her eyes and bit down on her bottom lip. "I'm not out of office yet. I still have some power."

"Okay." What did that mean, though?

Dawn stood. "I'm going to put together a strike team and we'll target one. Which one would you prefer?"

Paige wasn't even sure, but the Voudon had specifically asked for and offered their help, so... "New Orleans."

Dawn raised a surprised eyebrow. "We'll start there then. We'll get the evidence we need."

That sounded great. "I and my people can be down on the ground."

"You're a Secretary," Dawn said with a shake of her head.

Like that meant something. "It just means I *don't have* to do a lot. I haven't found a law stating I can't."

The look on Dawn's face said there were, in fact, laws to the contrary.

"Okay, not in actual government. I know I can't do much of anything in a meeting, but this? This is what I'm actually good at."

Dawn thought about that for a moment then released a long breath on her way to her desk. "No. We can't risk it."

"What about some of my people?"

"We'll handle this."

"And if they attack with magick?" Which they would.

Dawn thought about that. "If the strike team gets into trouble, you can help them. But no setting anyone fire."

It seemed stupid that she'd have to get *that* line of advice from a woman who'd threatened war on her just weeks before. "Understood." Paige stood and headed for the door.

"And one more thing, Paige."

She turned, one hand on the doorknob. "Yes, Madame President?"

Dawn tipped her head down and to the side, her lips set in a grim line. "Interviews are only going to save you so many times. Well done, but stop flaunting your kids around like a banner flag. It's gross."

Yeah. She knew, but hearing that said from, again, someone like Dawn Flynn was like a slap in the face. "I'll be a *person* to the American people as often as it takes. And I'll keep doing that to remind people what it *means* to be a monster."

"And what is that?" Dawn asked, raising her chin.

It was time for Paige remind Dawn they *weren't* exactly allies either. "When we turn people into things so we can abuse them *and* sleep at night, *that's* when *we* become the monsters we hide from."

Dawn flinched, then looked away sharply, sitting gingerly.

Yeah. Paige had to remind herself that she might be siding with Dawn for now, but it was only to best protect her people. Paige wasn't forgetting that Dawn was indeed responsible for *putting* them in this position.

So, any hole Dawn had dug was one she'd have to personally drown in herself.

Paige was offering lifelines to her people. Not to the president. Not to the vice president.

That was the side she chose.

Paige went back to Troutdale to wait for the call for deployment. She made a call to Chuck, telling him to be prepared just in case a paranormal strike team was called to save some mundane soldiers' asses. But when her brain suddenly shut off, she closed up her laptop and head home, telling everyone else to close it up for the night. She told them to take a walk around the place, laying down a few ground rules like what to do if they saw someone naked. That sort of thing. But they were to also get themselves settled and if they needed anything in town to just ask and they could likely get a ride or borrow a car.

She didn't have the full staff there, but it *was* starting to fill up. Would it start to feel like a comfortable normal just in time to disappear? Paige didn't want to jinx it, but she also just had a feeling that someone was going to make sure she didn't fulfill her job the way she needed to.

Paige went to the house and spent some time with the kids. Ember and Bobby were pretty inseparable from Tyler and Toby—the original Toby, not Naomi's Toby.

So, she went to check on the girls and they were having a

hen party. Literally, a party with hens. She didn't know when they'd gotten chickens. When had that even happened? But tucked inside the wood line was a fenced in chicken yard with a couple of houses and several chickens.

"They're our experiment," Mandy said matter-of-factly. "And Mom said it was fine as long as she didn't have to do anything with them."

"And she's not?" Because that seemed a little odd, kids actually handling…work. Paige didn't know anything about chicken maintenance, but she did understand they were a little more work than one might think.

Mandy ignored that.

Actually, all of the girls ignored her.

So, Paige did what any grown adult did when they were blown off by children. She went to the boys and invaded their space, inserting herself in their "war games." They were playing an RPG game of some sort but without pieces or a board. It was "live action" because they didn't have enough "miniatures." So this *had* to be something similar to what Barn had been talking about the other day. It was a big game of pretend with rules she was learning on the fly. She was a "floating NPC," which she quickly learned meant she was filling in for the in-game characters. She was giving Tyler a run for his money by doing and saying things he hadn't planned for.

Eventually, though, she had to bow out because adulting wasn't all about playing. Actually, it was never about playing.

She was doing something wrong in life. All work? No play? Yeah. She was definitely doing *something* wrong.

Merry called her on her way back to her room. "I have a possible solution for you, but I need to know you're willing to listen."

Solution to what? "It depends. What are we talking about?"

Merry didn't answer immediately. "What if you didn't have to sell your soul to the monkeys in government?"

This was sounding like a conspiracy theory or the beginnings of a really bad joke. It didn't escape her notice that Merry I'm-Better-Than-Everyone-Else Eastwood had called politians monkeys, though. "I'm listening."

"I'm coming to you." Then she hung up.

Paige's pocket buzzed. She couldn't figure out what it was until she pulled out the phone Quinn had given her. She unlocked it and it had a message. *I have information for you. Need meeting.*

Great. Well, she *wanted* that information. But when would she be able to get it? *Bit busy. Give me a bit to give you a time. Eager to hear.*

She didn't get a response.

Someone knocked on the front door and when she went to answer it, she found Merry Eastwood standing there, looking very well put together. A bit more so than normal, actually. Her hair and make-up were done supremely well, and her outfit looked like she was prepared to hunt big money-game. Well, okay. The expensive looking necklace, earrings, rings, bracelet, and hair adornments actually said that. Her clothes looked pretty normal for her.

"Escape the monkeys in the government?" Paige asked, suddenly wary.

Merry gestured to the side-porch with her hand. They walked over as silently as her high heals afforded. Then, Merry leaned against the railing and turned to Paige. "I am offering an invitation to meet the real people who run our country. The *real* government, if you will."

This *was* a conspiracy theory. "I don't have time for that."

Merry shook her head, and her dark hair didn't even move. "You're fighting a system that doesn't even work.

You're applying your energy into things doomed to fail because you lack the *power* to make them happen."

That got Paige's attention. "Sounds like you have a plan. What are you proposing?"

Merry rose to her feet, standing a little taller than Paige in the pumps her pants hid. "To show you where the real power lies."

Paige didn't want to do anything dirty. Not after as many karma spells as she'd laid, but she also didn't want to lose. Too many people would be adversely affected if she failed. She was fairly certain there was a strong chance she'd fail by sticking with President Flynn, and she wasn't confident Vice President Walton was even on her side. She nodded.

Merry gestured to someone behind her.

He was a witch she hadn't met yet. He cut open a door that wasn't black. It was a mage door.

Was this a trap?

Merry disappeared on the other side.

Paige couldn't *see* through to the other side. All she saw was a white screen that reflected her silhouette back at her. Reaching into herself, she touched on her magick and stepped through.

The room she entered was large, like a hotel lobby, but it was ornately decorated with many old portraits and paintings hanging on the rather busy walls. Bookshelves and a rolling ladder lined two of the walls. A hallway slipped among them, also lined with books for as far as she could see.

There were several high-dollar lounge chairs and tables, and the air smelled like cigar smoke. A glass was slipped into her hand.

Paige turned, startled.

A slight woman with curly blue hair smiled at her, her fingers delicate as she took Paige's fingers and wrapped them around the glass. When Paige had the glass in hand, the woman evaporated.

The wall sconces were moving hands holding balls of living flame of different colors. The lamps were made from trees that seemed to move, and upon further inspection, the *leaves* were giving off light, not some light bulb.

Even the lounge chairs, as she looked closer, seemed to have personality with a mouth just below the seat. Everything in this room seemed to be... alive.

Merry stalked forward, her glass in hand to her side, a superior look on her perfect face. She gestured to the room at large. "Welcome to real power, Paige. I had honestly suspected the Whiskeys would never make it here."

What the hell place had Paige just stepped into? First, she'd met a witch with a living broom. And now she'd walked into a *living* room? Her world was getting... large. Uncomfortably so.

"You can come out now," Merry said with a long-drawn sigh.

Ken Waugh, the leader of the dragons, was the first person to appear. He literally stepped through the wall, and as he did so, the wall sconce where his head had appeared changed color from blue to gold. "Good evening, Paige," he said in his dark, deep dragon voice.

She tipped her head to him.

A few more people stepped through the walls, the sconces changing from the different colors to gold with each one. Some, she knew.

Balnore was one of them. He stepped through and glanced at Paige, gracing her with a warm smile, but didn't approach. Daenys, the elf queen, also appeared, as did Llyntomi, the fairy queen.

The rest of the paranormal council was not there.

But when Paige took a look and really assessed those

before her, she realized who she was talking to. These were rulers; queens, gods, commanders. These weren't merely leaders or alphas.

Oh, shit. Paige shot her whiskey back and released a surprised breath at how smooth it was.

The blue-haired woman popped into existence again with a smile and filled it back up. She chittered something that made no sense to Paige's ears, but inside her mind, she heard, *Drink slowly. It is powerful.*

Okay.

Merry set her glass down and clapped her hands. "Now that we're all here, I think it's time to determine our intentions. Don't you?" She regally sank into a red chair with a toothy grin. She lifted a dark eyebrow at Paige and flared her eyes as if telling her to sit.

All Paige had to do was survive this.

No. She reached inside herself and got a grip. All she had to do was to determine what *these* people had to offer and determine what was best for the paranormal people of America. She chose the striped and furry chair closest to her.

It wrapped around her, massaging her back gently, and purred.

Oh geez. Living chairs.

Daenys glanced at Paige, but her green eyes didn't hold the faint chill they had in their first meeting. "Reparations must be made."

The United States had invaded a foreign *world,* so yeah. Paige was pretty sure "reparations" needed to be made. But she wasn't taking point in this conversation. She'd watch, listen, and learn before speaking.

Ken leaned his dark-haired head back, relaxing into a powerful massage, a plume of smoke issuing out of his nostrils. "I stand by our original plan."

Did Paige know the original plan? Secession? But wouldn't that bankrupt a lot of the people at the top?

One of the men who joined them, a tall black man in a fine suit, perched on the edge of his chair, his elbows on his knees. He looked human except his eyes were the color of sand and appeared to be moving. "It is not that easy," he said with a slight accent that daggered each syllable.

Ken carefully watched Paige. "Splitting the U.S. will bring things back into more manageable powers."

"But it will disrupt many of my assets," the black man with the sandy eyes said.

"Then, shift things so they are disrupted to your benefit," Merry said. "We hold the power. So, let's build that power to suit our needs."

This didn't seem like the type of meeting Paige even *wanted* to be a part of. She wasn't a power player. She didn't have a wealth of money or influence. She had a top government job where she had very little actual control or influence.

"Our lives," an Indian woman said in the back corner, her gold and orange scarf draped carefully around her face, "have been displaced for far too long."

Paige watched the woman's lips, and what she'd said weren't the words she heard in her head. Paige doubted she had a translator chip or whatever, so something magickal in the air? If so, she needed something like it.

"We grow less powerful as time slips," the Indian woman continued. "Others wrestle it away from us."

"And that is why," Merry said carefully, "this is a prime opportunity to take it back." She met Paige's gaze and held it for a long moment as if inviting her to speak.

She hadn't learned enough *to* speak yet. "Why am I here? I'm not like you. I'm not rich. I don't have… power."

Ken raised an eyebrow and let it fall. "I am glad your elevated position hasn't inflated your ego."

"I can just as easily lose this position as I gained it."

"Agreed." Ken resituated in his chair and it growled at him. He tapped the chair's arm lightly and the growling stopped. "You were opposed to the breaking of the Union before. Are you now?"

Paige really hadn't thought about it since then. She'd *thought* she'd provided a viable solution. "Yes."

"Why?" The Indian woman asked. She wasn't demanding or attacking. It was a simple question.

"Because…" Paige took in a deep breath and thought about her reasoning. She'd been brought up to love her country. "It's too big a problem." That was a bad answer. "It's too massive. Who can take this on? Not me. So, who? People hiding in the dark? Can we trust them?"

Daenys snorted and looked around the grand room. "Do you know when we created this place?"

Paige was certain she wasn't supposed to answer.

"Before rules were made to govern magick. We were among the first. We have carefully sculpted the world in the shape that suited us best."

"And what suits you best now?" Paige needed to know what moral compass was being used here. "Power? Prestige? Money?"

"Money changes shape," the Indian woman said, her voice ringing out like a bell. "What holds power now might not later."

Sandy-man held out a palm toward Paige. "We seek," he said quietly, "to do what is right for as many people as possible. Our people. We are the reason you were able to remain in hiding for so long. We grew and developed the groups made to guide you, like your Council of Elders. We are the reason your people were able to live in safety for so long."

That was kind of an eye-opening moment for Paige. She'd

wondered what kind of wizard was behind the Elder curtain for so long, and here they were.

"You are here because you are heralding a new era," the Indian woman said. "You are not immortal like we are, but you hold within you a power long-since dead and forgotten. Within your veins lies the power to recharge our world, replenish our Earth, and to provide the people with a new way of life, but this will not be an easy change."

"And," Ken said, "it must be one you want."

Wait. Paige let all of that sink in a little. She kinda got that Miss India was talking about her ability to feed the ley lines, or whatever it was she did. And she got that maybe it was a lot more powerful than she'd hoped. She really *did* just kinda want to be a little normal.

But was she *also* saying that these people would follow *her* lead? That wasn't...right. Was it?

"Why?"

Balnore stood and strode slowly toward her, his black gaze lighting with a fire she'd never seen before. "We learned long ago that we do not always know what is best for the world. And so, at each major change, we look to someone who lives among the people, who seems to have the best interest of those around them, and we give them our strength."

Watching her old guidance counselor slash instructor slash father figure, she finally saw the puzzle pieces sliding into place. He had inserted himself into her life for *this* day, guiding her, teaching her. He'd probably helped Rachel take Leah from her so she'd have the strength of heart to meet this day.

She wanted to punch him.

"So, when you consider the ramifications of your decisions," Balnore continued, kneeling before her, "do not discount bigger solutions out of fear or because you think the solution is 'too big' to handle. This was the moment you were born for."

Paige looked around the room, shaking her head. This was preposterous and dumb.

But so was letting an entire nation—an entire world—of paranormals fall because she refused to listen. "Tell me how this would work. Seceding? Civil war? How each new nation would flourish or falter? The systems that could be put in place to make it work. Tell me that, and I'll consider it."

Balnore gave her a wry grin, stood, then spun on the balls of his feet and nodded at Ken with a look that told the old dragon the demigod's student was ready to graduate.

Probably not. But Paige would give it one hell of a go.

Even though the thought terrified the ever lovin' shit out of her.

They gave her information that, frankly, didn't feel real. She kinda felt like if they'd told her the Tooth Fairy was real. She could believe that, but all this stuff about ancient magicks and power and controlling the world's strings... It was all a little much.

They'd also gone to great lengths to discuss which states should go where. Who would want to go it alone—Texas—and who needed to be talked into joining someone—Alaska and Hawaii. What to do when other countries attacked, or what to do with the massive deficit owned by the federal government.

It was all just... a lot to ingest.

Secession wasn't just *possible*. It might actually be practical.

Practical.

That was the point Paige was having a hard time wrapping her head around, to the point where she hadn't *really* taken the information in. It was all about resource management, investment planning, threat assessments. They were all things she'd never had to pay attention to before. She'd done a *little* digging into state resources when they'd first started *talking* about secession, but it hadn't gone beyond that.

Now that America's fate rested on her shoulders, that decision was hers to make. That didn't make sense at all.

Balnore had offered to escort her home, but she hadn't been ready to talk to him. He'd been grooming her for *this* her entire life? It kind of felt like a betrayal, a little. Like, he couldn't have given her a heads up?

What she really wanted was to tell them all to screw themselves and their fucking deficit talks, and fix the system they currently had. And she'd *tried* to have that conversation.

They hadn't been inclined to listen.

So, she'd gone home, checked on her sleeping kids, and paced in her bedroom until three in the morning. She'd passed out only to be rudely awakened what felt like a few hours later by a knock on her bedroom door.

She muttered something like, "Go away," but the door opened anyway.

Willow stepped through. "We have a situation. You've been asleep all day."

"What?" Had to be the fairy whiskey. But great. Just what Paige needed. Another situation. "What kind?"

"Another ghost attack."

Oh, shit. Paige pulled herself to a seated position. She hadn't even *made* it to bed. She'd just kinda fallen on top of it. She sat there for a moment, blinking. Fuck. Get up. Ghosts. Attacking. DoDO back at it.

Right. Time to get her shit together.

She forced herself up and at least throw on some deodorant if not a clean shirt, and managed to not stumble too bad going down the stairs. Everyone else was still asleep and there was no need to wake them. She went to the kitchen to grab a cup of coffee, but Willow directed her out the front door, across the driveway the darkening driveway as the sun set around them—damn. Paige really *had* been knocked out all day—and into the office suite.

Having work *that* close was going to suck.

A cup was shoved in her hand, warm and smelling delicious. Okay, maybe it wasn't going to suck *too bad*. She followed Willow to a conference room on the south end of the building that had actual finished walls. Still without paint, but the drywall was up and the seams were hidden. That was a step in the right direction.

Had people been working on this through the night? How had her staff been able to sleep through that?

Lovejoy turned around when Paige walked in. "You look like shit."

Paige didn't know if it was the fact that she'd gone to bed only a few hours before or if it had been the fairy whiskey, but either way, she wasn't feeling great. "What do we have?"

"The attack," Lovejoy said, briskly, watching two monitors, "is near New Orleans."

Huh. Interesting. Why there? That was the location Paige had given the president to focus her strike force attack team on.

"This time, it seems a little... strategic." Lovejoy went to her computer and flipped through a few windows, pulling up victim sheets. "Look at who was attacked. They're influential people. Not just random like before. They're all people who have verbalized they wanted DoDO out of our government."

Wait. "What?"

Lovejoy nodded. "Congresswoman Hernandez was one of them."

No. Jardena? "Holy shit."

"That's what I said." Lovejoy's tone was grim. "I hate to say it, but I think DoDO figured out how to extract the paranormal soul. Maybe not the way they thought or wanted, but well enough to hurt us and help them."

"Or," Paige said carefully, "they learned how to focus the soul's energy."

Lovejoy nodded. "Either way, not good."

Paige looked to the ceiling, trying to think quickly in the bog of her brain. "If this was the old me, I'd gather some people and we'd move to counter-attack."

"And I'd tell you good luck, but don't tell me." Lovejoy shook her head. "You've got to tell the president."

"If she doesn't already know."

Lovejoy shrugged. "Would she have alerts for ghost attacks?"

"I'm sure she'd know one of her congresswomen was killed."

"That." Lovejoy crossed her arms then shook her head, her lips firm. "What do you think she'll do?"

"Only one way to find out." Paige unfurled herself, hugging her coffee to her. Even the news of more death didn't awaken her. That was a sign she was getting used to this.

That wasn't good.

She sent Willow to wake Derrick as she gathered her things. She told everyone else to stay there, even though Ismail informed her that was a terrible idea.

So, she pushed him into his office and gave him the lowdown of the current events.

Horror crashed over his bearded face.

"So, when I tell you I need you at your stations ready to perform your damned job, understand that's what I fucking well need you to fucking do. And do it well."

Ismail nodded. He pulled out his phone, his hand shaking, and shook his head. "I don—"

It hit Paige then. Jardena had been his previous boss as of just a day or two ago. How long had he worked with her? How close had they been? And now she was dead. How would that affect him? "I am…so sorry. I don't know how, but I forgot."

"No, it's…" He trailed off, licking his lips and running a hand over his head. "Uh, it's okay. You know. You're right. I need ta—" He looked at Paige. "I need to call her family. Shez is good but she doesn't know everyone. I need to—"

"Yeah." Paige waived him out the door. "Find Bonnie. She'll get you where you need to go." Fuck. She headed into Willow's office which was now enclosed, but still lacked a door. "You're on your own. Ismail's off to handle Hernandez's… stuff."

Willow's eyes widened. "Right. Yes. Of course. We'll be fine."

"Hold down the fort."

"Okay." Willow's phone chirped. "And, Paige?"

"Yeah?"

"Don't die."

Paige frowned, but nodded as she left.

Derrick met her in her office, his expression grim. He wore a long trench coat she hadn't seen. "I assume we're going to war."

She shrugged. "I don't know that." But it was her guess as well.

Derrick cut a door open and they walked into Pearl's office.

Paige didn't wait. She barged into Ruben's office with quiet force, but he wasn't there. She walked into the Oval Office and was met with a few other people she barely knew. There were a few people in uniform. Paige didn't know military insignias, only police, but they had stars on their collars, so she assumed they were generals.

Dawn looked up, her eyes flashing with anger upon seeing Paige then relaxing. "You're here."

"This was a strategic attack," Paige said, continuing into the room. "Do you have a full list of the victims?"

"Victims?" the female general asked.

"Yeah." Paige brought out her laptop and opened it with her fingerprint. It popped up readily with the victim sheets ready. "It wasn't *just* Congresswoman Hernandez."

"What are you talking about?" Dawn asked.

Wait. "What are you guys here for?"

"We've uncovered a weakness in one of their bases," the female general said. "We're planning our attack. What are you talking about?"

"The attack DoDO made on American citizens in New Orleans. The one that took out Congresswoman Hernandez and several others, all people who'd been rather vocal about DoDO getting out of our government."

The generals looked to one another in confusion.

"New Orleans?" the female general asked, her gaze hooded as she looked around the room.

Yeah. So, the coincident hadn't escaped her either. Good to see.

"And Jardena?" Dawn asked in confusion. "You're sure."

"I don't know how you haven't heard of it yet." That confused the hell out of Paige.

About that time, several of them looked down or around, searching for their phones.

Dawn picked hers up and horror softened then twisted her expression. "You have proof it was DoDO."

Not concrete, but it was enough. It was really hard to scientifically prove the existence of killer ghosts. "Yes."

Dawn looked to the tallest general in the room and nodded.

He started barking orders and the other military

personnel shuffled out of the room.

Dawn assessed Paige after the room had been emptied. "We're taking the fight to DoDO."

"Good."

"But not for your sake."

Why the change in dialogue all of a sudden? "What happened?"

"I was impeached. That's what happened. Likely by your testimony."

Paige gnashed her teeth and looked away. She clenched and released her hands, battling with her foggy emotions. "I spoke the truth. You're the one thing that frustrates me the most about the world we live in."

Dawn said nothing.

"According to you and your ilk, truth is the one thing that must *never* be spoken out loud." Paige advanced on Dawn. "Look, I get that you're pissed that you were played. I would be too, but at the end of the day, you acted on the intel you had. You chose not to question it because it fit your vendetta. And, just like everyone else, you've got to pay the price of your actions."

Dawn turned her glare to the door Paige had never had the chance to use. "Follow me." She led Paige down a hallway, passed several doors where people glanced at her with surprise.

Then she opened a door. There was a conference room and a monitor up on one wall. Dawn gestured to a chair for Paige to sit in.

This had to be some kind of war room? Maybe?

The female general manned the phone that was on speaker. She was talking to ground troops. "Cameras coming online," she said just as the monitor flickered and green images filled the screen.

The men on the ground were coming up on a complex,

but they were well outside it. With the night vision, Paige could see shapes, and that was good, but she couldn't see much more.

"Switch to infrared," Paige said, her eyes glued to the set, ignoring everyone else there.

They ignored her too.

"Switch to infrared," Paige commanded, letting her alpha will slip forward.

The female general issued the order.

As soon as they did, a different view showed up. One of the men stood dangerously close to a hex pattern that pulsed slightly. Another camera showed a dome. Another man saw a glowing box.

"That box," Paige said, pointing, "needs to be taken out."

The tall general didn't think about it. He issued the command. A burst of ammunition rained out and the box sizzled, sparked, and stopped glowing.

The dome went down.

"Hurry through," Paige said. "That's not the only box to power that thing. It'll be back up." She was pretty sure.

Being on the sidelines watching was weird. It felt like being near a fight with her hands tied behind her back.

The men continued forward in infrared until they came up on the building. Several sigils lit up the entrance.

"Stop," Paige said, studying the sigils. They were all protection marks. If she was there, she could find a way to plow through. "Find a window, an entrance that isn't marked."

The men followed the orders given to them by the female general and finally found a window that was mark free.

"Is it safe to go in?" General Tall asked Paige.

"With the information I have in front of me?" She had no fucking idea. "Yeah."

He nodded to General Female who issued the order to

move in.

The soldiers did so, sliding the window open. No alarms. Nothing tripped. They made it inside the building into what looked like a classroom.

"What the hell?" General Tall asked.

Paige vaguely remembered Dexx mentioning something about classrooms. "Be careful." She wasn't there with her witch vision and her magick to save them.

"Roger that," the leader said.

They had an objective. Paige understood that. She just didn't know what it was. And the only thing she could do was to offer her eyes through their limited scope.

But when they stepped into a room that flared, she knew the team was in danger.

"Stop moving," she ordered.

"What's —?" General Tall demanded.

"Shh!" Paige waited for the lens to clear so she could see what trap they'd just sprung.

They'd walked into a room riddled with traps. Demon traps. Angel traps. Some she didn't even know.

There'd been a reason that window hadn't been protected.

And the soldiers should be okay.

Except that on either of the doors was a trap release.

DoDO had known Dawn would send in soldiers.

And they were willing to release demons and angels or both on those men.

"Hold your position," Paige said into the speaker phone on her way out the door. "Don't move. I'm coming to you."

Because she was the only way those guys were going to make it out.

Which was probably exactly what DoDO had planned on.

Fuck, fuck, fuck, fuck.

But it didn't matter either way. She wasn't going to let those men die. Not when she could save them.

2 9

—————————

When Paige arrived at the area marked off for doors, Derrick was already there. He didn't ask any questions. He just took the location from her.

General Tall chased her down the hall. "What exactly do you think you're going to do?"

They didn't have time for this.

Derrick cut open the door. It was quiet and dark on the other side.

"Hold it right there," General Tall shouted. "That's an order."

Silence was good. But how long would that last? "I don't serve you." She took a step toward the door.

Sounds of gunfire erupted on the other side.

They were out of time.

Derrick stopped her before she went through. "You're not bullet proof and neither am I."

"Tell your men to stop shooting," Paige said, and pulled out her witch hands. If she was right, and she was, she'd need to start ripping demons out of that room before her feet touched ground.

"I will do no such—"

A body flew across the door.

"Those are demons," Paige said quietly. "I can fight those, but not bullets."

General Tall's eye twitched. Then he made the call in his earpiece. "Cease fire. Reinforcements on the way."

It took a bit, but the room stopped exploding bullets.

Paige didn't wait. With her witch hands called, she activated the Hell gate embedded in her bones and reached for the first demon she saw as she stepped through the doorway, and shoved him back where he came from.

The room was large and dark. She switched to infrared, using her shifter sight, to better see the soldiers. One was down, two others gathered around him.

There were at least a dozen demons oozing out of the traps in the wall.

One stopped, cracking his neck as if in anticipation of her arrival. "We were expecting you, summoner."

"I was looking forward to doing something other than give speeches." She reached out with her left witch hand and grabbed another demon, pulling him toward her.

He fought, digging in, his demonic head twisting.

Derrick stepped through and clapped a door in front of the demon's face.

Startled, the demon released his clawhold on the walls and fell through the door in Paige's chest.

Neck Cracker demon stared at her for a long moment. "We need to speak with you."

"I need the people being held inside."

"Let's make a bargain."

If the demon was looking to deal, Paige wasn't interested.

"Squad leader," she called, not knowing what else to call the man. "Can your men walk?"

"Yes, ma'am," he said.

"Derrick, open a door and get the injured back. You go with them. I've got this."

"Paige," Derrick said, his voice low.

This was basically like getting back to the basics. *This* was something she could handle.

Derrick growled low, then cut a door behind her.

Paige appraised the demon. It was rare to find them in true demon form. Usually, they came up and rode shotgun to humans, being unable to take on a human form of their own. She wasn't sure of the science here. The demon body was physical. They had two legs and two arms, though both were longer. Their heads were wider at top, and some had horns while others didn't. Their ears were typically flat against their heads, though there must be species differences because others had longer ears that protruded.

They also came in different skin colors, but not flesh colors as Paige knew them. These were the colors of different minerals.

"Squad leader?" Paige said calmly once the wounded were doing as they were told.

The demons were calmly waiting.

"Yes, ma'am," the soldier said in a clipped tone.

"Continue. I'll follow."

He didn't answer immediately. "Yes, ma'am." He then led them out the door on the far side.

"What are you doing here?" Paige asked the lead demon warily.

Crack Neck bared his sharp, long teeth on one side almost as if smirking.

"You were trapped. You got caught." Maybe all she had to do was release them.

"Not as simple as that, darling." Crack Neck appraised her. "You tell us what you want. We tell you want we want. Let's cut a deal."

Hmm. She could. Or she could send them all back to Hell, even though the gate was harder to access, it was still a part of her, still embedded in her chest. "We're getting the paranormals released."

"The ones still alive, you mean," Crack Neck said.

Drill Head—this one had a garnet colored head that looked like a hand drill—took a step closer.

She reached out with her witch hand and grabbed him by his throat, not taking her eyes off Crack Neck.

Something isn't right here, Cawli said.

You're not wrong. Can you scout ahead? See what we're missing?

He didn't answer, but appeared beside her and walked off.

None of the demons reacted to him, so she felt pretty certain none of them saw him.

Paige pulled Drill Head through the gate in her bones. "Tell me what's going on here."

"Let's discuss price first," the demon said, a frown flickering across his forehead as if he was mildly miffed she'd just sent Drill Head to Hell.

Fine. She'd listen to buy herself some time. "What do you want?"

"Freedom." Crack Neck jerked his long chin toward Drill Head. "We've been trapped here for..." He tipped his head to the side in exaggerated disdain. "A long time."

As intriguing as that was, she was certain her answer was going to be no. She was a Cabinet Secretary now. She couldn't just let demons wander the Earth all willy-nilly. "What do you intend to do?"

"Cause a little chaos?" He shrugged. "Make a few people pay for their crimes?"

"Sven's been taken care of." She wasn't sure if all the

demons had been a part of the Sven invasion or if this demon was outside that sphere, but she didn't want him going out there thinking things were the same as they always had been.

"What the hell do I care about that twat for?"

Paige raised her eyebrows in surprise. "I can't just let you guys leave."

Crack Neck smiled. "Well, then, I hope you came prepared to fight."

Paige didn't need another invitation. She reached out with her witch hands and dragged two demons toward her.

Another door opened and Derrick shouted at her.

She sent the demons his way, wondering briefly why he hadn't gone like she'd told him to. She didn't have time to ask where the door led. She didn't care. Yet. She would later. She doubted Derrick had opened a gate to Hell, so where was he sending them?

Another demon let out a shriek and headed for the door, following the team.

Paige wasn't stupid. She was outnumbered. She needed to let a few leave of their own volition, but she also knew the strike team wouldn't be able to handle *demons*. They weren't armed with anything that would even scratch them.

She reached for the screeching demon and threw him through Derrick's door.

"Why can't you just let us go?" Crack Neck bellowed, tossing another demon aside to strike at her with his fist.

This guy wasn't too smart. She called up the power of the Earth to reinforce her arm and slammed her hand to meet his fist. Even with the strength of Earth, it wasn't like she was the Incredible Hulk or anything. He was still stronger than she was. Demons were physically designed for… she actually didn't know. But he was *stronger* than she was. She called on her shifting ability and partially shifted her arm into that of a gorilla, pushing him back with that force.

Gorillas were kind of amazing.

He grunted and stumbled back.

She reached for another demon with her inky black hands who was swinging at Derrick. The demon's solid form transformed into syrupy smoke as her witch hands changed his substance to be pulled through the gate Derrick had opened.

He yelled something at another demon, using a large stick that cracked the demon's leg at the knee. His jacket seemed to be enchanted and he punched harder than he should have been able to. He managed to trip the demon and push it through the door.

Derrick was doing fine and didn't need Paige to worry over him.

She gave Crack Neck her almost undivided attention.

Two other demons—smaller and wiry—looked around, chattering at each other, running in small circles like they were confused.

Another demon cut sigils into the walls, scratching out others, and filled them with power.

They weren't all attacking her, which was a good thing.

She reached out her witch hand toward Crack Neck and he dodged, tipping his head to the side. "Really?"

What? Like she wouldn't try that?

"Why can't you simply let us leave?" Crack Neck asked.

"We're a world on fire right now," Paige said, grabbing a demon with the witch hand Crack Neck had dodged. She sent that demon through the gate in her chest, the demon screaming as he went. "I can't just let demons walk the Earth."

"But why not?" Crack Neck frowned at her and batted one of the circling demons toward Derrick.

Derrick took his stick and whacked the hurtling demon further toward the door. The demon's cry quickly cut off.

"Because demons are bad." Paige grunted as a demon

crashed into her back, let out a startled yelp, and then fell through her soul-door backwards. She hadn't realized it'd work that way.

"Except," Crack Neck said calmly, "you know they are not."

"Do I?"

Something banged on the wall annoyingly.

She turned, grabbed a smaller demon playing the wall like a drum, and sent him through Derrick's gate. These demons didn't *seem* like the worst of the worst. Either that, or she was getting stronger and wiser? "Do you know how many times I've had to stop the world from ending because of demons?"

Crack Neck shook his head. "We are no different than any other paranormal out there."

She wanted to argue. When she'd just been a demon summoner and a detective, she'd not only allowed demons to run around, she'd summoned them to help her do her job in keeping the streets safe. Demons didn't live under the same rules as humans.

But here she was, the paranormal Secretary, and she was telling these demons they weren't allowed to live on her streets? Weren't they paranormal?

Paige stopped and looked Crack Neck in the eye. "Tell me why DoDO trapped you as a weapon."

He narrowed his eyes at her. "You think we were all trapped here as weapons? Like those?" He jammed a long thumb toward the remaining circling demon.

Paige rolled her eyes then caught sight of the demon who was carving symbols into the walls. She reached out with her witch hand to grab him.

But Crack Neck stopped her with his physical hand. That hand remained physical even after he held her.

No one had been able to lay a hand one of her magickal hands before. Oh... fuck.

Crack Neck gave Paige a full smile. "I see I have your attention now."

He did. She tried to take her hand back, but he held it firmly, though not roughly. "What do you want?"

"Freedom."

"For what?"

His seething red gaze met and held hers. "I have something I must do."

"You do know that after Sven, things aren't the same. Hell is further away."

He appraised her, his right eye twitching. "I *did* feel that."

Paige didn't know what kind of demon could *touch* her magick, but she didn't like it. She also wasn't sure what she could do about him. Her witch hands were literally the *only* weapon she *had* against demons.

"You can send everyone else back," he said, smoothly changing his grip from her inky black witch arm to her smoky fingers. "But I... stay."

"What's your name?" Because if she had that, she could summon him again at any time.

He appraised her for a long moment.

Cawli reappeared. *Hurry.* He looked over at Threknal and her spirit cat's hackles rose.

Several people shouted down the hall the strike team had disappeared down and gunfire filled the small area.

Shit. She was out of time.

Crack Neck raised his long chin. "Threknal," he said quietly then brushed his lips against her magick fingers.

She felt the caress all along her body. What the...

Cawli growled low in his throat, preparing to pounce.

What could her spirit cat do?

Wait. He might be able to actually do something since this demon seemed able to hold onto her magick.

But Threknal didn't appear to even see Cawli.

She knew she wasn't good at opening doors anywhere other than Hell and they were out of time. "Derrick."

Another burst of gunfire sounded down the hall, along with the shouts of men.

Open a door."

"To where?" Derrick slammed his stick into a demon gut.

"Anywhere but home."

"Or Hell," Threknal said with a smile. "Then I'll be out of your hair."

Paige wasn't sure what Threknal was or what he might do, but he was a problem for another day.

Cawli's front end lowered further.

She just had to hope that this wouldn't bite her in the butt later.

Derrick didn't look pleased by the pinch of his face, but he closed his door, opened another, then gestured for Threknal to leave.

The demon saluted Paige and stepped through the door, shifting as he left. A clean-shaved man in a blue suit continued on the other side.

"Are we done letting them go?" Derrick asked as another demon slipped through with a screech.

She was. She made the last four go through her demon gate together. It felt like trying to swallow too much food all at once. Not very comfortable.

Derrick's gate closed after his last demon went through. Wherever he dumped them.

The sound of gun fire still rang out down the hall.

Kitten, Cawli said, rising to his paws.

"Where did you send them?" she asked Derrick as they made their way down the hallway, following the sounds of more fighting and Cawli's ethereal tail.

"Hell," Derrick said, his voice hedged. "Wyoming."

Paige chuckled, but focused forward. The strike team

sounded like they might be holding their own, but if the DoDO agents were using mage magick, it wouldn't be for long.

Paige stepped into the room, her magick raised...

And found chaos of a level she hadn't anticipated. She couldn't make heads or tails of the room for several seconds.

The paranormals in the room were easy to pick out. They were in collars and writhing on the floor. Short arcs of electricity jolted them from the collars.

The black-clothed agents around the room *were* flinging mage magick at the strike team, but the bullets the soldiers used were making an impact.

Cawli attacked a collar, though it was zapping him with white sparks.

Paige needed to find a way to disable those collars. Rai had been able to use electricity. Maybe there was a way she could use that?

But it looked like they were already *being* electrocuted, so would that even work?

Before she had a chance to try, three of the DoDO agents turned to her, their hands raised, and shot mage energy at her.

She didn't think about it. She let it hit her, let it roll over and through her.

But she wasn't going to call on the Earth to set these agents on fire. She wasn't that dumb. The president and the entire war room were watching. So she called on the Earth to shake as she fed the energy *back*, allowing it to seek a new path to the ley lines running nearby.

The building shook and cracked. People cried out.

The paranormals—there were dozens of them of all ages —raised their voices, crying out louder, harder, desperation clear.

Cawli, she cried. *What do I do?*

He didn't have an answer for her.

As the building shook, harder now as if the Earth itself sought revenge, Paige ran toward the closest writhing person.

He looked at her, his eyes going wide, his mouth wider than she'd ever seen on a human, such *pain* rippling across his face.

And then... it exploded.

They all did.

Paige couldn't believe what she'd just seen.

Wearing the blood of those she'd intended to save, she grabbed onto the power one mage threw at her and held it in her fist. She couldn't bury them alive, but they couldn't get away with this either.

She held the ball of energy in her hand, letting it fill her. It spoke to her in different languages, visions, sounds her ears couldn't hear. She whispered into it, "Sleep," and released it onto every black-clad person in the building.

The mage ball turned blue then dispersed into the air, shooting out in every direction.

The DoDO agents dropped to the ground, laying in the blood their collars had spilled.

Someone was going to pay for this.

She looked at Derrick. "Take me back," she growled low.

His eyes were dark and his expression grim as he cut a door for her.

She had to hope they'd take her seriously now.

Still wearing the blood of those she'd sworn to protect, Paige stepped back into the war room. "Anyone want to take me serious now? There's your proof. And prisoners. I could not possibly make this any easier for you." She growled as she slammed the door shut behind her and took her seat, not caring she was smearing blood on the grey suede.

"Maybe you should get cleaned up," Dawn said, slightly leaning away from Paige.

"Maybe you should see the real consequences of our shared actions," Paige said tightly. "Are we getting reports in from anywhere?" The only thing Paige knew for certain was that DoDO hadn't done this on a whim. There was a reason and she needed to discover that as quickly as possible.

"A few," General Tall said, his tone professional and the snideness that had gilded the edges of his words before was gone. "It appears they changed their torture method."

She didn't understand him at all.

"The videos you shared with us about their torture. You believed the… ah… *ghosts* were tied to the torture."

Ah. Paige was starting to catch on. She *had* seen those videos and the torture highlighted had been *quite* different. Those victims had been strapped in chairs. They'd had magick applied to them. They'd screamed as though they were being flayed. "You believe the collars were doing that."

"We do."

"And now," General Female said briskly, "we have proof."

"Good." Now, what were they going to do about it? "Was this a ghost attack?"

General Tall turned to her directly. "Yes." He held up his phone, his expression tight and grim. "Reports of unexplained deaths all over New Orleans."

"People in other areas—" General Red-Head injected, "—are reporting people falling into comas. The hospitals are filling beyond capacity." There wasn't much of his balding hair that was still red, but the freckles would never leave him—

Shit. Troutdale. Her home. She pulled out her phone. She had dozens of messages. Her heart hammering, she opened them.

Troutdale was under siege. "I have to go."

General Tall held out his hand, palm down. "We need information."

She agreed. "I'll provide that with boots on the ground."

"You should get cleaned up first," Dawn said quietly.

If Paige had time for that, sure. "I'll get information," she promised General Tall as she stood, leaving behind the blood of some of the people she'd been unable to save.

He took her phone out of her hand and programmed his number into it. "Lovejoy already has it."

"I'll use her if I can, or transmit directly to you if I can't." Paige retrieved her phone and slipped out of the room quickly.

Derrick came out of a room looking a little cleaner. "Where're we headed?"

"Home," she said tightly. "They were attacked."

He stepped back and pointed to the room he'd just left. "Clean up a little."

Paige was about to argue, but realized that she wouldn't really be able to *help* with ghosts. She just wanted to be there for her family and to make sure *they* were safe. But it was more than just the Whiskeys. The entire town had become her family. She went into the bathroom and locked the door behind her, closing her eyes for a moment.

The shit on shit storm of shittastic proportions had literally just exploded in her face.

She had no idea how to even *deal* with this.

Not paying much attention to her reflection, she grabbed paper towels, getting them wet and cleaning herself up the best she could. There was still blood on her jacket, so she took it off. Her blouse was relatively fine. Her hair was a mess, so she pulled it back into a tight braid, unable to tie it off. It didn't matter.

When she looked up again, it was to see that people were still in her hair and along the edges of her face, on her clothes. She took a few of the chunks off.

Then rushed to the toilet as her stomach heaved. She stayed there, just breathing, trying to be okay with her situation. There was *no way* to *be* okay with this.

But she had to not be falling apart. Too many people *needed* her to be strong. She could fall apart later. Maybe the next day. Maybe the next week. Maybe the next month or year or decade. But she had to pull herself together *now*.

So she spent a few more moments flicking things that didn't belong in her hair or on her clothes into the toilet and flushed everything away.

When she stepped out, her hands were shaking and she was close to the emotional edge, but she was holding herself together. Barely.

Generals Tall and Red-Head were out in the hallway, talking to people. They nodded to her, acknowledging her on her way by.

Derrick opened a door and Paige stepped through into the main lobby of her new office suite.

Chaos reigned. People shouted. Aaron ran through the room, not even noticing Paige and Derrick.

Someone was on the floor of the lobby with two others knelt beside them. She remembered what she'd hired them for, but not their names.

The brown-haired woman looked up, her grey eyes slightly crazed with overwhelm. "She just collapsed."

The air caught in Paige's throat as she stared down at the unconscious woman. "Willow." She reached toward her assistant's neck. "Is she breathing?"

The brown-haired woman shook her head.

Paige couldn't find a pulse either. "Do you know CPR?"

The woman shook her head.

But the man kneed his way closer and started compressions.

Paige couldn't sit there and help Willow. She needed to assess the entire area, check on her kids, her sister, the rest of the town. "When I tell you, breathe for her." Paige showed the woman how to lift the chin and pinch the nose, pushing aside her growing panic. How were people *dying* now inside the safety of the wards?

Maybe this was just a one-time thing. Maybe Willow had a bad heart.

Paige got up and made her way through the offices. Almost half of her people were on the floor either unconscious or being worked on.

Ismail grabbed her, his tone serious. "The entire town was attacked," he said briskly. "There aren't enough emergency personnel to take everyone to the hospital."

Shit. "Then find a way to get these people there."

He grabbed someone running by and issued the order, then turned back to her before she had a chance to move on to the next thing. "The hospital will be overrun. We're going to lose people on that fact alone."

It was hard to push down her rising panic. "Have we heard from the town?"

"Slowly. The mayor is down. A few others."

Paige pulled out her phone and dialed Tuck. "How are we getting information?"

Ismail shook his head. "Social media. We don't have a line for this."

The phone rang but he wasn't picking up. "Come on, boss. Pick up." Fuck, fuck, fuck. She didn't even know what to tell him. "Where's Lovejoy?"

He shook his head. "Haven't heard from her."

Shit. She *needed* Lovejoy. "Find her." Tuck picked up, issuing orders on his end. "You're alive," she said into the phone.

"You too," he said, his tone filled with relief.

"How bad are we hit?"

"Still don't know. What the hell hit us?"

"Ghosts." Paige wished she was joking. "We know where they came from. We know how. We know who. I need to know how bad."

"Reports still coming in. I'll let you know."

"Good. You see Lovejoy?"

"Got her here. You need to come into town."

"On it. Stay alive." Because, fuck, she needed him. The whole town did.

"You too."

She wasn't sure who hung up on who.

She dialed Leslie on her way out of the office suite.

Derrick opened a doorway for the people working on Willow directly into the ER room.

Shit! That was the answer she needed!

She hung up from calling Leslie who hadn't picked up yet and called Phoebe.

The Blackman witch picked up on the second ring.

"How bad are you hit?"

"Not extensive," Phoebe said quickly. "You're calling, so you need something."

"Doors to the ER. To *any* ER. We might have to send them to unaffected cities. I don't know."

"And where would those be?"

"Still trying to figure that out."

Phoebe sighed. "And how do we know where to send *my* people?"

"Fuck. Everywhere?"

"Okay." Phoebe growled low in her throat. "What the hell happened?"

"DoDO attacked us with ghosts."

"You're fucking kidding me," the Blackman witch said through clenched teeth.

"I wish I was. And it looks like we aren't just going into comas. The wards *were* protecting us, but it looks like they found a way to overload them."

"Shit."

Paige hadn't realized Phoebe was a curser.

"Okay. We'll… send everyone out everywhere. I need Leah. Fuck and Ollie."

Paige crested the door from the office building and stepped onto the driveway nearly flying on her feet. "Checking on Leah now. Send her to you if she's okay?" Paige didn't want to think about it if she wasn't.

"Yup."

"Message me if you need anything." Paige didn't want to be the message center, but she needed to set something up and the people she would normally set up for this were falling like flies.

Damn it.

She burst through the front door of the Whiskey household and was met with silence.

Fucking shit.

She ran upstairs to see if there was anyone there.

She found Bobby on the floor in front of his room, his blue eyes open, his body surrounded in a glow. She ran to him, sliding the last couple of feet as panic welled inside her.

As soon as she touched his shoulder, the glow stopped and he took in a deep breath, closing his eyes for a long blink.

"Bobby," Paige breathed. What the fuck was going on? "Are you okay?"

"It's bad," he whispered with a slight whimper. He tried to sit up. "I tried, Mom. I really did."

She didn't know what he'd tried, but if he'd been glowing, that could be just about anything. "Are you okay?"

"They're not." Bobby looked at her, his blue eyes swimming with tears as she helped him off the floor. "They're *not.*"

"I know." She didn't know who "they" he was talking about. She got him off the floor and took him to the room he shared with Kamden. He still hadn't moved out. They'd run out of bedrooms for everyone, something they hadn't thought had been possible when they'd moved in. "We might need your healing magick. You up for that?" She thought of Willow whose heart had stopped. Who was in the ER but might not even be served depending on how busy they were with other people.

Shit. Shit. Shit.

He shook his head and took in a deep breath. "Yeah."

Which was she supposed to believe? His negative head shake or his words? Probably the head shake. She set him down on his bed and pressed a kiss onto the top of his head. "Rest."

"Mom, I can help."

"And Leah can take you where you're needed when I find her." If she was up and feeling okay.

Bobby nodded and curled up on his bed, his tears sliding across his eyes as he closed them.

She went to Leah, Mandy, and Rai's room next—aka, the attic. There, she found three bodies on the floor, on top of each other, all holding hands.

Paige ran to them, pulling Rai off of Leah and checking for a pulse.

Rai's heartbeat jumped, stuttered, and jumped again.

Kissing the girl's head quickly, Paige set her down then checked Leah's and Mandy's.

Leah took in a deep breath and released a scream as she regained consciousness.

A wave of relief washed over Paige, but she didn't' have time for that. Mandy wasn't breathing. She set Leah aside and scooted to lean over her niece. She checked for breath and pulse, still found none, and started CPR. In the office, surrounded by people, she didn't need to be the person focused on reviving one. But here?

She focused on counting, not recalling if it was thirty pumps then two breaths, or if it was continual pumps now. But it didn't matter. She needed to get the girl's heart started. That was it.

Leah panicked beside her. "Mandy!"

Rai sat up, lightning dazzling her eyes.

If Paige couldn't get Mandy jumpstarted, then maybe Rai could with her electricity. But how much was too much and could Rai control it?

At this point, it didn't matter. Paige heard one of Mandy's ribs crunch and a sob threatened to surge forward. "Rai," she barked and gestured to Mandy with her head. "Can you restart her?"

Rai just scrambled to all fours and pushed Leah out of the way, her hands crackling with baby lightning already. Paige lifted her hands off Mandy's chest and made sure her knees weren't touching the girl.

Rai set her fingertips on Mandy's chest and focused.

The moments stretched on for what felt like hours. Jolt after jolt until Paige worried that Mandy might not be okay.

"Bobby," Paige shouted, her tone laced with a terror she probably shouldn't have voiced.

His thundering footsteps pounded up the stairs.

"Mandy," Leah moaned, not touching her.

Bobby tripped up the last stair and crawled the rest of the way.

Mandy coughed heavily, groaned, then took in a sharp breath that sounded like it hurt.

Fuck.

Rai released her hand, her breath shaking as her chin quivered with unshed tears.

Paige reached over and took her daughter's hand and gave it a squeeze. "You did good, Rai. Bobs, I broke one of her ribs. Can you heal that?"

He nodded, calling up his golden glow over one hand and held it over Mandy's chest.

Mandy's breathing was raspy. "Aunt Paige?"

"Don't talk, baby girl," Paige said, fighting the tears. She needed to stay but she had to leave. She had to check on everyone else. Where the hell was Leslie? The pack? Tyler? Ember? Kamden? Kate? Nick? Mark? "You guys okay?"

Leah shook her head.

Rai nodded, swallowing hard.

There was no way Paige could send Leah to Phoebe but they needed all working door magick witches on emergency call right now. "Bean," Paige said, forcing down her emotions with a metal fist of resolution. "Go to Phoebe. We need help."

"I can't," Leah said around her tears. "This is—" She shook her head.

"Big. I know. Stash it. Bury it. Deal with this and cry later."

Anger flashed across Leah's face. "Like always."

Paige wished that wasn't so, but her heart pounded with the ferocity of pride at the fiery will of her daughter. "Like always."

Leah got to her feet, pushing Paige's hand away angrily, and cut open a door, disappearing through it.

Paige understood Leah was pissed and she was okay with that if it got the girl moving. "You guys good?"

Mandy's breathing was better.

Rai nodded.

"We might need you." Paige looked to Rai and Bobby. "Both of you. So, you get yourselves settled and find those who needs your help. Like Willow. She... her heart stopped. Last I saw, Derrick took her to a hospital." This wasn't a time for them to be kids.

And Paige hated that.

Rai nodded. "We'll find Derrick and have him take us to the hospital."

"Thank you," Paige whispered, cupping her daughter's cheek. Then she turned to her son. "Don't push yourself too hard."

Bobby bowed his head.

She looked at Rai. "Don't let him."

"Got it, Mom."

Paige shifted to four paws in the form of a fox and ran down the stairs, using her nose to guide her.

The boys were in Tyler's room and were pulling themselves off the floor, all three relatively okay, but a dark singe mark had been scorched along the floor and ceiling. Paige wasn't going to stop and ask. They were alive. That's what mattered.

Her nose searched for Leslie and located her freshest scent overlaid with everyone else. Paige followed it into the kitchen.

Where Leslie lay convulsing on the floor.

Paige ran to her and shifted into human form, not sure what to even fucking do. "Bobby," she yelled. "Get down here now!"

He ran loudly down the stairs like a fumbling gazelle and slid along the floor to his auntie's side. He didn't ask. His blue eyes were already glowing gold, as were his hands as he reached for Leslie.

But the convulsing seemed to get worse.

Leah stepped through a door and came toward them, shouting. "Get away from her!" She focused those words on the air, not Paige or Bobby.

Paige looked up, seeing nothing, unable to assist either of her children or her sister.

Waiving her arms, Leah screamed, the high pitch turning gravelly as she reached deeper into her magick.

The room released with a concussive whoosh that hurt Paige's eardrums.

Then Leslie went still, breathing deeply.

Paige sat in the silence, Leah collapsing beside her, Bobby's non-glowing hands splayed on the floor.

They were so fucked. She reached out and grabbed her kids close to her, moving her knee to feel the warmth of her sister's prone form.

Shit. They were...soooooo fucked.

Paige didn't know who to call because in a situation like this, Leslie was her go-to gal. So, she called Mama Gee.

"You heard about de ghost attacks," Mama Gee said, her voice strained.

"Heard? I was there." How many places had been attacked? "So, you were hit?"

"Yes."

Paige had guessed. "I need..." She didn't know what she needed. "I need someone smarter than me, better at magick."

"What do you need exactly?" Mama Gee asked, her accent emphasizing her words.

"Leslie was attacked by ghosts. She's—"

"A lot of them," Leah added. "There were a lot of them. All around her. Attacking."

"Right." Paige had to hope the Voudon witch had heard that. "She's unresponsive."

"And you think I can help?" Mama Gee asked in high surprise.

"You're *the* goddamned Voudon witch of Voudon witches.

Yes, the fuck ma'am, I think you can help." But only if her hands weren't already overly full. "Leslie's spirit animal is a griffin and he doesn't react well to ghosts. If she does come out of this and he's in control?" Paige didn't know how bad that could get.

"Send me a door," Mama Gee grumbled.

"How badly are you guys hit?" Paige asked because she had to. She *couldn't* take resources from one critical area to another.

"Badly. Your wood witch was here earlier. Much earlier. So, we had some protections, but…" The Vodoun witch sighed. "I will need to come immediately back."

"Okay. I'll send my daughter."

Leah's eyes widened in surprise.

"I'll need an assessment of your situation if you have it. Do you—I'll ask when you get here." She hung up the phone after getting the witch's location. "Bean," Paige said after quieting Leah with her alpha will. "We don't have time for this. I love you. Buck up. And get me Mama Gee."

Leah's face screwed up with thirty-one flavors of anger, but she stood, opened a door, then disappeared.

Mandy and Rai came down the stairs.

Bobby looked…thin. Razor fucking thin.

She wasn't going to ask if Bobby could do anything else for Leslie or the hospitals. They didn't have a healer for the healer.

Ember, Tyler, and Kamden followed the girls, Tyler talking a mile a minute until he saw his mom on the floor.

It was chaos after that as Paige fielded questions from the kids. She still had no idea where Kate was, or the rest of the pack. If any of them were okay. So, the kids who were better off were sent to go look for them.

Rai was given instructions to resuscitate those she could

but to stop before exhaustion set in because they didn't need an implosion bomb to top everything else.

Leah returned with Mama Gee and the Voudon witch simply went to work, her expression grim as she opened a bag and started pulling things out.

Paige wanted to stay and help, but she knew she'd be absolutely useless. She needed to get downtown and see what the damage was there. But before she left, she asked, "Do you need door magick in New Orleans?"

"No." Mama Gee's voice was brisk. "We have our ways."

That's all Paige needed. She scrambled to her feet. "I'll need details. Later."

"I'll send word through Wy."

Sounded good. "Bean," Paige said on her way out the door, "take her home when she's done and then report to Phoebe." Paige stopped at the backdoor and looked at her daughter standing fierce guard over the Voudon witch and her comatose and very powerful aunt. "I love you, Bean."

"Love you back," Leah whispered.

Paige turned and shifted into owl form. She needed speed, but she needed quiet, too. She flew over the Whiskey lands and was rewarded with seeing several of her pack up and walking. Margo was okay. Her brother wasn't. Kate was dealing with Nick who was getting up. Mark still wasn't up yet. Paige couldn't stop to see if Mark would make it, but her heart hurt.

Was Dexx okay?

She had to hope he was.

There were two car accidents on the road to town from the house. She winged over the Eastwood estate to discover that they *all* appeared to be good. She stopped long enough to talk to Oliver about helping the Blackmans and about putting up a patrol because of everyone, they seemed the least affected. He said he would do both.

Then, she went to the police station, but she was stopped by the appearance of several new trees, some having sprung up right in the middle of the road. Dryads?

The police station was in chaos as she sought out Tuck.

He latched onto her gaze and met her in the middle of the small bullpen. "What the hell?"

Paige licked her lips, feeling the brunt of too much emotion being forcibly repressed. "Where are we?"

Lovejoy joined them, looking well within her element. "We've got a communication network. Danny managed to get a social media board for people to reach out if they need to. The emergency lines are being diverted to national lines." She led the way to the conference room she'd taken over. A map was on the wall with pins in eight locations. "So far, we know that these areas were hit the hardest, each with coma patients and dead."

This was good. Well, not good. But thorough. "Give me a sec." Paige pulled out her phone and dialed Billie Black. "The dead. Are they humans? Paranormals?"

"Mostly humans."

"Paige," Billie said as she picked up. "I'm watching the news."

"DoDO fought back. You don't want details. Look, I need to know where you put up wards."

"Uh, yeah, sure. Denver—"

Paige put her on speaker phone so Lovejoy and Tuck could hear her.

"—Orleans—"

Lovejoy nodded and pressed a fingertip to the red thumbtack on that city already.

"New York City, Boston, San Francisco, Seattle, and Oakland. Why?"

The eight cities hit.

"The wards are being targeted," Paige said to both

Lovejoy and Billie. "Is there any way of making them harder to be located?"

"If I knew *how* they were finding us?" Billie sounded flummoxed. "But they worked, didn't they?"

Lovejoy went down the list. Denver had suffered the least with lots of people in comas, and only one reported death. Troutdale had been hit the worst. Hundreds in comas. Several people dead with the body count rising as they continued to search.

"Yeah. They worked." Paige thanked Billie and hung up. "They were targeting me."

Lovejoy nodded. "Most likely."

"You stood up to 'em." Tuck shoved his tongue between his lips and sucked. "You told the world to get them out. How'd they do this?"

Paige shook her head, disgusted by this whole situation. How many people had died to make this attack happen? How many had been in the room in the New Orleans DoDO facility? How many people was she wearing? "The collars. They were…" Bile rose in her throat. She swallowed it down. "They were tortured with them and then their heads literally exploded."

"And the ghosts were released and attacked people," Lovejoy said, staring at the map thoughtfully.

Paige nodded slowly. "Who would have thought to use ghosts as weapons?"

"It's my thought," Lovejoy said, "that wasn't what they'd intended."

"Mine as well." Paige perched on the edge of the conference table, knowing she couldn't relax yet. She couldn't allow herself to come unglued *yet*. "They were trying to find a way to transfer the powers of the paranormals into humans of their choosing."

"And your research," Lovejoy said, waving her hand. "The information you got from them. Were they successful?"

Paige shook her head, biting her lips. But was Dexx's information current? She hoped so.

"This might have been a last-ditch effort." Lovejoy looked at Paige and took in a deep breath, releasing it slowly. "A way to get rid of the evidence."

"Or check for weaknesses?" Paige didn't like that idea.

"Whatever it was," Tuck said gruffly. "I want my county safe. So, can you make that happen?" He met Paige's gaze. "Get your information and then fix this."

Paige nodded, accepting his orders. She turned to Lovejoy. "Keep doing what you're doing. Right now, you're the only one who seems to know what the fuck they're doing and we need that. Not just here. Everywhere."

"We serve the nation," Lovejoy said, acknowledging it. "I know. I've been using old contacts."

"Good." Paige picked up her phone and called the number General Tall had given her.

"McCormick," he answered.

Finally. A name. "Whiskey. I've got information." She gave him everything she had, including Lovejoy's contact information.

"This was a terrorist attack on U.S. soil," he said.

She hadn't thought of it that way, but sure. "It certainly looks like it."

"And they used ghosts."

"They've *been* using ghosts."

"Did they break through your defenses?"

She didn't want to tell him, mostly because she wasn't sure she could trust him. "Yes."

"How bad is it there?" General McCormick asked.

"Severe."

"Take care of it. Keep us informed."

She was pretty sure she didn't answer to him, but she grunted and hung up, then called the line Dawn had given her. She repeated herself as she walked on two human feet down the steep hill from the police department to downtown Troutdale.

The citizens were rising to the occasion, stepping in where they could, directing the Blackman witches where they were needed. More than a few made passes at the ward tree, touching it, as if refueling it. That was a good call and one Paige hadn't thought of.

"Thank you," Dawn said over the phone. "I'll do what I can."

Paige hoped she did. "I don't know when I'll be free."

"Understood."

Hanging up on the president, Paige stashed her phone in her pocket and walked up to a tree that had pushed an SUV to the side and into the blue Volkswagen Bug beside it. She touched the bark.

It quivered.

Damn. Why had the dryads been so affected?

Paige went to the mayor's office. It was like the eye of a hurricane. People went about their business there, some doing so with tears flowing down their cheeks, others in stiff resolve. They did what needed to be done, but they were all somber.

Paige went to Suzanne's admin assistant. "Any word on how she's doing?"

The woman shook her head and clamped her lips tight for a long moment. "She didn't make it."

Fuck. Paige raised her face to the ceiling. "Who else?"

The woman gave her a scribbled list. "That's only what I have so far and only the people who'd..." She shook her head. "We lost a lot of good people today."

Paige perused the list and bit off a curse. They really had.

A few of the names, she knew. Most, she didn't. But there were also titles beside their names.

The person who handled housing. Dead.

The person who'd handled food distribution. Dead.

Security. Dead.

One of the energy efficiency brothers. Dead.

The mayor. Dead.

Wendy. In a coma.

DoDO might as well have gutted Troutdale.

"Update me as this list grows," Paige said quietly.

The secretary nodded.

"And, um." Paige swallowed hard. "Could I get your name?"

"Lizette," the woman said tightly. "Lizette Velez."

Paige nodded then took the woman's phone number, programming it into her phone with a name and a title because she was collecting names faster than she could keep up. She shot Lizette a text message. "If you need me, I'm a text away."

"My family," Lizette whispered. "I haven't' been able to get a hold of them."

"Where are they?"

"Sacramento."

"That wasn't a city that was attacked."

Lizette released a relieved puff of breath. "Thank God. The lines...they just must be jammed."

"They probably are." Paige had been able to get all of her calls out. "If you need to take time off, do it. Take care of yourself."

"Suzanne wouldn't want it that way. She really cared about this city." Lizette's face crumpled with tears.

Paige had to get out of there before she joined in. "Call me if you need me."

Lizette nodded and took in a deep breath. "And collect information."

"As much as you can." With that order issued, she continued on her way to Red Star, trying to think of anyone else she might have missed. Chuck. She pulled out her phone again. He didn't answer. So, she tried Faith. She didn't answer.

Shit. So, she shifted and flew over to his place, but found him miles away from his home.

Shifters littered the woods outside the wards. Chuck was fighting to contain a fully shifted wolf who snarled and lashed out, drooling excessively.

There was an entire pack of them. They looked feral.

Or rabid.

Paige touched down and shifted.

Faith was throwing down her alpha will on the pack.

What was going on here? Maybe the ghosts had attacked and affected them differently? They'd been outside the Trout-dale wards, so they'd had very little protection.

One of the wolves caught Paige's scent on the wind. He was a timber wolf, grey and white. He lunged for her.

She wasn't going to use her magick on him. He wasn't the enemy. She called on her alpha will and released it with all the frustration and pent-up emotions welled up inside her.

The wolf stopped, lowering his belly to the ground, and whined up at her.

The rest of the pack did as well.

Chuck glanced over at Paige and inched his way backward toward her, his hands out, his eyes on the wolves.

"I came to check on you," Paige said. "See how things were going, but I think I have my answer."

Faith edged toward her as well. "Over half of our packs have been hit like this."

Fuck. "What's the plan?"

Chuck shrugged, his softly accented voice quiet. "We are restraining them and bringing them home. We don't know what else to do."

"How long are they staying like this?"

Faith shrugged, her hands flopping to her sides. "A few have already snapped out of it and seem fine. But..." She shook her head. "We were attacked."

By how many? How many people had died to lay this attack on the Troutdale wards? Dozens? Hundreds? More? Would they ever know?

Paige helped Chuck and Faith round up a few more of the feral shifters. *Her* alpha will had a bit more punch, but... it didn't *feel* like alpha will. It felt like...she didn't know. Something else.

But that was yet another thing to ponder at another time when she had more luxury for such things.

"So, regional pack alpha, you think it might be time to move the pack inside the wards. I'm offering to create a ward tree on your estate and connect it to Troutdale." He'd declined Paige so many times before.

"I don't think I have a choice. Do it."

Paige started it, using a massive stone as it's grounding point, and showed them how to add themselves to it.

"We'll grab the pack and continue as best we can. Thank you for your help."

She left with a feeling that she'd outgrown him. Before, when she'd been just another member in his pack, he'd done little things to make her realize she was a part of something bigger, that she was safe and secure.

This time, it felt like the roles had been reversed.

And she didn't ache for it to be otherwise.

Growth, she guessed. Or she was just tired of constantly second guessing herself. Either way, it was progress.

She flew to Red Star.

Scout was a flurry of information.

She had names of missing—likely dead, she now assumed.

She was able to match a few of those names to ghost reports, things that had been said, impressions, even the smells, which was strange. Maybe Paige would have to consider making a scent directory? No. That was too invasive and too...weird.

But this was good work.

And Joel, the goblin, and had been instrumental in protecting everyone at Red Star. Thank goodness for small favors.

But he'd also been instrumental, under Scout's guidance, in getting names.

Roc had been helpful in that area as well. There was an entire untapped network of gargoyles out in metropolises.

The only disturbing issue was the ash tree taking up the conference room. Michelle, apparently, had opted to stay behind when Dexx had left. She'd said something about needing to be with the grove or something. Scout was a little fuzzy on the details. And when the attack had started, Michelle had been the first one affected. She was the reason Joel had known to throw out protections in the first place.

But she, and the other dryads, had been forced into tree-form upon attack. And Paige had no idea how to communicate with any of them.

Paige went back to Dexx's office and shut the door, shaky and spent, not knowing what she should do next and just needing... a moment.

So much had happened.

Real danger had hit her in an area she'd begun to think of as safe.

And she wasn't sure she was ready for whatever might come next. She let her head fall back, drawing in Dexx's smell. She needed Dexx home. Beside her. With him by her side, she could take on anything. He might be a wildcard at times, but he was her rock and her partner.

She took in one deep breath, recalling the fear and anger on Leah's face.

She released it, pulling on Lizette's resolve to make Suzanne—who hadn't been great, but hadn't been bad either—proud.

Taking in another deep breath, she remembered Tuck looking up at her, wondering what to do next with his wizened eyes.

Releasing that breath, she touched on Lovejoy's resolve to handle the situation and to do what was necessary, knowing what to do, who to call.

Another breath, and she thought of those who had fallen, people she'd begun to count on, had thought of as friends.

As she walked down that list, she stopped at Leslie and closed her eyes, wishing this hell was over.

DoDO had gotten close. Really close. They'd won a battle, a painful one.

She couldn't let them win the war.

3 2

Paige went home, sprayed herself down outside with the hose, then took a shower. There, she finally broke down. Being the strong one was hard, but it wasn't a role she was about to shirk just *because* it was hard and she didn't have all the answers.

She was busy most of the next day, calling the family members of those she'd hired who had died during the attack. It sucked that she barely knew most of them because they hadn't even worked for her for long. One had only been on the job a matter of hours. Her parents had put her on speaker phone and had yelled at her for over an hour.

Paige had let them.

She just replayed running into a silent Whiskey house, of finding all the kids on the floor, of almost losing Mandy, of how gaunt Bobby still was after a night of rest and eight meals—the kid couldn't stop eating. She understood why they were upset.

That didn't mean she could stop.

But the media was *hounding* her for a comment. Something.

President Flynn and General McCormick had taken all the information she'd gathered. She'd included Lovejoy in that conversation. Lovejoy was also taking point directly with Scout and the new Red Star team. That part of the situation was now running on its own, giving Paige the time to handle things here.

Ismail was going through the resumes and finding quick replacements for the people they'd lost. He'd run a few of them past her and she'd approved them with barely more than a glance.

She'd just lost nearly half her team because they'd decided to join her staff. Some had just wanted a chance at advancement. Some actually believed in what they'd been doing.

Wendy was still in the hospital, fighting for her life. She wasn't in Troutdale or Portland. She'd been sent to Seattle, which was nearby and hadn't been affected by the recent attack. Troutdale and Portland hospitals had been too overrun to take anyone else, including Wendy. And so many others.

Troutdale itself had been decimated.

Danny Miller sat across from her, silent, his gaze distant his reporter's notepad forgotten in his lap. "We need to get camera crews in here."

"People are still mourning," Paige said quietly. She knew he was right, but this wasn't some parade. This wasn't some event. This was people's lives.

He just met her gaze and held it, something in those irises telling her he knew what she meant, that he knew what she was trying to convey.

She closed her eyes and nodded. Waving him off, she opened her eyes again and returned to work. "Keep it respectful and don't get in people's faces."

"Honestly," he said, clamping the arms of his chair, but

not standing, "it's like you have no idea what true journalism is."

She didn't. She just stared at her monitor, not having the energy to read what was on her screen.

"Are you okay?" he asked quietly.

"No," she whispered. "Not even a little. How can I be?"

His lips flattened as he steepled his fingers on his chest, leaning back as if settling in.

She knew Danny was the wrong guy to talk to about this. He was a reporter, but he'd *proven* himself time and time again. She turned to him, sagging onto her desk as if the steel holding her up had evaporated. "We were prepared. Danny, we..." She licked her lips, recalling the *smell* of the destruction, the feel of the... blood she'd worn for almost an entire evening. "We had the strongest wards. I made sure of that. Our house? My house? Had double the protection. *Angels* couldn't get through my wards, but DoDO figured a way through."

Danny nodded, his nostrils flaring. "You cornered them."

"They threw..." How many people? She had the lists. "Hundreds of ghosts against our wards, most of them here."

"You think they've been watching you for a while?"

"Yeah." She knew it. "They had these black boxes set up. I had thought they were trying to build their own wards, but now? I don't know. Maybe they were just testing our weaknesses."

"Well, they found them. But will they be able to do that again? Will they ever have that many..." His Adam's apple bobbed. "...prisoners again?"

"I hope not." She looked down at her desk, not seeing the scattered paperwork and onboarding forms. "Are we on the record?"

"Of course not." Danny didn't shift his stance. "The

people *need* this story. I know that. You do, too, but sometimes, people need the room to just be… human.”

That hit Paige in the feels and she beat back the tears.

“We need *you* to be human.” Danny scooted back to lean forward, propping his elbows on his knees, his notepad falling to the floor. “Whatever you need to do, you can't go cold. Too many people are counting on you to care, to…” He twisted his lips as if the words he was about to say were distasteful. He stooped down to retrieve his notepad and set it on her desk. “To give a damn. So you give a damn. You give a big god damn. And you make DoDO understand they can *never* do something like this again.”

How the hell was she going to do that? She didn't voice that doubt, though. She just nodded then straightened. “Bring them in. Tell the story.”

He stood and pressed his fingertips into her desk. He opened his mouth to say something, but closed his lips and rapped his knuckles against the desktop instead, grabbing his notebook and shoving it in his pocket.

It was time to take the offensive. It'd only been less than a day. The people *were* getting their stories out there on social media. It wasn't like they were being told they couldn't. They were throwing their views and opinions out there. The people did know.

And Paige didn't need to lead *that* assault.

She just needed to get DoDO off U.S. soil. For good.

Paige called Ruben. “It's time to strategize.”

“Was about to call you and say the same thing. Lick your wounds enough?”

His tone wasn't harsh. He wasn't asking if she'd had a chance to tend her girly feelings. He was asking if she was okay. Sometimes, gruff people *sounded* like assholes with their word choice, but their tones and body language could change the intent. “No. But it'll have to do.”

"Okay. Have *Derrick* bring you by my office. But *only* Derrick."

She didn't know why that was, and she'd be asking when she got there.

But for now, she went to the house and checked in with her kids.

With Leslie laid up still, Nick and Mark had moved in. Mark was awake and had only been temporarily knocked out by something Kate had done to protect them. She wasn't really great at elven magic yet. Tru was busy with Leslie, his entire attention wrapped up in her. Yeah, she was comatose, but that didn't mean he couldn't do everything in his power to make her life amazing when she got up.

Including finishing the brake job on her car. Or finishing the bird house she'd requested three years ago. Or fixing the light switch in their bedroom closet. Or rehanging the –

He was keeping himself busy while his hands were completely useless. She couldn't blame him.

The kids were similarly keeping themselves busy to the point where the house was the cleanest it'd *ever* been. Well, except for when they'd moved in. Now, that wasn't to say that the kids were moving *quickly*. They weren't. But the house was *clean*. The dishes were done *and* put away. The washing machine *and* the dryer were working. Someone was vacuuming upstairs. Both the working brooms were missing. The furniture had been moved. The lamps had been fixed. The one sofa had been *sewn* back together where Ember had clawed through it.

Everyone worked through their worry differently.

Mandy was still laid up in bed because none of the adults were letting her get up. She'd nearly died. Bobby was on bed rest too. Mark actually sat with him, reading to him from a book—*20,000 Leagues Under the Sea*—and wasn't leaving the boy's side.

Nick hugged her on the landing outside Bobby's room and just held onto her, not letting her go. As an empath, he could *feel* what she was going through. She didn't have to explain herself.

She just held onto him, letting him hold onto her, letting him keep her stable in the onslaught and emotional battle raging through her. But she had a lot of people to check on and didn't have a ton of time. So, she eventually pulled back and kissed his cheek.

He held onto her hands, giving them a good squeeze, staring into her eyes with his melted chocolate gaze. "I love you."

She might barely know this man, but… "Love you, too."

Rai was…angry and wanted to go with Paige to D.C. to talk to the president and to get her to *understand* what was going on. Paige had to remind the girl she didn't have the clearance.

"But Leah does?" Rai asked incredulously.

"You can shift into any animal you want," Paige said, trying to find a cork for this bottle. "She can open doors."

Rai rolled her eyes and paced away, throwing her arms in the air then slapping them against her thighs. "I hate this. I hate all of this. What are we supposed to do? Wait?"

Paige felt like she was talking to an adult. "Prepare."

"How?" Rai spun, shouting at Paige. "We *were* prepared. They…" She blinked back tears then roared in anger.

Paige closed the gap between them and wrapped her light-ning charged daughter in a bear hug.

"I'm so scared," Rai whispered against Paige's chest.

"Me too," Paige said into the girl's dark hair. "Me too." She pulled away. "And that's why I'm going. Alone. With your Uncle Derrick."

Rai nodded, her lips pursed in dark thought, her brow furrowing deeply. "That's good. He's good in a fight."

He certainly had been. "I'll be back for dinner."

"Promise?"

"Can't. But that's what I'm going to try to do."

Rai swallowed and a lost look filled her eyes as the lightning died. "Come home for dinner. Okay?"

Paige cuffed her daughter's cheek. "Okay, baby girl. I will."

A knock sounded downstairs. She went downstairs, grabbing only her computer bag. "Hey." She was glad to see Derrick and, for the first time in her life, actually felt like she was looking up to a big brother.

He stood tall, wrapped in his jacket, wearing more rings than he needed and a couple of bracelets. He didn't look like he was going to a rock concert. He looked more like a Viking going to war.

"You know why Ruben wants you?"

He nodded briefly and cut a door open. "When you're going into anything that could be a battle, I'm your guy."

"Oh." That made her feel a bit better.

"Yeah. And I'm getting a security briefing for the next time."

"Oh." Pearl's office showed through on the other side. Paige wanted to ask more questions about that, but stepped through. Ruben's door was already open, so, she just walked into that office as well.

He looked up and grunted at Derrick to take a seat and flagged Paige through to Dawn's door.

Paige didn't wait and found the president on one of the couches as two people in uniform walked out the other one.

Dawn picked up a remote and turned on the TV, flipping it to a channel. It showed Walton addressing the press corps. "She went too far," he said. "We should never have invaded their corporate spaces."

Corporate spaces?

Dawn turned the volume down. "They've been playing this basically on repeat for the last hour."

"Is he completely missing the part where those 'corporate' goons killed dozens of innocent people? Just in that one location where we caught it on camera?"

Sighing, the president gestured for Paige to sit on the couch opposite her. "I have a decision to make."

"Well, if it's a decision between telling the truth and hiding it, I say tell it. Get your story out there."

Dawn nodded thoughtfully, but didn't answer.

"We weren't at fault. We *had* probable cause. They sent *demons* after us." Which sounded a lot worse than it'd actually turned out to be. "And they were *torturing* those people with the collars until *their heads exploded*. En mass. *That* information *must* get out."

"Except that I forced you to wear one."

Which was true, but so far, Paige wasn't seeing the down side here.

"And I forced your babies to wear them."

Okay. Paige could perhaps see how that wasn't *great* for the president. But she'd also been impeached, so just what was she trying to save, exactly?

"And if we show that, they're going to replay the video of little Rai breaking out of her collar."

"Which is fine." And which had probably taught DoDO a few ways to improve them.

"I'm trying to remain a sitting president," Dawn explained. "I can't help you if I'm removed from office."

And Walton had basically just showed his hand. He wasn't going to support paranormals. He was siding with DoDO.

For Paige, this wasn't in question. "You tell them the truth. You get in front of this and you level with the people. You show the footage. You tell them about the collars and their *true* intent, which—did you know about that when you put it on my babies?"

Dawn shook her head.

Great. "And you let them know just how far DoDO is willing to go. And then you label them as terrorists and you get them as far away from our country as possible."

Straightening her shoulders, Dawn squeezed her knees with her fingertips. "Okay." She nodded firmly at Paige. "That's all I needed."

Really? She'd been called in for this? "No. That's not all you need. They declared war on *your* people. They attacked with ghosts, not bullets, but it was an attack nonetheless. People are dead."

"Paranormals are dead."

"No, Madam President." Paige tried to push down her anger enough to remain respectful, but after the evening she'd just had, she barely had enough room in her heart for *respect.* "Paranormals were sent into feral crazes like they were made rabid. You don't think that was *planned?* That DoDO isn't *hoping* that word will get out about that? That they're *betting* that *someone* will be injured by that and that the nation will simply go to war on their own? Humans are in morgues across your nation. And let me just remind you that mundanes and paranormals both fall under your umbrella of protection. We're *all* your people." It pissed Paige off that she was *still* trying to get this woman to see that. "Not just the ones you want to claim."

Dawn stared at a point on Paige's face then nodded as she met Paige's gaze. "One nation. *All* Americans." She stood.

Paige rose to her feet. "You go out there and fulfill your damned oath to protect the people you serve. Madam *President,*" she said, emphasizing the last word for effect, leaning in and lowering her voice, "do your damned job."

Dawn raised her chin, her expression grim. "All."

Technically speaking, as a Secretary, Paige's job was now done. She'd advised the president.

But if Dawn didn't spin it the way they needed, if she found some other way to soften the blow, to save face for whatever reason, Paige was going to take the matter into her own hands.

Paige would save the paranormals of the United States. Failure was not an option.

3 3

With Dawn taking over getting the story out there—for now—Paige was free to work on other matters.

Yes. DoDO needed to be removed from U.S. soil and the government was probably the best way to do that. There had to be reasons for government, one of which was handling jobs that were too big for normal people. Like DoDO.

But *she* could track down *where* the collars were being made and stop *that*.

She went back to Red Star, completely side-stepping her office. She had a bunch of funerals to attend in the next couple of days, people she'd hired and should have sworn to protect. She had to consider that as she brought new people on, as Chuck's pack—those who were recovered and back, anyway—continued their work on the office suite. And was that even a good idea?

Really? Was it? Because…if she was thinking this one through to the end, the likelihood of President Flynn keeping her seat was slim. The woman had been impeached. Getting her out of office was just a ceremonial measure. Paige couldn't see a world where an impeached president was able to retain her seat as the leader of one of the most powerful nations in the world.

And if she lost her seat, then what was the likelihood that Paige would even remain in *her* position? Walton didn't seem to like her or paranormals. Or maybe she was reading too much into his statements, but he'd sided with DoDO after what they'd done. She didn't know if he was changing his views.

But Dawn had been good on her word. She'd released the videos of the strike team. She showed the demons being released from their traps. She showed the paranormals being tortured. She didn't show what happened. It was too… gory. But she'd followed it up with the reports of the dead and the coma patients and how the two were tied to DoDO. But she didn't say how it'd seemed to be strategic, in how Jardena had been killed along with several other highly influential people who had spoken against DoDO.

"This is a new world we find ourselves in and the dangers they present are far beyond what we ever could have imagined," President Flynn said, addressing the press. "Be assured that we are doing everything in our power to take care of this terrorist threat."

Paige didn't appreciate how it was kind of implied that the paranormals were to blame for this new threat because that wasn't true, but she did agree with the term terrorist in regard to DoDO. That's what they were.

Scout and her team were tracking down the information as best they could. They were narrowing it down, using the information they had. Paige wanted to apply her focus there. She felt on edge and unable to concentrate on the paperwork ahead of her. She kept looking at the legislation ideas she was bringing to those who could actually put it into law and all she saw were things that would never see the light of day.

She wanted to go talk to Wendy, but knew that their ideas of school integration would likely never happen even if Wendy could be awakened.

Equal rights? Probably off the board.

Ability to buy a house? Who even knew if that'd be allowed?

Paige realized she was allowing herself to feel defeated when she shouldn't, but…

She was shaken. She would get up and check on Leslie every hour or so, but there was no change.

DoDO had managed to get… close. Really… *close.*

Paige had been too confident for too long with her growing powers. Though, she did hope that *that* was coming to an end. Like, there was only so much *more power* she could gain before she just… she didn't even know what. But the truth was, she'd become complacent. Yeah, okay. She'd gone out of her way to make sure her wards were strong. And the town of Troutdale had probably felt a little safe because—even though they were blockaded *again*—she was there to protect them. The wards were there to protect them.

But Dexx had been taken from them when that shouldn't have been possible. By DoDO.

The wards had been breached by being overrun. By DoDO.

They were studying her and were learning her weaknesses.

To what end? What was their end game? Did they want to see all paranormals die? Be enslaved? What?

She didn't know if she'd ever learn that. She had to hope that Dexx would take care of Cardinal Bussemi, and President Flynn would take care of DoDO, so Paige could go back to taking care of her family.

Which was what she wanted.

That was the other thing eating at her. She'd been handed a big fight. She'd won.

Then she'd been blindsided and hit *hard*.

In that moment, the thrill of her new position was stripped away and she realized she wanted nothing to do with politics or the spotlight. She wanted paranormals to be safe. Yes. She wanted them to be able to live within the boundaries of society again. Yes.

But she wanted out of politics.

So, looking around this office suite, she realized she wanted to tear it down. She didn't want to hire anyone new. She wanted to send them all away.

She wanted Willow back.

Paige closed her eyes and fell back into her chair. She knew what this was. She was grieving. This... was grief.

She was still not quite over the loss of Alma. It didn't feel like she'd had *time* to cope with that. She hadn't been *allowed* time to deal with any of it. To let her grandmother go, to deal with her relationship with Dexx, to be a new mom and an old mom. Her *kids* hadn't been *allowed* to be babies, for crying out loud. She felt like she'd cheated the system, but each time she looked at Rai and Ember, she just felt as if *she'd* been cheated. She'd lost so many years of Leah's life and now she had missed out on theirs as well?

She wanted to rail and scream and throw things. She wanted to punch things, to go to the obstacle course out back and scream at scarecrows like Tyler. She wanted to hold Bobby and tell him things would be okay.

But since the attack, he'd gone quiet. He'd gotten his color back, sure. He wasn't as gaunt as he had been. But he was... haunted.

And Paige didn't know what to do about that.

More than anything, Paige wanted to be handed a situation she could *actually* handle. Like a normal person. She just wanted to go back to normal life. Be a normal detective—or running a detective agency. She'd be okay with running a department. She had never been a normal witch, but she wanted Leslie to have that chance.

She wasn't certain any of that was ever going to happen.

But she also knew she had to pull herself out of this funk if she was going to *make* it happen.

Five…four…three…two… one.

She breathed in and out with each numeral, pulling herself further from the edge of the emotional cliff.

She *could* make a difference.

She *did* have a position of power and influence. Mostly influence. Not really power.

She *was doing* a good job.

She was *positively* impacting lives.

She'd lost a lot of them. Just the night before. But that wasn't her fault. That wasn't on her. She hadn't—

They hadn't lost all of those people because she'd been weak or late or misinformed. They'd lost those people because there was an organization hell bent on destroying paranormal society and bending it to their own will. That wasn't on her.

Paige kept counting and kept repeating that, ignoring the messages coming to her phone. Each time her phone buzzed, her heartrate sped up a bit, wondering what new hell had just opened up, until she put it on silent to kill even the buzz.

Finally, when she'd gotten a handle on her emotions— grief, anxiety, overwhelm, the *weight* of the day—she flipped her phone over and scanned through the messages.

Most of it was just information. She was being copied on it. She wasn't the main recipient. The acting person was also given the information. So, Ismail and Lovejoy. They were the recipients of most of it.

But there was one message they didn't get.

Check it. From an Unknown number.

Oh, crap. Paige had totally forgotten to respond back to Quinn. She pulled out the other phone and saw another message from her. *Saw the news. Still have information. Come see me.*

There were coordinates.

There was *nothing* else she could do there, so she gathered her phones and Derrick.

Paige stepped through his door and into a room that looked very similar to the one under the Denver building that had crumbled. It had a bunch of doors and lots of symbols. When she switched to her witch vision, she was able to see the magick lacing each wall, each panel, each door.

A statue of a winged gremlin-like creature stood guard over the room.

"Gargoyle?" She reached a hesitant hand up, but didn't touch it.

It didn't move.

A door lit with a violet light and Quinn Winters stepped through dressed in tactical black. She didn't have the vest on, but she did have thigh belts with knives, and she wore the tactical boots. But she also carried with her a computer. She acknowledged Paige on the way to the stone alter in the middle of the room and set down her laptop.

"What is this place?"

Quinn shrugged. "There are a lot of old organizations. You're unlikely to find them all."

Great. So, she wasn't even going to learn about it. "What do you have?"

Quinn appraised Paige for a moment. "How are you doing?"

"Fine." Paige glanced at the screen, wondering if the *reason* Quinn was asking was because of what she saw on the readings.

Quinn rolled her dark eyes and nodded. "Yes. Your readings have been a little… off." She shrugged and took Paige through what they'd found.

Paige's magic *wasn't* growing in power. It just seemed like it because she was starting to access more of it. And, Quinn suspected, the other Whiskey witches were also capable of similar things.

"It's not connected to your door magick, though it does help it. In a weird way, I guess. There's a reason your door magick doesn't work the same as, like, his." She gestured at Derrick.

"You actually let her study you?" he asked with a thick frown on his brow.

Paige frowned a shut-up look at him. "Why is that?" Paige asked Quinn.

"Well, from what we can gather, your 'life magick' as you call it is what let you tap into the ley lines."

"Like mages."

Quinn shook her head. "Not even close. They dip in, take the ley energy, and have to change it to suit their needs. You don't need that. When you touch the ley energy, it doesn't have to change. That's the reason you're able to feed it."

"I— I don't even know what that means."

So, Quinn took Paige back to the studies she and the organization she worked for—not DoDO—had conducted on the Whiskeys over the years. Apparently, when Alma had been younger, she'd made a name for herself and had managed to put herself on their radar.

Each time Alma made her garden grow, a spike in ley line magick had manifested as the energies from the plants were then refed into the Earth.

When Paige had made the plants grow in Red Star, she'd inadvertently created a small yet growing ley-pool under the headquarters.

It wasn't that Paige was growing more powerful. She was simply developing a better latent understanding of her abilities. And her abilities had less to do with war and protecting people and had more to do with filling Earth's magickal energies it needed.

"With you and your family actively putting magick *back* into the Earth," Quinn said, "you're making magick more alive."

Derrick scratched his head. "She's... what?"

Quinn took in a breath that straightened her spine and looked at Derrick. "Even if this hadn't come to a head now—with Flynn and DoDO and everything—there would have been a natural explosion of magickal people. *More* witches. *More* humans developing magickal abilities, latent abilities."

How could this backfire on Paige? "So, there are going to be more paranormals?"

Quinn nodded. "We had a feeling this would happen. And it would make sense why you were granted Bobby. Because in time, he'll be needed as a guide."

"As a guide." Paige didn't want to sound like an idiot, but Bobby was her *son* who'd been a *toddler* just a few weeks before. She didn't *want* to think of him as some savior to the world. She hadn't had a chance to *raise* him yet.

Quinn held out her hands. "The people I work for—they've seen the future. Several versions of the future, actually. And you play a pivotal role in most of the good ones. But this? This wasn't supposed to happen yet. Not for years."

"How do you know?"

"I just do." Quinn said with a hard but open look in her almond-shaped eyes. "You were supposed to live a nice long life refilling the reservoirs of magick. People were supposed to wake up on their own, in their own good time. Your kids were supposed to age properly—well, the twins weren't supposed to house a rajasi and a thunderbird. I think the

spirit animals saw what was coming and decided to help. I—"
She stopped and closed her eyes for a moment. "The rajasi is not going to be able to stay much longer. We believe he will fulfill his role and then he will return to the spirit realm."

"The Vaada Bhoomi."

Quinn's face registered pleased surprise. "Yes."

"And what will happen to Ember after that?"

"We—" Quinn licked her lips and tipped her head to the side. "We don't now."

"But Rai and her thunderbird?"

"Will *probably* leave as well? She doesn't typically stay long."

"Typically?"

Quinn nodded but didn't offer more information. "Something in this timeline changed. Something big. And when it changed here, it changed in the others."

"Timelines?" Now, Paige *knew* they'd entered into science fiction. "You have time travelers?"

"No. Just seers. People who have spent lifetimes watching the futures—all the futures. Sven? He wasn't supposed to happen at all. He was shrouded in secret for the longest time. Your daughter was never supposed to have been taken from you. None of this was supposed to happen."

And yet, here they were. "So, you're telling me someone *made* this happen, starting all those years ago when Rachel took Leah."

"I'm saying," Quinn said, nodding, "that someone else can not only see futures, but they can make them."

"Who could do that?"

Quinn shrugged. "*That* is what I and the people I work for are trying to figure out."

"Who *do* you work for?"

Quinn shook her head and closed her laptop.

"Can you even be trusted?"

"Yes." Quinn nodded once, tipping her head to the side.

"You need to be a better liar." Paige paced away then came back. "So, what am I supposed to *do* with this information?"

Quinn stared at her like she was insane. "Don't you see? Whoever is behind all of this has an agenda. If you look at it, they're targeting *you*."

"To do what?"

"Destroy you? Your family? End your line? Your magick?" Quinn threw her hands up, taking a step back. "We don't know. But you need to be *very* careful. Because you're the center of everything."

That was... dumb. Paige licked her lips and bit them. She didn't even know what to do with this information.

"You're not *powerful*, Paige. That's the reason your magick's been 'glitching'." Quinn gathered her laptop. "You simply have the ability to *channel* the energy you touch, the power you gain, and you're able to return it to the Earth."

That... none of that made any sense. "I need you to stop watching us."

Quinn's eyebrow crinkled, but she released it with a nod. "If you need me..."

"You'll be buried deep inside DoDO trying to tear it down from within," Paige finished for her.

"Yeah." Quinn licked her lips, raising her chin, then frowned and shook her head. "I just thought you should know. Anyway."

"When you arrived in Troutdale..." Paige called to Quinn before the siren could leave.

Quinn stopped and turned back toward Paige. "Yeah?"

"You intended to get on my team to watch me."

Quinn opened her mouth, then pulled her bottom lip in and raked her top teeth across it. "Actually no. I meant to get close to Tyler because in the timelines I'd been sent to monitor and keep track of, he was the important one. He was the one who brought about this level of change. But when you arrived and things kept going off the recorded visions, we suspected something was going on. And that's when we discovered that DoDO might have a bigger role to play."

"Bussemi."

Quinn narrowed her eyes. "Yeah. Stay away from him, if you can. Your magick and all your abilities will be no match for him."

Good to know. "I'll do what I can."

"Great. Now, I really must go." Quinn disappeared through a violet-lit door.

That...hadn't been the information Paige had thought she'd receive.

But it did make her think. Who was behind all of this? And what did they want from her and her family? And did that mean this person wanted to attack the Whiskeys? Or just use them?

And would she give them the opportunity to show her?

Paige wasn't sure what to do with the information Quinn had given her. Feel elated? She was too worried and stressed and tired for that. Feel scared? There were too many real-world things in her life to make her scared. Who had that kind of time?

She scrolled through the news, reading headlines, her mind too fuddled to read the actual articles. She watched a few clips of videos, but again, her mind was too *full*. Going to the news was bad. The only thing she got was that the people —and maybe it was a PR spin. Who knew? Paige certainly didn't—didn't trust Dawn. They didn't know if what she was telling them was the truth. The Senate was compiling the information on the impeachment and were getting ready to put it to a vote to either let her serve her remaining term or force her to leave office immediately.

Paige… needed to care a little less because she was exhausted.

So, she went to the house and spent time with her kids. She didn't let them ignore her. Yeah. They were busy entertaining themselves with whatever projects they had going on, but she needed family time. So, she gathered them all up and played UNO and board games and made a mess of the kitchen while making dinner.

And she tried really hard to forget the fact that the world was a complete an utter mess. Her soul needed the reset.

The next day, she woke up feeling a little better, but her dreams or nightmares had been filled with danger just out of her view. Lots of dark colors and weird noises. There were a lot of notes, actually. She couldn't remember any of them, but she did remember that *notes* in dreams were weird because you couldn't *read* in dreams. Well, *she* couldn't read in dreams.

She received a new visitor the next afternoon, and a welcome one: Sam Waugh from Nederland. He knocked on her office door and let himself in, walking slowly with his blue cane and sagging back. His long, white hair hung over his shoulders, but his eyes met hers with a sharpness she remembered.

She greeted him and invited him to sit. "What are you doing here?"

"I wanted to see how you were doing," Sam said, resting his head against the back of the couch.

"Okay, I guess." Not even a little, but she was trying. "I need information, but what I'm looking for is so…" Damned hard to find.

"What are you looking for?"

"I need to know where DoDO's collars are being made."

"Like a factory?" he asked, setting both hands atop his cane and leaning forward. He pinched his eyes narrower and looked at her like she was missing something obvious.

She recalled everything that had happened in Denver during the time she'd met Sam and couldn't—Oh. "The chip."

His expression widened as he nodded.

Sven had been working on a chip of some sort, a shifter spirit inhibitor. She'd stopped that. "Is that what started DoDO on their…" She didn't know what to call it. Quest seemed too noble to be suitable.

Sam shook his head. "I can tell you that collars come out of that area. Same warehouses the demon used."

But where had those been? She'd never found out. She'd been so dumb before. But Barn might know. Tony might, too. "Thanks, Sam." She pulled out her phone and called Barn.

Sam smiled and waved at her. "Thank you for the invitation," he said quietly then saw himself out.

It certainly felt like things were starting to make sense, finally—things that had been nonsensical before, when they'd happened to her, when they'd been just a random string of events. But now… all those gaps she'd missed before were coming to a close.

Would things be different now if she'd *even thought* to search for the factory making the chips? That hadn't even crossed her mind. She'd been so concerned with discovering shifters then worrying about Dexx as he turned.

"Yeah, Paige," Barn said brightly, though he sounded a bit distracted.

"Hey, remember that Sven case in Denver?"

"No." His tone was firm. "Remember in Denver when Tony wanted to just shut me out of everything because I was human and so I didn't know anything?"

Oh, right. "There were chips in some of those victims."

"I remember that."

"Did you ever figure out where they were being made?"

"Yeah," he said, keys clacking. "Though, that's pretty old. I don't remember where I would have—I can call—you know what? Just—how about I call you back in a bit?"

"Sounds great. Thanks." Paige hung up then called Ruben.

"What?" he asked grouchily. "Complaining about the coverage?"

Why would she do that? It wasn't going horribly. Granted, she still didn't know *entirely* how government worked, but *if* she was able to keep her job, she should still be able to make the changes they needed to make happen. Maybe. Hopefully. "How much trouble would I be in if I stopped the manufacturing of the collars?"

"Hypothetically speaking?"

"Yeah." Which meant she'd be crossing a line or two.

"If you happened to be at a location and was hypothetically attacked, you'd be well within your right to defend yourself."

Which also meant she couldn't just go in. That *did* make sense, though she understood there *were* circumstances she *could* use to get her in the door. "Got it. Thank you."

"Hypothetically speaking, should I warn the president about anything?"

Uh. Yes. "I might be having a meeting."

"Where?"

She didn't want to say. "I'm still getting that buttoned down."

"Okay." Ruben sighed. "Just don't make anything worse for her than it already is."

"Try to remember that's a hole she dug on her own."

"Oh, I do," he said with a grunt then hung up.

Paige called Ismail into her office to make sure she wasn't disturbed for a while. "Hey," she said to him before he left. "Are you okay?"

He turned back to her. His eyes had dark bags under them and his shoulders looked weary. "I just lost one boss and now I'm about to lose another. So, you know? I don't know."

"I'm not going anywhere."

"You're going to do something reckless, aren't you?"

Yes. "It's just a mission to see what I can find, see who might be there."

"You're going to blow something up."

Absolutely. Yes. "I'm meeting someone to discuss a way to keep the collars from being manufactured. That's all." She had an inside gal. Quinn. Could she get the location verified? Paige was sure Barn was double-checking the information against what Dexx had been able to bring out of DoDO. She'd have to make sure he was, though. Without insulting him.

Ishmail narrowed his gaze. "What do we need to do?"

"Stay within the wards." She'd also powered them up a little more than before. She wasn't certain that'd work, that it'd be enough, but she had to try.

"I'll have the team draw up a statement."

"You don't even know how it's going to go down."

He flared his dark eyes as he walked out of her office, closing her new door with a soft slam.

Barn called with the information she needed. She pulled up the location on the internet and looked at it from the street view. She'd *been* there. Before. She could have taken the whole place down then.

That still might not have stopped DoDO. She couldn't kick herself for this one. She'd done her best at the time. Had it been enough? Obviously not, but that didn't mean it hadn't been her absolute best.

But it had been.

At some point, that just had to be enough.

She then called Chuck. "Can you gather the local leaders? I think I know where we need to go to kneecap DoDO."

"Meet at my place. We'll be there."

She stopped at the house first to talk with her kids.

They wanted to go too.

"No." Hadn't they learned their lesson already? "You can't go."

"We go with you, or we go behind you." Leah wore her hurt and angry face.

Paige rose to tell them no, to stay where they were safe. Then, she remembered them all passed out and nearly dying in the "safety" of their house. "Fine. You can come to Chuck's with me."

Leah shared a look with her friend, Ashley.

They went together, even though riding a horse would take longer than taking a door. Ember and Rai flew ahead. Bobby needed a ride, though.

So, Paige opted to go as a horse as well, and walked beside Ashley. They cut through the countryside and through yards. When they didn't have to travel by road, it was faster.

The trip gave Chuck's people more time to gather.

The kids almost immediately disappeared, meeting up and playing with the other kids from Chuck's pack.

Paige met Faith on the porch. "How're the affected shifters?"

Faith opened the door and motioned Paige in. "Back to normal." Faith's facial scar twitched as she winced.

"What?"

Faith shook her head. "Their shifter animals took most of the attack, which is why they acted so rabid. It's almost as if —" Faith held the screen door open, trying to find the right words.

Paige had no idea what she was about to say, so she had nothing to offer.

"It's almost as if the spirits were still collared. The wolves, the spirits, they were suffering from being repressed when they attacked in ghost form."

Interesting. "But the living are okay?" Paige asked, stepping into Chuck's large living room. Where had all those ghosts gone? Had reapers managed to take them all away? She had to hope so.

Faith lifted a shoulder in a shrug.

Paige had to hope they were because she was greeted by a room full of shifters. Pack alphas. She recognized a few of them from her interactions with them.

Once Chuck had everyone's attention, he gave the floor to Paige. She filled them in on the chips—at the time—that had then turned into collars. She told them of how they'd progressed and how she'd seen them used the other day. "They're weapons now."

"But they won't be used on us," Doe, the Utah alpha, said, her voice ringing clear in the large, rustic room. "You're making sure of that."

"You need to understand something," Paige said. These people, these leaders, needed to fully comprehend the severity of their situation. "In politics, I have no powers. I'm not a witch. I'm not a shifter. I'm a person. And not a very influential one at that. I don't know people. I don't have a ton of money. I often don't know the right thing to say, the best word-dagger to use, because I'm still learning the playing field."

"But I was under the impression you're doing well," Roger from Montana said. He was a coyote, which was rare as an alpha. He hadn't let her "in" at the time. That'd been one of the many "bust" trips, but he'd been fair.

She shook her head. "I am. But for how long? President Flynn, who assigned me to this position, is getting fired."

"Impeached," Faith grunted.

Same thing. "Vice President Walton doesn't seem to share the same opinion as she does."

"But that's good for us," Doe said fervently.

"Except that things have shifted." Paige then brought them up to speed on the president's views. "She still thinks the paranormals aren't completely in the right and we're not. We *have been* operating outside the law. We *have been* doctoring police and medical reports to cover our trails. But she's realized she'd gone too far. That, I think, is real."

"She could be playing you," Chuck said, his accent softening his tone.

"Yes. She could be." Paige wasn't a complete fool. "But Walton knows all this information and he's still backing DoDO. That speaks volumes to me. He's seen the videos. He's seen the data and the information. He's seen the proof of just how far they've gone, that they've far surpassed their grounds, and he still backs them instead of President Flynn."

A blonde female alpha who always seemed to rub Paige wrong curled her lips in disdain. "He seeks power. That's something we can all understand."

"Seeks power at the sake of others, though?" Paige asked. "That's not something we can tolerate."

The group erupted into chaos.

Chuck held up a hand for silence. "What do you suggest?"

She met the gaze of as many of the alphas as she could. "We take down the factory making the collars. That way, no matter who's in power, they can't use those against us."

"Wouldn't they still have the plans?" Faith asked. "Those would still be stored somewhere. We can't just magick those away."

"Agreed." Paige didn't' have an answer for everything. "But if they have none in stock, they can't use them against us until they've had a chance to make new ones."

"And do we know if there are other factories?" Chuck asked.

Paige shook her head. "We have a *lot* of their information and we're putting the pieces together as quickly as possible. Right now, we *believe* they have one hub making these, and they're in Denver. I have the location."

Chuck raised his face to the ceiling, clamping his hands between his knees. "And when we get caught?"

"We should probably *not* get caught." Paige was trying to figure out a way around that one, but the best way to make sure there was no blow back, that no one could rally behind a war cry and bring war to Troutdale's wards again, was to make sure that the only people who knew who was attacking was DoDO.

Then gaslight the crap out of them.

"We'll need one hell of a good plan," Faith grumbled.

"That's why you're here," Paige said. "Because if there's one thing I've learned, it's that I'm not the smartest person in the room."

People broke off in pairs and groups, but they were talking.

Paige wasn't sure this would work, but she couldn't let go of the idea, the notion, that if she was kicked out, if she lost her position, if paranormals were again made enemies of the state, those collars could be used to *torture* then *kill* them.

And that was something she couldn't allow to happen.

One battle—the battle of impeachment—was beyond Paige.

But this was something she *could* do. And this *did* involve her strengths. It was time to use them.

3 5

Paige and the kids went home later in the afternoon. She made sure the kids were safe and put them to bed.

They were a little upset about that because it was early, but she didn't care. They were going to take down the warehouse that evening. She understood that the Whiskey house wasn't as safe as she'd thought. Paige didn't care. She needed to feel like she'd done something right. She *knew* the battle itself wasn't the smartest idea. Everything was a tinderbox right now, and here she was striking a match.

But she couldn't erase the visual of what had happened outside New Orleans. It was *more* than the visual. It was the feel. She still remembered how it had felt to wear those she'd been trying to save.

That was what she was fighting against. She needed to make sure that no matter what else happened, those collars weren't able to be used against paranormals again.

Quinn agreed to do what she could about scrubbing the internal servers of the plans, so that would certainly help.

Paige was going to focus on destroying evidence. They'd

all agreed that her type of magick left a signature, so she wasn't going to join the fight directly. But she could destroy research. She'd be looking for the servers. She'd have a few other shifters with her who'd all be going after as many computers as they could find.

Then when it was all over, they'd claim they'd never been there. Destroy all the evidence. Make sure they weren't seen on any cameras. Nothing recording them. Deny everything.

It was the best plan they had.

It *could* work.

Paige wasn't calling in any of her new contacts. No four-star generals. No president or chief of staff. She wasn't calling in Merry or the—

That was one power move she couldn't ignore.

What were the stakes? As she kissed Bobby goodnight and tucked him into bed, his eyes falling shut almost instantly, she realized she was staring at the consequences. If she messed this up, she'd lose her kids. All her kids. Her life. And not just her. All paranormals. If this went wrong, there were a lot of people who could lose their kids, their homes, their lives.

She used the amulet Merry had given her.

The hallway mirror flashed and Merry's face shone through. She blinked coolly. "Yes?"

What was this? "What are you doing in my mirror?"

"Nothing." Merry looked bored, but her tone said she was irritated that Paige wasn't smarter. "I can't be expected to just show up each time you call. You're very needy."

Paige wasn't *needy.* "I call it getting stuff done."

"Like a wrecking ball." Merry shook her head and waved off Paige's concern. "It's magick."

There were limits to even Merry's magick, though. Paige gave her the mom stare.

"Not my own," Merry said, tipping her head to the side,

her dark eyes wide. "I stole the stone from a goddess. Are you happy now?"

Paige recalled Bastet liked to use pools of water to watch things play out. "Okay. As long as my—"

"Yes, yes. What did you want?"

They didn't have time to waste. "I'm going to attack a warehouse."

"You think that's wise?"

Paige leaned her head on her fingertips, not quite comfortable with this conversation. "I'm destroying their ability to create more collars."

Merry made a guttural noise then nodded. "I suppose those weapons would merit a little destruction at a time like this."

"That's kinda what I thought."

"A word of caution, Paige," Merry said, her voice rising a smidge. "Don't get caught."

"That's why I'm calling. You have some pretty powerful friends."

Merry's expression flashed with mild disgust before realization relaxed it again. "Yes. I do. They come with a price, though."

"I'm sure they do. Look, they said they wanted war, right?"

Merry nodded but said nothing.

Paige wasn't going to say she was *leading* them *to* war, but if this could potentially buy her some help? "This will be a good stone to throw."

Merry's lips wrinkled as she pursed them. "They're going to want more than a thrown stone, Paige. They're going to want a battle cry. A bell. They're going to want a midnight ride."

Wax eloquent, why didn't she? At least she understood the intent. "You know I'm not ready for that."

"I do," Merry said, a film of relief raising the corners of her lips and dropping the corners of her eyes. "You had me worried."

"I don't know how to play with these kinds of people."

"I'm glad to see you're not taking it completely off the table."

Paige hadn't thought about what they'd offered. Not really. "I still want to find a peaceful solution."

"And you think this will do that? You would be striking at them."

Paige closed her eyes and nodded slowly.

"You'd be putting them on the defensive."

"And possibly leveraging myself to maintain my position after President Flynn is removed from office."

Merry's face blossomed into a smile. "Oh, Paige." She smiled proudly, looking up and away, shaking her head. "I never thought I'd see the day."

"Yeah, yeah, yeah. Will you help?" Because Paige was done whoring herself out.

"As far as my help, what do you need?"

"To not get caught. I have someone wiping their internal servers."

Merry's lips rounded in a surprised "o," with a raised eyebrow.

"I'll be getting rid of hard copies on sight. I've got people working on destroying computers. But that's not to say there aren't copies out there somewhere, or that there aren't cameras that could catch us. I need to be able to deny being there or even knowing anything about it. I can't have proof showing otherwise."

Raising her chin, Merry nodded shallowly. Another smile graced her thin lips. "I'll see what I can do. When is this happening?"

"We have the information now. We're acting on it before anything changes."

Irritation flashed across Merry's eyes. "Of course. I'll see what I can do." She waved a hand, and Paige's mirror was just a mirror again.

With that out of the way, it was time to get into position.

Paige wasn't like Derrick who prepared spells on rings and tokens and daggers and...who knew what else. She just had to show up and be ready, which... was she wrong? That didn't seem very... witchy of her.

Several Blackman witches and shifters were gathering outside Chuck's house. It felt a little like old times.

She wasn't in charge of this operation, though. Chuck was. She was to follow his orders, especially if she wasn't going to get caught. She wasn't there for battle. She was there to destroy information. Maybe save people if there were people left to save. Denver *had been* one of the hit cities. That could simply mean they had a stash of paranormals imprisoned, but that didn't mean they had "extras" to spare in fighting the packs.

Paige wasn't going without her magick, though. She touched on it, getting it ready. She still wasn't *quite* certain what Quinn was getting at with her magick not "getting stronger" but that she was finally learning how to use it.

For that evening, she simply had to fall back on instinct. Old school magick. Old school approach.

But hopefully smarter.

Chuck gave the command and doors opened all around them. The first wave of shifters disappeared. It seemed like forever, but eventually, more doors opened and more shifters went through to the sounds of battle on the other side. It wasn't a lot, not like she'd become accustomed to.

Finally, Chuck turned to Paige and the handful of shifters

with her. "We've located the areas where they store information and the computer room."

Paige nodded, not knowing if he meant a server room or a room of computers. She'd find out when she got there. She wasn't planning on using explosives. She was going to use good old magick, and another trick she got from Tru. The other shifters were intent on using their claws. No need to worry about things going wrong or alerting local police if they didn't have to.

Pulling on her magick, she stepped through her door, ready for just about everything. She slipped into witch vision.

On the other side, she stood in front of a lab of sorts. The walls were temporary plastic sheets on wood studs. Her witch vision didn't show a lot of extra information, and she couldn't switch to shifter vision because she was surrounded by shifters.

Going in with her team and not necessarily being the lead was refreshing. She was on the lookout for potential trouble, sure. But she wasn't the one leading the charge. She wasn't the one causing the damage. She might not have to go home with the gore.

The warehouse area she walked into was cordoned off by more plastic sheets, this time on metal studs. The sounds of fighting—mostly grunts and people and not necessarily gunfire—was to her left. There was a large, open area and a wall with three doors. She didn't head in that direction like she normally would have. Instead, she crept toward the partitions, which were slightly opaque. She didn't see any bodies or the shadows of moving people. Just tables and beds and machines.

She slipped behind the first curtain as those with her chose others. An empty hospital bed dominated the small space with equipment on all sides of it. On one table were reports. She pulled out her phone and took a few pictures to send to Barn when she was done. She didn't know what they meant, but he might. And maybe he could use that information to reverse what had been done with the coma patients.

With Leslie.

She could hope. She took out her lighter and started a fire, using the air to bring it to life and contain it. She didn't need to set the entire place ablaze. She was just there to take away their research.

She repeated the process in each room she found. All the curtained areas seemed to be where they'd held their victims and had been gauging responses. There were even reports on their pain threshold and when they saw results.

From what little she could understand, they'd managed to find a way to monitor the shifter spirit and they were working to separate that from the human soul it had been bound to.

The science was well above her head, but it made a sick sort of sense.

There was something else about this place. It seemed to be draining her. Not quickly. She wasn't staggering or anything, but doing any magick was difficult.

It was like the area was starved.

Taking the information Quinn had given her, she turned on her witch vision again and looked around. Many things pulsed with a dull blue light. The machines had been lined with it, as if they'd managed to somehow combine technology and magick together.

But below her feet was a roiling mass of darkness laced with blue light that seemed to disappear as if being extinguished.

Experimentally, she reached out with her witch hand, focusing on her life magick. She'd never actually paid attention to *that* magick alone. She'd never tried to isolate it. But instead of focusing on her door magick, instead of trying to grab souls and sending them back to Hell, she focused on the feel of *energy*.

That was draining.

Black boxes lay scattered all around the site, similar to the ones that had been outside the Whiskey lands, with leaching roots digging into the concrete floor. Unlike on the Whiskey lands, Paige could *see* what these boxes were doing. They were taking energy from the Earth, tapping into the ley lines—though she could only feel that, not quite see it—and were pulling the stolen energy into the machines.

Remnants of the disposed energy lined the beds as well.

What the hell had been going on here?

She searched for an office among the doors lining the walls and found one. Inside, boards with information plastered on them hung on one wall. Not all of it made sense to her, but she took pictures to show to smart people. She had to have *someone* who could figure out what was going on here.

A massive black box took up a large portion of one of the corners of this office. She'd have to destroy that. But before she did, she grabbed a crate from outside the office and shoved as much of this research into it as she could. She called to their Blackman witch and told her to send the crate through a door to Troutdale.

But that wasn't enough. There was so much information here and just taking pictures of it wasn't enough.

So, together, Paige and the Blackman witch opened a door and shoved *everything* through, or as much of it as they could. "If you find more stuff like this, send it on. Go."

The woman nodded and left the now mostly stripped room.

Leaving Paige to face the black box on her own.

It reeked. Not with… a smell. At least, not with anything her human nose could detect, but her magick did. It shied away from the black box and as she drew closer to it, tendrils of a thick dark smoke rose from it, seeking her out.

Like snakes searching for something to eat.

If this devoured ley energy, then what would it do to someone who *fed* ley lines?

Shit. Paige backpedaled.

She'd *touched* the box the last time *with* her magick.

But those boxes had been different. She looked around with her witch gaze and didn't *see* the red haze of a dome. *Those* black boxes had been designed to mark, maim, and murder.

She needed to know the intent of these *and* to free the Mother from the constraints put on her. But the last time Paige had done that, she'd used the pull of the pack to keep her grounded, and she'd injected the light of her soul into the box.

But that had destroyed the boxes.

Fuck.

Paige shook out her hands. This area *felt* different than the areas outside the Whiskey lands. These *boxes* felt different. They felt… invasive? Contagious?

She didn't know *how* to be careful on this one. But she did know one thing. These boxes needed to be undone. They needed to be broken.

So, she reached out with her witch hands and grabbed two of the roots.

The pull on her magick was immediate. She didn't have to offer up the light of her soul. This box was sucking her dry.

Panicking, she reached deeper inside herself, trying to gain her connection to her pack. Anything.

She found the demon door.

The box unraveled it. It found a thread to the door itself and tugged. It felt as though the connection between Paige and the Hell realm was being eaten away.

She opened her mouth to scream, to tell someone—anyone—she needed help. But no sound came out. She tried to release her hold on the roots, the energy abyss below her feet beating in time to her racing heart. The box wrapped leaching roots around her witch hands, keeping her in place.

The door opened behind her and a familiar voice filled the sucking silence. "Well," Mario said, "aren't you a bit of a surprise?"

Jeezus. Paige wasn't going to make it out of this one. Fuck.

Being unable to disconnect herself from the soul sucking black box was one thing. Knowing that someone who viewed her as an enemy was an added thing. The two together? Paige tried to disengage herself enough to be able to shift, to call out to the pack for help.

With the box firmly attached to her magick, there was no way of doing that.

Cawli's presence struggled in her mind. His ethereal form pulled his head to the side, parts of him being dragged into the box. *I'll get help.*

Mario walked around Paige, his nearly white hair smoothed back and finding some sort of light source to reflect. His brilliantly blue eyes practically shone as he stared between her and the box with a wide smile of victorious joy. "I must say," he said, his British accent softening the blow of his words, "you *are* a sight for sore eyes."

Not what she needed to hear.

She called to the elements, bringing them to her.

It was as if they couldn't even hear her.

"I've been trying for *months* to get that box to work."

Mario turned, studying it closely. "Just look at it. Doing exactly what it's supposed to." He turned a narrowed gaze to her. "No wonder Sven was so deeply interested in you."

She turned her attention away from Mario and focused on the box. Maybe instead of *panicking,* she could focus. What did it want?

It didn't answer. It merely ate.

Was Mario trying to *eat the souls* of the paranormals he'd captured? She recalled the look of Cawli trying to withstand the storm of the box's assault. The collars hadn't merely been about repressing the shifter spirit. "You're trying to devour them," she grunted out. At least those were the words she'd intended. They came out sounding a bit thinner, not quite as formed.

Mario took a step back and folded his hands in front of him, perusing her as if she was something he was thinking of purchasing. "Yes, Paige. In the simplest of senses, that is exactly what I'm doing."

"Why?" If she could figure that out, she might be able to figure out how to stop the box. Or tear herself away from it.

"Because the mages, in all their glory and dumb sense, have depleted the one source we once had."

He didn't sound like the Mario she'd come to know. Her Mario had been kind of a nincompoop. He'd been shallow, a follower. This man seemed... older, wiser, as if he'd seen things. "Who am I speaking to?" she asked with her demon summoning ability. Well, at least she tried. But that ability was being funneled away from her because it was part of her door magick.

Mario threw his head back and laughed heartily. "You were always smarter than the rest."

She didn't feel like that at the moment.

"I made a pact, a deal." He turned a semi-serious though overly pleased smile to her. "With something... powerful."

Something like a bahlrok? She had to hope not. But she had information now. He was trying to find a new energy source. "Human souls not enough?"

Mario rolled his eyes and waved her off almost comically as if she'd told the funniest joke of the century. "I have no idea why demons and angels fight over those puny things. They're practically worthless. But shifter spirits?" He advanced on her. "Imagine harnessing the power of a being capable of creating an entire plane of existence for themselves?"

Paige didn't know much about that. She didn't know how the Vaada Bhoomi had come to be. And she wasn't certain they'd been the ones to create it in the first place.

But she did know that the shifter spirit was strong enough to not *need* containment. Cawli had shown her that. She didn't *know why* they chose to team up with humans and to be bound by the rules of a physical form, but Cawli could exist outside her body.

A shout went out in the area outside the door.

She had to hope it was the cavalry. Paige needed a diversion so she could try to break this damned box.

Mario tipped his head to the side and leaned to see around her. Then he straightened and met her gaze with a smile, raising his invisible eyebrows. "I'll be right back."

She didn't know how to warn them that they were in trouble, that he was stronger somehow, that he'd made a deal with some sort of demon. She opted not to waste the time whoever had shown up had allotted her.

The box needed to feed. It was searching for the energy of shifter spirits.

She couldn't let Mario get to them.

She did have one thing, though. A Hell's gate seared into her bones.

But for how much longer? The damned thing was unraveling. Fast.

Cawli appeared in the room with her again, his fur dragging from him in wispy tendrils as if he was made of dust.

She might not be able to destroy it. But if she could *overload* it. But not with animal spirits.

With demon souls.

She knew this was a bad idea. They were people. Ones she didn't entirely understand, but they were people.

But this *could be* one of those deciding moments that could bring another ally to their door in the coming war. If DoDO *invaded* their realm as well and tapped into their souls, drained them... then when Paige went to meet DoDO in war, they might help.

It was a long shot, and she didn't know if her logic was entirely viable. The only thing she knew for certain was that she was running out of time because the door to Hell was disappearing.

Disappearing.

The one thing she'd *tried* to get rid of for years had bonded to a shifter spirit in order to cure, and it was being eaten by a magickal item.

Calling on the power of her hands, she dug into the fabric of their world and *reached* for Hell. Normally, she'd call for demon names, but she couldn't this time. For one, her mind was scrambling as she felt her essence being pulled from her.

For another, she didn't want to leave a trail leading to her. She wanted that trail of dead demon souls to lead straight to DoDO.

Her mind slipped, memories racing around in her head, creating a maelstrom of noise. A few voices popped up that didn't belong to her. She didn't know exactly what was going on. The visions. The voices. The emotions.

They weren't hers.

Kitten, Cawli called through the storm. He appeared in her mind's eye, something black and inky in his teeth. *Take this.*

She grabbed it with her witch fingertips, trying to hold onto it as the black box fought to devour it and her and every bit of energy she had in her soul.

But as parts of her were stripped away, new parts shone through, like the castle in the *Dark Crystal* once the stone was healed.

Not allowing herself to be distracted by that, she focused on the rope, the thread Cawli had given her.

A thread to her door to Hell.

Calling on her energy, pulling it from her toes, through her legs, her hips, abdomen, chest, arms, and into her fingertips, she called a door to be opened.

And invited the box through it.

It hesitated like a starving dog, then dropped her like a bad bone and leapt for the delicious goodness on the other side. Tendrils of darkness shot from it, stabbing things on the other side she couldn't quite see. She could *tell* she'd made a connection to the other side more by the fact that she'd gotten a reprieve.

The power built inside the box.

Paige stood in place, her feet grounded, her arms held rigid on either side of her body. She turned her head to see if she could tell how the battle was going.

Not well. Mario's form filled the door frame, and he didn't appear to be touched in the slightest.

Shit. She was nearly out of time.

What do we do? Cawli asked, his fur still drifting from him like stardust in a black hole.

She didn't know. Did the box feel like it was overheating? No. There was no heat. Over—whatever? Her mind struggled to find the right words, the right terms.

Overpowering? Overloading?

A shaft of wind shot through the office as the air finally rose to her call.

The Earth groaned, the concrete cracking as it heaved upward.

Magma seeped upward, the heat beating at her.

Water poured from her, evaporating from her skin, from anything with water nearby.

Mario turned with a little surprise. "*What* are you doing?"

Paige couldn't give him any attention. She used the elements to shift the box. To move it. To break the roots and to disengage it from its location.

The cries of demons still sounded through the door she'd cut open.

If she could dump it into the other realm…

Would it work?

Would it split their world?

Hers?

Tear the two worlds further apart?

There were so many unanswered questions. But she knew one thing. If it remained here, it would drain her and everyone with her.

It's moving, Cawli grunted.

It was.

But she needed *more*. So, she dug in deep. She pulled on her door magick, taking energy from it and using that to push. She pulled on her soul and fed that into the move to push.

Cawli gave Paige a long look, something lighting his flickering cat eyes.

Paige cried out, not quite knowing why, but it almost looked as if he was saying… goodbye.

Then the small cat leapt at the box, throwing his ethereal form at it with a tiny house-cat roar.

The box fell through the door she'd made—taking Cawli as well—collapsing the door behind it.

Paige staggered as the abyss let go of her. Her witch hands retracted back into her. The wind buffeted her, wild and out of control. Water droplets fell on her only to sizzle away as the lava continued to spill forth from the cracks in the concrete.

She turned to Mario, enraged and empowered, carried by the force of the elements alone.

His startling blue eyes widened as he stumbled backward.

Paige needed to feel her teeth sink into his neck. She thought of a mighty tiger and shifted—

Only to discover she'd maintained the same form.

Cawli, she called in her mind.

Nothing answered her back.

She tried to shift into a fox, a gorilla. Anything.

Nothing.

Mario took another step back and clapped his hands with a smile. "Well done, Paige."

Bodies littered the concrete floor. Bodies of shifters in partial shift, some in full shift. She knew *they* were still alive, at least. The ones in full human, naked form, though?

They were probably dead.

Paige shook off her shock at no longer being able to shift. Cawli might be trying to find his way back to her. She might just need to cut another door to Hell. Or he might find a long road back to her.

She couldn't fight that battle now. First, she had to defeat Mario.

So, she turned to the magicks she still possessed. Elements, door, and… life.

The smaller boxes around the place were shrinking, disappearing, shriveling as if the disappearance of the one box had broken their ability to exist. Her life magick—the stuff that came from her very soul—was safe.

But could she use that on him?

She pummeled him with wind, creating a massive storm inside the warehouse. The metal roof screeched as it was pulled inward.

Mario batted one panel away with his hand. He tipped his head, irritated, and unbuttoned his sleeve, rolling it up.

She didn't have time for that. She flung her hand at him, screaming her rage.

Earth's fire surged forward to answer, shooting from the cracked concrete and crashing into him. Smoke flared up as things melted and vaporized—the curtains behind Mario, his clothes and body, perhaps?

Paige pulled at the lava that swallowed Mario. She piled as much onto him as she could stand. The heat from it rose into the air, making it difficult to breathe.

As the liquid stone turned from a blinding white to a darker red, cracks appeared on the surface, then a hole appeared. A charred fist broke out, followed by an arm, then…

Mario stepped out, his shirt and most of his pants burned and peeled back, but his skin healing and pink.

What the hell had he teamed up with?

He lowered his head, bowing his shoulders slightly as he pulled up power, reaching with his hands.

The blue light of the energy he'd gathered sputtered out before it could reach him.

Paige smiled, deciding to keep *her* magick to herself. She wasn't going to *feed* him with the power of her soul. The Earth? Yes. Him? No.

So, instead, she threw every bit of elemental rage she could.

The elements fed off her anger and answered with their

own, coiling around him, constricting, building, rising, squeezing.

He released a guttural squawk then pulled something small out of his pocket. It flashed in the light of her lava. His blue eyes lit with the promise of reciprocation.

Then he vanished.

Paige released the elements, allowing them to disperse back to where they belonged. The lava, of course, could only harden as it cooled. But the Earth settled, leaving giant cracks in its place. The storm abated, the once dark clouds evaporating through the massive holes in the ceiling.

Leaving Paige to stand in the middle of the warehouse, panting.

They'd won.

Hadn't they?

Well, they were alive. *She* was alive.

But this time, that wasn't enough. She'd managed to stop Mario. She'd managed to slow him down. She didn't know to what extent at the moment, but she hoped it was enough.

What was the cost?

It was time to find out.

P aige stumbled until she located a Blackman witch who could open a door for her. Paige was tired, but not *exhausted* like she had been from past battles. But *something* was missing.

Cawli.

The Blackman witch dumped Paige in Chuck's driveway. She made her way to the woods, reaching for the door embedded in her bones.

It wasn't there.

Her bones were fine. She was fine.

But the door was gone.

That…was good. Right?

She had to hope so.

She pulled out her witch hands and cut a door to Hell. It wasn't super stable. Door magick wasn't something she was good at. She was about to walk through when Derrick grabbed her, stopping her.

"What are you doing," he demanded.

"I've got to get Cawli," she mumbled. She might not be exhausted, but she wasn't working on all thrusters either.

She'd just lost part of her soul to a box, so maybe she could cut herself a little slack.

He shook his head but didn't let go of her arm. "I'm going with you."

Paige opened her mouth to tell him no, that she was going to Hell, but she couldn't. Mainly because she knew she might not have a way back if she didn't bring him. *Her* door magick was great for a one-way trip.

Taking in a deep breath, she moved to step through.

But the door was slammed closed before she could.

Balnore stood where it had been, furious disbelief on his face. "What do you think you're doing?"

"I'm getting Cawli back," she said. Because she wasn't just going to leave her shifter spirit over there.

"He didn't—" Balnore gripped her arms. "He didn't make it."

That wasn't possible. "How do you know that?"

The demigod raised his face and took in a deep breath. Then, like she was a toddler throwing a tantrum, he dragged her over to Chuck.

The alpha knelt beside someone lying on the ground. Chuck looked up as they approached. His blue eyes closed briefly, then he stood up, saying something softly to the shifter on the ground.

Paige couldn't hear what he'd said. She should have been able to. Why couldn't she—The answer hit her, but she didn't want to believe it. She just had to *find* Cawli. She just had to *get to* him.

Chuck met her halfway then licked his lips as if bracing himself. "I'm so sorry, Paige."

She didn't need him to be sorry. "He's just in Hell," she said. "I just have to go get him. Bring him back."

Chuck started shaking his head almost as soon as she'd started talking. "He disappeared from our connections when he went across."

Paige ran through the logic of it. Cawli had gone through. They'd been able to feel him. So, there was hope—

The box.

The box had devoured him.

Paige let that knowledge roll over her.

Cawli was dead.

That knowledge left her feeling… heavy and numb.

"What about the box?" she asked quietly. "Is it disabled?"

"Finally?" Balnore asked, his voice low as well as he shifted his weight. "Yes. Though there were heavy casualties. Demons want war."

"Good," she said, not feeling victorious. "We'll point them at DoDO and have them help."

"That's a dangerous road to travel."

"DoDO's a dangerous adversary." Paige swallowed hard, not even able to dredge up tears. She was just so… numb. Just so… overwhelmed. Too many things had happened. She'd *done* too many things. She'd taken *too much* action.

And not enough.

"The numbers?" she asked, turning her face to Chuck, who would never be her alpha again. She'd never have to ask that question or hope for that answer. She was what she had been before all of this, before Denver, before shifters, before Sven. She was a witch.

A terrible witch.

"We lost a few," Chuck acknowledged. "But we will be fine. Did you destroy the information?"

She shook her head and pulled out her phone, not really able to focus. She needed to call someone. But who?

Cawli.

She closed her eyes.

It wasn't like she really needed to mourn him. He'd been

in the back of her mind, but he hadn't been a part of her. Not like other shifters. He hadn't bound his soul to hers.

If he had, he might still be alive.

That's when she realized what was going on inside her head. It wasn't that she was numb. Well, not entirely.

It was that her mind was silent.

She was alone. Inside her own head.

Staring into the dark caverns of her mind, she felt the echoey emptiness. She'd never *asked* for him. She'd never really felt him with her, had always felt as though he spent more time *away* than with her.

But now that he was gone, she realized just how much time he'd been there. Comforting her when she'd needed it, bolstering her when she'd faltered. How much of her success, of her capabilities, was thanks to him?

She needed the Blackman witch who had helped her steal the information. She turned away to search for her.

Derrick grabbed her arm, peering into her face with concern. "What are you doing?"

She shook her head. She didn't *need* his concern. She just had to focus.

He shook her.

But hands pushed his away, and arms enveloped her, holding her tight. She knew those arms. They were Balnore's, a demigod she'd always seen as a demon, who—even so— had been a type of father figure to her. She stepped into his hug, holding him tight, burying her head in his chest.

He whispered a few words to her in a language she didn't understand, but he laid his cheek against the top of her head, then his chin.

The chin wasn't comfortable, but his arms were. She didn't need someone to tell her things would be okay. She'd find a way to *make* them okay. She just wished the world would stop getting so much bigger. At some point, bigger monsters *had* to stop happening.

Though, if that was truly the case, then why was Bobby older? Why had his abilities needed to manifest now?

And why were Rai and Ember not babies? She believed the witch world kept things in balance. So, what did that mean for her? Was she about to face something even worse?

Without Cawli, though, she felt like part of her was missing. That she'd somehow lost half of her power.

But... also the demon door.

No Dexx. No door. No Cawli.

She forced herself to raise her head. "I need the witch who helped me gather their research."

Derrick nodded and cut a door, bringing her along with him, though he was gentle about it. "Bigs," he called as he stepped onto the Blackman porch.

Phoebe walked out of the house. "Derrick? Is it over?"

He shook his head. "Where's Bigsby?"

"I don't know." Phoebe took a look at Paige, and concern washed over her slight face. "Are you okay?"

"No," Derrick said, his face folded with a look that said he didn't know what to do. "It's been a really hard couple of days." He pulled out his phone and dialed.

That's when Paige remembered she still had *her* phone in her hands. She'd been about to call someone. But who? She couldn't remember.

She needed Dexx. Not to fix this. Not to make her feel better. But just...to lean against. She just felt so damned alone.

With no one to call, she stashed her phone.

Derrick hung up and gave Paige an open look with almost a smile. "Found her."

Paige nodded.

Phoebe touched Paige's arm. "Can I get you anything?"

Paige shook her head. If she wanted people to stop showing concern, she'd have to plaster on a smile. But that took energy she didn't have. "No. I'm…" Fine? She *wasn't* fine. She looked at Derrick. "Bigsby?"

Derrick cut another door, and this time, they stepped into Red Star's bullpen. It looked like a storm had rolled through. Paper was everywhere. The boards were shoved in between two cubicles, the plant wall pitched at an angle.

Bigsby looked up, her dark hair pulled back in a hasty ponytail.

Sitting at a laptop in front of one of the boards, Barn looked excited as hell.

Scout came out of the back with a fresh mug. She stopped. "Hey, boss. You look like shit."

"Feel like it," Paige said, her voice harsh. "Tell me we got something good."

"We do!" Barn's voice trembled with excitement. "I know what they were doing."

He went into a very long and very complicated description of what the collars had been intended for. It wasn't to make shifters more susceptible to bursting out. It had, as she'd theorized after seeing how the box reacted to Cawli, been an attempt to separate the animal spirit in order to turn it into pure energy.

"But why?" Barn asked, holding up a finger. "I don't know." He looked thrilled about that.

"The ley lines are drained," Paige answered, her voice even and almost mechanical. "Mages need power. They're running out."

"Mages," Barn repeated.

"DoDO," Scout said shortly, setting down her mug to cross her arms over her chest. "And they were doing this. Do we know if the internal files got scrubbed?"

That's what Paige had been trying to do. She pulled out

the phone Quinn had given her and found she had a message. *Done. Tru's virus worked.*

That was all she needed, though she hadn't realized Tru had given Quinn a virus. It was good thinking. "Yeah." She stashed the phone back in her pocket. "Good work, everyone."

Scout uncrossed her arms. "We need to make sure they never get their hands on this."

"Agreed. So, make sure that doesn't happen. Whatever it takes." Even if it meant destroying everything.

"I think I can use this," Barn said, "to wake them up."

The people in comas. Leslie. The others. "Good." Paige didn't have anything left in her.

Derrick touched her arm, then held it, breathing in a deep breath. "I'm taking you home."

She didn't argue.

When she made it into the house, she was met with darkness she didn't have shifter vision to penetrate. So, she felt around with her toes, trying not to stumble into anything. She opened one door then another, checking on her family.

They all slept. They were all safe. Safe and sound.

She closed the door to Leslie's room and walked to the window of the reading nook, staring into the backyard, tired and spent.

Leaning against the wall, she slid to the floor, pressing her elbows into her knees and her palms to her eyes.

They'd won.

The threat of the collars was no longer on the table. DoDO couldn't use them against the paranormals any longer. They couldn't make new ones. They couldn't strip people of their shifter spirits to use as a replacement to ley energy. DoDO would be stopped. She could see the end.

At least... she hoped.

This had to end. She didn't know if she had another battle in her if she could face a bigger, badder bad guy.

She let her hands drop and stared down the hall, listening to people snore.

She was tired of being alone. *If* she continued this war, she'd need to regain her people. Leslie needed to wake up. Dexx needed to come back.

But she'd never get Cawli back. She'd never have a voice inside her mind, guiding her, offering her strength and a second opinion.

She let her head fall back against the wall, hitting the windowsill with a dull pain. *This* was the price of peace. And it wasn't even a peace she could claim was fully hers yet. She wasn't certain she'd wake up the next morning and still have it.

This wasn't going to work.

But she still wasn't prepared to admit they needed to go to war.

Because the United States Government was just another bigger, badder monster.

And Paige was just…

…tired.

But tired enough to accept peace at the loss of freedom if it came to that?

She had to hope it wouldn't because she wasn't sure of her answer. For now, she'd go to sleep, get up, continue working on her peace, putting it in cement before Dawn was removed from office. She'd try to make that work.

And she'd be staying close to home. A *lot* closer to home. She'd ventured too far. Tried to do too much.

She wouldn't do that again. She had too much to lose.

They all did.

The end

This concludes Book 3 of the Midnight Rising Whiskey
Witches Saga.

Join us for the next book in this saga, *International Team of
Mystery* as Dexx is running from DoDO, is trapped in Europe,
and dying from ward sickness in his pursuit to keep his
family safe from Cardinal Bussemi.
He finds answers—and more mysteries—and is forced to
make an incredible sacrifice.

Be sure to order it now!
https://www.fjblooding.com/pre-order-wwmr-book-4

We hope you enjoyed *Midnight Whiskey*.
Be sure to visit my site, fjblooding.com, to sign up for our
newsletter, get free books, join the forum discussions, and
find out more about our latest books!

And don't forget to leave reviews!

WHISKEY MAGICK & MENTAL
HEALTH

Sign up to learn more about our books and receive this free e-zine about Whiskey Magick and Mental Health. https://www.fjblooding.com/books-lp

F.J. Blooding lives in hard-as-nails Alaska, growing grey hair in the midnight sun with Shane, her writing partner and husband, his two part-time kids, his BrotherTwin, SistaWitch, TeenMan, and SnarkGirl, along with a small menagerie of animals which includes several cats, an army of chickens, a rabbit or two, but only one dog.

She enjoys writing and creating with her wonderful husband and dreaming about sleeping. She's dated vampires, werewolves, sorcerers, weapons smugglers, U.S. Government assassins, and slingshot terrorists. No. She is *not* kidding. She even married one of them.

Sign up for her newsletter, get free books, and join the discussions on the forums when you visit her website at FJBlooding.com